D0471227

ORION AND THE CONQUEROR

Tor books by Ben Bova

As on a Darkling Plain
The Astral Mirror
Battle Station
The Best of the Nebulas (ed.)
Challenges
Colony
Cyberbooks
Escape Plus
Gremlins Go Home (with Gordon R. Dickson)
The Kinsman Saga
The Multiple Man
Orion
Orion in the Dying Time
Out of the Sun
Peacekeepers
Privateers
Prometheans
Star Peace: Assured Survival
The Starcrossed
Test of Fire
To Save the Sun (with A. J. Austin)
The Trikon Deception (with Bill Pogue)
Triumph
Vengeance of Orion
Voyagers
Voyagers II: The Alien Within
Voyagers III: Star Brothers
The Winds of Altair

ORION AND THE CONQUEROR

BEN BOVA

A TOM DOHERTY ASSOCIATES BOOK
NEW YORK

This is a work of fiction. Any references to real people, events, or locales are intended only to give the fiction a sense of historical authenticity. Other names, characters, and incidents are either a product of the author's imagination or are used fictitiously, as are those fictionalized events and incidents which involve real persons and did not occur or are set in the future.

ORION AND THE CONQUEROR

This book is printed on acid-free paper.

A Tor Book
Published by Tom Doherty Associates, Inc.
175 Fifth Avenue
New York, N.Y. 10010

Library of Congress Cataloging-in-Publication Data

Bova, Ben, 1932–
Orion and the conqueror / Ben Bova.
p. cm.
"A Tom Doherty Associates Book."
ISBN 0-312-85447-1
1. Macedonia—History—To 168 B.C.—Fiction. 2. Time travel—Fiction. I. Title.
PS3552.O84O68 1994 93-42545
813′.54—dc20 CIP

First edition: February 1994

Printed in the United States of America

0 9 8 7 6 5 4 3 2 1

To Michael, Michelle, Michael, Lindsey and Hayley

As flies to wanton boys, are we to the gods;
They kill us for their sport.

Prologue

In the timeless city beneath the golden energy dome, Anya healed me of my wounds, both physical and spiritual. The other Creators left us alone in that empty mausoleum of a city, alone among the temples and monuments that the Creators had built for themselves.

My burns healed quickly. The gulf between us caused by her seeming betrayal, less so. I realized that Anya had had to make me think she had abandoned me; otherwise Set would have seen her trap when he probed my mind. Yet the pain was still there, the awful memory of feeling deserted. As the days quietly passed and the nights, the love we felt for each other slowly began to bridge even that gap.

Anya and I stood on the outskirts of the city before the massive bulk of the enormous Pyramid of Khufu, its dazzling white coat of polished limestone gleaming gloriously in the morning light, the great Eye of Amon just starting to form as the sun moved across the sky toward the position that created the shadow-sculpture.

I felt restless. Even though we had the entire empty city to ourselves I could not overcome the uncomfortable feeling that we were not truly alone. The other Creators might be scattered across the universes, striving to maintain the spacetime continuum that they themselves had unwittingly unravelled, yet I had the prickly sensation in the back of my neck that told me we were being watched.

"You are not happy here," Anya said as we walked unhurriedly around the base of the huge, massive pyramid.

I had to admit she was right. "It was better when we were back in the forest of Paradise."

"Yes," she agreed. "I liked it there, too, even though I didn't appreciate it at the time."

"We could go back there."

She smiled at me. "Is that what you wish?"

Before I could answer a shimmering sphere of glowing gold appeared before us, hovering a few inches above the polished stone slabs that made up the walkway around the pyramid's base. The globe touched lightly on the paving, then contracted to form the human shape of Aten, dressed in a splendid military tunic of metallic gold with a high choker collar and epaulets bearing a sunburst insignia.

"Surely you're not thinking of retiring, Orion," he said, his tone just a shade less mocking than usual, his smile radiating more scorn than warmth.

Turning to Anya, he added, "And you, dearest companion, have responsibilities that cannot be avoided."

Anya moved closer to me. "I am not your 'dearest companion,' Aten. And if Orion and I want to spend some time alone in a different era, what is that to you?"

"There is work to be done," he said, the smile fading, his tone more serious.

He was jealous of me, I realized. Jealous of the love that Anya and I shared.

Then the old smug cynicism came back into his face. He cocked a golden eyebrow at me. "Jealous?" He read my thoughts. "How can a god be jealous of a creature? Don't be ridiculous, Orion."

"Haven't I done enough for you?" I growled. "Haven't I earned a rest?"

"No. And no. My fellow Creators tell me that you have grown much like us in your powers and wisdom. They congratulate me on producing such a useful . . . creature."

He was going to say "toy" until he noticed my fists clenching.

"Well, Orion," he went on, "if you are going to assume godlike powers then you must be prepared to shoulder godlike responsibilities, just like the rest of us."

"You told me that I was your creature, a tool to be used as you see fit."

He shrugged, glancing at Anya. "It comes out to the same thing. Either you bear responsibilities like the rest of us or you obey my commands. Take your choice."

Anya put her hand on my shoulder. "You have the right to refuse him, my love. You have earned that right."

Smirking, Aten replied, "Perhaps so. But *you,* goddess, cannot evade your responsibilities. No more than I can."

"The continuum can struggle along without me for a while," she said, almost as haughty as Aten himself.

"No, it can't." Suddenly he was utterly serious. "The crisis is real and urgent. The conflict has spread across the stars and threatens the entire galaxy now."

Anya paled. She turned her fathomless silver-gray eyes to me, and I saw real pain in them.

I knew that we could escape to Paradise if we wanted to. To those who can control time, what matter days or years or even centuries spent in one era or another? We could always return to this exact point in spacetime, this individual nexus in the continuum. The crisis that Aten feared would still be waiting for us.

Yet how could we be happy, knowing that our time in Paradise was limited? Even if we remained there for a thousand years, the task awaiting us would loom in our minds like the edge of a cliff, like a sword hanging over our heads.

Before Anya could reply I said, "Paradise will have to wait, won't it?"

She nodded sadly. "Yes, my love. Paradise will have to wait."

BOOK I

MERCENARY

War therefore is an act of violence
intended to compel our opponent
to fulfil our will. . . . War is a mere
continuation of policy by other means.

Chapter 1

Their tread was like the pacing of a giant, some ten thousand men marching in perfect unison, making the air quiver and the ground shake with the weight of each booted step.

They were coming straight toward us, the heavy long sarissas of their front ranks pointed at our eyes, those in the rear still held upright. It looked like a forest of spears advancing upon us.

"Steady," yelled our phalanx commander. "Let them tire themselves out marching toward us. Hold your places."

We stood at the crest of a modest rise in the stony, bare ground. Hardly a blade of grass was growing here. The morning sun was already hot, the sky so bright it almost hurt to look at it. On the other side of the rocky hills before us stood the besieged city of Perinthos; we were here to lift the siege.

I was in the tenth rank of our twelve-deep phalanx, on the right end of the row, with no man's shield to protect my right side. The officers were up front, of course, except for the quarter-file and end-file commanders, who had stationed themselves on the left ends of their ranks. I was bigger than most of the other hoplites and could handle a twelve-foot spear easily. But the army we faced had those sixteen-foot-long sarissas and a reputation for winning their battles.

Their right wing was the heavy one, as usual. At least sixteen ranks deep; it was hard to tell because they were kicking up a fair amount of dust as they advanced across the open ground toward us. Behind them and to our left, off by the scrawny trees that dotted the hillside, I could see their cavalry shuffling nervously, waiting for the order to strike. We had no cavalry, and I feared that once the fighting began the Perinthians' own hoplites would quickly turn tail, leaving us to be butchered. They were civilians, after all, citizens of the city we had been hired to help protect. I doubted that they could stand up before the professional army advancing upon us.

"Steady," our commander repeated. He was a tough old vulture, his bronze breastplate and shield dulled and dented from many a battle, his arms covered with white puckered scars. Diopeithes, the leader of our mercenary band, was mounted on a lovely white steed well to the rear, ready to run all the way back to Athens if the going got bad. He was more of an opportunist than a soldier; I doubted that he had ever led his men against trained professional troops.

I worked a finger through the chin strap of my helmet. I was sweating, and not merely from the hot morning sun. We were professional soldiers, mercenaries, but we were badly outnumbered and forced to fight at a time and place of the enemy's choosing. The politicians of Perinthos may have known how to govern their city, but they made poor generals. Their biggest mistake was to expect that Athens would fight for them. The Athenians had not even paid Diopeithes; or so he told us. We were forced to live off the land, which hardly pleased the Perinthians we were supposed to be defending.

The distance between our spear points and theirs was shrinking steadily. Our commander stepped out in front of the phalanx and bellowed, "On my word—*forward!*"

We started marching toward the advancing enemy, each one of us stepping out with his left foot, spears levelled, shields raised. I felt exposed on the right end of our rank, with no shield to protect my right side, though I knew I could take care of myself once the fighting started. Yet, as I marched in step toward the advancing enemy, my thoughts churning, I found I could remember nothing about the battles I had fought. Nothing at all. My brows knit in puzzlement. My memory was as blank as a newborn baby's. I could remember nothing earlier than a few hours ago, when we had picked up our weapons and formed our ranks.

This was no time for soul-searching. Skirmishers appeared from behind the files of the advancing phalanx, firing arrows into us, pelting us with stones and javelins. Someone screamed and went down with an arrow in his neck. A fist-sized stone banged off my shield. They wanted us to raise our shields against their missiles, or, better yet, break ranks. Then their phalanx would hit us at the run and shatter us completely. We were trained to ignore the skirmishers and close ranks whenever a man went down. I knew that but I could not remember when or where I had learned it.

Their cavalry off in the woods started to move. Horsemen could never attack a solid phalanx; our spears were like the spines of a hedgehog, and the horses shied away no matter how much their riders urged them. But cavalry could swing around our flank and attack us in the rear. And once a phalanx is broken the cavalry enjoys riding down individual soldiers. More men are slaughtered in the flight after the battle than during the battle itself.

The skirmishers melted away like the annoying insects they were. The bare stony ground between us and the enemy was shrinking rapidly. Our pace quickened. So did theirs. Trumpets on both sides blared and we yelled as loud as we could and broke into a run and the two phalanxes smashed into each other with a thunderous bloodthirsty roar and the screeching, clanging, terrifying clamor of iron spearpoints against shields and bronze breastplates—and flesh.

The world seemed to slow down for me. Time stretched out like an elastic ribbon. Everyone around me began to move in sluggish, torpid slow motion, as if they were all underwater or in a labored blood-soaked dream. I saw the men in our front ranks go down under those six-teen-foot-long sarissas, skewered or pummelled or just shocked off their feet before their own spears could reach the enemy soldiers. Men were trampled underfoot as the two phalanxes ground into each other, each still advancing despite the shredding of our front ranks. Spears snapped, men howled with anger or pain or blood-lust, shields split apart under the tremendous impact of collision.

I reached over the men in front of me and drove my spear into one of the enemy hoplites. I saw him raise his shield as my point came toward him so I hooked the edge of his shield with the rear barb of my point, jerked the shield aside, then rammed the point into his throat. He looked surprised and then his gushing blood spattered me as he began to fall and I wrenched the spear point free.

Our front ranks had collapsed under the enemy's im-pact and I was suddenly shield-to-shield with them, shoving and struggling, pushing against the men in front of me as I jabbed with my spear. It was too long for this close-in work and out of the corner of my eye I saw their skirmishers sneaking around our right flank, firing arrows and javelins into our exposed side.

I ducked an arrow as it flew in lazy slow-motion to-ward me, then rammed my spear through the shield and breastplate and body of a hoplite. The battle was becoming a chaos of screaming, bloodied, falling men; all order gone among our side. My rank was being shredded by the enemy. I saw a javelin coming at me. Leaving my spear in the falling body of the man I had skewered, I batted the lighter javelin aside and then reached for my sword before the two hoplites in front of me could react in their dream-like slow motion. I cut them both down but there were more of them moving with mechanical discipline, spearing, stabbing, using their shields to knock men off balance, moving forward in an unstoppable tide.

There were too many of them and they were too well led, too disciplined, for us to overcome. My fellow mercenaries fought well, but we were clearly outmatched. We did not turn and run because we knew that would be sure death. But we were cut off from the Perinthian citizen troops, separated from what remained of their phalanx and driven backward across the field toward the trees. Sure enough, the Perinthians broke and fled. And, even surer, the enemy's cavalry came thundering out of the woods, shrilling their exultant battle cries, and started to cut them down without mercy. The cavalry leader could not have been more than a boy, golden hair streaming in the wind as he bent eagerly over the mane of his magnificent black charger, sword held high and eyes intent on the fleeing men who had foolishly thrown down their shields and helmets in their frenzy to escape.

There was hardly more than a handful of us left as we retreated slowly, grudgingly, up the slight slope toward the trees. Our phalanx had been slashed to ribbons; there were only a few knots of individual men fighting now. Still, everything seemed to be moving as slowly as a beetle trapped in honey. Sword in hand, I could see the moves my enemies were going to make by the shifting of their eyes, the knotting of muscles in their legs or arms. I ducked under one of the long sarissas and drove my sword point through the man's leather cuirass into his belly. He shrieked and I wrenched his long spear from him with my left hand.

And saw that I was alone now, my back to a tree, sarissa in one hand and sword in the other. A dozen wary soldiers ringed around me, eyes ablaze, armor smeared with blood, watching me, waiting for an opening. Most of them had lost their sarissas and were gripping swords. They were veteran troops; they intended to take no chances against a man who had killed so many of their own. But they were not going to let me escape them, either. The best I could hope for was to take as many of them down with me as I could before they finally did me in. Then I saw one of them signalling to a handful of archers. They were going to take no risks at all.

"Hold!" called a gruff-voiced man on horseback. He rode up and stopped at the edge of the ring facing me. His armor was white with gold filigree, but caked now with dust. His helmet was topped with a white horsehair plume, and he had unfastened the cheek flaps so I could see his face. A bristling black beard, streaked with what looked like crusted blood on one side. Then I saw that he had lost the eye on that side of his face long ago. It was half closed, and beneath its drooping lid I could see the blank whiteness of dead flesh.

He was obviously one of their generals. The men backed away from me slightly, but none of them lowered their weapons. Another general rode up and I realized that both of them were mounted on powerful chestnut brown horses, but had neither saddles nor stirrups, only a pad that seemed to be made of layers of blankets.

"There's been enough killing," said the black-bearded one. Some of his men nodded. To me he raised his voice, "I have need of good soldiers. Would you accept employment in my army?"

I looked around. My companions were either dead or

prisoners. I did not have much of a choice, but at least he was offering me something better than being sold into slavery or slaughtered outright.

I thought it over for all of a half-second. "Yes," I replied. "I would like to be on the winning side, for a change."

He threw his head back and laughed. "Very well, then! How are you called?"

"My name is Orion."

"From where?"

I started to reply, then realized that I did not know. I could not remember anything more than a few hours ago.

"From the North," I temporized.

"Must be a Scythian, from the size of you. I'd recognize those gray eyes anywhere. But where's your beard? Why are you shaved?"

I hadn't the faintest idea. "A beard gives your enemy a handhold to grab," I heard myself answer.

He tugged at his own thick beard. "Does it, now? You sound like my son." Then he turned and called to one of the soldiers standing closest to him, "Nikkos, take him into your troop. I don't think he'll need much training. Looks to me as if he already knows how to use a sarissa."

He pulled at the reins and trotted off, grinning, the other officer riding beside him.

That was my first sight of Philip, King of the Macedonians. The golden-haired boy who led the cavalry turned out to be his son, Alexandros.

Chapter 2

We camped at the battlefield that night, to burn the dead and then rest after the long hard day's exertions. Nikkos, to my surprise, was a Thracian, not a Macedonian at all.

"In my father's time we raided into Macedon and stole their horses and cattle," he told me as we sat by a crackling wood fire and chewed on roasted mutton. "And their women, too," he added with a leering wink.

He could not have been thirty. His hair was dark brown and wild as an untamed forest. His black beard was smeared and sticky with mutton drippings. About a dozen of us were sitting around the fire while a physician from far-off Corinth went around applying salves and bandages to men's wounds.

"And now you serve the Macedonians," I said.

He gulped at his goatskin of wine, splashing much of it over his beard and chest. "You bet we do! Old One-Eye has changed everything. When he became king he beat the shit out of us. And everybody else around him. Struck us in the winter, in the summer. Made no difference to him. He never lost a battle. He knows how many beans makes five, he does."

"Philip conquered your people," I murmured.

Nikkos shook his shaggy head vigorously. "No. Not conquered. We still have our own king. He just showed us that we'd be better off allied with him than fighting against him."

A diplomat, I thought. Then I realized that Philip had done the same thing to me this day.

"Now all the country tribes are allied with Macedon," Nikkos went on, "and Philip even makes war against Athens."

If Nikkos was unhappy with this situation he did not show it. Indeed, he seemed to be quite pleased with it all.

Then he leaned closer to me. "D'you know what I think?" he asked in a low voice.

His breath was foul and I could see things crawling in his beard. "What?" I asked, trying to keep the distance of a flea's jump between us.

"I think it's her that's done it."

"Her?"

"The witch. Philip's wife."

"The king's wife is a witch?"

He lowered his voice even more. "Priestess of the Old Cult. Worships the Snake Goddess and all that. She's a sorceress, all right. How else can you explain it? I was already big enough to help my father tend his flock when Philip pushed his brother off the throne. Macedonia was being sliced up by all the tribes around it. Not just us, but the Illyrians, the Paionians—all of us. We raided and plundered every year."

"Philip put a stop to that?"

"In the blink of his one eye, or so it seems. Now all the tribes serve him. It must be that Molossian bitch of his; that's the only way to explain it."

I glanced uneasily at the other men sitting around the fire.

Nikkos laughed. "Don't worry, I can't say anything about the witch that Old One-Eye hasn't said himself. He hates her."

"Hates his wife?"

Several of the men nodded agreement, grinning.

"If it weren't that she's the mother of his son and heir he would have sent her packing back to Epeiros long ago."

"He can't do that," said one of the others. "He's afraid of her."

"She can cast spells."

"Spells my ass. She poisons people."

"Not poison. Magic."

"Look what she did to the other son, the one by the Thessalian woman."

"Arrhidaios? The idiot?"

"He was a healthy baby. She fed him poison that made him feeble-minded."

"Or cast a spell to make certain her own son would be Philip's heir, even though he's a couple of years younger."

The men fell to arguing over whether the king's wife was a poisoner or a sorceress. I listened with only half an ear. The men around me, the battle we had gone through, this chill, dark night with the black bowl of the heavens strewn with brilliant glittering stars—all of it was strange and new to me. I had no memory of anything farther back than that morning. Each of the men around me had a family and clan and tribe, each of them could recall their kings and histories from generations back.

I had nothing. A blank where my memory should have been. The men spoke of the gods they worshipped; their names meant nothing to me. Until one of them mentioned Athena, the warrior goddess, the patroness of Athens.

"She's more than a warrior goddess," said Nikkos grudgingly. "She's the goddess of wisdom. Or at least, the Athenians think so."

"They should," one of the others said. "She gave them the olive tree, didn't she?"

"And the spinning wheel."

Athena. A picture of her formed in my mind: tall and slim and incredibly beautiful, with lustrous dark hair and solemn silver-gray eyes.

"We're all playthings for the gods," Nikkos was saying. "They pull the strings and we jump."

"I don't believe that," said the man next to him. "I live my own life; nobody pulls *my* strings."

But we are here to do the gods' bidding, I thought. *At least I am.* I felt certain of that. Yet—what did the gods want me to do? Who was I, really, and why was I here? There was no answer in my mind, no message from the gods to enlighten me.

The fire sputtered low and the men began to wrap themselves in cloaks or blankets and stretch out for sleep. I had nothing but the grimy, skirted chiton of sweat-stained linen that I was wearing. My bronze breastplate and greaves and helmet rested on the ground beside me. Yet as soon as I realized that the night wind was chilling me, I clamped down on my peripheral circulation and consciously speeded my heartbeat to raise my body temperature enough to compensate for the cold.

I did that almost without thinking about it. But then I began to wonder how I could control my body so minutely. And how I knew what I was doing. Somehow I realized that this was far beyond the capabilities of other men. In the battle I had been able to fight and kill without being scratched. I could see everything in slow motion, yet my own reactions were always faster than anyone else's.

Who am I? I wondered as I laid myself on the hard ground and closed my eyes. *Where am I from?*

For hours I lay on my back staring sleeplessly at the gleaming stars wheeling majestically above me. I recognized the two Dippers, and Cassiopeia on her throne. Nearby her daughter, Andromeda, chained to the rock with Perseus the hero beside her. My own constellation, Orion, was still below the horizon, although I could see the Dog Star blazing like a sapphire just above the rim of the hills.

At last I closed my eyes in sleep. Or was it sleep? I seemed to be transported to another place, in some other world far removed in time and distance from the battlefield near the walled city of Perinthos.

This is a dream, I told myself, even though I did not truly believe it. I stood on a grassy hillside dotted with wildflowers beneath a warm summer sun. Below me on the plain was a magnificent city shimmering in the day's heat, lofty towers and mighty monuments lining stately broad avenues. And beyond the city was the sea, dazzlingly blue-green in the bright sunshine, waves marching up onto a white sand beach in tireless procession.

The city seemed empty, dead, yet perfectly preserved. I began to realize that the shimmering I saw was some sort of protective dome over it, thin as a soap bubble, pure energy.

My life was tied to that city. I knew that with an absolute certainty. Yet I could remember none of it. Nothing except the concrete conviction that my life began with that city. And my love, as well. The woman I loved, the goddess who loved me, was part of that dead, empty, abandoned city.

When I tried to walk down the hill toward the city I found that my feet would not obey me. I stood rooted to the spot. In the distance, so far and so faint that I could not be entirely sure of it, I heard someone laughing sardonically. Almost crying, so bitter was the laughter. A man's twisted laughter, I thought, although I could not be altogether sure.

With all the force I could muster I tried to break free of whatever held me immobile and start on the way down the hill toward the city.

Only to wake up on the threadbare grass of the stony

battlefield outside Perinthos with the first rays of the sun glinting over the rugged hilltops.

Who am I? The question echoed in my mind. Then another question arose to haunt me: *Why am I here?*

Chapter 3

That morning we marched to Perinthos, where the main body of Philip's army was camped outside the city's wall. It was embarrassing to realize that Philip had used only a small part of his army to defeat my mercenary troops. Most of the Macedonian forces were besieging Perinthos, while still another contingent of his troops was marching swiftly toward Byzantion, on the narrow strait of Bosporus that separated Europe from Asia.

The city was no great affair. I could not see much of it, huddled behind its wall and locked gates, but it seemed small and cramped to me. The main wall was rough and uneven; crenelated towers stood by each of its two gates and only a few buildings inside were tall enough to rise above the wall's top. It sat at the edge of the water, where the rocky plain that descended from the distant hills met the Propontis, the sea that lay between the narrows of the Hellespont and the Bosporus.

Yet there was something familiar about the city, something that tugged at my memory. When I tried to recall what it was, though, I struck a blank wall much more obdurate than the city wall of Perinthos.

Philip's camp lay sprawled on the threadbare plain, almost within an arrow's shot of the city wall. I sensed an edginess in the air. The camp reeked with a restless, disgruntled mood, the kind of irritation that arises when soldiers have been sitting too long in one place with neither the comforts of their home base nor the prospect of getting home any time in the near future.

The siege was going badly. Perinthos was a seaport, so it could stay behind its locked gates and defy the Macedonians while ships brought in fresh supplies and, occasionally, reinforcements from Athenian allies such as Byzantion. Philip, supreme on land, had no navy. It must have been sheer madness for the Perinthians to try to relieve the siege with the handful of mercenaries that Athens had sent. Philip had made short work of them, but now that the battle was over, the siege went on and the city remained defiant.

The horses kicking up clouds of dust in their corrals seemed to be more active than the soldiers. Men loafed about as we marched into the camp. I saw that they had been here long enough to have built log huts for themselves with well-trampled paths between them. Mules brayed as slaves led them past us, their backs piled high with fodder and stacks of firewood.

The only soldiers who seemed busy were the engineers swearing and sweating over a massive catapult, yelling at a quartet of bare-chested slaves straining to load a heavy iron bolt onto it while another squad of half-naked slaves sat waiting to start the mules pulling the thick ropes that would cock the catapult's arm. I saw that someone had scratched onto the dark iron bolt the words, *From Philip.*

I heard the thump of another catapult being fired and, turning, saw its missile tumbling high into the morning sun. It cleared the wall and disappeared behind it. Then came a thunderous crunching boom as it hit. Voices wailed, a woman's high-pitched shriek cut through the air as a cloud of dust rose above the wall like a dark blot against the sky. From Philip.

Troy. Vaguely I remembered another siege of another city, long ago: Troy. Had I been there, or had I merely heard tales about it? My right hand pressed against my thigh and I felt the dagger that I kept strapped beneath the skirt of my chiton. What had it to do with my faint recollection of Troy?

Nikkos directed our phalanx to a relatively clear area of the camp, as far from the smell and dust of the corrals as possible. I saw that Philip's army was much larger than the Macedonians could field by themselves. He had added troops from all the tribes allied to his kingdom, such as Nikkos' Thracians, and still hired mercenaries, as well.

"See those gilded lilies there?" Nikkos prodded my ribs with his elbow as we were unloading our equipment from the mule train that had followed us into camp.

I looked in the direction he was staring. A troop of men in identical polished armor and helmets of gleaming bronze was forming up in well-ordered ranks under the flinty eyes of a trio of officers. Their breastplates were molded to look like a well-muscled torso; their helmets were plumed with horsehair dyed red. They seemed to sparkle in the sun.

"Argives," said Nikkos. "Fresh meat from the Peloponnesos."

"More mercenaries?" I asked.

He nodded and spat into the dusty ground. "Look at 'em. All prettied up in their fine bright armor. I bet they've never done anything more than parade around and tell tall tales. They must think they can get the Perinthians to swoon at the sight of 'em."

I had to laugh, especially when I looked down at my own battered armor, dented and scratched and caked with dust. But then I had to wonder: armor like that cost a great deal of money. Where did I get it? What other battles had I fought, to dent and scratch it so? Where was I from?

Philip and his generals seemed to understand full well that soldiers with little do to begin to rot from the inside. We were drilled every day, trained in the close-order formations of the phalanx until handling our sixteen-foot-long sarissas seemed as natural as using a soup spoon. The mercenaries loafed and laughed at us while we of the Macedonian phalanxes marched and wheeled and turned and charged at the bawling commands of our unit leaders.

It was dull, sweaty work; endless repetition. But I had seen how Philip's machine had ground up my mercenary phalanx like a meat chopper with ten thousand arms and one brain. I went through the drills without complaint and ignored the jeers of the mercenaries.

Most of the tribesmen served not as hoplites in a phalanx but as peltasts, archers or slingers or javelin throwers, light infantry that could skirmish against the heavier-armed phalanxes and dash away before the hoplites could close with them. The mercenaries were all hoplites, of course, heavy infantry.

"The country's full of mercenary troops," Nikkos told me. "Any poor boy who wants to make something of himself joins a mercenary troop and goes off soldiering. Every city in the land grows soldiers nowadays. Except Athens, of course."

"What do they grow in Athens?" I asked.

"Lawyers." And he spat again.

Some of the other men near us laughed. I let it pass.

The men fell to arguing over which city produced the best soldiers. Some felt that the Spartans were the bravest, but most agreed that Thebes had an even better reputation.

"Especially their Sacred Band," said one of the men.

"The Sacred Band aren't mercenaries," Nikkos pointed out. "They fight only for Thebes."

"And damned well, too."

"They're all lovers. Each man in the Sacred Band is part of a pair."

"The philosophers say that makes the best kind of soldier, a man who's fighting alongside his lover. They'll never let each other down."

"Fuck the philosophers. The Sacred Band's the best damned bunch of soldiers in the world."

"Better than us?"

"Better."

"We have a better general!"

"But they're not mercenaries. As long as we don't make war against Thebes we don't have to worry about them."

"There are plenty of Theban mercenaries, though. Even the Great King, over in Asia, hires mercenaries from Thebes."

"The Great King?" I asked.

Nikkos gave me a peculiar look. "Of Persia," he said. "Don't you know anything?"

I could only shake my head.

Nikkos did not trust the newly-arrived Argives. He kept calling them "pretty boys" who would be next to worthless in a real battle. For their part, the Argives swaggered through the camp as if they were each personally descended from Achilles, and laughed at our constant drilling.

"Why doesn't the king send them against the wall?" Nikkos grumbled. "Then we'd see what they're really made of."

But Philip apparently had no intention of attacking the city wall. The army sat outside and did little more than drill—and fire a few missiles into the city each day. The Perinthians sat tight and cheered each time a ship sailed into their wall-protected harbor.

Our phalanx was camped next to the strutting Argives,

and there was plenty of bad blood between us. It was natural, I suppose; if we were not allowed to fight the real enemy we fought each other. There were rows and fistfights almost every night. The officers on both sides sternly punished the men involved; Nikkos himself took ten lashes one morning while we were all made to stand at attention and watch. One of Philip's generals, Parmenio, threatened to stop our wine supply if we did not behave.

"We'll see how belligerent you are on water," he growled at us. I had heard that Parmenio was a wine lover, and he looked it: heavy and red-faced, with broken blood vessels splotching his cheeks and bulbous nose.

The Argives were punished by their own officers, of course, but it seemed to us that their punishments were much lighter than our own.

I tried to stay out of the squabbling. Without quite remembering the details I recalled how another army had been almost destroyed because of a quarrel between its leaders. Was that at Troy?

Then came the night that changed everything.

"Where is Troy?" I asked Nikkos that evening, as we reclined on our blankets in front of the dinner fire.

He furrowed his brow at me. "Who knows? Maybe it's only a story."

"No," said one of the other men. "It's on the other side of the Hellespont."

"It's still there? I thought it was burned to the ground."

"That's where it was."

"How do you know? If it ever existed it was so long ago—"

"In the time of heroes."

"Heroes?" I asked.

"Like Achilles and Odysseus and Agamemnon."

Odysseus. That name rang a bell in my mind. Was it he who gave me the dagger I kept strapped to my thigh?

"What do you horse thieves know about Agamemnon?" shouted one of the Argives, barely a stone's throw from our fire.

"He was one of the leaders of the Achaians at Troy," I answered.

"He was an Argive," said the mercenary, stepping into the light from our fire. "King of Mycenae. Not some shit-footed farmer from the hills like you bunch."

I got to my feet. The Argive was big, and wearing his muscled cuirass plus a short stabbing sword at his hip, but I was taller by half a head and wider across the shoulders.

"I am of the house of Odysseus," I said, half-dreaming. "I remember that."

His jaw dropped open, then he laughed and planted his fists on his hips. "You've taken one too many blows on your head, Scythian. You're crazy."

I wondered how he knew that I was believed to be a Scythian.

Another Argive stepped up beside the first one. He too was armed. Nikkos and several others of my band scrambled to their feet.

"Odysseus has been dead for a thousand years," said the second Argive. He had a nasty sneer on his bearded face. "If he ever lived at all."

"He lived," I said. "I was with him."

"At Troy, I suppose."

They both laughed at me. Then the second one stepped close and looked up into my face. He barely came to my shoulders.

"You're crazy, all right," he said.

"Or a champion liar," said the first Argive.

I could feel Nikkos and the other men behind me stiffen with tension.

"No, look," I said, reaching for my dagger. "Odysseus gave me—"

The Argive jumped back and pulled the sword at his belt. "Trying to knife me!"

"No, I—"

He lunged at me. I parried with the dagger and punched him in the jaw with my left hand. He went down like a slaughtered ox.

And the camp around me erupted into violence. Men were punching, kicking, biting, wrestling each other onto the ground. I stood in the midst of it, the dagger still in my hand, while the fight swirled around me.

Feeling dumbfounded, I backed away, out of the firelight. At least they weren't using weapons, I thought. The one man who had drawn his sword lay unconscious by the fire.

Officers were bellowing in the night. I sheathed the dagger and stepped back into the fray, trying to separate the fighting men.

Philip himself rode up on a chestnut horse, bareheaded, without armor, his one good eye blazing with anger.

"Stop this at once!" he roared. And we stopped. The authority in his powerful voice was unmistakable.

For a moment everything was quite still. Men stood or knelt or lay stretched on the ground, all of us covered with dust, some of us bloody. Nikkos, his shirt torn and the welts on his back still livid, had one knee on the chest of an Argive and his teeth clamped on the man's bloody ear.

Before Philip could say another word a stone came hurtling out of the darkness and struck him squarely on the back of his head. It sounded almost as loud as one of the catapult bolts landing. Philip's head snapped forward, he slumped and fell off the horse. An Argive ran up with a spear in his hand and I saw that about a dozen of the

Argives had formed a ring around Philip's prostrate body. All of them had swords in their hands.

I charged forward, head down, and bulled through the ring of armored men, grabbed the spear and wrested it from the Argive's hands before he could plunge it into the unconscious king.

Battle fury seized me again and the world slowed down around me. Holding the spear like a quarter-staff I smashed its weighted end into the face of the man I had taken it from. He fell like a stone. Then I stood over Philip's body, my back to his nervously stamping horse, ready to protect the king. The circle of armed Argives looked stunned with surprise. Beyond them Nikkos and the others of my troop seemed just as shocked and frozen into immobility.

Then a fresh commotion erupted out in the darkness beyond the firelight. A man's rough voice choked off in a bloody gargle, others shouted, and suddenly young Alexandros burst upon us, golden hair glowing, eyes wild, the sword in his hand bloodied.

"The king!" he shouted, pushing men out of his way and advancing upon me.

"I think he's merely stunned, sir," I said.

He stared hard at me, then turned to the ring of Argives who still held their swords. "Take them," he snapped. "All of them."

Nikkos and the others disarmed the Argives and led them off into the darkness.

"You saved my father's life," said Alexandros to me.

Parmenio and other officers came rushing up now and knelt beside Philip.

"I want those assassins hanged," Alexandros said into the night air. "But not until they tell us who paid them."

No one seemed to be listening to him. He fixed his blazing eyes on me. "Go with the king. I will join you presently."

And he stalked off into the darkness. If ever a man had murder on his face, it was Alexandros at that moment. It was difficult to realize that he was scarcely eighteen years old.

Chapter 4

An hour later Philip was still woozy. I had followed the officers who carried him to his cabin, a rough log hut with horse blankets covering the dirt floor. I stood at the open doorway, the Argive spear still in my hands. The officers had carried Philip to his cot with a tenderness I had seldom seen. Several physicians and generals crowded around the king. A frightened-looking slave girl brought a flagon of wine to the cot.

Philip regained consciousness slowly. Although the physicians urged him to remain on the cot, he insisted on sitting up. His officers helped him to a folding camp chair. He gripped its arms weakly.

A scream of agony ripped through the night. Philip looked up sharply. Another scream, longer and more tortured than the first.

Philip gestured to one of the generals, who bent his ear to his king's lips. Philip spoke, the general nodded and strode out of the hut, past me.

The physicians bustled about. One of them bathed the back of the king's head. I saw that the cloth came away bloody. Another seemed to be preparing some kind of ointment in a shallow bowl over a candle flame. It smelled of camphor.

"Wine." It was the first word I had heard from him since he'd been felled. "More wine."

The girl's eyes lit up. She smiled with relief. She could not have been more than thirteen or fourteen.

A few moments later I saw a small parade approaching the hut. I recognized the general that Philip had sent out, a big, burly, hard-faced man with a beard blacker than Philip's own and outrageously bowed legs. Antipatros was his name, I learned later. Beside him strode Alexandros, his face white with anger or something else, his eyes still ablaze. And behind Alexandros marched a half-dozen other young men from his chosen Companions, all of them clean-shaven as Alexandros himself was. It made them look even younger than they were.

The Companions stopped at the doorway. Alexandros went through, followed by Antipatros.

Alexandros went straight to his father. "Thank the gods you're all right!"

Philip grinned crookedly. "I have a thicker skull than they thought, eh?"

If they were father and son they did not look it. Philip was dark of hair and swarthy of skin, his beard bristling, his arms thick and hairy where they were not laced with scars. Alexandros shone like gold; his hair was golden, his skin fair, his eyes gleaming. I thought of someone I had once known, a Golden One, and for some reason the hazy memory made me shudder.

"I'll find out who's responsible for this," Alexandros said grimly.

But Philip waved a hand at him. "We know who's responsible. Athens. Demosthenes or some of his friends."

"They bought out the Argives. I'll hang every one of them."

"No," said Philip. "Only the ones who had weapons in their hands. The rest of them had nothing to do with it."

"How can you be sure? Let me get the truth out of them."

"The truth?" Philip's face twisted into sardonic laughter. "Hold a man's feet in the fire and he'll tell you whatever you want to hear. What kind of truth is that? Is that what Aristotle taught you?"

Before Alexandros could reply, Parmenio spoke up. "This man saved your life." He pointed to me.

Philip fixed his good eye on me.

"When you were down and they were about to spear you, he broke through them and wrestled the spear away from the assassin."

Philip frowned, trying to remember. At last he said, "Orion, isn't it?"

"Yes, sir," I said.

He beckoned me to him. "What troop are you with?"

"Nikkos' phalanx, sir."

"Nikkos, eh? Well, since you've done such a good job of protecting me, you're now part of my personal guard. Tell the quartermaster to outfit you properly. Antipatros, show him where the guard is camped, eh?"

Antipatros nodded curtly. "Come with me," he said.

He led me outside the hut. "Scythian, eh? I suppose you can ride a horse," he said.

"I think so."

He gave me a sour look. "Well, you'd better."

Thus I became one of Philip's bodyguards.

My new companions of the royal guard were almost all Macedonians, most of them sons of very ancient and noble families, although there were a few newcomers and foreigners, such as I. I quickly learned that a true Macedonian nobleman learns to ride a horse before he learns to walk. At least, that is what they told me, and it seemed true enough. They were born riders. My first morning as a guardsman I spent watching the others mount their powerful steeds and ride galloping along the bare earth where they exercised the horses.

Before the sun was at zenith I had learned what I needed to know. With neither saddle nor stirrups, a man had to clamp his knees tight against the horse's flanks and grip the reins in his left hand to keep the right free to hold a lance or sword. That seemed simple enough. I told the wrangler in charge of the corral that I was ready to ride. He trotted out a dun-colored stallion while several of the other guardsmen stopped what they were doing to watch me.

I swung myself onto the back of the stallion and, gripping with my knees, off I went. The horse had ideas of his own. It broke into a frenzied bucking, kicking and twisting, trying to throw me off its back. The men back by the corral were slapping their thighs with laughter. Obviously they had given me the nastiest beast in the corral, to initiate me into their company.

I leaned forward against the stallion's neck and, gripping his mane, said aloud, "You can't shake loose of me, wild one. You and I are a pair from now on."

I clung with every ounce of strength in me and, after several very rough minutes, the stallion settled down and trotted to a stop, snorting and blowing, flanks heaving. I let it rest a few moments, then urged it forward with a nudge of my heels. We flew like the wind, off toward the distant hills. I turned it around and we cantered back to the corral where the other men stood open mouthed.

"Good horse," I said. "What do you call him?"

"Thunderbolt," one of the men said, almost sullen with disappointment, as I slid to the ground.

"I like him," I said.

The wrangler's weatherbeaten face showed an expression halfway between disbelief and amusement. He shook his head at me. "Haven't seen anything like that since the Little King tamed old Ox-Head."

The Little King was Alexandros, I knew.

"Well, if you like him that much," said the captain of the guard, Pausanias, "he's yours."

I thanked him and led Thunderbolt off to where the slave boys were rubbing down the horses after their exercise.

The siege of Perinthos ended a few weeks later. The city still defied Philip from behind its wall, and still received supplies from the sea. Philip gave the order to break camp and head back to Pella, his capital.

"I don't understand it," I said to Pausanias, the highborn Macedonian who headed the king's guard. "Why are we leaving without either taking the city or being driven away?"

Riding beside me, Pausanias gave a bitter little chuckle. The captain of the guard may have been born to the nobility, but there was something dark and festering in him. The men made jokes about him behind his back that I did not understand, jokes that had to do with stableboys and too much wine.

"There are more ways to win a city than by storming it or starving it out," he told me as we rode. "The king has a thousand tricks, one more devious than the other."

"Why did he want Perinthos in the first place?"

"It's allied to Athens."

"And why make war on Athens?"

Pausanias had a handsome face, with a well-kept light brown beard. But that grim moodiness showed through the humorless smile he was giving me.

"Why not ask the king? I'm only one of his distant nephews." And he pulled his horse away from mine, tired of my endless questions.

A short time later Alexandros came dashing up on Ox-Head, his powerful midnight-black charger, almost breathless with excitement.

"We're turning back!" he shouted to the group of us. "The king wants us to go back!"

"Back to Perinthos?"

"No, but to the coast. Quickly. Follow me!"

We turned and followed. Up ahead I could see Philip with others of his guard and a clutch of officers urging their horses into a swift trot. Something was up.

I rode with Pausanias and the rest of the royal guard, following Philip and his generals. Alexandros led the remainder of the cavalry behind us. The sun was high and hot by the time we slowed to a walk and nosed our mounts through a thin screen of trees and shrubbery atop the low ridge that lined the seashore. Alexandros rode up to his father's side, leaving the main body of the cavalry down at the bottom of the ridge.

Down on the beach below us a great flotilla of boats had been pulled up on the sand. There must have been two hundred and more of them, fat round-bottomed cargo carriers for the most part, although I saw more than a dozen sleek oar-driven war galleys among them.

Pausanias smiled wickedly as we sat astride our horses, stroking their necks to keep them calm and silent.

"You see?" he said to me, in a low voice, almost a whisper. "There is the Athenian grain fleet, ripe for the taking."

Men were lolling around the ships, dozing on their decks in the midday sun. A few of the grain carriers were keeled over on their sides while teams of slaves daubed hot pitch on their hulls.

"The gods know who he bribed to get them to stop here," Pausanias muttered. "The One-Eyed Fox has more tricks than Hermes."

I knew he meant the king, Philip. From the little I had gleaned of the situation, it appeared that this fleet was carrying the grain harvest from the rich farm lands of the

Black Sea, beyond Byzantion and the Bosporus, the annual harvest that fed the land-poor city of Athens.

"The Athenians don't work the land," Nikkos had told me one evening. "They don't work at anything any more. They live on a public dole and bring the grain in through the Bosporus and the Hellespont. That's why Old One-Eye wants the seaport cities like Perinthos and Byzantion. The Athenians have the finest navy in the world, but it won't do them any good without ports to tie up in each night, will it?"

Obviously the grain fleet had been afraid to put in at Perinthos, with Philip's army besieging the city. So they had beached for the night here, nearly a day's ride below Perinthos, thinking themselves safe. Philip must have had spies along the coast—perhaps even among the sailors of the fleet, if Pausanias' wry comment had any truth in it.

Philip backed us away from the wooded ridge line, down to where the rest of the cavalry waited, hidden from the beach. We were ordered to feed and water the horses and to take a cold midday meal of preserved strips of goat's meat and water. The meat chewed like leather.

Presently I saw a long line of soldiers winding along the trail that led toward us. Peltasts, not the heavily armored hoplites, trotting at an easy gait. This was going to be a fast strike, and the lighter-armed peltasts would be more useful than the clanking heavy infantry.

With Pausanias' permission I crawled up to the ridge line to join the handful of scouts already lying on their bellies, keeping watch on the enemy. The Athenians had not even posted any guards! I saw a few armed men standing near the war galleys, but otherwise their camp was as undefended as air.

The sun had swung behind us and was heading for the rugged bare hills at our backs when Philip gave the order to mount up. I was dressed and armored exactly like all the others of the king's personal guard: a bronze cuirass molded to resemble a man's well-muscled torso, leather windings to protect my lower legs, and a bronze Corinthian-type helmet with cheek flaps. I bore a lance in my right hand and a sword in its scabbard against my hip. I also had my ancient dagger strapped to my thigh beneath the skirt of my chiton.

We did not charge. The word came from the king that we were to ride slowly down from the ridge toward the beach, ready to break into a gallop if the trumpets so ordered. It was not necessary. The sailors froze where they stood at the sight of more than a thousand of Philip's cavalry ambling out of the woods toward their beached boats. As I rode toward them, my lance upright in my hand, I saw the shock and terror on their faces. The peltasts came in at either end of the curving beach, javelins and bows ready. The sailors were trapped against the sea.

There was no fight in them. They surrendered meekly and the entire year's grain harvest became Philip's prize. There would be hunger in Athens this winter. Or so I thought.

Chapter 5

Philip was in high spirits as we rode toward Pella, his capital. He had failed to capture Perinthos, and had done little more to Byzantion than throw a scare into its citizens. But he had the grain harvest. An army of slaves had loaded it all onto creaking ox carts and then we had burned the Athenian ships, every last one of them. The black smoke rose like an offering to the gods and stained the crystal blue sky for days. The Athenian sailors he sent home on foot, despite the urgings of Alexandros and several others to enslave them.

None of us was disappointed that we had won the grain without a fight. Except for Alexandros.

"The young hothead thinks he's a new Achilles," grumbled Pausanias as we rode toward the capital. "He wants glory and the only way he can get it is by bloodshed."

"How young is he?" I asked.

"Eighteen."

I made myself chuckle. "It's understandable, isn't it? Didn't you want to be a hero when you were eighteen?"

Pausanias did not reply to my question. Instead, he told me, "A few years ago, while we were campaigning in northern Thrace, Philip left Alexandros in Pella, to govern while he was in the field. Gave him the ring and the seal and everything. That's when people started calling him the Little King. He couldn't have been more than sixteen."

"He was left in charge at sixteen?" I marvelled.

"Antipatros was left with him, of course, to steer him by the elbow, but Alexandros took himself very seriously, even then. One of the hill tribes, the Maeti, stirred up some trouble. They're always raiding one another, those cattle herders, or trying to get away from paying the king's taxes."

"Alexandros went after them?"

Pausanias nodded. "Left the capital in Antipatros' hands, and he and his boyfriends went galloping out to deal with this miserable handful of cattle thieves."

He broke into a sour grin, the closest I had seen Pausanias come to laughter. "The Maeti ran off to the hills, of course, and left their pitiful little village empty. So Alexandros sent back to Pella for a dozen or so Macedonian families, resettled them in the village, and changed its name to Alexandropolis."

I waited for the rest of the story. Pausanias gave me an exasperated look.

"No one is allowed to put his name to a city," he explained impatiently. "Only the king."

I said, "Oh."

"Do you know what Philip said when he heard about it?"

"What?"

" 'At least he might have waited until I'm dead.' "

I laughed. "He must be fond of the boy."

"He was proud of him. Proud! The little snot slaps him in the face and he's proud of it."

I looked around us. We were riding at the head of the group but there were others of the guard close enough to overhear us. It was not wise to call Alexandros names.

"Don't worry," Pausanias said, seeing the concern on

my face. "None of *my* men will inform on us. They all feel the same way."

I wondered if that were true.

Pausanias went silent for a while and we rode with no sound but the soft padding of the horses' hooves on the dusty ground and the occasional jingle of metal from their harnesses.

"It's his mother, if you want to know where the fault lies," Pausanias muttered, almost as if talking to himself. "Olympias has filled the boy's head with crazy tales ever since he suckled at her breast. She's the one who's made him think he's a godling. Made him believe that he's too good for us, too good even for his own father."

I said nothing. There was nothing that I could say.

"All those tales that Philip isn't his true father, that he was sired by Herakles—that's Olympias' twaddle, for sure. Sired by Herakles! She would've loved to have Herakles plow her, all right. But she settled for Philip."

I recalled that Nikkos had called Olympias a witch, and the other men had argued about her supernatural powers. And her reputation as a poisoner.

For my part, Alexandros seemed like a typical teen-age lad—albeit a teen-age boy whose father was king of Macedonia; a teenager who had already led cavalry in battle a half-dozen times. To me he seemed eager to show the men around him that he too was a man and no longer a boy. And even more desperate to prove himself in his father's eyes, I thought. He was heir to the kingdom, but his accession to the throne was apparently not all that certain: the Macedonians elected their kings, and if anything happened to Philip, young Alexandros might have a difficult time convincing the elders that he was ready for the throne.

He had his Companions, though: the lads he had grown up with, mostly the sons of Macedonian noble families. He was their natural leader, and they seemed almost to worship him. Four of them seemed especially close to him: smiling Ptolemaios, gangling Harpalos, the Cretan Near-kos, and especially the handsome Hephaistion vied with one another to shine in Alexandros' eyes. In battle they rode together, each trying to outdo the other. They even shaved their chins clean, as Alexandros did, although the word among the guards was that Alexandros hardly needed to shave at all.

"He's effeminate that way," Pausanias told me, more than once. He seemed to take pleasure in saying it. I wondered if he realized that my own beard grew so slowly that I shaved only rarely.

There was something in Alexandros' eyes, though, that disturbed me. More than ambition, more than an avid quest for glory. His eyes seemed to me far older than eighteen. Something glittered in those golden eyes that seemed ageless, timeless. Something that seemed faintly mocking whenever the Little King looked my way.

As the days passed, my memory did not improve. It was as if I had been born, fully grown and dressed in a mercenary hoplite's armor, just a few days earlier. The men around me took me for a Scythian, since I was tall and broad of shoulder, and had gray eyes. Yet I understood their language—the various dialects and even the outright foreign tongues that some of the men spoke.

I tried to remember who I was and why I was here. I could not avoid the feeling that I had been sent here purposely, dispatched to this time and place for a reason that I could not fathom.

The dagger strapped to my thigh was a clue. It had been there for so long that even when I removed it the straps and sheath left their imprint against my flesh. I had not shown it to anyone since the night the Argives had tried to assassinate Philip.

But on the trail back to Pella one night I removed it

from beneath my skirt and one of the other guardsmen noticed its polished onyx hilt glint in the firelight.

"Where did you get that?" he asked, eyeing the beautifully crafted dagger appreciatively.

From Odysseus, I started to say. But I held my tongue. No one would believe that. I was not certain that I believed it myself.

"I don't know," I said, letting him take it from my hand and examine it closely. "I have no memory beyond a week or so ago."

Soon the other members of the guard were admiring it. They began to argue over its origin.

"That's a Cretan dagger," said one of the men. "See the way the hilt is curved. Cretan."

"Pah! You don't know what you're talking about. Take a good look at the *design* on the hilt. You ever see a Cretan design that used flying cranes? Never!"

"All right, hawkeye, where's it from, then?"

"Egypt."

"Egypt? You've had too much wine!"

"It's an Egyptian piece, I tell you."

"So's your mother."

The men nearly came to blows. Pausanias and I had to push them apart and change the subject.

But the following night the armorer of the guardsmen asked to see my dagger. It was becoming famous, which worried me. I had always kept it hidden so that I could use it in an emergency when all else failed. If everyone knew about it, how could I use it as a surprise weapon?

"That blade," said the armorer admiringly. "I've never seen work like that. Nobody makes an iron blade like that. It's a damned work of art."

The flying cranes were the symbol of the House of Odysseus, I knew. Somehow I had received that dagger from Odysseus, king of Ithaca, in the Achaian camp outside the walls of Troy.

A thousand years ago.

It could not be, yet I seemed to remember it. I could see in my mind's eye those high thick walls and the single combats between heroes on the plain before the city. I could see valiant Hector and fiery Achilles and stout Agamemnon and wary Odysseus as clearly as if I were with them now.

When I stretched myself out on the ground beneath my guardsman's cloak that night I clutched the dagger in my hand, determined to dream a dream about it, and about who I was and why I could remember a war from a thousand years in the past yet could not remember anything from a month ago.

I dreamed.

It was a confused, troubling dream, whirling and moving and filled with half-hidden faces and voices I could not quite hear.

I saw Alexandros, golden hair streaming in the wind as he galloped on his midnight steed over a stark desert made of human skulls. His face changed ever so subtly, still the golden-haired intense face of that royal youth, yet now he was someone else, someone mocking and scornful who laughed as he rode roughshod over living men, crushing their bodies beneath his horse's hooves.

Everything shifted, changed, melted like hot wax into a different scene where Philip slumped drunkenly against a dining couch, wine cup in one hand, his good eye glaring balefully at me.

"I trusted you," he mumbled at me. "I trusted you."

He was not drunk, he was dying, blood spurting from a sword gash in his belly. In my right hand I held a bloodied sword as I backed away from Philip's throne.

Someone laughed behind me and I turned, nearly slipping on the blood-slicked stones of the floor, and saw that it was Alexandros. Yet it was not him, but a different person, the Golden One, age-old yet ageless, youthful flesh with eyes that had seen the millennia pass by. He laughed with a bitterness and scorn that chilled my soul.

And beyond him stood a tall, regal, utterly beautiful woman with flowing red hair and skin as white as alabaster. She smiled at me grimly.

"Well done, Orion," she said. And she stepped past the Golden One to put her hands on my shoulders and then slide her arms around my neck and kiss me full on the lips.

"You are not Athena," I said.

"No, Orion. I am not. You may address me as Hera."

"But I love—" I was about to say Athena, then I realized that that was not her true name.

"You will love me, Orion," said flame-haired Hera. "I will make you forget about the one you call Athena."

"But . . ." I wanted to tell her something, but I could no longer think of what it was.

"Go back to the timeflow, Orion," said the Golden One, still smirking. "Go back and play out the role we have written for you."

His eyes were on the dead form of Philip as he commanded me. The bloodied sword was still tight in my grip.

I awoke in the camp with Philip's other guardsmen, still clutching the ancient dagger, sick at heart at my dream.

We resumed our march along the rocky trail through the coastal hills back to Pella. Following along behind us was the long, long train of wagons bearing the grain harvest that we had taken. Already there was talk in the camp each night that Philip would sell the grain harvest to raise more troops and then attack Athens. Or sell the grain *to* Athens in exchange for Perinthos and Byzantion. Or store the grain at Pella in preparation for an Athenian attack on the capital.

If Philip expected an attack on Pella, however, the city

certainly did not look it. My first glimpse of Philip's capital, on the morning when we finally rode into sight of it, impressed me. There was no wall around the city. It sat on the rolling plain by the high road, a sizeable city of stone buildings, as open and defenseless as the Athenian grain fleet had been.

"We are its defense," Pausanias said. "The army. Philip fights his wars in the enemy's territory. They never get the chance to threaten his cities."

Pella was a new city, Pausanias explained to me. "The old capital, Aigai, up in the mountains, it's got walls around it, all right. Built to be a fortress, Aigai is. But Olympias hated it there, so Philip moved his capital here, by the high road, just to please her."

The city was still being built, I saw as we rode closer. Houses and temples were being constructed from stone and masonry; before us as we approached was a large theater carved into the hillside. Up on the highest ground stood a cluster of columned buildings of polished granite: Philip's palace, Pausanias informed me.

"It's big," I said, meaning the palace.

"The biggest city I've ever seen," said Pausanias.

"You haven't seen Athens," came a voice from behind us.

Turning on my mount I saw it was Alexandros, golden hair shining in the morning sun, eyes aflame with inner passion.

"Athens is built in marble, not this gray, dull granite," he said. His voice was sharp, high-pitched. "Thebes, Corinth—even Sparta is more beautiful than this pile of rocks."

"When were you in Athens?" Pausanias asked icily. "Or Thebes. Or Corinth. Or—"

Alexandros shot him a glance of pure fury and darted past us, his black Ox-Head kicking dust in our faces as he galloped away.

Pausanias spat. "To hear him talk, you'd think he's been around the whole world in a chariot."

Half a moment later Alexandros' Companions dashed past and we got more dust in our mouths.

When we stopped for the noon meal Pausanias made us clean up our gear. Grooms brushed our horses, slaves polished our armor. We trooped into the city bright and shining, and the citizens of Pella came out into the streets to welcome us with flowers and warm shouts of victory. I did not feel particularly victorious, and my dream still troubled me. I wondered if there were anyone in the city whom I could trust to interpret the dream without denouncing me as a traitor for even dreaming of slaying the king.

Philip rode in our midst, and the people showered him with flowers and cheers. From what I had heard among the soldiers, when Philip had become king, less than twenty years ago, Macedonia was being carved up by its neighbors. Now Macedonia had either conquered those neighbors or forced them into alliances. Philip was so successful that his capital needed no wall around it. Now he was struggling to make himself master of all the region, from the Illyrians along the Adriatic Sea to the Byzantines on the Bosporus, from wild northern tribes along the Ister River to the mighty cities of Thebes and Corinth and even Athens herself.

There was even talk of invading Asia, once the issue with Athens was settled, to free the Greek cities of Ionia and pluck the beard of the Persian High King.

Up the wide main thoroughfare of Pella we rode, enjoying the crowd's welcome, until we passed through the gates of the palace wall. At home now, Philip prodded his horse to the front and thus was the first to arrive at the steps of the palace.

Standing at the top of the gray stone stairs, proud and regal, her flame-red hair tied up in spirals that made her seem even taller than she was naturally, her royal gown purest white with shimmering crimson borders, her incredibly beautiful face haughty and imperious, stood the woman from my dream who had called herself Hera.

I gaped at her.

"Close your mouth, Orion," whispered Pausanias harshly. "That's the queen you're staring at: Olympias."

It was Hera.

And she recognized me. She looked past Philip, who was stumping painfully up the stairs. I realized for the first time that in addition to all the other wounds he had suffered, Philip was nearly crippled. But that is not what stunned me. It was Olympias. Hera. She looked straight at me and gave me an icy shadow of a smile. Her blood-red lips moved ever so slightly, mouthing a single word:

"Orion."

She knew me. My dream had not been a dream, after all.

Chapter 6

Somehow I was not surprised when I was told that the queen commanded me to appear in her presence.

Most of the royal guard were young Macedonian nobles; once we were relieved of duty they quickly dispersed to their homes and families. Only those few of us foreigners or men who had no house in Pella remained in the barracks.

We were quartered in one of the buildings adjacent to the palace, where slaves of all ages and both sexes bustled about to make us comfortable. Our quarters were almost luxurious, for a barracks. There were good beds in a wide room with strong rafters holding up a wooden ceiling. Plenty of room for us to stretch out. The room was well-aired, too, with windows that looked out on the parade ground.

I saw that the men knew these household slaves well. Several of the women, and some of the younger boys as well, seemed to be lovers of certain of the guardsmen.

A messenger informed me of the queen's command as I was bathing in the spring-fed pool outside the exercise yard. The water was icy but I did not mind it, nor did I care that some of the men laughed at me for washing myself.

"It will rain soon enough, Orion," called one of them from the stone benches lining the yard.

"What are you, one of those Athenian dainties who has to take a bath every month?" jeered another.

But when the queen's messenger arrived they quickly fell silent. To them it must have seemed as if I had known the queen would summon me. Or as if the queen had magically made me wash so that I would be sweet-smelling in her presence.

So I followed the messenger, a smooth-cheeked youth who smelled of perfume, through the many rooms of the palace to the queen's audience chamber.

She was Hera, the flame-haired, imperious beauty who had told me in my dream that I would love her. It *had* to be a dream, I told myself as I walked from the entrance of her audience room to her throne and bowed low before her. How could it be otherwise? Men sometimes glimpse their futures in dreams. And she recognized me and knew my name because she had been informed by messengers from Philip's camp. Messengers—or spies.

That could explain how she recognized me, I thought. Yet how could I explain that the Hera in my dream looked exactly like the Olympias, queen of Macedon, who sat before me on a throne of polished ebony? I had never seen her before, except for my dream.

Two guards in handsomely burnished armor stood behind her throne, staring stonily into infinity. Several women sat off in a corner of the large room. The floor was polished wood. Her throne was flanked by tall red-figured vases filled with vibrant flowers.

"Your name is Orion, I am told," she said to me.

"Yes, Your Majesty," I replied formally, thinking that she knew perfectly well what my name was. Then a new thought surfaced in my mind: *Perhaps she knows more than my name; perhaps she knows who I truly am, why I am here, everything!*

"I am told that you saved the king's life."

"I did what any loyal man would have done," I said.

Again that ghostly smile animated her lips briefly. I

realized that if Philip had been assassinated, her son might now be king.

"Olympias, Queen of the Macedonians, offers her thanks to you, Orion."

I bowed again.

"What reward would you have?" she asked. "Speak freely."

I heard the words on my tongue before I had a chance to think about them. "I have no memory, Your Majesty, beyond a few days ago. If it is in your power, I would like to know who I am and why I am here."

She arched an eyebrow at me, as if half-amused, half-affronted by my request.

But she smiled once more and murmured, "Come to this room at midnight, Orion. Come alone and tell no one. Do you understand?"

"I understand."

"Until midnight, then."

I hurried out of her audience chamber. Come alone and tell no one. That sounded dangerous. What would the king think if he learned of it?

As it turned out, the king was also thinking about my lack of memory. The messenger who had conveyed me to the queen's chamber was still waiting outside in the anteroom when I left Olympias. He told me that Parmenio wanted to see me now.

It was difficult not to like red-nosed Parmenio. He was an older man, probably almost fifty, his hair and beard grizzled with gray. He was built like a boar, low to the ground, thick in the chest and arms. Blunt as a boar, too; there was not a trace of dissemblance in him.

"The king wants you to talk with Alexandros' teacher," he said once I was ushered into his quarters. It was a sparse, spare room in the palace. If he had a family and a real home, they must have been elsewhere.

"Alexandros' teacher?" I asked.

"He's heard about your lack of memory and he wants to see you. His name's Aristotle. Fancies himself a philosopher, although he's from these parts—Stagyra. Spent some time in Athens, though; that must be where he got all the weird ideas he's always mumbling about."

I was getting a good tour of the palace and its surrounding buildings. I followed the same perfumed young man out of the palace, through the gate we had ridden past earlier in the day, and down one of the noisy streets of Pella to the house of Aristotle the Stagyrite.

The air in the streets seemed thick with dust—whether from all the construction that seemed to be going on everywhere, or blown in by the cutting wind from the plain beyond the city, I could not tell. The city was raucous with the sounds of hammering and yammering, builders and vendors and street hawkers and housewives and men of business all conducting their affairs at the top of their lungs. I saw a slim young girl, hardly into her teens, leaning against the freshly plastered wall of a new house, fiddling with one of her sandals. She was a pretty little thing, her long brown hair done up nicely, her short-skirted blue dress slipping over one bare shoulder. Then I realized that she was applying ink to her sandal. Wherever she stepped she left an advertising imprint for the brothel of Dionysia of Amphipolis. I laughed: Dionysia must have a high-class clientele if she expected new customers to be able to read.

The house that Philip had furnished Aristotle was large and spacious, although not imposing. Some of the new houses I had passed, and others still under construction, seemed much grander, with fluted columns and impressive staircases fronting them. Most of them were set well back from the street, separated from the traffic by low walls and flower gardens.

Everyone who was anyone, it seemed to me, was pouring into the capital. Men whose fathers had been horse-thieving hill-clan leaders were now vying with one another to build the most impressive house and lavish garden. These new noblemen had left their ancestors' homes in the hills to be in Philip's capital and to serve the king.

Aristotle's house was low and wide, with a newly-timbered roof the only sign that anyone cared about it. The garden in front of it had gone to weeds. The gravel path was also weed-choked and obviously had not been raked in months. The shutters on the windows were unpainted, cracked with age; a few of them were dangling lopsidedly.

Yet once I was ushered inside everything changed. I had thought the house much too large for one man, since I had been told that the philosopher lived alone. I saw that I was wrong: the house was barely large enough for him, because he was far from alone in it.

The house was a museum, a library, a repository for every kind of book and specimen and drawing and sample of all the myriad kinds of things that interested the Stagyrite's far-ranging mind. The pretty young messenger left me at the front door, after it was opened to me by a bright-eyed servant with a ragged sandy brown beard and thinning hair. His chiton was clean but seemed very old and frayed.

I stepped from the untended garden into a room that had originally been an entryway. Now its walls were lined with shelves and the shelves were crammed with book scrolls, all of them well-worn. Down a hallway narrowed by more bookshelves I was conducted by the balding servant until we came to the back of the house where Aristotle stood bent over a long table covered with seashells. No two of them were alike.

He looked up, blinked at me, and then dismissed the servant with an abrupt flick of his hand.

Aristotle looked almost like a gnome. Short and lean almost to the point of emaciation, his head was large and high-domed, dominating his tiny, shrivelled body. His hair was thinning but still dark; his beard neatly trimmed. His eyes were small and he blinked constantly as if they pained him.

"You are the one called Orion?" he asked, in a voice that was surprisingly deep and strong.

"I am Orion," I said.

"Son of?"

I could only shrug.

He smiled, showing ragged yellow teeth. "Pardon me, young man. That was a trick. Four times before I have seen men who have lost their memory. Sometimes an innocent question brings an answer before they can think about it and the memory returns. Or at least part of it."

He sat me on a stool next to his worktable and examined my head in the afternoon light streaming through the long windows.

"No scars," he muttered. "No sign of a head wound."

"I heal very quickly," I said.

He fixed me with those burning eyes. "You remember that?"

"No," I replied truthfully. "I *know* it. Just as I know that my name is Orion."

"You remember nothing that happened to you beyond a few days ago?"

"It is as if I were born as an adult. The first thing I remember is marching with the mercenaries of Diopeithes on the plain of Perinthos, little more than a week ago."

"Born fully-formed, with shield and spear in hand," he said, half smiling. "Like Athena."

"Athena? You know her?"

"I know of all the gods, Orion."

"I dream of them."

"Do you?"

I hesitated, wondering how much I could tell him.

Would he consider me insane? Would he consider it treason against Philip to dream that Olympias, the queen, was also Hera the goddess? And that she intended that I should slay the king?

"What does Athena look like?" I asked.

He blinked several times. "Usually she is portrayed in armor and helmet. Phydias' great statue of her shows her bearing shield and spear. Often she has an owl with her, the symbol of her wisdom."

"But her face," I insisted. "Her form. What does she look like?"

Aristotle's eyes widened at my question. "She is a goddess, Orion. No one has seen her features."

"I have."

"In your dreams?"

I had blurted enough, I decided. So I merely replied, "Yes, in my dreams."

Aristotle considered this a moment, his large dome of a head tilted slightly to one side on his frail shoulders. "Is she beautiful?" he asked at length.

"Extremely beautiful. Her eyes are silver-gray, her hair as black as the midnight sky. Her face . . ." I could not find the words to describe her.

"Do you love her?" he asked.

I nodded.

"And she loves you? In your dreams?"

She loved me in the barren snowy wastes of the Ice Age, I knew. She loved me in the green forests of Paradise. We had loved each other through a hundred million years: in the dusty camps of the Great Khan, in the electric cities of the industrial world, on the shores of the methane sea of ringed Saturn's largest moon.

All this I kept to myself. He would think me a raving madman if I told him a hundredth of it. So I answered merely:

"Yes. In my dreams we love each other."

He must have sensed that there was much I was holding back from him. We talked until the sunlight faded from the windows and slaves entered the room softly to light the oil lamps. The balding major-domo who had admitted me to the house came and whispered in his master's ear.

"You are wanted back at your barracks, Orion," said Aristotle to me.

I got up from the stool, surprised that we had been talking for so long that my joints popped when I stood up.

"Thank you for your time," I said.

"I hope I have been helpful."

"Yes. A little."

"Come see me again. I am almost always here and I will be happy to see you."

"Thank you," I said.

He walked with me around the long table toward the door to the room. "I think that perhaps the key to your memory lies in those dreams you described. Often men dream of things that they do not think of when they are awake."

"The gods use dreams to give us messages," I suggested.

He smiled and reached up to pat my shoulder. "The gods have other fish to fry, Orion, if they actually take any interest in human affairs at all. They are far too busy to meddle in our dreams, I fear."

His words sent a shock through me. Somehow I knew he was right, and I wondered how he knew so much about the gods. Yet, at the same instant, I knew he was also wrong. The gods' principal interest is to meddle in human affairs.

I had been recalled to barracks because I was assigned to duty that evening. Most of the royal guard had gone off to their homes scattered through the city, so the handful of us who lived in the barracks got the chore of standing like statues through the king's long, loud, wine-soaked dinners.

Pausanias was one of the few Macedonian nobles who actually did his guard duty that night. Sour-faced and grumbling, he complained that he should be reclining on a dinner couch with the others rather than standing around in armor and helmet while his fellow nobles drank themselves into a stupor.

"I'm as good as they are," I heard him growl as he inspected my uniform. We were all decked out as if we were marching into battle. We even carried our shields with us.

My post was by the main entrance to the dining hall. It was a big room with a huge fireplace at one end of it, roaring hot although no cooking was done on it. Even in summer the Macedonian nights could be chill. The food was brought in on long trays by sweating servants and set down on the dinner tables, while the dogs, lolling by the fireplace, watched silently with hungry eyes that caught the flickering of the flames.

Philip reclined on a couch at the front of the hall, raised up on a two-step dais, beneath a strikingly vivid mosaic of a roaring lion done in colored pebbles. Flanking him along the table were his generals Parmenio and Antipatros, and Antigonos, gray and lean as an old wolf. Like Philip, Antigonos had lost an eye in battle long ago.

The dinner guests sitting below them were all male, of course. At first. There were plenty of women servants, most of them young and slim and smiling as the men ogled and pawed at them. The boys among the servants were treated much the same. Even Philip pinched buttocks without regard to gender. Wine was poured liberally, and the laughter and rowdiness rose with each gulp.

I saw that Alexandros was not present, nor any of his young Companions. This was a dinner for the king's friends and companions-in-arms. And for relatives, close and distant, such as Attalos, a fat and beady-eyed clan leader who owned, it was said, the biggest house in Pella and the richest horse ranch in Macedonia.

Attalos also had a fourteen-year-old niece who was being dangled as bait before Philip's eyes, according to the barracks gossip.

"Philip likes 'em young," one of my barracks mates had told me while we were suiting up for duty. "Girls, boys, makes no difference."

"How old was Olympias when he married her?" I had asked.

"Ahh, that was different. That was a state marriage. Brought the Molossians and all of Epeiros over to Philip's side with that marriage."

"He was mad about her, though," said one of the other men.

"Bewitched by her, you mean."

"Well, whatever it was, it wore off as soon as she bore him Alexandros."

"Doesn't matter; the old fox casts his one good eye on anything with smooth skin."

They all laughed approvingly, wishing they had the kingly prerogatives of Philip.

As the dinner stretched into a long drinking bout I wondered if I would be able to keep my midnight appointment with the queen. Philip looked half-unconscious from the wine he had drunk, yet he had a boy of ten or so pouring still more into his gold goblet. Some of the dinner guests were drowsing on their couches; those who weren't were fondling the prettier servants.

Then the hetairai were admitted into the dining hall and the servants scampered away, many of them looking grateful. These professional women were older and looked quite sure of themselves. It seemed to me that they picked out the men they wished to be with. No one argued with their choices. And the men's behavior actually improved. The lewd jokes and roaring laughter quieted down as one of the courtesans pointed to the musicians who had been sitting idly in a corner. They struck up their lyres and flutes and lovely soft music filled the dining hall. The stench of spilled wine and vomit still hung in the air. But now the perfumes of distant lands began to make the room more pleasant.

In less than an hour the dining hall emptied out. No one could leave before the king did, of course, but soon after the hetairai appeared he lumbered off with one of the serving boys, leaning heavily on the lad's shoulders, dragging his bad leg. One by one the other men went off with their female companions until at last the hall was emptied of all except the servants, who wearily began cleaning off the tables and throwing scraps to the dogs who had been waiting by the fire all evening long.

At last Pausanias strode past my post at the entrance. "Dismissed," was all that he managed to say.

I hurried back to the barracks, took off my armor, and rushed back to the palace to find Olympias' audience chamber.

Chapter 7

The queen was not in her audience chamber. But a sloe-eyed maid with flowing dark hair and a knowing smile was waiting for me. Holding a clay oil lamp in one upraised hand, she guided me through the upper levels of the palace, a dizzying labyrinth of stairs and corridors and rooms. I thought she was deliberately trying to confuse me.

"Is the queen's room in a hidden place?" I asked, half joking.

She looked up at me in the yellow light of the lamp, her smile full of secrets. "You will see," she said.

And I did. Soon we came to a low wooden door at the end of an otherwise blank corridor. I could hear the night wind moaning even though we had passed no window. We must be up high, I reasoned.

The servant scratched at the door and it swung inward on silent hinges. She went through and beckoned me enter. I had to duck to get through the arched doorway. The servant slipped behind me and went out again, closing the door behind her.

It was dark inside. Blacker than the darkest moonless night, a darkness so deep and all-engulfing that I felt as if I had stepped into oblivion, an emptiness where nothing at all existed. Dark and cold, frigid, as if I had been plunged into the void where warmth and light could not exist. My breath froze in my throat. I stretched out my arms like a blind man, reaching for some reference point in this stygian abyss, searching sightlessly while my senses told me I was falling, tumbling through a nothingness where neither time nor space existed. Panic rose within me as I struggled to breathe.

Then I saw the faintest, faintest glow of a distant light. Like the flicker of the first star of evening, so tenuous that I could not be certain it was there at all. Gradually, though, the light brightened. I heard a slithering of bare feet, the faintest suggestion of distant laughter. I could breathe again. My fear subsided. I stood immobile, silent, waiting for the light to brighten further, my right hand resting gently on the dagger strapped beneath my skirt.

Slowly, lamps came aglow, low and guttering at first, then gradually brightening. I saw that the room I stood in was immense, impossibly long and wide, its vast ceiling lost in shadows, its floor polished white marble, massive columns of green marble marching in rows along either side of me.

At the far end sat Olympias—Hera?—on a throne of ivory inlaid with gold. She glowed with splendor. Snakes slithered on the dais of her throne, on the steps of the marble platform, on the high back of her throne itself. Some were small and deadly poisonous. Others were huge constrictors, their eyes glittering in the lamplight.

This colossal opulent room could not possibly have been part of Philip's palace. Somehow I had passed through a gateway into another world, another universe. This was witchcraft, I realized, beyond anything that Philip's rough soldiers could imagine.

"Come to me, Orion," Olympias called. Her voice was low and melodious, yet it carried the distance from her throne to me as if she had been standing at my side.

I walked as if in a trance. It seemed to take hours. I

heard nothing but the clacking of my boots against the marble floor. I watched the snakes watching me with their glittering eyes.

At last I stood at the foot of her throne. Olympias wore a copper-red robe that matched the color of her hair and left her shoulders and arms bare. Its slitted skirt revealed her long smooth legs. Bright jewelry bedecked her throat, her arms and wrists. She looked down on me and smiled a cruelly beautiful smile.

"Do you fear me, Orion?"

"No," I replied truthfully. One of the pythons was entwining its mottled body of brown and green around my leg, climbing me as if I were a tree. And I stood immobile as a tree, unable to turn away, unable to run, unable even to move my arms or fingers. Yet I felt no fear. I was truly under her spell.

Olympias leaned back in her throne as a sleek cobra slithered over her bare shoulder and across her bosom.

"Do you love me, Orion?"

"No," I said. "I love—Athena."

Her smile turned cold. "A mortal man cannot love a goddess, Orion. You need a woman of flesh and blood. You love me."

"I mean no offense, but—"

"You *will* love me!" she snapped. "And no other."

I found that I was unable to speak. The python had coiled itself around my chest. Its head rose to my eye level and its flickering tongue touched my face. I stared into its slitted yellow eyes and saw nothing, no purpose, no reason. It was being controlled just as I was.

"You will love me," Olympias repeated. "And you will do my bidding. Not merely here, but wherever and whenever I command you."

It was if my body did not belong to me, as if it were a machine under someone else's control. I could think, I could feel the massive strength of the python's muscular coils gripping me tightly, feel the tingling jabs of its tongue on my face. I could hear Olympias' words and see her leaning forward on her throne, her eyes as glittery as the snakes'. But I could not move. I knew that if she willed it, my heart would stop.

The cobra glided across her lap and down the leg of the throne. I saw that what I had at first thought to be a bright metal armband was actually a small snake that she now removed from her forearm and considered silently for a moment.

Then she got up from her throne, holding the little coral snake in both hands, and came down the three steps of the dais to me.

"You will love me," she repeated, "and do whatever I command you to do."

She held the snake to my throat. I felt its tiny fangs penetrate my flesh and a hot surge of flaming agony raced along my veins with the speed of an electrical shock. I realized why Olympias had made the python coil around me. Without it I would have collapsed to the cold marble floor.

I never lost consciousness. The pain passed and my body felt frozen, totally numb. Yet when Olympias commanded me to follow her, I found that the python had slid off me and I could walk almost normally. She led me to a bedchamber that seemed suspended in emptiness. I felt a solid floor beneath my feet, but when I looked down I saw nothing but tiny pinpoints of light winking in swirling clouds of cold mist that billowed pink and blue and golden yellow.

We reclined on a bed as soft and yielding as the gentle swells of a becalmed sea, stars gleaming out of the darkness all around us. Olympias unfastened her robe; her body was magnificent, perfect skin glowing in the darkness, a form as divine as a goddess.

"Do you like what you see, Orion?" she asked as she knelt beside me.

I could not help but answer, "Yes."

She took my clothes off me, clucking her tongue slightly at the dagger strapped to my thigh.

"The gift of Odysseus," I explained. "At Troy."

Wordlessly she unstrapped the dagger and tossed it off into the darkness surrounding our bed.

"Now you are mine, Orion," she murmured.

We made love, slowly at first but then with increasing ardor. Every time she climaxed she screamed, "You're *mine! Mine!*"

In the lulls between times she asked, "Who do you love, Orion?"

I could not answer. I could not say her name, and her control of my body would not permit me to speak the name of Athena. Then we would begin anew and the passion would surge in us both as we thrashed and tumbled and sweated wildly. "Did she ever do *this* for you?" Olympias would ask. "Did she ever make you do *this*?"

How long we spent coupling was impossible for me to reckon. But at last we lay side by side, staring into the infinite sea of stars, panting like a pair of rutting animals.

"Speak the name of the woman you love, Orion," she commanded me.

"You will not like what you hear," I replied.

I had expected anger. Instead, she laughed. "Her hold on you is deeper than I had expected."

"We love each other."

"That was a dream, Orion. Nothing more than a dream of yours. Forget it. Accept this reality."

"She loves me. Athena. Anya."

For long moments she was silent in the darkness.

Then, "A goddess may take on human form and make love to a mortal. That is not love, Orion."

"Who am I?" I asked while her control over me was relaxed. "Why am I here?"

"Who are you? Why, Orion, you are nothing more than any other human creature—a plaything of the gods." And her laughter turned cruel once more.

I closed my eyes and wondered how I could escape this evil woman's grasp. She had to be the goddess Hera that I had seen in my dream. Or was she merely the witch Olympias, controlling me, bewitching me, with the power of her dark magic? Were my memories of Athena and the other gods and goddesses merely vivid dreams hatched by my own longing for a knowledge of my origins, my own yearning for someone to love, for someone who could love me? Was Olympias' powerful magic truly witchcraft, or the superhuman abilities of an actual goddess? I fell asleep trying to fathom the mystery.

When I opened my eyes again early morning sunlight was filtering through the beaded curtain of a window. I was lying beside a naked woman in a rumpled bed. The makeup smeared across her face told me that she was one of the hetairai who had attended Philip's dinner the night before.

I sat up slowly, not wanting to wake her. In the milky early light she looked older, tired.

Softly I rose from the bed and gathered my clothes, which had been neatly piled on a curved chair in the corner of the bedroom. Even my dagger was there, at the bottom of the pile. I dressed, ducked through the curtained doorway of the bedroom, and bumped right into Pausanias.

"You've had a busy night of it," he growled.

I had no idea of how I had gotten here, so I said nothing.

"Damned Thais just picks out whoever she likes, like a man," said Pausanias as he led me down the corridor toward a flight of stairs. We went down to the ground floor and out into the street. It was still early, quiet outside.

"How did you get there?" Pausanias asked grumpily, jerking a thumb back toward Thais' house. It was a modest two-story building, but well kept, with flower boxes blooming brightly beneath every window.

With a shrug that I hoped was convincing, I replied, "I don't really know."

"If you can't hold your wine you shouldn't drink."

"Yes, you're right."

We marched along the empty street, heading uphill toward the palace.

"Trouble is," Pausanias said, "that young Ptolemaios has his eye on her. And she taps *you* on the shoulder instead."

Ptolemaios was one of Alexandros' Companions, I knew. Rumored to be a bastard son of Philip, as well.

"Perhaps she's merely trying to make him jealous," I half-joked, still wondering how I did get into Thais' house. And bed.

"That kind of jealousy leads to murder, Orion. And blood feuds."

I shrugged light-heartedly. "I have no family to carry on a blood feud after I'm gone."

"Thank the gods for small favors," he muttered.

As we neared the palace wall a question popped into my mind. "How did you know where I was?"

Pausanias fixed me with a surly glance. "One of the queen's servants woke me before cock's crow and warned me of it. Said I'd better get you out of there before Ptolemaios finds out about it."

"And how did this servant know?"

"I told you she was one of the queen's servants. The witch knows everything that happens in the palace—sometimes before it even happens."

Chapter 8

The air of the palace seethed with intrigue. The king was conducting one military campaign after another along his borders while at the same time negotiating with delegations from regions as far-flung as the Peloponnesus and Syracuse in Sicily, as well as receiving ambassadors from the Great King of Persia.

No one seemed to know what Philip was aiming at, what his goals were. There was no dearth of opinions on the subject, however. I heard as many different guesses as there were men speaking on the subject. Philip wanted to rule all of the Greeks, said one. He wanted to conquer the Persian Empire, said another. No, he wanted to be dictator of Thebes, the city where he had spent several of his younger years as a royal hostage. No, he wanted to humiliate Athens and hang Demosthenes by his scrawny neck. Nonsense, said still another, his real intention is to expand Macedonian colonies northward into the backward, bickering tribes of the Balkans, but to do that he must safeguard the kingdom's southern borders, where the great cities of Thebes and Athens and the others are waiting for him to turn his back.

I was one of the guards standing behind Philip's throne the afternoon that the Persians were presented to the king. They were exotic in their long silk robes of many colors, bedecked with sparkling jewels. They brought magnificent gifts of spices and incense from their new king, Dareios III. Philip accepted them as if they were his due and gave in return a hundred cavalry horses: all geldings, I learned later. The other guardsmen laughed themselves sick over Philip's trick.

The king himself was not even smiling after the Persians left his court.

"Spies," he said grimly to Parmenio and Antipatros, after the Persians had left. "They're here to see how strong we are, how well we're getting along against Athens."

"I'll bet they're heading straight for Athens now, to tell Demosthenes everything they learned here," said Antipatros.

"And to pour more gold into his hands," added Parmenio.

There were other intrigues, as well, much closer to the court. Attalos was pushing his young niece, Kleopatra, as a fitting bride for Philip. I knew that the king had taken several wives, mainly as diplomatic gestures, and he had a powerful sexual appetite: male or female did not much concern him as long as they were young and pretty.

Kleopatra was such a common name among the Macedonians that many of the nobles at court referred to the fourteen-year-old niece of Attalos by an honorary name that Philip had bestowed on her: Eurydice, the name of the supernally beautiful wife of legendary Orpheos. Orpheos had voluntarily descended into Hades to recover his dead love. I thought that Olympias would rather see Philip in hell before she would accept his marriage to Kleopatra/Eurydice.

Olympias was scheming constantly. She had driven all of Philip's other wives out of the court, although she resolutely refused to sleep with him, according to the palace gossip. She wanted to make certain that her son, Alexandros, would be the only possible heir to Philip's throne. That meant that there must be no new marriages and no new legitimate sons. I knew that all the tales about her powers of witchcraft were more than true, and that she could somehow command me at her whim. What she planned for me I did not know, and after that first wild night of lovemaking she did not so much as glance at me.

For his part, Philip was also scheming. A marriage into the house of Attalos would benefit the throne. So would an advantageous marriage of his daughter by Olympias, who was also named Kleopatra. Even younger than Attalos' niece, and painfully shy, Philip's daughter was a very valuable pawn in the game of nations.

And that game went on without cease. Ambassadors and couriers arrived at the court almost every day. From my post as one of the king's guards I saw that Philip could be tactful, generous, flexible, patient, a good host, a firm friend, a reasonable enemy ready to make peace even when he had the upper hand. Especially when he had the upper hand.

But I began to see, also, that he was implacable in his pursuit of one goal. No matter how generous or flexible or reasonable he was, each agreement he made, each objective he sought, was aimed at making Macedonia supreme, not merely over the surrounding tribes and the port cities along the coast; Philip wanted supremacy over the major city-states to the south—Thebes, Corinth, Sparta, and especially Athens.

"Demosthenes rouses the rabble down there against us time and again," Philip complained to a visiting Athenian merchant. "I have no reason to fight against Athens. I revere the city of Perikles and Sokrates; I honor its ancient traditions. But the Athenians think they are the lords of the earth; they are trying to strangle us by cutting us off from the sea."

The merchant had been sent to negotiate for the year's grain harvest that we had seized. Philip wanted Athens to cede control of Perinthos and the other port cities along the Bosporus.

"All the port cities?" gasped the Athenian. "But that, most honored king, would put your mighty hands at the throat of our people. Macedonia would be able to shut off the grain supply whenever you chose to."

Leaning an elbow on the withered thigh of his crippled leg, Philip looked down at the white-robed merchant from his throne. "It would make us friends, Athenian," he said. "Friends trust one another. And they do not rouse their people to make war against one another."

"You speak of Demosthenes."

"None other."

The merchant tugged at his beard for a moment, then smoothed the front of his robe. At last he replied, "Athens, sir, is a democracy. In the past, our city was ruled by an oligarchy. Even earlier, by tyrants. We prefer democracy."

Patiently, Philip said, "I have no intention of ruling Athens. All I want is for Athens to stop making war on us."

"I shall so inform the Assembly when I return."

"Very well."

Philip traded the grain for a promise that Athens would no longer support Perinthos against him. Nothing was said about Byzantion.

Philip saw the merchant off with full diplomatic honors. The royal guard was lined up at the palace gate for him. Unfortunately, it was in the middle of an autumn storm, and cold driving rain made everything gray and miserable. Philip limped back to his rooms with me and three other picked guardsmen following close behind him. The cold raw weather must have bothered his bad leg intensely.

His three chief generals were waiting for him in his work room, together with slaves bearing pitchers of strong red wine. It was a smallish room, dominated by a heavy trestle table on which a large map of the Aegean coast was held down by heavy iron paperweights.

"The agreement means nothing," Parmenio grumbled as he put down his first goblet on the edge of the sheepskin map. "The Athenians will keep their word only as long as they choose to. In the meantime they get the grain."

"And their navy can strike anywhere along the coast, unhindered," Antigonos pointed out.

Antipatros agreed vigorously. "You should have held onto the grain. Let them feel hungry for a while. Then they'd be more reasonable."

Philip took a deep grateful draught of the wine. Then he said, "They'd get hungry, all right. And blame us for it. Then we'd just be proving what Demosthenes has been telling them for years: that I'm a bloodthirsty tyrant intent on conquest."

"Tyrant," spat Parmenio. "As if you rule all by yourself, without the Council or the elders to account to."

But Philip was hardly listening. His mind was already spinning out the next move. I stood guard at the door until it was dark, when I was relieved. When I got to the barracks Pausanias told me that the queen had sent for me.

He eyed me suspiciously. "Why is the queen interested in you?"

I returned his gaze without blinking. "You will have to ask her, captain. She has summoned me; I didn't ask to see her."

He looked away, then warned, "Be careful, Orion. She plays a dangerous game."

"Do I have any choice?"

"If she says a word against the king—even a hint of a thought against him—you must tell me."

I admired his loyalty. "I will, captain. I am the king's man, not the queen's."

Yet, as I made my way through the deepening shadows of night toward Olympias' rooms in the palace, I knew that she could control me whenever she chose to. I was hopelessly under her spell.

To my surprise and relief, Alexandros was with her. A slave woman met me at the door to the queen's suite of rooms and guided me to a small chamber where she sat on a cushioned chair talking earnestly with her son. Even in an ordinary wool robe she looked magnificent, copper-red hair tumbling past her shoulders, slender arms bare, lithe body taut beneath the light-blue robe.

Alexandros was pacing the small room like a caged panther. He radiated energy, all golden impatience, pent-up emotion that made his smooth handsome face seem petulant, moody.

"But I'm his only legitimate heir," Alexandros was saying when I was ushered into the room.

Olympias acknowledged my presence with a glance and gestured for the servant who had brought me to depart. She closed the door softly behind me and I stood there, silent and immobile, waiting to be commanded.

Alexandros was no taller than my shoulder, but he was solidly built, with wide shoulders and strong limbs. His golden hair curled down the back of his neck. His eyes glowed with restless passion.

"There's no one else," he said to his mother. "Unless you count Arrhidaios, the idiot."

Olympias gave him a pained smile. "You forget that the Council may elect whom it chooses. The throne does not automatically pass to you."

"They wouldn't dare elect anyone else!"

She shrugged. "You are still very young, in the eyes of many. They could elect Parmenio or—"

"Parmenio! That fat old man! I'd kill him!"

"—or they could appoint a regent," Olympias continued, unshaken in the slightest by her son's outburst, "until you are old enough to rule."

"But I'm old enough now," Alexandros insisted, almost whining. "I've already served as regent while the king was off at his wars. What do they expect of me?"

"Vision," said Olympias.

"A vision? Like an oracle?"

"No," she said, in a slightly disappointed tone. "The kind of vision that excites men's souls. A goal for the future that is so daring that men will flock to you and follow wherever you lead them."

He stopped his pacing and stared at her. "What are you talking about?"

"You must lead the Greeks against the Persian Empire."

Alexandros frowned at his mother. "By the gods, Philip has been talking about fighting the Persians for ten years or more. There's nothing new or daring in that."

Olympias gestured to the chair next to hers. I saw that her fingernails were long and lacquered blood-red.

Alexandros sat.

"Philip talks about fighting the Persians. You will speak of conquering the Persian Empire. Philip uses the Persians as an excuse in his drive to bring all the Greek cities under his dominion. You will tell all the Greeks that no Greek city can be free as long the Persian Empire threatens us."

"That's what Aristotle told me—"

"Of course he did." Olympias smiled knowingly.

"But the Persians aren't threatening us," Alexandros said. "Their new king is struggling to hold his empire together. They have no intention of invading us."

"Little matter. People remember the tales of their grandfathers, and *their* grandfathers before them. The Persians have invaded us in times past; they all know that.

Even today the Persians control the Greek cities of Ionia and interfere in our politics, paying one city to war against another, keeping us weak and divided. Only by crushing the Persian Empire can cities such as Athens be truly free."

Alexandros gaped at her. At last he said, "You could be a better orator than Demosthenes himself."

Olympias smiled and patted her son on his golden curls. "Philip has an army. Demosthenes has a cause. You can have both."

"To conquer the Persian Empire." Alexandros breathed the words, inhaled the idea like heady perfume. "To conquer the *world*!"

Still smiling, Olympias turned to me. "Orion, I have a command for you."

I knew that I must obey.

"This is my son," she said. "You will protect him at all times against all his enemies. Including the man who believes himself to be his father."

"Against Philip?" I asked.

"Against Philip and anyone else who would stand in his way," Olympias said to me.

"I understand."

Abruptly she turned back to Alexandros, still sitting there musing about conquering the world. "Be patient. Learn from the One-Eyed Fox himself. Bide your time. But when the moment finally comes, be prepared to strike."

"I will, mother," said Alexandros fervently. "I will."

Olympias dismissed me as soon as Alexandros left. I went to my barracks bed that night with my thoughts in a swirl. I owed my allegiance to Philip, yet Olympias had commanded me to protect Alexandros even against Philip himself. What did she fear? What did she plan?

I forced myself to sleep, willed myself to dream. Once again I found myself on the sunny hillside overlooking the magnificent city by the sea. It sat beneath its glittering dome of energy, looking totally empty, completely abandoned.

The woman I loved had lived there once. The woman I knew as Athena. Anya was her true name, or as true a name as any of the Creators possessed. They were far beyond the need for names, even the need for words. They were as far beyond mortal human form as the stars are beyond my reach.

The Creators. I remembered the word, the concept. One of them had created me. Hera had called me a creature, a being created by—by the Golden One, Aten. I remembered that much. My memory was slowly returning. Or were the Creators merely allowing me to remember some things so that I could serve them better?

Determined to learn more, I started walking toward the glowing city.

Only to find myself in my rumpled bed in the barracks at Pella, sunlight beaming through the high windows and roosters crowing in the distance.

Chapter 9

"Do you think you could make a good spy for me?" Philip asked.

I had been summoned into his work room. The trestle table was bare, except for a pile of scrolls in one corner. There were no servants, no wine.

"A spy?" I blurted.

"Why not?" Philip mused aloud, leaning back in his leather sling-chair. "The best spies are men who seem to be part of the background, men who are not noticed by the people they're spying on. Or women, of course, but that's something else altogether."

I stood at attention before him, not knowing what to say.

"Don't look so miserable, Orion," the king said with a crooked grin. "I'm not asking you to sneak around and pry into locked rooms."

"I don't understand, sir."

He scratched at his beard. Then, "I am sending Aristotle to Athens as an informal diplomat, to make contact with the men there who are against Demosthenes and in favor of making peace with me. He will need an escort. I would like you to head his escort."

"Yes, sir," I replied. "But spying?"

He laughed. "Just keep your eyes and ears open. See

everything. Listen to everyone. Remember it all and tell it to me when you return. That's what spying is."

I felt relieved. I could do that easily enough. And to leave Pella would mean leaving Olympias and her witch's spell over me. I felt far more than relieved over that. Philip dismissed me after telling me that Aristotle would depart the following morning. But as I started for the door I realized that this mission would take me away from Alexandros. What of the task Olympias gave me to protect her son?

"By the way," Philip called before I could reach the door latch. "My son will be going with you. He's never seen Athens. Neither have I, for that matter."

I turned back to the king.

"He'll have a few of his Companions with him. They'll be travelling incognito—if that young hothead can manage to keep his mouth shut, that is." He sighed like a worried father. "I want you to take special care of him, Orion. He is the future of this kingdom."

I must have smiled foolishly, for Philip looked surprised. Then he grinned back at me. As I left him I felt an immense sense of relief. Philip meant no harm to his son. He wanted me to protect Alexandros just as much as Olympias did. And Olympias must have known of this mission to Athens last night. Perhaps it was all her idea, to have her son see Athens, and Philip was just as much of a pawn in her hands as I was. Perhaps I would not be out of her grasp even in distant Athens.

Still, I felt a new sense of freedom once we had left Pella behind us. The crisp air of the open fields and wooded hills was like wine to me. The sky was bright and clean; the intrigues and intricacies of the capital faded away as we rode our mounts along the trail that wound through the rising, rocky countryside.

The trip turned into a travelling school. Aristotle had

been Alexandros' tutor until just about a year ago, and now as we rode our horses across the hills and through the mountain passes heading southward, the gnomish old man became engrossed with every fold of the land, every bird and beast and insect, every blade of grass or burr of thistle.

He sent Alexandros and his Companions scurrying across the countryside collecting samples of everything from grass seeds to rocks. Hephaistion, who seemed especially close to Alexandros, got himself half-killed by wasp stings when he tried to collect a sample of the nest they had constructed in a dead tree. Aristotle tended the lad himself with mudpacks and soothing ointments, all the while telling us that his father had been a physician and had been bitterly disappointed when Aristotle did not follow in his footsteps.

I had expected the old man to travel in one of the wagons, but he rode horseback as the rest of us did. The servants, of course, rode mules. We had hired professional teamsters to handle the ever-increasing number of wagons in our train.

The high road south wound its way through the rocky Vale of Tempe, between Ossa and craggy Mount Olympos, its lofty peak already gleaming with snow.

"The abode of the gods," said Aristotle to me as we rode through the brisk autumn morning. Brittle dead leaves strewed the trail; our horses snorted steam in the early chill.

"Only in legend," I replied.

He looked up at me, his brow furrowed. "You don't believe in the gods?"

I must have made a bitter little smile. "I believe in them, but they don't live up there in the cold. They take better care of themselves than that."

Aristotle shook his head. "Remarkable. For a man who has no memory, Orion, you seem very certain of your knowledge about the gods' residence."

"We could climb the mountain," I said, "and see for ourselves if the gods are living up there."

He laughed. "See for ourselves! Very good, Orion. Very good. The essence of truth is knowledge gained by examination. I'll make a philosopher of you yet!"

"The essence of truth," I muttered.

"Truth is often difficult to determine, Orion. Sokrates gave his life seeking for it. My own teacher, Plato, tried to determine exactly what truth is, and he died broken-hearted."

I wondered silently what the essence of truth might be. Were my dreams truer than my waking reality? Were my hazy recollections of other lives true memories or merely desperate fantasies of my mind?

He misinterpreted my silence. "Yes, I differ from Plato's teachings. He believed that ideas are the essence of truth: pure ideas, with no physical substance whatsoever. I cannot accept that. To me, the only way to discover truth is by examining the world about us with our five senses."

"You say that Plato died of a broken heart?"

The gnomish old man's face grew somber. "Dionysios invited Plato to his city of Syracuse, in distant Sicily. There Plato instructed him on how to be a philosopher-king, a great leader among men. It isn't every day that a philosopher has a king for his student."

"What happened?"

"Dionysios listened very carefully to Plato's ideas about the ideal republic. And he used those ideas to make himself absolute tyrant of Syracuse. His son was even worse. He threw Plato out of Syracuse, sent him packing home to Athens."

"So much for the philosopher-king," I said.

Aristotle gave me a troubled look, then fell silent.

Our little band was growing larger every day with Aristotle's constantly-growing collections. We had to buy more mules and wagons and more men to tend them. The pack train would be twice the size of our original group by the time we reached Athens. There was already snow on the lower mountaintops, and the trees were turning gauntly bare. I urged our band southward through the narrow pass of Thermopylai, where Leonidas and his Spartans had stood against the invading Persians of Xerxes more than a century and a half earlier.

Alexandros insisted that we stop and do homage to the brave Spartans, who died to the last man rather than surrender to the Persians.

So there on the narrow rocky shelf between the grim mountains and the heaving sea, near the hot springs for which the pass was named, we paid honor to ancient heroes while the winds keening down from the north warned of impending winter. Alexandros spoke of the Persians with contempt, ending with, "Never will our people be free until the Persian Empire is shattered completely."

Aristotle nodded agreement. The men were impressed with his words. I was more impressed with the smell of snow in the graying sky. We moved on.

"One thing that Alexandros did not mention," said Aristotle from the back of the gentle chestnut mare he rode, "was that the Macedonians allowed Xerxes and his army to travel through their territory without raising a finger against them. They even sold the Persians grain and horses and timber for their ships, as a matter of fact."

He spoke with a forgiving smile, and in a low voice so that no one could hear but me. Even so, he added, "But that was a long time ago, of course. Things have changed."

I had expected Attica to be somewhat like Macedonia, a wide fertile plain ringed with wooded mountains. But instead the mountains marched right to the edge of the sea, and they were mostly starkly bare rock.

"The Athenians cut down their forests over the generations to make ships for their incessant wars," Aristotle told me. "Now the country is fit for nothing but bees."

Alexandros rode up between us. "You can see why the Athenians took to the sea," he said excitedly. "There isn't enough farmland here to feed a village, let alone a great city."

"That's why they depend on the grain from beyond the Bosporus," I guessed.

"That's why they want to hold onto the port towns. We can strangle them by taking all their ports away," said Alexandros. Suddenly his eyes lit up. "When I make war against the Persians, the first thing I will do is to take all their port cities. That will make their fleet useless!"

And he galloped off to tell his friends of his sudden strategic insight.

Philip's command was that Alexandros and his Companions—he had brought four of them—should remain incognito while in Athens. They were to be nothing more than part of the guard for the revered teacher and philosopher, Aristotle. I knew it would be difficult to keep these high-born Macedonians from shining through any disguise; especially Alexandros, who wanted to see everything and be everywhere. He would never follow my orders. Any Athenian with half an eye would see that this was the golden-haired son of Philip who was already becoming something of a legend throughout the land.

We entered Athens without fanfare, stopping at the city gates only long enough to tell the guards on duty that this was Aristotle of Stagyra come to visit his old friend Aeschines, the lawyer. As we rode through the narrow, winding, noisy streets I saw the great white cliff of the Acropolis rising before us and, gleaming atop it, splendid marble temples and an immense statue of Athena, the city's protectress.

My heart leaped in my chest: *Of course! This is her city! This is the place where I will find her.*

As if he could read my thoughts, Alexandros said to Hephaistion, riding beside him. "We must go up there and see the Parthenon."

His young friend, tall and lean and dark where Alexandros was short and solid and blond, shook his head. "I don't think they allow visitors up there. It's sacred ground."

"It's where they keep their treasury," Ptolemaios said, laughing. "That's why they don't allow visitors."

"But I'm not merely a visitor," Alexandros snapped. "I am the son of a king."

"Not on this trip," said Ptolemaios, like a big brother. "We're just escorts for the old man."

Alexandros tried to stare Ptolemaios down, found he could not, then turned to stare at me. I looked the other way. *Yes,* I said to myself, *it's going to be very difficult to keep him under control.*

The house of Aeschines, the lawyer, was more magnificent than Philip's palace. It was smaller, of course, but not by much. Its portico was all marble, its walls decorated with colorful friezes of nymphs and satyrs. Statues crowded the garden like a marble forest: grave men in solemn robes and nubile young women in various stages of undress.

Aeschines himself was not at home when we arrived, his major domo told Aristotle. He spoke Attic Greek, not the Macedonian dialect, but I could understand him just as well. The lawyer was pleading a case before the Assembly and would probably not return until nightfall. We had several hours to unpack and settle into the spacious guest wing of the house.

"Is it true?" I asked Aristotle as we watched the slaves unload his specimens and cart them off into the room that had been given him for his studies. "Are all Athenians lawyers?"

The old man laughed softly. "No, not all Athenians are lawyers. Some are women. Many are slaves."

I took an especially heavy crate from a staggering, frail older slave and started off toward the philosopher's work room with it on my shoulder. Aristotle walked beside me as we entered the house.

"They say this city is a democracy," I said, "where all the citizens are equal. Yet they have slaves."

"Slaves are not citizens, Orion. Nor are women."

"Then how can it be a democracy if only a portion of the population has political power?"

He countered with another question. "How can the city manage without slaves? Will the looms run by themselves? Will crates carry themselves from place to place? You might as well ask that we give up horses and mules and oxen as give up slaves. They are necessary."

I fell silent. But once I had gently deposited the crate on the floor of his workroom, Aristotle carried his lesson a step farther.

"You have hit upon a sensitive point, Orion. Democracy is to be preferred over tyranny—the rule of one man—but democracy itself is far from perfect."

Deciding to play the student, I asked, "In what way?"

There were no chairs in the workroom as yet. Nothing but the crates that the slaves were bringing in. Aristotle peered at one, decided it was not too fragile to sit upon, and planted himself on it. I remained standing.

"When all political decisions are to be made by a vote of the citizens, then the man who can sway the citizens most easily is the man who makes the real decisions. Do you see the sense of that?"

"Yes. A demagogue can control the citizenry."

"You say 'demagogue' with scorn in your voice. The word merely means 'leader of the people.' "

"The Athenians have turned the word into something else, haven't they?"

He blinked at me. "How do you know so much, when you have no memory?"

"I am learning quickly," I said.

He did not look entirely satisfied. Still, he went on. "Yes, it's quite true that orators like Demosthenes can sway the Assembly on tides of passion and rhetoric. It is Demosthenes who has goaded the Athenians into making war against Philip. It is his demogoguery that I must counter."

"Are you an orator, also?"

He shook his head wearily. "No. Orators can be hired, Orion. They are merely lawyers who work for a fee."

"Then who does Demosthenes work for?"

The old man gave me a puzzled look. "He has clients, of course. Civil suits, damage claims, inheritances. That is what buys his bread."

"But who pays him to speak against Philip?"

"No one. At least he claims to do it as a free Athenian citizen."

"Do you believe that?"

Aristotle stroked his beard. "Now that I think on it, no, I do not."

"Then who pays him?"

He thought a moment longer, then replied, "Logically, it must be the Persians."

Aeschines arrived home shortly after sunset, full of apologies for being late and warm greetings for his old friend. He was a smallish man with a pot belly, a red face and bulging frog's eyes. Apparently he had been a student of Aristotle's when the philosopher had taught at Plato's school in the Academy district of the city some years earlier.

"Demades speaks to the Assembly tomorrow," he told

us, as his servants scurried to bring wine and goat cheese. His face went grim. "And then Demosthenes."

"I must hear them," said Aristotle.

Aeschines nodded.

Supper was served in a sumptuous room with an intricate tile mosaic for a floor and a meager fire crackling and spitting in the fireplace—just enough to ward off the autumnal night chill. Philip had ordered that Alexandros remain incognito, even to his host, so he and his beardless Companions were introduced merely as young noblemen. Alexandros was such a common name among the Macedonians that there was no need to give the Little King an alias. Most Macedonian nobles had at least a passing knowledge of Attic Greek, especially the younger ones. Philip had seen to that.

Aeschines gave Alexandros a crafty look when Aristotle introduced him, but said nothing more than he said to all the others, including me, when names were exchanged.

The talk around the supper table was all of Demosthenes.

"He is whipping up the people to a war frenzy," Aeschines told us unhappily. "They go to listen to him as if they were going to the theater, and he gives them a good performance. By the time he's finished speaking they're ready to arm themselves and march against Philip."

Aristotle shook his head, brow furrowed with worry.

"But Athens is already at war with us," Alexandros said.

Aeschines replied, "Technically, yes. But until now the Athenians have been content to let others do the fighting for them. They have sent silver against Philip, not Athenian troops."

I recalled that I was one of the mercenaries that Athenian silver had bought.

"And ships," added Ptolemaios. "Athens uses its navy against us."

"To little avail," Alexandros boasted. "Soon they won't have a port to put into north of Attica."

"There is talk," said Aeschines gloomily, "of making an alliance with Thebes."

"Thebes!" A stir went around the long table.

"They have the best army outside of Macedonia," Hephaistion blurted.

"Their Sacred Band has never been defeated," said dark-skinned Nearkos.

"Well, neither have we," Alexandros countered.

Harpalos, sitting on Alexandros' left, made a disappointed frown. "Maybe we haven't been defeated in battle, but the king has walked us away from victories. Perinthos isn't the first city that we've besieged without taking."

Alexandros' face started to turn red with anger. Aristotle spoke up. "Philip has gained more cities at the parley table than on the battlefield," he said mildly. "That is the art of a true king: to win without bloodshed."

"There will be blood between Athens and us," Alexandros predicted, his anger barely under control.

"I fear you're right," Aeschines agreed. "Demosthenes will not stop until he has them marching against the barbarians."

"Barbarians?"

"You," he said directly to Alexandros. "He calls you barbarians. And worse."

Again trying to ward off an explosion, Aristotle said, "To the Athenians, anyone not of their city is a barbarian. The word originally meant stranger, nothing more."

"But that's not how Demosthenes uses it now," Aeschines said.

I could see Alexandros was struggling to control his temper. "I saw him once, years ago," he muttered. "He came to Pella at the king's invitation. He was so flustered he became completely tongue-tied. He couldn't speak a complete sentence."

"He speaks whole sentences now," Aeschines said, somberly. "With devastating effect."

"I must hear him for myself," Alexandros said through tight lips.

But there was something else the prince wanted to see first. We were all quartered in one large room, all except Aristotle. After supper, as I was preparing for bed, I saw that Alexandros and his Companions were heading for the door, cloaks wrapped around their shoulders, swords at their sides.

"Where are you going?" I demanded.

"To the Acropolis," Alexandros replied, smiling like a boy setting off on an adventure.

"It's forbidden. The gates to the Sacred Street are locked."

"There's a trail up the cliff side. One of the servants told me of it."

"You're going to follow a servant?"

"Yes, why not? I want to see the temples up there."

"Maybe we'll raid their treasury." Ptolemaios laughed.

"Perhaps it's a trap," I said.

"We are armed."

"I'll go with you."

"That's not necessary, Orion."

"Your father commanded me to take good care of you. If you break your neck climbing the cliff in the moonlight, I'd better jump off and land beside you."

He laughed as I grabbed my sword and cloak and went with them, thinking that his mother had also ordered me to protect him.

The climb was much easier than I had feared. The moon was bright, although the night wind cut like a razor.

The servant turned out to be a young girl, no more than twelve, I guessed. Harpalos had spotted her in Aeschines' household. I imagined that he intended to reward her by taking her virginity.

We reached the flat top of the cliff without trouble and stood gazing at the Parthenon and the other temples. The Parthenon was absolutely breathtaking: graceful fluted columns, perfect Pythagorean symmetry, wonderful friezes along the roof line so marvelously carved that the cold marble figures seemed almost to come alive. I had seen it before, I realized. It stood, in all its original harmonious balance, in the empty city of the Creators that I had visited in my dreams.

It was wondrously beautiful, especially in the soft silver radiance of the moonlight. And standing in front of it was the giant statue of Athena, warrior goddess and patroness of the city, goddess of wisdom whose sacred symbol is the owl.

We all stood gaping at the marble splendors of temples and statues. All of us except Alexandros. He took everything in with a single glance, then strode purposefully toward the statue of Athena.

I hurried after him.

"They say you can see the sunlight glinting off her spear tip from the harbor of Piraeus," he told me.

The gigantic statue was clad in ivory. Her upraised spear reached higher than the Parthenon's peaked roof. In the moonlight Athena towered above us. Her face was painted, her eyes as gray as my own. But empty, blank, cold ivory.

Alexandros started up the temple steps. "There's a smaller statue inside. They say it's clothed in gold."

It was. This statue was merely twice life-size, much more graceful, much more lifelike. In the shadows inside the temple it seemed to glow with an inner radiance. *It's the gold leaf of her robe catching stray moonbeams,* I told myself. And then I looked up into her face.

I recognized her. Athena, Anya, Ardra, I had known her under many names in many times and places. Known her and loved her. And she had loved me. But now I was alone in this timeplace, without her, without my love, lost and abandoned.

I felt a cold dark misery enveloping me. I could remember so little, yet I remembered her. The face of this statue was the face of the woman I had loved. No, not a mortal woman. A goddess.

I was a creature, a mortal fashioned by the Creators to do their bidding. I had dared to fall in love with a goddess who had dared to take human form and fall in love with me. And now I was without her.

I strained with every fiber of my being to make that statue stir, to bring it to life, to have her breathe and move and smile at me.

But it remained cold marble sheathed in gold. I could not reach beyond its form to find the goddess it represented.

"Come on," said Alexandros brusquely. "I'm getting cold. Let's go back to our beds."

Feeling as cold and dead as the stone all around us, I followed him back to the house of Aeschines.

Chapter 10

The meeting of the Assembly was held in the open air, under the crisp clear blue sky, in the natural auditorium created by the hill slope facing the Acropolis. A huge crowd turned out. Although only free male citizens could vote in the Assembly, there was no law prohibiting the whole city from listening to the orators. I imagined that clever demagogues could work up the crowd to fever pitch and sway the voting citizens with mob passion.

The orators had to compete with the vendors from the market place hawking broiled lamb strips, wine, nuts, even honeyed fruits. And when the wind gusted from the direction of the Agora there were the smells of butchered meat and dried fish in the air. And flies.

The orators' stand was cut out of the natural rock of the hillside. Off to one side the fifty members of the city council sat on stone benches.

Demades was the first to speak. He was tall and slim, elegant-looking. His powerful deep voice carried well all the way to the rear of the crowd, where I stood with Alexandros and his Companions. I was tall enough to see over the heads of the throng, but Alexandros had to stand on tip-toe and try to see between those in front of us.

"Why should we tax ourselves to fight a man who harbors us no ill-will?" Demades asked. "What do we care of the petty squabbles in the northern lands? Philip has no intention of fighting us; why do we strive against him?"

A voice in the crowd shouted back, "He stole our grain!"

Seeming to ignore the heckler, Demades went on, "This pointless war increases our taxes, drains our treasury, and sends our navy out on foolhardy missions. Philip has no desire to harm us. Even when he seized the grain harvest from our ships he returned it to us in exchange for a city that we neither want nor need."

He went on for what seemed like hours, stressing the cost of the war against Philip and its pointlessness, pounding home again and again how high taxes had been raised to prosecute the fight against Philip.

"And what have we gained from our sacrifices? Nothing whatsoever. Philip remains in his own land, fighting against his fellow barbarians, not against us."

I saw Alexandros' face twitch in an angry tic at the word barbarian as he leaned on the shoulders of Ptolemaios and Hephaistion, both of them a good head taller than he.

At last Demades finished and Demosthenes took the platform. The crowd stirred. This was what they had come for.

He was a small man, with narrow shoulders and a slightly bent posture as he walked slowly to the center of the platform. His hairline was receding, although his hair was still quite dark and his beard thick and bushy. His eyes were deep-set beneath dark brows; I suspected that his beard hid a weak chin. His robe was plain, unadorned white wool. Clasping his hands in front of him, he stood with balding head slightly bowed until the vast throng stilled into absolute silence. I could hear the breeze sighing; a bird chirped in the trees behind us.

Demosthenes began slowly, dramatically, gestures measured to each phrase almost as if he were dancing in rhythm to his own words. His voice was higher than Demades', not as powerful, yet it carried back to us well enough. He did not try to counter Demades' arguments; indeed, he spoke as if he had not even heard them. And then I realized that Demosthenes had memorized his speech. He was not speaking extemporaneously; he was reciting a carefully-rehearsed performance, each gesture and stride across the platform perfectly timed to suit his lines. It was a long and intricate poem that he was delivering to the expectant audience, unrhymed but in careful cadence. The Athenians loved it, sighing with pleasure at his phrasing, his exact choice of words, his use of wit and even invective.

Alexandros' face reddened as Demosthenes spoke of "this barbarian king, this sly dog, this wine-besotted beast who wants to take our freedom from us." His attack on Philip was personal and highly emotional. Within a few minutes he had the crowd entirely in his hands.

"Athens is the light of the world, the best hope for freedom for every man. Our democracy shines like a beacon against the darkness of tyranny. Let Philip know that we are unwilling to permit the destruction of this democracy which our fathers and our fathers' fathers have bequeathed to us by their blood and sacrifice. Let Philip know, whether he wishes us well or ill, that we will pay any price, bear any burden, and oppose any foe to assure the survival of our democracy here in Athens and its spread across the world."

The crowd shook the city with its roar of approval. They applauded and cheered and whistled and stamped their feet on the bare ground for nearly a quarter of an hour. Demosthenes waited patiently for them to quiet down, hands folded and head bowed. Then he continued.

"There are those who claim that Philip bears us no ill will. How do they know this? Has Philip spoken to them of his ambitions toward us? Are they in Philip's employ, taking silver and gold from the tyrant to lull us into passivity and inaction? Nothing is so easy to deceive as one's self; for what we wish, we readily believe. Yet the facts speak for themselves.

"Philip continues to build his army. Why? Why does he march against democratic cities founded by Athenians and peopled by Athenian settlers? Does Philip have any enemy in the whole of Greece to justify the size of the mighty army he is building? No! He has none. His army is meant for us and it can be meant for no other. He intends to conquer our city, to enslave our people, to burn our buildings to the ground and put all of us in chains—your wives, your daughters, your sisters and mothers will be Philip's slaves. Your sons, too."

He castigated the very idea of kingship, insisting that a democracy and a tyrant can never be at peace.

"There is nothing, absolutely nothing, which needs to be more carefully guarded against than that one man should be allowed to become more powerful than the people. It would be better for us to be at war with all the states of Greece, provided they were democracies, than to be friends with them if they were ruled by kings. For with free states it would not be difficult to make peace when we wished, but with tyrants we could not even form an affiliation on which we could rely. Democracies and dictators cannot exist together! Every dictator is an enemy of freedom, and Philip means to end the freedom of Athens!"

Again the crowd roared with approval, stamping and clapping, cheering, whistling, waving scarves to show their enthusiasm.

And in the midst of the uproar the assassins struck.

I had been standing beside Alexandros and his four Companions, all of us dressed in plain homespun chitons and leather jerkins. None of us wore anything rich or conspicuous; Alexandros' fingers were bare, and the short swords we carried were plain and undecorated.

While Demosthenes spoke the crowd surged forward slightly, as if eager to be closer to their idol. A few men pushed between me and Hephaistion, who was standing directly beside Alexandros on one side. Alexandros had his arm upon the taller Hephaistion's shoulder, helping himself to stand tip-toe. Another man wedged himself between me and the young men. I turned and saw that three more were now standing just behind Ptolemaios and lanky Harpalos. Nearkos was too short for me to see in the crowd that was pressing around us.

But I could see Alexandros' golden mane easily enough, and realized that it stood as an easy identification for anyone who wanted to find him. As the crowd broke into its thunderous ovation one of the rough-clad men who had pushed up to us stepped sideways, behind Alexandros. I saw his hand go to his belt and I knew he was going to thrust a dagger into Alexandros' back.

"Behind you!" I shouted in the Macedonian dialect, bellowing as loud as I could over the roar of the crowd. I tried to plunge through the men separating us but suddenly my arms were pinned behind me and a swarthy short man with a scar halfway down his face was shoving a dagger at my belly.

My senses went into overdrive and the world around me slowed to a dreamlike lethargy. I kicked at the scar-faced man's leg as I twisted my body sideways, spoiling his aim enough so that I took his dagger in my side instead of straight-on. I felt it go in and slice through me as my body instantly dampened the pain messages along my nerves and clamped down on the severed blood vessels.

My kick knocked the scar-faced knife wielder backward a step. I stamped on the foot of the man pinning my right arm as hard as I could and yanked my arm free while I saw that Hephaistion had shoved the other assassin from

Alexandros' back, but now the boys were surrounded by at least a dozen armed men.

I punched the man holding my left arm between the eyes. As he collapsed I swung my right arm back and smashed the other one with my elbow. With my freed left hand I hit scar-face, still trying to recover his balance, squarely in the jaw and he went down, blood spurting from his mouth. Then I leaped into the ring of knife-wielding men who had surrounded Alexandros.

The fight ended as quickly as it started. They broke and turned tail, disappearing into the crowd. By the time a local constable came up, frowning and officious, it was all over. Hephaistion had been nicked in the arm; I had been sliced in my side but I was consciously willing the muscles beneath my skin to hold the wound tightly together, and the blood was already coagulating.

The constable wanted to know our names and what the fight was about.

"They were cutpurses, obviously," I said. "And stupid ones at that, since there isn't one purse among the five of us."

He scowled at me, then glanced back and forth among the youths. "Names," he demanded. "I must have your names and places of residence."

Alexandros, red-faced with fury, blurted, "I am Alexandros, son of Philip of Macedon. And if this is the way your noble city treats its guests, then my father is far too lenient with you."

With that he strode off, his Companions around him. I followed them, leaving the constable standing there dumbfounded.

"It was a deliberate assassination attempt. Deliberate!" Alexandros raged all the way back to Aeschines' house. "They tried to kill me."

"But who sent them?" Hephaistion asked. Alexandros had torn a strip from his own chiton and tenderly wrapped the scratch on his friend's forearm.

"Demosthenes," answered Ptolemaios. "Who else?"

"That's not logical," Alexandros said.

No one had bothered to wrap my wound. I knew I healed quickly, and it did not appear that any vital organ had been cut. My body responded to my conscious control; although I had shut off the pain receptors in my brain, I could sense that the wound was neither deep nor serious. Infection was the only thing I worried about, yet I knew that I could manufacture antibodies at a prodigious rate, when necessary.

I seemed to recall Aten, the Golden One, smirking at me, telling me that he had built me to be a warrior and had included all the self-repair that I needed for my task.

"What do you mean, not logical?" Harpalos asked.

A little more calmly, Alexandros replied, "It would not be logical for Demosthenes to try to have me assassinated. Not here. Not now."

"Not in Athens?" Harpalos wondered aloud.

"Not while he's making his speech," Ptolemaios joked.

Nearkos said nothing. He simply walked along with us, his dark Cretan eyes always on Alexandros.

"If you were assassinated in Athens," Hephaistion argued, "your father would come down here and raze the city to the ground."

"Or try to," said Ptolemaios.

"That would force the Athenians to fight us, which is just what Demosthenes wants."

Alexandros shook his head. "But Demosthenes wants the Athenians to fight a just war. You heard him; he claims that democracies have a higher spiritual standing than kingdoms."

"Yes, and crows can sing."

"He would not want to fight a war brought on by a cowardly assassination. In his own city, yet."

"During his own speech."

"The Athenians might refuse to fight such a war," Alexandros insisted. "No, it was not Demosthenes."

"Who then?"

We were climbing the cobblestoned street as it rose toward the residential area where Aeschines' house stood.

Alexandros made a fluttering gesture with both his hands. "Aristotle taught me to look for the logical answer to every question."

"So what's the logical answer to this one?"

"Yes, who sent the assassins—logically?"

"The man who would gain the most from my assassination, of course."

"But who would gain?"

Alexandros walked on for several silent steps, head bent, hands slowly balling into fists. I thought he was mulling over the question, but once he spoke I realized that he had known his answer all along.

"The king," he said.

"What?"

"Your father?"

They all stopped walking, stunned by the enormity of the accusation.

"I don't know if he is my true father," Alexandros said. He spoke not with shame, not even indecision. "My true father might be Herakles. Or Zeus himself."

The other youths fell silent. There was no sense arguing *that* point, each of them knew.

"But even to imagine that the king might have tried to have you assassinated . . ." Hephaistion's voice was hollow with fear.

"Think of it logically," Alexandros said quietly.

"What better pretext could he have for attacking Athens directly? You said so yourself, a moment ago."

"Yes, but—"

"Who would come to Athens' aid if Philip made war to avenge his son's murder?"

"No one."

"That's true enough."

"He'd have isolated Athens completely."

I spoke up. "Who would inherit the throne if Philip died in battle?"

"What difference does that make?"

"A great difference," I said. "Philip has spent his life molding Macedonia into a powerful and secure nation. Would he throw away all that by killing his son and heir? Would he *knowingly* throw the kingdom into such a turmoil that it might split apart once he dies?"

The youths were nodding among themselves.

I asked Alexandros, "Is that logical?"

He gave me a troubled gaze.

"Your father," I said, "sent me with you to protect you. Is that logical, if he wishes to have you assassinated?"

Very calmly, he looked up into my eyes and said, "You might be part of the plot, Orion. My father may have instructed you to let the assassins have me."

I could see cold fury in his golden eyes, and felt my own rage boil up within me at his accusation. But I held my emotions in check and replied, "I was the one who warned you, Alexandros. And took a knife in the ribs for it."

"Barely a scratch, from the look of it."

"Your father instructed me to protect you," I said firmly. "He is not your enemy."

Alexandros turned away from me and resumed his walk up the sloping street. "Perhaps you are right, Orion," he said, so low that I barely heard him. "I hope so."

* * *

We stayed in Athens only a few days longer. The news from the Assembly was not good. The Athenians had decided to send delegations to Thebes and several other cities to arrange an alliance against Philip. Aristotle was especially downcast.

"This will mean war," he told me as we packed his ever-growing collection. "Real war. Not the marching and petty skirmishes and sham sieges of the past few years."

I had taken part in one of those petty skirmishes. The men who had been killed were just as dead as heroes of a great battle.

The night before we were to leave I had another dream—if it was a dream.

I was at the Acropolis once more. This time by myself. It was the closest I could be to the goddess I loved, to my past lives, to the memories that had somehow been locked away from me. The night was black and windswept, the stars blotted out by roiling clouds that seemed so low they nearly touched the upraised spear of the giant statue of Athena.

I walked through the warm wind to the gigantic statue. Lightning flashed and briefly lit her face, but it remained coldly indifferent ivory, not flesh. Rain began to pelt down, stinging cold hard drops, almost sleet. I rushed up the steps and into the shelter of the magnificent Parthenon.

The gold-clad statue stared at me with painted eyes.

"I will find you," I said aloud, amidst peals of thunder. "Wherever you are, whenever you are, I will find you."

And the statue stirred. The stiff gold-leafed robe softened. The eyes warmed. Her face smiled sadly at me. Twice life-size, standing on a pedestal of marble, my goddess breathed into life.

"Orion? Orion, is it you?"

"Yes!" I shouted over the earthshaking thunder. "I am here!"

"Orion, I want to be with you. Always and forever. But it cannot be."

"Where are you? Why can't we be together?"

"They decided . . . the forces . . ."

Her voice grew faint. Lightning flickered through the sky, throwing blue-white strobes of light through the temple. Thunder roared and boomed like the voices of the gods railing against us.

Still I shouted, "Where are you? Tell me and I'll find you!"

"No," she said, her voice fading, fading, "Not yet. The time is not right."

"Why am I here?" I begged. "Why have they put me here?"

I thought she did not hear me. I thought she had left me. The lightning stopped and suddenly the temple was in utter darkness. I could not see her statue, could not sense her presence.

"Why am I here?" I repeated, almost sobbing.

No reply. Only black silence.

"What do they expect of me?" I shouted.

"Obedience," said another voice. A woman's voice. Hera's.

"I expect you to obey me, Orion," her voice slashed coldly through my mind. "And obey me you shall."

Chapter 11

I returned to Pella unwillingly, filled with dread and the inner emptiness of a hopeless longing. The trip north was cold and miserable: rain in the hills, driving snow in the mountain passes. With each step along the way I felt the power of Olympias returning, settling over me like a sickness, sapping my strength and my will. In my dreams she was Hera, the haughty and demanding goddess. In my waking hours she was Philip's queen, the witch who had cast her spell upon me, the woman I was powerless to resist.

On the day we returned to Pella the king summoned me to his presence. I reported on the assassination attempt.

He scowled darkly. "What fool tried that?"

We were alone in his small work room. The afternoon sunlight slanted through the one window, but the air was cold. Philip sat next to the meager fire, a dark woolen cloak over his shoulders, his aching leg propped on a stool, his black beard bristling, his one good eye piercing like a hawk's.

I decided that he wanted the truth. And so did I.

"He thinks that perhaps you did," I blurted.

"Wha—" His face went white with sudden anger. He gripped the armrests of his chair as if he were going to leap to his feet.

But the fury drained out of him almost immediately. I

watched him battle to control his emotions. I saw that he was shocked by the accusation, and not because his son had hit on the truth. Philip had not tried to kill his son. And now that his immediate wave of anger had passed he looked sorrowful to be falsely accused.

"That's his mother's doing," he grumbled. "She's always poisoning his mind against me."

I said nothing. But I realized that the assassination attempt might well have been Olympias' doing. The assassins had plenty of time to cut Alexandros down, and his Companions with him. Instead, all they did was to drive a wedge of suspicion between the prince and his father.

"She's a witch, Orion," he told me. "Entranced me when we first met. At the Dionysian rites on Samothrace. I was just about Alexandros' age and I fell completely mad for her. The most beautiful woman on earth, that was sure. And she seemed to love me just as wildly as I loved her. Once she had the boy, though, she wanted nothing more to do with me."

She is more than a witch, I thought. *She is the avatar of a goddess, or perhaps the goddess herself in human guise, with powers that could destroy us all at a whim.*

"She scorns me, Orion, and plots with her son to get him the throne."

"Alexandros wants to be a good son to you," I told him. "He wants to be worthy of your throne."

Philip smiled crookedly. "He wants to sit on my throne, and the only way he can do that is to kill me."

"No," I said. "I see nothing of that in him. He wants to show you that he's worthy. He wants your approval."

"Does he?"

"Despite all that his mother has poured into his ears, he admires you."

"Does he acknowledge that I'm his father?"

So he knows about Alexandros' personal mythology, I realized.

Aloud, I replied, "Boyish ego. He doesn't believe it himself."

Philip cast his good eye on me. "I wonder." He pulled the cloak tighter around him. "I wonder if maybe it's all true. Maybe Herakles or some god did beget him. Maybe he's not my true son, after all."

"No god begat him, sir," I said. "There are no gods. Only men and women."

"Sokrates was given hemlock on the accusation of not believing in the gods." He smiled again as he said it.

I smiled back. "If you poisoned everyone who did not believe in the gods, you would run out of hemlock long before the job was half finished."

He chuckled. "You jest, Orion. Yet it seems to me that you are serious, at the same time."

How could I tell him that the so-called gods and goddesses were as human as he was? The faint memory of them seethed in my mind: the deities were men and women from that city of my dreams, the city that existed in another time from this.

He mistook my silence. "You needn't fear, Orion. Your beliefs are safe with me."

"May I make a suggestion, sir?"

"What is it?"

"Keep the boy close to you. Don't allow him to see his mother—"

"That's easier said than done, unless I chain him up like a dog."

"The more he is with you the less his mother can influence him. Take him with you on campaign. Let him show his mettle before your eyes."

Philip cocked his head, as if giving my suggestion some

thought. Then he tapped a forefinger against the cheekbone below his empty eye socket.

"I only have one eye, Orion. But perhaps you're right. I'll bring the lad come on campaign with me."

"Another campaign?"

His expression went grim. "The damned Athenians are negotiating with Thebes and several other cities to form a league against me. I've never wanted to fight Athens directly, and I certainly don't want to tangle with Thebes. But now it looks as if I'll have to face them both together."

"Your army has never lost a major battle," I encouraged him.

He shook his head. "Do you know why, Orion?" Before I could reply he answered his own question. "Because if I had lost a major battle, just one, my whole kingdom would collapse like a house of cards."

"No, that could not be."

"It would, Orion, and I know it. It gnaws at me every minute of the day. It keeps me awake when I try to sleep. Macedonia is strong and free only so long as we keep winning. If my army is ever defeated, all the tribes that owe me allegiance will go back to their rebel ways. Thrace and Illyria and even the goddamned Molossians will rise against me—or Alexandros, assuming he survives. I'll be dead on the battlefield, you can rest assured."

That was the vision that haunted Philip. He feared his kingdom would be torn apart if he lost a major battle. He had to keep on winning, always fighting, always victorious, or lose everything. That is why he avoided battle with Athens. One throw of the dice could destroy everything that he had worked his entire life to create.

That night I decided to see the queen on my own terms. But my duty as a guardsman came first. I was serving once again as one of the formal guards at Philip's royal dinner, posted this time behind the king's couch, to stand there like a statue in armor and spear while Philip and his guests ate and drank and caroused. His guests were mostly Macedonian, including the oily Attalos, who fawned on the king and praised even his belches. There were a few foreigners reclining on dinner couches near the king: I thought one a Persian and recognized another as the Athenian merchant whom I had seen in Pella before. They were spies, I knew. But for which side? Did they spy on Athens and the Great King in Persia for Philip? Or did they spy on Philip for the Great King and Athens?

Probably both, I concluded. They would take gold from either side and praise the winner.

Parmenio and Philip's other generals were present, of course, but there was no talk over dinner of matters military. Only politics. Would Demosthenes' representatives be able to talk Thebes into an alliance with Athens?

"After all the patience you've shown with both cities," said Antipatros, "this is the thanks they give you."

"I never expected their thanks," Philip said, holding his wine goblet out for the serving boy to fill it.

From my post at the king's couch I saw with satisfaction that Alexandros had been placed next to his father.

"We should march on them now," he said, almost shouting to make his light tenor voice heard over the buzz of background talk. "First Thebes and then Athens."

"If we march now," Philip replied, "it will give them the excuse they need to cement their alliance."

Alexandros looked at his father. "You will let them prepare for war against us while we sit here drinking?"

His own wine cup had not been refilled since the eating had ended. He drank little; he ate little, as well. His old teacher Leonidas, I had been told, raised the boy with Spartan values and discipline.

Philip grinned at his son. "I will give them plenty of

time to argue over the terms of their alliance. With a bit of luck they'll fall out between themselves and there will be no alliance for us to worry about."

"But if the luck goes against us?" Alexandros asked. "What then?"

Philip took a long draft of his wine. "We'll just have to wait and see. Patience, my son. Patience. It's a virtue, I'm told."

"So is courage," Alexandros snapped.

The dining hall fell absolutely silent.

But Philip laughed. "I don't need to prove my courage, son. You can count my scars."

And Alexandros smiled back at his father. "Yes, that's true enough."

The tension eased. Men went back to talking with one another. Goblets were refilled. Philip fondled the thigh of the boy who was serving him. Alexandros bristled at that, but then looked across the room at the place where his Companions were reclining. Ptolemaios and the others were nuzzling the serving girls there. Except for Hephaistion. He stared back at Alexandros across the wide, noisy hall as if there were no one else in the room.

Then I noticed Pausanias, captain of the guard, standing at the doorway of the dining hall. His fists were planted on his hips, as if he were about to deliver one of his withering verbal blasts at the two guards posted there, his mouth set in its usual sour grimace. But his eyes were on Philip, and even from across the breadth of the dining hall I could see that Pausanias was burning with anger.

The hours toiled on, the wine goblets were refilled over and again, and the dinner guests became rowdier and bawdier. No one left until finally Philip pushed himself up from his couch, draped one arm heavily around the shoulders of the boy who had been serving him, and lurched off toward his bedchamber. Slowly the other guests struggled to their feet and staggered off, many of them with either girls or boys in their grip. Alexandros rose from his couch coldly sober. Hephaistion, equally restrained, crossed the hall to be with him.

As the kitchen slaves came in to clean the hall, Pausanias finally gave us leave to return to barracks. Clearly something had enraged him, but he gave no hint of what it was.

I pretended to go to sleep, but as soon as I heard the snores of my fellow guardsmen in the darkness, I got up and headed for the queen's rooms. I knew the layout of the palace well enough to get to her rooms on my own. But I did not want the guards or her serving women to get in my way.

So I went out onto the parade ground in the cold night, barefoot and wearing only my thin chiton. It was dark, moonless. Clouds were scudding low across the stars. The air felt damp, the wind cutting. Staying in the shadows of the barracks wall so that the sentries would not see me, I hurried the length of the parade ground and clambered softly up onto the roof of the stables. I had brought no weapon with me, nothing to clink in the night and alert a drowsy sentry. Nothing but the dagger that I always kept strapped to my thigh.

It was a good leap from the stable roof to the slightly higher roof next to it, but I made it almost silently and then climbed the rough stones of the wall to the still-higher roof of the palace proper. Then I made my way along the sloping timber beams of the roof until I figured I was above the queen's quarters. I lowered myself from the eave and swung my legs through the curtained window, landing with a soft thud.

"I have been waiting for you, Orion," said Olympias in the darkness.

I was in her bed chamber, crouched on the balls of my

feet, my fingertips touching the polished wood of the floor, ready to fight if I had to.

"Don't be afraid," she said, reading my thoughts. "I want you here with me this night."

"You knew I was coming?" In the shadows I could make out her form reclining on the bed.

"I commanded you to come to me," she said, her voice taunting. "You don't think you did this of your own volition, do you?"

I did not want to believe her. "Then why didn't you send a servant, as before?"

I could sense her smiling in the darkness. "Why encourage palace gossip? The king likes you. He trusts you. Even Alexandros admires your fighting prowess. Why spoil all that by letting the servants know you are my lover?"

"I'm not—"

"But you are, Orion," she snapped. Her body seemed to glow faintly in the darkness, stretched out languidly on the bed, naked and warm and inviting.

"I don't want to be your lover," I said, although it cost me pain to force the words through my gritted teeth.

"What you want is of no consequence," Olympias replied. "You will do what I command. You will be what I desire you to be. Don't force me to be cruel to you, Orion. I can make you grovel in slime if I wish it. I can make you do things that would destroy your spirit utterly."

"Why are you doing this?" I demanded. But even as I asked it, I shuffled closer to her bed. "What are you trying to accomplish?"

"No questions, Orion," she said. "Tonight is for pleasure. Tomorrow you will learn what your new duties are to be. Perhaps."

I was helpless. I could not resist her. Even when I saw that the bed she lay upon was writhing with snakes I was unable to turn away, unable even to turn my eyes from her. She laughed as I slowly stripped off my chiton.

"Take off the dagger, too," she commanded me. "You won't need it. Your natural equipment will be quite enough."

I did as she instructed me. The snakes were dry and cold against my bare skin. I felt them biting me, sinking their fangs into my flesh and filling my bloodstream with strange venoms that melted my willpower and heightened my senses to an excruciating pitch. Then it was Olympias' teeth and nails penetrating me, tearing me apart, giving me pain while she took pleasure from me. She laughed while I wept. She exulted while I abased myself for her.

Chapter 12

For weeks, for months, my life was bound to her whims. She would ignore me for long stretches of time and I would begin to think that she had tired of me, but then she would summon me again, and again I knew the tearing passions of physical pleasure and mental anguish. By day I served Philip and watched the love-hate relationship between the king and his son. By night I lay in my barracks bed fighting with every gram of strength in me against her domination. There were times when I almost thought I had thrown off her control.

But then she would call me again, in my mind, silent and invisible and completely irresistible. I would come to her and the snakes that she allowed to coil around her naked body. She would laugh and rend my flesh and rack me until I was utterly exhausted. Yet at dawn I always found myself in my barracks bed, refreshed and unhurt despite what Olympias and her witchcraft had done to me during the hours of darkness and passion.

By day, the news from the south grew steadily worse. Athens and Thebes had indeed concluded their treaty of alliance, backed by Persian gold. The bit of luck that Philip had waited upon turned out to be all bad: now he had to face the two most powerful cities of the south, knowing that if he lost to them he would lose his crown, his life, and all that he had struggled for since coming to the throne of Macedonia.

I wanted to ask Aristotle for his estimation of the situation. He was the wisest man I knew, except perhaps for Philip himself. But Philip's wisdom was of the kingly sort, centered on what he needed to accomplish to enlarge his kingdom and make it safer and stronger. Aristotle was wise in the ways of human behavior. He cared about understanding the world rather than ruling it.

During one of my off-duty hours I tracked the philosopher down; he was in a shed standing by itself out beyond the stables. In it, on a rough trestle table, he had placed a large box of dirt. He was sitting on a teetering off-balance stool, staring at the dirt intently.

"May I enter?" I called from the doorway of the shed. There was no door, merely a rough blanket hung over the opening, which was so low that I had to duck through. The morning was warm and sunny; spring was in the air.

Aristotle jerked with surprise so hard that his rickety stool nearly toppled over. He peered across the shed at me, blinking painfully.

"Oh! It's you, Orion. Yes, come in, come in."

I saw that the box of dirt held a colony of ants.

"We can learn much from the ants," said Aristotle. "They make kingdoms and even fight wars, much as men do."

"Why do men fight wars?" I asked.

Aristotle wrinkled his high-domed forehead at me. "You might as well ask why men breathe. It is in their nature."

I vaguely remembered one of the Creators, the Golden One, telling me arrogantly that he had designed me to be a warrior; me, and the other creatures he had sent into the time of the Neanderthals.

Aristotle mistook my silence for puzzlement. He took

my arm in one of his thin-fingered hands and pulled me to the ant colony.

"Do you see them, Orion? I put two queen ants in there, one in this corner and the other on the farther side. They had plenty of room and I saw to it that they had plenty of food."

The ants all looked exactly alike to me: tiny and black and terribly busy, scampering every which way across the sandy soil that filled the box.

"Yet look there," Aristotle pointed. "Battalions of ants were fighting each other, rending one another apart with fierce mandibles.

"They could live in peace, yet they fight. Each group wants to be master of the other. It is in their nature."

"But men are not ants," I said.

"No, they are like ravening dogs." With real anger in his voice, Aristotle told me, "They see a neighbor who has something they do not, or a neighbor who appears too weak to defend himself, and they want to steal what that neighbor has. War is theft, Orion, thievery on a grand scale. Murder and rape and plunder, that is why men fight wars."

"Does Philip intend to rape and plunder Athens and Thebes?"

"No, but they would do it to us."

"Really?"

"That is what we fear."

"But those cities lie far to the south. Why are we preparing to make war on them? Why do they want to make war against us?"

"Ah, your questions grow more specific. Good."

"Well?"

Aristotle got down off his stool and clasped his hands behind his back. He had to look up to see into my face.

"Are you prepared to listen to a lecture on history, Orion?"

I knew from his tone that this would be a long lecture. I nodded. He began to pace. And speak.

The Greeks have never been able to unite themselves, Aristotle said. That is their glory and their weakness. Not since Agamemnon led the Achaians against Troy, countless ages ago, have the Greek cities been able to stand together for more than a few years at a time.

They united briefly, a century and a half ago, when the Persians under the old Dareios invaded Greece as punishment for Athenian support of a rebellion against Persia by the Greek cities on the Ionian coast, across the Aegean from Athens. The Persians were driven off after the Athenians stopped them at Marathon. Ten years later, Dareios' son Xerxes invaded Greece again with an army that blackened the land with their numbers. Again the Persians were beaten off, even though they sacked Athens itself, because the cities of the south—principally Athens and Sparta—fought side by side against the invaders.

"Both times the Macedonians allowed the Persians to pass through their territory without a fight. They even sold the Persians horses for their cavalry and timber for their ships. Athens has never forgotten that."

"But that was more than a century ago," I said.

"Yes, and the Macedonians were little more than a bundle of cattlemen," said Aristotle. "No match for the power of the Persian Empire. They did not even consider themselves to be Greeks, in the sense that the Athenians did."

"The Athenians still call the Macedonians barbarians," I recalled.

Aristotle nodded. "To this day."

After their second defeat in Greece the Persians decided that these rugged fighters living at the edge of their empire were not worth the trouble to conquer them. But the Great King wanted to keep the rich Ionian cities on the

Aegean coast, despite the fact that those cities were as Greek as Athens or Sparta or Thebes.

"Ever since then," Aristotle continued, "the Persians have meddled in Greek politics. At one time they supported Sparta against Athens. At another, Athens against Corinth. Persian gold has been spent to keep the cities from uniting. Thus the Great King keeps us weak and no danger to his empire."

"And Philip wants to change that?"

Aristotle smiled, a bit ruefully, I thought. "No man is completely master of his own actions, Orion, not even a king."

Certainly not me, I knew.

"Philip came to the throne with Macedonia in chaos. The ravening dogs around us were tearing the country to pieces. Our neighbors to the north and the west and the east all invaded Macedonia, seizing whatever they could. No one was safe. Fire and savagery were everywhere. Every man's hand was raised against us.

"Philip was not the chosen king then. He had to push his own brother off the throne in order to save the country. He united the Macedonians and threw back the invaders. He enlarged the kingdom by conquering those who had invaded us. He has made the Thracians and Illyrians and Molossians and many other warring tribes into allies or outright colonies of Macedonia. He has stretched his power to the edge of the Adriatic Sea, where those primitive tribesmen kill one another for sport. He has expanded his influence into central Greece, where Thebes and Corinth oppose him. For the past several years he has fought a war—sometimes undeclared, but a war nonetheless—against Athens."

"But why?"

Aristotle's smile turned knowing. "The Athenians still believe that they are the greatest power among the Greeks.

They are loath to allow any other power to become strong enough to challenge them. Encouraged by Persian gold, Athens strives to limit Philip's power."

"So that Athens can remain supreme among the Greek cities?"

He nodded. "For his part, Philip believes that he must bend Athens to his will or Athens will destroy Macedonia."

"Is that the truth?"

"Close enough for Philip. And for Demosthenes."

"But for you?"

"I see the hand of the Great King behind it all. Like his forebears, this new Dareios fears the power of a united Greece. Philip is the only man who can unite all the Greeks, so young Dareios encourages Athens and the other cities to work against Macedonia."

"He sees Philip as a threat to the Persian Empire?" I knew that there had been talk from time to time about wresting the Ionian cities from the Persians, but I had taken it to be little more than talk.

Now Aristotle became very serious, even grave. "Orion, it is our destiny to unite the Greeks and conquer the Persians. Unless we do, the Greeks will always be as disunited and quarrelsome as those barbarous Balkan tribes."

I must have gaped at him. This gnomish philosopher with the weak eyes, this studier of ants and espouser of moral codes, he wanted Philip to make war against the greatest empire in the world.

"And that, in the end, is why men make war upon one another," said Aristotle. "It is just as natural as a lion chasing down a deer. Kill or be killed. The world must be either one thing or the other. If we do not destroy the Persians they will destroy us."

I was almost dumbfounded. "But you say that the

Persians have tried to destroy Greece for more than a century and a half. They have not been able to do so."

"Not as yet," he said calmly. "But what is a century and a half in the affairs of mankind? What is a thousand years? I speak of the long term, Orion, of the ebb and flow of human affairs that takes a thousand generations or more. The Persians can afford to be patient. They have an immense empire and wealth beyond compare. Slowly, slowly they are grinding us down. They paid Sparta to conquer Athens, and when the Spartans became too powerful they paid Thebes to beat down Sparta."

"And now they play Athens *and* Thebes against us," I said.

"Exactly. And every year, every generation, we grow weaker and more tired. Eventually all the Greeks will fall prey to the Persians and we will be swallowed up entirely."

"Unless we swallow them."

"Precisely," he said. "The Greeks and the Persians cannot exist peacefully together. Either we conquer them or they conquer us. There is no other alternative."

"You are certain of this?"

Aristotle nodded solemnly. "That is what I have trained young Alexandros for. To conquer the world."

To conquer the world.

Aristotle may have trained young Alexandros to conquer the Persian Empire—which was all the world worth conquering, in his eyes—but to accomplish that, Alexandros needed a united Greece behind him, and only his father Philip could bring all the Greek cities together under Macedonian hegemony. And Olympias, I knew, was scheming to set Alexandros against his father.

"Why?" I asked her, the next time she summoned me to her bed. "Why do you try to make Alexandros hate Philip?"

"You ask too many questions, Orion," she said, lazily twining her bare arms around my neck.

I put one thumb on her lovely throat. "I want to know."

Her eyes widened. "You dare to threaten me?"

"I want to know," I repeated in a whisper, applying a bit of pressure to her windpipe.

One of the pythons slithered up onto my back. I pressed my body close to Hera's. "Your snake will have to crush us both."

A viper slid past her face, hissing at me. "The poison will not work fast enough to stop me from snapping your lovely neck," I said.

Olympias' eyes glittered like the snake's. But then I saw something different in them, as if another person were looking out at me through her jade-green eyes. "I have never died before. What is it like, Orion?"

I must have looked surprised. She said, "Oh, you have died countless times. Don't you remember? No, of course not."

A word drifted into my mind. A name. "Osiris."

Her smile widened. "Yes, Osiris. The god who dies each winter and is reborn in the spring. That was you, Orion, in another life. And Prometheus. Do you remember the band of warriors?"

"In the Ice Age." Vaguely I recalled a battle in the snowy wastes of a distant time. "Anya was there."

"Is it exciting to die?" she asked me. I could feel the pulse in her throat quickening. "Is it arousing?"

Try as I might, I could remember nothing definite of those earlier incarnations. And then I realized what was happening.

"You're playing with me," I said. "Toying with my mind."

But Hera's thoughts were on death. "Tell me, Orion.

What is it like to die? What does the ultimate adventure feel like?"

I remembered falling down the endless pit into the molten core of the Earth. I remembered the cave bear that ripped my body apart.

"Pain," I said. "The deaths I have suffered have been painful ones."

"And afterward?"

I rolled off her naked body. I could feel the snakes slithering out from under me.

"Afterward it begins all over again. Another life, another death. What does it matter?"

She was Hera. No more pretense of being Olympias, no need for witchcraft. Undisguised now, she revealed herself as the goddess, one of the Creators. Propping herself up on one elbow she traced a red fingernail across my chest. "What's the matter, creature? Don't tell me you're bored with life."

"What reason do I have for living?"

"What reason?" She laughed. "Why, to serve your creators. That is your reason for living. To do whatever I want you to."

I stared up at the shadowy ceiling, avoiding her eyes, and asked, "And what might that be?"

"To see how far this hotheaded princeling called Alexandros can reach."

"Your son."

"Olympias' son," she acknowledged.

"What was it like to give birth?" I asked her.

She replied haughtily, "I wouldn't know. That is a human ordeal that I want no part of."

"Then you—" I hesitated, groping for words. "You inhabit Olympias' body only when you choose to?"

Again her disdainful laughter. "Don't torture yourself trying to understand us, Orion."

"Us?"

"We Creators. Your mind can't comprehend our powers, don't even bother to try." Then she leaned against me and ran her hand down my abdomen to my crotch. "Your task is to satisfy my desires, creature."

"That's easy enough to do in bed," I countered, still avoiding her eyes, trying to maintain control of myself long enough to learn more. "But what am I to do about Alexandros and Philip?"

"Serve Philip well," she said. "Protect Alexandros, as you did in Athens. And wait."

"Wait? For what?"

"No more questions," she murmured.

"One more. Why did you send those assassins against Alexandros?"

I felt her body twitch with shocked surprise. "How did you—" Then she caught herself. For a startled moment she stared down at me, speechless. At last she broke into a bitter laughter. "My creature exhibits some powers of intelligence, after all."

"No one could profit by having Alexandros assassinated," I reasoned. "But someone might profit by having me save Alexandros from assassination."

"I wanted Alexandros to accept you. To trust you. When you started out for Athens he regarded you as one of his father's men. Now he owes his life to you."

"He hardly thinks so."

"I know what he thinks better than you do, Orion," she said. "Alexandros trusts you now."

Again I asked, "But why did you—"

"I said no more questions." And she slid her body over mine, supple as one of her snakes, eyes burning with human passion and something beyond.

Chapter 13

The army was on the move again, this time heading south, toward Attica. Long columns of troops winding along the roads, stirring up clouds of dust that could be seen for miles. Cavalry flanking the roads, moving up along the hillsides where there was grass enough for the horses. Threading through the narrow mountain passes, the cavalry went first and the foot soldiers ate dust. In the rear was the long train of mules and ox-carts, laden with armor and weapons and supplies.

It felt good to be out of the palace, away from Olympias' grasp. Once again I breathed the crisp clear air of the mountains. Even with the dust and smell of the horses and mules it tasted like nectar to me.

I was assigned to Alexandros' guard and rode along with his Companions. They bantered good-naturedly about Thunderbolt and even compared my mount favorably to Alexandros' own Ox-head—but never when he was within hearing.

Alexandros was a young man of moods. I could see that he was being torn up within himself. He admired his father and hated him at the same time. Olympias had filled his mind with the central idea that Philip did not love him and did not truly accept him as his son and heir. Still,

Alexandros wanted his father to admire him; yet he feared that such a desire was treason to his mother.

Young, ambitious, uncertain of his abilities or his acceptance by his own father, Alexandros did what so many frightened, self-conscious teenagers do: he went to extremes. He boasted that his true father was Zeus himself, or at least Herakles. He claimed that he wanted to be like Achilles, who chose glory over a long life. He had to be braver and more daring than anyone else. He took risks that others would blanch at.

My job was to keep him alive.

"He's a young hothead," Philip told me the day we began our march southward. "And his Companions are completely in awe of him. They even shave their faces clean, just as he does. It's up to you to see that he doesn't break his foolish neck."

No easy task.

When the cavalry had to forage in the hills of Pieria, Alexandros took it upon himself to raise fresh recruits for the army by galloping his Companions into each miserable little village along the way and giving a speech from Ox-Head's back.

"We march to glory!" he shouted in his thin tenor voice. "Who will come with me?"

Inevitably some of the village youths would step forward, faces burning with visions of fame and honor—and loot. Just as inevitably the village elders would tug them back into the crowd. Or worse, their mothers would while the rest of the villagers laughed. Still, Alexandros got a handful of newcomers along the way.

As we approached Thessaly, though, the responses became decidedly more hostile. At one of the mountain passes the local sheep herders even tried to ambush us.

All they saw, I'm sure, was a gaggle of beardless lads on horseback, all of them richly adorned. The horses alone would be worth a fortune to a man who spent his life scrabbling out a living on those rocky hillsides.

Our job was to scout the pass, make certain it was safe for the main body of the army to come through. We knew full well that a handful of determined men could hold up an army for days or even weeks, as Leonidas had at Thermopylae long ago. Philip wanted to get to Thebes before the Athenians could bring their army up to unite with the Thebans. To be held up in these mountain passes could be disastrous.

The local hill folk held scant allegiance to Thebes or anyone else except their own villages. To them, the world was bounded by their mountains and valleys. They knew nothing of the impending war. So when they saw a half-dozen young dandies riding through one of their passes, they thought they had received a windfall from the gods.

They chose their spot well, where the rocky mountain walls nearly touched one another and a rider had to nose his horse carefully around the boulders strewn along the trail.

Alexandros was in the lead, as he usually insisted on, with Hephaistion close behind him. Strung out further behind were Ptolemaios, Nearkos and Harpalos. Ptolemaios was singing a bawdy song, enjoying the echo of his own voice against the mountain walls. I brought up the rear, constantly searching the rugged crests of the mountains and looking behind us for any signs of peril.

I heard the danger, rather than saw it. A rumbling, crunching sound. Looking up, I saw a boulder bouncing down the steep mountainside, kicking up more rocks as it fell.

"Look out!" I bellowed, pulling up on Thunderbolt's reins.

Alexandros heard it too. With a single glance upward he kicked Ox-Head forward, Hephaistion right beside him.

The rest of us turned our horses around, away from the rock slide.

The boulders thundered down and crashed to the floor of the pass in a shower of gritty dust and flying pebbles. Our mounts shied and whinnied. Thunderbolt would have taken off altogether; it took all my strength to hold him where he was.

Eerie war cries echoed through the canyon and I saw men racing along the top of the cliffs. A spear came flying toward me. I saw it in slow-motion, flexing as it glided through the air. Men were scrambling down the rocky face of the cliffs on both sides of us.

And Alexandros was on the other side of the boulders that they had rolled down.

I ducked under the spear and let it fall clattering to the bare ground. Ptolemaios, Harpalos, and Nearkos were being swarmed under by more than a dozen half-naked men armed with spears and staves, but they had their swords out and were slashing at their attackers from horseback. I urged Thunderbolt through the melee, bashing a few heads with my own sword as I approached the rock slide.

The boulders formed a barrier that I could not ride past. I could hear shouting and swearing from the other side, and the scream of a man in death-agony. Swiftly I climbed onto Thunderbolt's back and leaped atop the nearest boulder, then jumped to the next one.

Alexandros and Hephaistion were on their feet, back to back, surrounded by hill tribesmen with murder in their eyes. Two half-grown boys were leading Hephaistion's horse down the canyon. Ox-Head was nowhere in sight.

With the greatest roar my lungs could give I leaped from the boulder onto the mass of men attacking Alexandros. Spears snapped and bones crunched. I rolled to my feet and slashed the nearest man almost in two. They were all moving with languid dreamy slowness. I ducked a spear and thrust my sword into the man's belly, dodged sideways as I yanked the sword out and grabbed the next man's spear with my left hand. I cracked the spearman's skull apart with an overhand swing of my sword just as another spear pierced my leather corselet and sliced into my ribs.

I hit the spear with a backhand sword thrust and it pulled free of my flesh. I felt no pain, only the exultation of battle fever. Alexandros killed the man who had speared me and suddenly the attackers broke and ran.

"The others!" I yelled and started scrabbling up the boulders that separated us from Ptolemaios, Harpalos, and Nearkos.

They were still on their horses, although Nearkos' mount was bleeding in half a dozen places. We roared down on the hill men, slashing and killing until they tried to escape our fearful swords, but Harpalos rode down two of them as they ran in blind panic along the canyon trail. Alexandros pulled down another who was scrambling up the rocks and took his head off with a single blow. I saw one climbing madly up the cliff face. I took half an instant to calculate the throw, then flung my sword at him. It struck him squarely between the shoulder blades. He screamed and fell face-first at my feet with a wet thump, the sword sticking out of his back.

Turning, I saw that Hephaistion held the last of the hill men by the hair. He could not have been more than thirteen: dirty, clothed in rags, on his knees, eyes bulging at the bloody sword Hephaistion held in his other hand. His mouth was wide open but no sound came from it. He was petrified with fear, looking at his death inches away.

"Wait," Alexandros commanded. "These dogs have taken Ox-Head. I want him to lead us to their village."

The boy did as he was told. We wound through the narrow pass, out onto a wider trail, and then up a rocky hillside where sheep had cropped the grass almost to its roots. Beyond the second row of hills, nested in the cup of a wooded valley, was the boy's village.

All the way there, Alexandros raged and fumed about Ox-Head. "Steal him from me, will they? I'll roast them alive, each and every one of them. They'll curse the day they were born. If they don't return Ox-Head to me I'll kill them all with my own hands!"

I saw that his hands were shaking: the aftermath of battle. He had nearly been killed, although he actually suffered nothing more serious than a few nicks and bruises and a bad fright.

We must have made a grim sight, six bloodied warriors, three of us on foot. I had given Alexandros my mount to ride. Nearkos walked beside me, slim and small, silent and dark as a shadow, leading his bleeding horse with one hand, his sword in the other.

The village elders came out to meet us, trembling visibly. A pair of half-naked boys, silent and round-eyed, led Ox-Head and Hephaistion's mount toward us.

The elders stopped a few paces before us, dithering and jittering, glancing uneasily at us and each other.

Before they worked up the courage to say anything, Alexandros spoke. "Where are your young men?"

The elders looked back and forth among themselves.

"Well?" Alexandros demanded.

One of the elders was completely bald, but had a white beard that ran halfway down his chest. His fellows nudged him forward.

"Our young men, lord, are dead. You have killed them all."

Alexandros snorted. "Don't lie to me, grandfather! We allowed ten or more of them to escape. I want to see them. Now! Else I will burn your miserable village to the ground and sell your women and children into slavery."

"But, brave sir—"

"Now!"

"Sir, they have run away. They fear your wrath and they have hidden themselves in the hills."

"Send your boys to find them. Have your women prepare a meal for us. See to it!"

They jumped to his command. It struck me that half a dozen men could be swarmed under if the whole village attacked us at once. But they were cowed, terrified. The boys scampered out toward the hills. The women bustled around their cook fires. The elders led us to their village's central green, where a feast was prepared for us.

By nightfall, seventeen young men stood sullenly before Alexandros, firelight flickering on their grimy, frightened faces. Several of them wore blood-soaked bandages on their arms or legs.

We had eaten a decent meal of roast lamb. The local wine was thin and bitter; Alexandros had made certain that we drank no more than one cup apiece.

Now he strutted up and down before the failed ambushers, fists on his hips, firelight glinting off the jeweled pommel of his sheathed sword. The meal seemed to have taken the edge off his rage. That, and the fact that Ox-Head had been returned unharmed.

Turning on the white-bearded village leader, Alexandros demanded, "What retribution should I exact on men who tried to kill me?"

The old man had recovered some of his courage, too. "You have already slain enough men to keep our village in mourning for the rest of the year, young lord."

"Is that your answer?"

He bowed his head. "You may take whatever vengeance you desire, my master."

"I will take, then, these young men."

"You would slay them all?" Beyond the fire's dancing shadows I sensed a stir among the villagers.

"I will not slay any of them. They will join my army and fight against my enemies."

His army! I wondered what Philip would say to that.

"But, sir," said the old man, "if you take all of them we will have no one to tend the sheep, no one to defend our village from the marauders of the next valley."

"You would prefer that I hang them, here and now?"

"Hang me," said the old man, trying to draw himself up straight. "I am the leader of these people. I am responsible for their crime."

Alexandros stared at the white-beard. Then he broke into a wide grin. "You're right, old man. Your village has been punished enough." He turned to the waiting younger men. "Go back to your homes. And thank the gods that you have a man of courage leading your village."

The old man sank to his knees. "Thank you, brave lord! Thank you for your mercy."

Alexandros pulled him up to his feet. "There is one thing that I want you to do, however."

"What is it, lord?"

"Raise a statue to me and place it here, on this spot, as a reminder to your people to cease their thieving ways."

"I will have it done, lord. But I don't know your name."

"Alexandros of Macedon."

"The son of Philip?" The whole village gasped.

Alexandros' smile vanished. "The son of Zeus," he answered.

When we returned to the main body of the army we received more bad news. The Athenians had already marched their army to Thebes and now the two armies, together with other allies from among the smaller cities nearby, stood ready to block our path to Thebes and Attica.

"Can we maneuver around them?" Alexandros suggested. "Take Thebes while they stand in the field waiting for us to appear from the north?"

Philip's one good eye widened. "Clever thinking, son."

We were huddled in Philip's tent, bent over a folding table that bore a map of the area. Alexandros stood across the table from Philip, who was flanked by Parmenio and Antipatros. Antigonos the One-Eyed stood beside Alexandros; Ptolemaios and the other Companions crowded behind them. I was at the tent's entrance flap.

"Can you find a route that the whole army could pass over without being detected by the enemy?" Philip asked Alexandros.

Barely glancing at the map, Alexandros replied, "No, not the whole army. We would be seen and reported on, no matter which route we took."

Philip nodded.

"But," Alexandros went on, "a smaller group of men, a striking force of cavalry with a phalanx or two of hoplites, could swing around the enemy army and take Thebes while they're still in the field awaiting your advance."

Parmenio blurted, "That's foolhardy! A small force could never take the city by storm and wouldn't be able to lay siege to it."

"We would have the advantage of surprise," Alexandros shot back.

"D'you expect the Theban garrison to drop dead of shock at the sight of you?" Parmenio quipped.

No one laughed. The tent fell deathly silent.

Philip broke the silence. "If you could take the city it would be a great advantage to us. But it would not eliminate the army that faces us. They'd still be there, and we'd still have to deal with them."

"And we'd be weaker," said Antipatros, "because your striking force would no longer be with the main body of our army."

Alexandros said nothing. He simply stared down at the map, his face red with suppressed anger.

"Do you understand the situation?" Philip asked gently. "We must defeat their army in the field. Seizing Thebes won't accomplish that."

"I understand," Alexandros said tightly, without looking up.

"The question, then," said Antigonos, "is where do we fight them?"

"And how many of them are there? What's their order of battle? Who's leading them?" Parmenio was full of questions.

"We'll get some information along those lines shortly," said Philip.

"From spies?" Antipatros asked.

Philip nodded.

"I don't trust spies," grumbled Antigonos. "They can lie to you as often as not. I prefer to see the enemy's dispositions with my own eye." And he put a forefinger below his one good eye.

"Perhaps you and I should scout out the enemy together," suggested Philip, pointing to his own single eye. "Between us we equal one whole scout."

Everyone broke into laughter, the king loudest of all.

"We need to scout them out," agreed Parmenio. "Even the best of spies doesn't have a military head. We need to find out exactly what we're facing."

"You won't like what you see," Philip warned. "They'll outnumber us by quite a bit."

"And the Theban Sacred Band is worth two or three times its numbers," said Antigonos.

"We need some scouts," Parmenio insisted.

"I'll take a look at them," Alexandros said.

"No. It's too risky. You stay in camp."

"But I can do it!"

"So could I," said the king. "But I'm too valuable to risk on a mission that others can do as well."

"All our necks will be beneath the blade once the battle begins," Antipatros said, trying to make peace. "There's no sense taking risks now that we can avoid."

Alexandros raised no further objections, and the meeting broke up with the agreement that Parmenio would pick the men who would cautiously scout the enemy encampments.

But as I followed Alexandros and his Companions back toward their tents, Alexandros pulled me aside. Waving the others to go on, he walked me toward a small clump of trees near one of the horse corrals. I had become accustomed to the smell of the horses and their nervous snuffling when they were penned into the makeshift corrals. It was almost sundown and the horses were anticipating the arrival of the slaves with their bundles of hay.

"Orion," said Alexandros, in a low, confidential tone, "it is clear to me that my father and his generals need information from inside the enemy's camp."

"I'm sure—"

He cut me off, impatient to have his say. "Parmenio's scouts won't be able to glean the kind of information we need."

"Your father has spies in the enemy camp, though. Surely they'll bring out—"

"No, no! We need someone from the army to go into the enemy camp and see for himself how they are arrayed, who their leaders are, what their plans are."

I thought I understood what he was driving at.

"You want me to do this?"

He had to crane his neck to look up into my face. "Not exactly, Orion. I am going to do it myself."

"You!" I was thunderstruck.

"But since my mother told me I must not go anywhere

without you," he went on, unperturbed, "you will have to accompany me."

"But you can't—"

"I can't let Hephaistion and the others know; they'll want to come with me."

Appalled, I blurted, "You can't go into the enemy's camp!"

"And why not?"

"You'd be recognized! You'd be killed or captured and held for ransom. You could wreck your father's entire plan!"

Alexandros smiled at me, pityingly. "How little you understand, Orion. I cannot be killed. Not before my time. My mother is a priestess of the Old Gods and she has prophesied that I will not die until I have conquered all the world."

"Not all prophecies come true."

"You doubt my mother?" he asked coldly.

I knew where that would lead, so I evaded with, "Even if you are not killed, if the enemy captures you they will hold you a hostage until your father surrenders to them."

"In the first place, Orion, my father is more likely to be Zeus than mortal Philip. In the second place, if I am discovered I will fight to the death rather than allow myself to be captured."

"But—"

"And since I am not destined to die until I have conquered the world," he overrode me, "I obviously will not be killed now."

There was no way to penetrate such logic.

"You must accompany me; that is my mother's command."

"And the king's," I reminded him. "Your father commanded me to protect you at all times."

He laughed and headed for his tent.

Chapter 14

We waited until the crescent moon was setting behind the jagged mountains to the west. All our camp was asleep, except for the sentries standing muffled in their cloaks against the night's chill.

I slipped out of my tent without waking the other men of the royal guard sleeping there, and wrapped the scabbard of my sword with a long strip of cloth as I made my way to Alexandros' tent. Silence would be our ally, and I wanted no clink of metal to reveal our presence—either to the enemy or to our own sentries. I wore a dark woolen vest over my chiton, leaving my arms and legs free. The cool night air was no discomfort to me; I simply adjusted my body's circulation to keep myself warm.

There were two guards on duty before Alexandros' tent, leaning sleepily on their spears at its entrance. They allowed me inside without challenge. Alexandros was awake and bristling with energy, pacing the length of his tent, which was larger than the one in which six of us guardsmen slept and furnished almost as handsomely as his quarters in the palace. As soon as he saw me he wordlessly took up a dark half-length cloak and fastened it across his shoulders.

"Do you have a hat or a hood?" I asked. "That golden hair of yours is a dead giveaway."

He nodded and went to a chest at the foot of his cot. From it he pulled out a dark woolen cap and tugged it over his hair.

As far as the guards were concerned, the prince was going for a late-night stroll through the camp with his personal bodyguard. The sentries were a different matter. We had to slip past them without being seen.

"Follow me," whispered Alexandros. "I scouted our own camp this afternoon."

He led me to the little stream that meandered through the camp. Tangled bushes grew at its banks, except for the places where the soldiers had cut them down to get at the water. We waded knee-deep into the icy water and made our way out of the camp. When we came to sentries posted on either bank, we ducked low and let the shrubbery screen us. When the stream turned at an angle that hid us from the sentries' sight, we clambered out, struggling through the thorny bushes onto bare dry ground.

Alexandros shivered, but I thought it was more excitement than the cold. He was happy as a little boy at play. We pressed on toward the enemy camp.

"We should tell Parmenio or one of the other generals that someone can sneak into our camp through that stream," I whispered.

He made a grunt that might have been an affirmative.

Up ahead I could see camp fires, thousands of them. It looked as if the dark countryside had been visited by a plague of fireflies. But these lights did not dart and flicker through the shadows; they remained fixed in place. I knew that each of them represented anywhere from six to a dozen or more soldiers. There must be fifty thousand troops facing us, I figured.

Far in the distance a few other lights gleamed wanly. I touched Alexandros' shoulder and pointed.

"That's the town," he whispered to me. "Chaeroneia."

We went down on our bellies and crawled like beetles to get past the enemy sentries. It took a long time; we would inch along, then stop, wait, glance around to see where the sentries were and if they were looking our way. Then we dragged ourselves across a few more feet of the dusty hard ground.

At last we were deep enough inside the camp to get to our hands and knees and scamper behind the shelter of a decent-sized rock.

Alexandros was grinning. "We used to play at this when we were boys, Ptolemaios and Harpalos and I."

He was little more than a boy now, I thought. But I said nothing.

Once inside the camp's guarded perimeter it was almost easy to walk around. There were men from many different cities and tribes, and even though they tended to camp amongst their own, we saw that many others were walking through the camp, talking with friends or strangers or drifting alone with their thoughts, unable to sleep on the night before battle.

Alexandros could distinguish among them by their accents. He spoke to several men, low and brief in his words. I noticed that he used the Attic accent rather well, disguising his native Macedonian tongue.

Finally we were among the Athenians. I saw a very large tent, bright with candles within and guarded by half a dozen men in armor.

"Their generals must be there," I said to Alexandros as we stood in the shadows between lesser tents. "Making their last-minute plans."

"I wish we could get close enough to listen." But even reckless Alexandros saw that it would be impossible. The area around the tent was cleared for a good fifty feet and lit at all four corners of the open space by watch fires. The guards could see anyone approaching the tent from any direction.

Then we saw a familiar figure leave the tent: thin, stoop-shouldered, balding, combing the fingers of one hand through his bushy beard.

"Demosthenes!" Alexandros hissed.

"Their generals don't need his oratory now," I said.

We watched Demosthenes make his way to his own tent, head bent, walking slowly, like a man deep in thought. The instant he stepped through the tent's entrance Alexandros started after him.

I tried to stop him. "Are you mad? One yell from him and you're a prisoner."

But he pulled away from me. "He won't yell with my sword's point at his throat."

I could either overpower the young hothead or go with him. I went with him.

There was no guard at Demosthenes' tent. We pushed right inside, drawing our swords.

He looked up, startled. The tent was no great affair, big enough for a cot and a table, little more. Demosthenes was at the table. A dark-skinned man in a colorful robe, his head wrapped in a white turban, stood next to him.

"A Persian!" Alexandros snapped.

"Who are you?" Demosthenes demanded.

"I am Alexandros, prince of Macedon."

I swiftly took in the tent's furnishings. The table was bare except for a pitcher of wine and two cups. A hoplite's panoply of armor stood arrayed on a wooden form in one corner. Next to it rested a large round shield painted blue, with the words "With Fortune" in white around its edge. Four spears stood behind the armor, poking up into the shadowed ceiling of the tent. A chest next to the cot, a sword in its scabbard atop the chest. Nothing else.

"I am not a Persian," said the dark-skinned man, in strangely accented Attic Greek. "I am from Hindustan."

"Hindustan?" Alexandros seemed almost to ignore Demosthenes. "Where is that?"

The turbanned man smiled condescendingly. "Far from this place. It lies on the other side of the Persian Empire." He had large dark liquid eyes. His skin seemed to shine in the lamplight, as if it were oiled.

"Young Alexandros," said Demosthenes, his voice trembling slightly.

Alexandros suddenly remembered why he was here. Pointing his sword at Demosthenes' throat, he advanced on the Athenian. "And you are the man who calls my father a sly dog and a vicious beast."

"One c-c-cry from m-me and you're a d-d-dead man," Demosthenes stuttered.

"It will be the last sound you ever make," Alexandros said.

"Wait," I snapped. Turning to the Hindi, I said, "Who are you? Why are you here?"

"I serve the Great King," he answered in singsong cadence. "I carry gold and instructions to this man here."

"Gold and instructions from the Great King," muttered Alexandros. "The man who preaches the glories of democracy over tyranny serves the Great King of the Persians, the tyrant who holds the Greek cities of Ionia in bondage."

Demosthenes pulled himself to his full height, little taller than Alexandros. "I serve no m-m-master except the de-democracy of Athens."

"This man says otherwise."

With a lopsided smile, Demosthenes answered, "The Great K-King serves me, Alexandros. His g-g-gold helps me to fight your f-father."

"Politics," Alexandros spat.

"What do you know of politics, princeling?" Demosthenes shot back. Suddenly his nervous stuttering was gone, vanished in the heat of anger. "You play at war and think that conquest is everything. What do you know about ruling people, about getting free men to follow where you lead?"

"I will rule when my father dies," said Alexandros. "And I will conquer all the world."

"Yes, I see. You were born to be a ruler of slaves, like your tyrant father before you. All you have known all your life has been luxury and pleasure—"

"Luxury and pleasure?" Alexandros' voice nearly broke. "I was raised like a Spartan helot. I can run twenty miles and live for weeks on roots and berries. My body is trained and hard, not a soft slug of a worm like you."

"But all your life you have known you would be king one day. You have never doubted it. You have never had to wonder where your next meal would come from, or if you would have a roof over your head."

"I've spent more nights in the open air than with a roof over my head."

"What of it?" Demosthenes challenged. "I was born in poverty. All my life the only safety I have had has been from my wits. I have *worked* all my life, since earliest childhood. No one gave me a place at the table; I had to struggle to get where I am. No one named me prince and assured my future. I had to *earn* my position as a leader of Athens. And even today, even at this moment, my position can be taken from me. I have no security, no father to protect me, no wealth to shelter me from hunger and cold."

"By the gods," Alexandros almost whispered. "You're jealous of me!"

"Jealous? Me? Never! *Never!*"

I kept one eye on the Hindi. He was not armed, and he made no move toward the sword on the chest behind him.

He seemed to be following the argument with intense interest.

"You envy my position," Alexandros insisted. "You think that you should be a prince, instead of me."

"Never!" Demosthenes repeated, so vehemently that I thought Alexandros had touched the most sensitive nerve of all. "I want no princes, no kings, no tyrants to rule over men. I want democracy, where men rule themselves."

"Where men are swayed by demagogues such as yourself," Alexandros said. "You want a nation of obedient idiots swept by emotion and your rhetoric. You want followers, slaves to your words."

"And you want slaves outright!"

"Not so. The king of Macedonia is not a birthright, as you seem to believe, Athenian. The king must be elected—"

"By your army, yes, I know."

"And our army is all the able-bodied men of the kingdom. How does that differ from your democracy?"

"Because your army will elect the son of the old king, and well you know it!"

"They will elect the son of the old king if they deem him worthy. Soldiers do not willingly elect fools to lead them. But from what I've seen of your democracy, anyone can be a leader if he promises enough and has enough fancy words to stir the mob."

Demosthenes took in a deep, shuddering breath. Eyes squeezed shut, he said in a low voice, "You represent the power of the sword and the privilege of birth. I represent the will of the people. Tomorrow we will shall see which is stronger."

"If you live to see tomorrow," said Alexandros.

Demosthenes' eyes popped open. "I should h-have expected n-n-nothing less from the s-son of Philip. You would kill an unarmed m-man."

"I would decapitate a poisonous snake."

"That's not why we came here," I reminded Alexandros. "And making a martyr of this man will only make the Athenians fight harder."

Alexandros glanced at me, then returned his gaze to Demosthenes. "Where will the Athenians be placed in tomorrow's formation?"

"On the far left," said the Hindi, before Demosthenes could open his mouth. "The Thebans will be on the right, which will be the stronger side."

Alexandros blinked at him.

"I will tell you whatever you wish to know, so long as you do not kill this man."

"Why?"

The Hindi made a sad little smile. "It is my religion. No man should kill another, or allow one to be killed if he can help it."

"What kind of a religion is that?" Alexandros wondered.

"It is The Eightfold Path. The Way of the Buddha."

I asked, "Do you know all the dispositions of the troops for tomorrow's battle?"

"Oh yes."

"Can we believe that?" Alexandros demanded.

"I am the representative of the Great King," he replied easily. "My lord Dareios and his advisors will want to know every detail of tomorrow's battle. I am to carry that information back to them."

"You'll give it to Philip and his generals first," said Alexandros.

"Willingly, if you will spare this man."

Curious, I asked him, "You will help us to slay thousands tomorrow if we spare this one individual?"

"Tomorrow you will fight and thousands will be slain no matter what I do. I have no control over that. But if I can save the life of this one man, I must do it. That is the Way."

I turned to Demosthenes. "Can we trust you to remain silent while we take this man to our camp?"

He glanced at Alexandros, still brandishing his sword, then nodded.

"You may trust this demagogue, Orion," said Alexandros, "but I don't."

Sheathing his sword, Alexandros went to the armor standing in the corner of the tent. He pulled the straps from the cuirass and greaves and used them to bind Demosthenes hand and foot. Finally he stuffed a gag in the orator's mouth and tied it with a strip of cloth.

"Now we can trust him," Alexandros muttered, "for a little while."

Standing by the blue shield with its lettering, Alexandros looked back at Demosthenes, lying helpless on the bare ground.

"With Fortune," he read grimly. "I will look for you on the battlefield tomorrow."

Then we left with the Hindi and started back toward our own camp.

The Hindi's name was Svertaketu. "It is acceptable for you to call me Ketu," he said modestly as we made our way through the predawn shadows back to the Macedonian camp. "The words of my native language are difficult for your tongues to pronounce."

All the way back to the camp Alexandros pressed Ketu for information about his native land.

"Tell me of the lands beyond the Persian Empire," the young prince asked as we hurried across the grassy, rolling ground between the camps, where tomorrow's battle would be fought.

"It is so large that it has many names," replied Ketu.

"Indra, Hind, Kush—many names and principalities. A far land, very large, very distant. A great, great empire with vast palaces and temples of gold. And lands beyond that, too. Cathay is an even larger empire, far to the east. It stretches as far as the great eastern ocean."

"The world is much larger than I knew. I must tell Aristotle of this."

I wondered what was going through his mind. Alexandros felt it was destiny to conquer the whole world. Was he dismayed that there was so much more to it than he had thought? Or was he excited at the prospect of new lands to see, new empires to conquer? He sounded more excited than dismayed to me.

We let the sentries of our camp see us, and when they challenged us Alexandros pulled off his dark cap and shouted his name to them. Swiftly we strode through the camp, while the sky began to turn milky with the first hint of dawn, and went straight to Philip's tent.

True to his word, Ketu told Philip and his generals everything he knew about the enemy's battle plans.

"How do we know this man is telling us the truth?" Parmenio grumbled. "And even if he is, won't Demosthenes and the Athenian generals change their plans?"

Philip made a wry grin. "Do you think they have enough time to bring the Thebans and all the others together and change their order of battle? From what my spies tell me, it took them more than a week to work out the plan they've agreed on."

Scratching at his beard, Parmenio admitted, "Yes, it would probably take them another week of arguing to get them to make any changes."

Philip nodded and dismissed Ketu, indicating with a gesture that I should go with him. I saw in his one good eye a conflict of anger and admiration for his son. For me he had nothing but anger, I thought. Yet he knew as well as I that no one could prevent Alexandros from doing whatever he wished to do. He could not blame me for the Little King's foolish risk-taking. Or could he?

Alexandros remained in the tent with Parmenio and the other generals, digesting the intelligence Ketu had provided and altering their plans for the imminent battle.

As Ketu and I stepped outside into the brightening morning, I could hear Parmenio asking bluntly, "How do we know he's telling us the truth? He could have been planted here to give us false information."

Alexandros immediately objected. I showed Ketu the direction to the tent I shared with some of the other guardsmen.

"They do not trust me," he said as we walked along.

"It does seem very fortunate," I said, "that you are so knowledgeable—and cooperative."

He shrugged his slim shoulders. "We are all directed by fate. What purpose would it serve for me to be obstinate?"

"What would your master, the Great King, say?"

Again he shrugged. "I served the Great King because I was commanded to by my king. He gave me to the Great King as a gift, to curry favor with the Persians. I am a professional diplomat, and I know I will never see my home again."

"Then you don't care who wins this battle?"

"It makes little difference. We are all bound up on the wheel of life. Those who die tomorrow will return to life again and again. The great goal is to get off the wheel, to achieve final nothingness."

I stopped him with a touch on his arm. "You believe that men live more than one life?"

"Oh yes. We are reborn into this world of pain and suffering until we can purify ourselves sufficiently to attain Nirvana."

"Nirvana?"

"Nothingness. The end of all sensation. The end of desire and pain."

"I have had other lives before this one."

"We all have."

"I can remember some of them."

His large liquid eyes went wide. "Remember? Your past lives?"

"Parts of them. Some of them."

"That is a sign of great holiness. You may be a Bodhisattva, a holy being."

I had to smile at that. "No, I was created to be a warrior. Even my name means 'hunter.' I am a slayer of men; that is my destiny."

"But if you remember your former lives—that is something that only a Buddha can do truly."

"Do you believe in the gods?" I asked him.

"There are gods, yes. And demons, too."

I nodded, old memories stirring inside me. "I have fought demons. Devils. Long ago."

He stared hard at me. "We must speak further of this. It is of great importance, Orion."

"Yes, I agree."

Horses were stirring in the growing light of dawn. And men. The camp was bustling.

"But the battle comes first," said Ketu. "May the gods favor you, Orion."

I thanked him. The first trumpet blew. We would be forming up for battle within the hour.

Chapter 15

Just as Ketu had told us, the Athenians were on the extreme left of their battle line, opposite our right. By long tradition, the right side of an army's line was the stronger. The Thebans with their invincible Sacred Band stood on their right. The middle of the enemy line was filled with allies from Corinth, Megara and other cities opposed to Philip.

Demosthenes must have talked their generals into letting the Athenians take the position most likely to be opposite Philip himself. Or perhaps they reasoned that the Thebans, led by their Sacred Band, would crush our weaker left flank and roll up our line like an unstoppable juggernaut.

They had no cavalry, but their line stretched from the steep hill of Chaeroneia's acropolis to the marshy ground by the river. There was no way for the Macedonian cavalry to round either of their flanks, one anchored on the temple-topped acropolis and other on the muddy flats. We would have to break their line, one way or the other.

I sat astride Thunderbolt, who was flicking his ears nervously and snuffling as we waited at the extreme left end of the Macedonian line. In front of us were only light troops, peltast. Beyond them, facing us, stood the Thebans in phalanxes twelve men deep. The Sacred Band stood on the extreme right of their formation, at the edge of the mud flats, their polished armor gleaming in the morning sun, their spears bristling like a forest of death.

Alexandros, sitting on black Ox-Head in front of me, was in command of the entire heavy cavalry. We had some lighter horsemen off to our left, by the river. As I waited for the trumpet to sound the advance, I remembered Philip's final word to us, less than an hour before, when the commanders had gathered for their final conference before the fighting began. From the back of his horse Philip looked up and down the two assembled armies with his good eye.

"Now we'll see how well this nation of lawyers can fight," Antigonos had joked.

"Well enough, I expect," said Philip. "They have a fair number of mercenaries among them."

"Yes," agreed Antipatros, "but most of the Athenians are citizen hoplites, not professional soldiers."

"The same kind of citizen hoplites that defeated the Persians more than once," said Parmenio, eyeing the Athenian phalanxes.

Philip had shaken his head. "That was a long time ago, my friend. They've spent the generations in between getting soft."

"Lawyers, all of them," Antigonos repeated.

"Well," said Parmenio, pointing to the other side of the line, "the Thebans aren't soft, and their Sacred Band aren't citizen-soldiers. They're as professional as they come."

"That's why I've put the cavalry against them," Philip had answered.

Alexandros, standing bareheaded beside his father, pulled himself up a little taller. He had never commanded the entire cavalry before, only smaller detachments. His father was showing enormous faith in him.

"You know what to do?" Philip asked him.

"Wait for your signal."

"No matter what happens, you wait for my signal."

"No matter what, I will wait."

"Whether my side of the line advances or retreats, you wait for my signal."

Alexandros nodded.

"If the earth should open up and swallow the whole army—"

"I will wait for your signal."

"Good." Philip laughed and reached out to tousle Alexandros' hair. "Better get your helmet on, son. You're going to need some protection for those pretty curls."

Alexandros flushed as the generals laughed. As we rode back to our position in the line he complained, "He always gives with one hand and takes away with the other."

"He's put you in the most important position," I said. "He's showing great faith in you."

"He's put me in the spot where I'm most likely to get killed," Alexandros grumbled.

I could not let that stand. "I thought your destiny was not to get killed until you've conquered the whole world."

His grin told me that he understood the irony of the situation. "Yes, and now I know that there's a lot more of it to conquer: Hindustan and Cathay and the gods know what else."

That was an hour ago. Now we sat waiting for the order to charge, grooms standing beside us to help keep the horses steady, squires holding the lances we would use when we went into action. Nerves were screwed up tight, palms sweating, the very air crackling with that special electricity that comes when nearly a hundred thousand men are ready to do their utmost to slaughter one another.

The enemy stood their ground, content to wait for Philip to make the first move. They were defending their homeland; to get to Thebes and Athens we would have to get past them. If we beat them, there was nothing between us and the cities of the south. If they beat us Philip's kingdom would collapse. This one battle would determine the outcome of the war.

The sun climbed higher. The two lines of armed men stood facing one another, sweating not entirely from the heat, waiting, waiting.

A single trumpet sounded. Like a single creature, Philip's phalanxes on his far right began to march forward toward the Athenians. Not a charge, just a slow methodical march of some twenty thousand hoplites, shaking the ground with each step they took.

The Athenian line seemed to shudder. Then their spears came down to point at the advancing Macedonians. A battle between phalanxes often turned into a pushing match. The two lines would meet with a clashing of spears and roar of fury and each would try to push down the other. That was why Philip ordered his phalanxes sixteen men deep; the extra weight was often the difference between victory and defeat.

The Athenians were twelve men deep. They began to move forward, toward the advancing Macedonians, with an equally slow, measured tread.

From our horses we saw it all unfolding. Thunderbolt was quivering with excitement, eager to go. I stroked his neck and glanced at Alexandros. Even with his helmet on and his cheek flaps strapped on I could see that he, too, was eager to charge. But true to his promise he kept his place, even though the rest of the enemy line was now moving toward us, keeping pace with the Athenians. The Thebans were marching straight toward us, as methodical and inexorable as death itself.

From out of the Macedonian phalanxes a flurry of peltasts scampered, showering the advancing Athenians with arrows and javelins and rocks. The second and more rearward ranks raised their shields over their heads, protecting themselves and their first rank, who kept their shields before them. I saw a few men fall, but by and large the peltasts did little more than irritate the Athenians.

I was more worried about the advancing Thebans. Horses will not charge spears, no matter how you urge them. And a forest of Theban spears was approaching us, with nothing between us and them except a scattering of our own peltasts. They annoyed the Thebans but could not stop them.

Philip's troops were advancing in oblique order, their farthest right phalanxes leading the others. It was a technique Philip had learned from the great Theban commander Epaminondas when, as a boy, he had lived in Thebes for several years, a royal hostage after Macedonia had been trounced by the Thebans.

I heard Alexandros gasp. The peltasts in front of Philip's line turned away from the advancing Athenians and fled from the field. *And the phalanxes began to retreat, as well.*

"They're running away!" Alexandros said. His voice was low, breathless.

Not running, I saw. They were retreating in good order. But retreating. Even before they had come to grips with the enemy line.

A great exultant shout went up from the Athenians and they broke into a headlong charge to close the distance with the retreating Macedonians.

"Should we send some of the cavalry to go help them?" I asked Alexandros.

"No," he said grimly. "We stand here until he gives us the signal."

The Thebans were moving toward us faster, now, but they were not charging wildly, as the Athenians were. The allied troops in the center of the enemy line were struggling to keep the line intact, with the Athenians rushing pell-mell on the left side of them and the Thebans advancing more slowly on the right.

Not a blow had yet been struck by the hoplites anywhere on either line, yet it looked to me as if the battle had already been lost.

And it had. But not by the wily One-Eyed Fox.

The allied hoplites could not keep up with the charging Athenians. Gaps opened up in their line. The Theban commander must have seen this, for now he began to move his phalanxes more toward the center of their formation, trying to close the gap—leaving some firm ground open between his own right flank and the marshland by the river.

Another trumpet sounded, blasting the air like the crack of doom. Alexandros grabbed the lance from the hands of his squire, raised it over his helmeted head and screamed, "Follow me!"

We charged headlong into the gap between the allies and the Thebans, thundering across the sloping ground like a torrent of death. The world around me slowed once again as my body went into overdrive. Right behind Alexandros I rode, gripping Thunderbolt with my thighs, levelling my lance as I leaned forward against the horse's flowing mane.

We poured into the gap between the Thebans and the allied phalanxes before they could close the ground between them. Wheeling around faster than the phalanxes could turn, we hit them from the rear and sides. The allied hoplites broke and ran. The Thebans held their ground and fought back. But our light cavalry swung around their other flank, skirting the marshy ground, and completed their encirclement. In front of the Theban phalanxes our light troops harried them with arrows and javelins. They could not turn their backs on the peltasts. They could not turn their backs to our cavalry. Their commanders bellowed orders but their voices were lost in the thunder of the battle. They tried to form a circle of shields, but we cut through them and sliced their formation into smaller and smaller bits. I left my lance buried in a man's chest and pulled out my sword, hacking and swinging madly at the milling, frightened, disorganized men all around me.

When an army loses discipline it loses the battle. The Thebans, good as they were, had lost the cohesion a phalanx needs to make it effective. They were not an army now, they had no phalanxes, only knots of shaken and confused men who were being cut to pieces by our cavalry.

On the other side of the battlefield, I learned later, the Macedonians stopped their planned retreat the instant the trumpet blast gave us the order to charge. Suddenly the Athenians were facing those sixteen-man-deep phalanxes. The two sides clashed briefly, then the Athenians broke and started to run away. Philip's men pursued them, slaughtering them as they ran, until he saw that the Thebans were still fighting for their lives against us. He ordered an end to the pursuit of the Athenians and brought his phalanxes over to our side of the field to finish off the Thebans.

For even though we had won our battle, the fighting was far from over. The Thebans refused to surrender. Hopeless, they fought on, especially their Sacred Band. Those men lived up to their reputation; even when we had cut them down to scattered pairs of men they fought on, back to back, on their knees when they were too badly wounded to stand. They refused to give up.

"You may kill us, but you will never see our backs," shouted one of them as he stood over the drooping body of his companion, dying from several spear thrusts.

It was grisly work, and costly. Thunderbolt took a spear thrust through his ribs and went down with a hideous shriek, almost pinning me beneath him. I leaped clear and skewered the Theban who had killed him. I saw Alexandros still on Ox-Head, his helmet gone, golden hair flowing in the breeze, hacking at the enemy with a fierce grin pulling his lips back from his teeth. His Companions were scattered through the melee, killing with equal ruthlessness, their swords and sword-arms dripping with hot blood.

A pair of Thebans must have recognized Alexandros' blond mane, for they pushed their way past the peltasts in front of them and headed for the prince. Coming up behind him they raised their spears simultaneously at his unprotected back.

Unprotected except for me. I had tried to stay as close to Alexandros as I could, but in this awful slaughter the excitement of battle, the passions of fear and blood-lust, and the sheer exhilaration of killing had almost made me lose my head. Almost. I knew somehow that this craving for violence had been built into me by the Creators; I was their instrument of destruction, their Hunter.

But despite the battle-fury that drove me on I saw the two Thebans ready to strike Alexandros from the rear. I was fighting a pair of them myself, both of them protecting themselves from my sword with their big shields, one of them still holding a spear, which he used to keep me at a distance from them.

The spear point seemed to waver in slow-motion before my eyes, almost hypnotically, while the other Theban tried to work himself over to my left side, where he could thrust at me with his bloodied sword.

I had no time to waste on them. I ducked beneath the spear point, rolled to the ground and kicked the spear-wielder in the groin. As he collapsed onto his own shield I jumped to my feet and slammed my shoulder into the shield of the other Theban. He jounced backward a step and I dashed off toward the men who were about to kill Alexandros.

I could not close the distance in time. So I threw my sword as hard as I could as I yelled, "Alexandros! Behind you!"

My sword point went completely through the nearer Theban's shoulder. He screamed and the spear dropped from his paralyzed fingers as his companion jabbed his own weapon at Alexandros. But the young prince had turned slightly at my shouted warning and the spear point slid across the belly of his bronze cuirass harmlessly as Alexandros raised his sword and brought it down on the Theban's neck hard enough to take his head almost completely off his shoulders. Blood geysered as the man gasped his death agony.

I had reached the other Theban by then. He had fallen almost beneath Ox-Head's shuffling hooves. Wrenching my sword from his shoulder, I plunged it into his throat. He died with a look of surprise on his face.

Philip's phalanxes reached us then, marching up in good order to dispatch the last of the Sacred Band.

The king rode up just behind his phalanxes and went straight to Alexandros. Looking him over with his one good eye, Philip broke into a tired smile.

"Not a scratch on you!" He seemed pleased. "Not even on Ox-Head. The gods must work overtime protecting you."

Alexandros smiled back as if he had received nothing more than his due. If he realized that I had saved his life he made no mention of it.

I stood, panting and suddenly very weary, on grassy ground made slippery with blood and entrails. All around me the field was littered with corpses and the writhing, moaning bodies of the wounded. The battle was over. Now some of the troops were moving among the wounded, giving them the final merciful dagger in the throat. Others were stripping the dead of their arms and armor.

Ignoring the men, I staggered across the battlefield looking for Thunderbolt. Philip's strategy had worked almost perfectly. The enemy commanders had known that cavalry could not attack a well-formed line of spears. So Philip had induced the Athenian citizen-soldiers to break ranks and ruin the solidarity of their line. Then our cavalry could destroy their foot soldiers, and we did. But it had cost me a valiant steed.

Thunderbolt was already dead when I found him, the spear still sticking in his flank. I hoped that he had not suffered too much, then found it ludicrous that I cared more for this horse than for all the men who had fallen.

I began to laugh, at myself, at the folly of men who slaughter one another, at the so-called gods to whom men pray. If they knew that the gods were nothing more than selfish humans like themselves, what would they do? How would they re-order their lives if they rejected the gods they worshiped?

I had to get off by myself. Slowly, painfully I climbed the steep hill of Chaeroneia's acropolis. The sun was going down behind the distant mountains, and from the steps of the temple atop the hill I could see the entire battlefield in the long shadows of the setting sun. Thousands of bodies lay strewn like broken toys the breadth of the field.

"Are you pleased?" I muttered. "Is this the kind of human sacrifice that you enjoy watching?"

Turning to the temple, I climbed its steps and entered its shadowed interior. Statues of gods loomed around me: Zeus, Ares, Apollo, Poseidon.

"You made me part of this," I said to them. "You created me to kill my fellow men. I hate you! I hate all of you! For making me in the first place, for using me as a puppet, a tool, a toy. All I want is to get out, to get off this wheel of life, to find the final peace of oblivion."

And I knew that I had to learn from Ketu how to seek that ultimate death.

The statues remained silent and cold. The sun dipped behind the mountains and the temple became utterly dark.

Yet my eyes adjusted to the darkness; I could still make out the statues, their aloof faces, their blankly staring eyes. Yes, there was Hera, proud and cruel. And Aphrodite, sensuousness personified.

And Athena, with a warrior's helmet and a spear in her hand. She too was lifeless, inanimate marble. As distant from me as the pale cold moon.

Yet I thought I heard her voice within my mind, saying, "Be brave, Orion. Bear the pain."

No, I thought. *Not even for you. I can't bear this pain any longer. If there is a way out of life, I want to find it.*

Chapter 16

It was full dark as I made my way back down to the camp that Philip had set up on the battlefield. Men were still carrying the bodies of the slain to the funeral pyres dotting the plain; others were stacking the armor and weapons they had collected.

Pausanias cast a baleful eye at me as I showed up before the cook fire in front of his tent.

"Where've you been, Orion? The king assigned you to young Alexandros; you don't have leave to wander wherever you choose."

"I was communing with the gods," I said drily.

"Never mind that," he snapped. "Your post is at Alexandros' side. Find him and stay with him."

"Yes, sir."

He softened somewhat. "I hear you did well in the battle. Have something to eat before you go on duty again."

I was not hungry, but I thanked him and sat by the fire. Women camp-followers had shown up, and one of them was cooking for us. She was middle-aged, missing several teeth, but some of the guardsmen were already ogling her. After a bit more wine she would look ravishing.

I gnawed on a leg of goat, took a cup of wine, and then went to the river to clean the blood and grime of battle off me. Within the hour I was presentable enough to report for duty. I went searching for Alexandros.

All of the generals, I was told, were at Philip's tent, enjoying the fruits of victory. Alexandros was considered a general now. He had commanded the cavalry that had struck the crushing blow of victory.

There was much wine at Philip's tent. And the women pouring it were young and slim and smiling. Alexandros sat in a corner of the tent, his wine cup untouched on the ground beside his chair. Parmenio was lurching after one of the young wine pourers. Antipatros snored loudly on his chair, head thrown back and arms hanging almost to the ground.

Philip was joking with Antigonos and a few of the younger officers. Alexandros' Companions were nowhere in sight.

I went to the prince. "I am reporting for duty, sir."

He gave me a wan smile. "I won't need a bodyguard this night, Orion. I'm more in danger from boredom than anything else."

"I will stand watch outside the tent, then."

He nodded.

"Do you want to leave and return to your own quarters?" I asked.

"The king has commanded me to stay with him. I am a general of the army now, he says, and I must be part of all the conferences that the generals attend."

I looked around the tent. Philip had clutched one of the serving girls around the waist. With his free hand he was beckoning to another of them.

"It doesn't appear that military strategy will be discussed this night," I said.

Before Alexandros could reply, Philip staggered toward us, half supported by the two serving girls.

"We've won!" he said drunkenly to his son. "Why aren't you celebrating?"

"I am celebrating, sir," replied Alexandros. "I am with you."

Philip grunted. "I suppose you'd rather be with your own Companions, eh? I'll bet Ptolemaios' got a girl or two with him."

"I wouldn't be surprised," Alexandros said.

"But Hephaistion won't. He'll be waiting for you, won't he?"

"Yes. Of course."

Taking a deep breath, Philip clutched the two young women closer to him. Then he asked, "D'you know *what* we've won today, my son?"

"A great battle."

"No, more than that." Philip wagged his head from side to side. "We've won peace, my boy. Peace! There is no other power in all of the Greek states to oppose us. Macedonia is safe now. We can dictate terms to the Athenians and stop them from nibbling at our coastal cities. The tribes of the north and those savages in the Balkans will all calm down now, because they know we can turn our full power against them whenever we choose to. We'll have peace, Alexandros, for the first time since I took the throne."

Alexandros' brows knit. "But what about the Persians?"

"They'll accept us as supreme in Europe, we'll accept them as supreme in Asia. That will do it."

"But—"

"I know, I know. There's the Greek cities in Ionia. Dareios will tax them lightly, you'll see. He has enough troubles holding his empire together without stirring up the Ionian cities."

Alexandros rose to his feet. I realized that, short though he was, he was the same height as his father. Somehow Philip had always given the impression of being taller, even when his bad leg made him stoop.

"We are destined to conquer the Persian Empire. It's my fate," Alexandros said.

Philip grinned crookedly at him. "Perhaps it is *your* fate, young godling. But *my* fate is to rule a strong and secure Macedonia. When you're king—if you are accepted as king after me—you can go off and conquer the whole world. If the army will follow you."

I saw Alexandros' hands tightening into fists. His face went red. Not trusting himself to speak another word, he brushed past his father and the two young women supporting him and strode out of the tent. I followed him into the cool night air.

Behind us, Philip lurched and staggered through the tent's entrance, shouting, "We've won the peace, young fool! I've worked all my life for this and I'm not going to ruin it now. I'm not going to let *anybody* ruin it!"

Alexandros stalked off into the night, with me trailing dutifully behind him.

Among the spoils the soldiers collected from the battlefield was a large round shield, painted blue, with the word "With Fortune" lettered on it. When Alexandros heard of it, the morning after the battle, he ordered the shield brought to his tent—and the man who had found it, as well.

"Was the man whose shield this was also found on the battlefield?" he asked the young man. He was a Dardanian shepherd's son who had joined the army as a slinger.

"No, sire," said the youngster, clutching his felt cap in both hands, half bent over into a sort of bowing posture before the Little King. He might have been a year or so older than Alexandros, but he seemed much less sure of himself than the prince.

"The shield was found by itself?"

"Yes, sire. The man who owned it must have thrown it away as he fled from our phalanxes."

"I will keep it," said Alexandros. Turning to the servant at his left hand, he ordered, "Give this lad coins to make up for the value of the shield."

The young Dardanian bowed and thanked his way out of the tent, beaming. He had never seen so much money in his life.

Alexandros called me from my post at his tent's entrance and pointed to the shield, resting against his table.

"This is Demosthenes' shield."

"Yes," I agreed.

An icy smile flickered across his lips. "I would enjoy returning it to him."

"Assuming he survived the battle."

"Oh, he survived, all right. He threw down his shield and ran for his life. He probably ran all the way back to Athens."

Philip, merciless in battle, was generous in victory. He called Alexandros to his tent to discuss with his generals the peace terms he would exact.

"We will put a garrison of picked men into the acropolis of Thebes," he said flatly. "That will keep the city under control."

"That," added Parmenio, "and the fact that their army no longer exists."

"Their Sacred Band fought almost to the last men," Antigonos said, a bit of awe still in his voice.

Philip gave a snort. "Yes, they'll be celebrated in poems for all time to come. All we've got is the victory."

Everyone laughed. Except Alexandros. I could see that he was still smoldering over his father's pronouncement of the previous night.

"So what do you propose to do about Athens?" Parmenio asked.

"I want to send you, Alexandros," Philip replied, "into Athens to give them my terms."

"Which are?" asked Antigonos.

"They must sign a treaty that promises they will not make war against us again. They must recognize that we control the coastal cities up to and including Byzantion."

"And?"

"That's all."

"That's all?" Antigonos challenged. "Don't you want to install your own men in their government? Don't you want them to lay out their silver to pay for the cost of this war?"

Parmenio winked and said, "At least we can parade the army through their city."

"None of that," said Philip, quite seriously. "They're beaten and they know it. If we rub their noses in it they'll resent it and start a new war as soon as they're able to."

"They'll do that anyway," mumbled Parmenio.

Philip shook his head. "No, I don't think so. Demosthenes and his war party are discredited now. Their democracy will turn on them and toss them out of power, maybe exile them from the city."

"I'd rather see him hanging from his golden throat," Antipatros said.

"All I want from Athens is that they leave us in charge of the seaports and stop making war against us."

"And what about the Persians?" Alexandros asked, his voice as thin and hard as a knife blade.

"The Great King will make his settlement with us. If we offer no threat to him, he'll offer no threat to us."

"For how long?"

Philip fixed his son with his one good eye. "For as long

as we control all of Greece. Which will be for as long as I sit on the throne of Macedonia."

I wondered. Philip had forged a powerful instrument in his army, and armies need enemies to fight. Otherwise they go to rot. Or worse, their officers begin to scheme against the king. Still, I could not see Parmenio or Antipatros or One-Eyed Antigonos plotting to overthrow Philip.

Alexandros, however, was a different matter. And there was his mother to consider.

This time Alexandros entered Athens openly. No disguises, no deception. He rode bareheaded in a gold-leafed chariot pulled by a brace of magnificent white stallions, followed by his Companions, all mounted on their war chargers, and then a squadron of the heavy cavalry that had crushed the Thebans.

The whole city turned out to see the boy-hero of Chaeroneia. If they resented the Macedonian conquest of their army they did not show it. The narrow winding streets of Athens were thronged with citizens shouting and waving to Alexandros, even throwing flowers. *Many of these men must have been marching against us in the battle,* I thought. *Many of the women must be widows because of Chaeroneia. How can they cheer for their conqueror?*

Perhaps because they were still alive, I reasoned, and not enslaved. Philip did not pursue the fleeing Athenian hoplites as ruthlessly as he might have. Instead of harrying them to their deaths he turned his phalanxes against the Thebans, coming to the aid of us in the cavalry.

Apparently the news of Philip's lenient terms had already been spread through the city. They thought he admired Athens, revered it so highly that he felt himself too humble to enter the city himself. Actually Philip was busy settling with Thebes and the other cities that had arrayed themselves against him. He was working at a king's tasks; he had no time for glory and adulation.

But Alexandros took the city's homage as his personal due.

The city's leaders were obsequious, hailing Alexandros before the crowd at the Agora as if he had won the victory for their side. In private they seemed unable to believe their good fortune.

"Philip will not send troops to occupy the city?"

"No," said Alexandros.

"He does not demand reparations or ransom for the prisoners he took?"

"No."

"All he wants is for us to confirm his control of the seaports along the Hellespont and Bosporus?"

"That, and a guarantee that you will no longer make war against us." Sullenly.

The Athenian leaders could hardly suppress their delight.

"After all, he controls the ports already."

"It was Demosthenes and his faction that wanted to war against Philip. I never believed in it."

"Nor I."

"Nor I!"

"Where is Demosthenes?" Alexandros asked. "I have something of his to return to him."

Chapter 17

I accompanied Alexandros to Demosthenes' house, carrying his heavy blue shield with me, a combination bodyguard and porter. The other Companions had wanted to come and gloat, but Alexandros—in a very sober, serious mood—told them to stay behind.

Ptolemaios, who had brought his mistress Thais with him to see her native Athens once again, laughingly said to the others, "Let the Little King go see the golden-throated coward. We have better things to do!" And he shaped the curves of a woman in the air with his hands.

The other Companions agreed, laughing. Except for Hephaistion, who came to Alexandros and pleaded to come along with him.

"No, I want to see Demosthenes alone, eye to eye. If you or any of the others were there it would seem as if we're flaunting our victory over him."

"Well, aren't we?" Hephaistion asked. "Shouldn't we?"

Alexandros said merely, "That isn't what I want to do. I must see him alone."

"But you're taking Orion with you."

Without even glancing my way, Alexandros replied, "Orion is a servant, a bodyguard. He doesn't count."

Perhaps I should have been annoyed or even angered

at that. I could not work up any resentment; he was right. I was a servant, a bodyguard, a hired soldier. In thrall to his witch mother, as well. And a slave of the Creators who let their creatures worship themselves as gods. What right had I to be angry at the truth?

I arranged an honor guard of six uniformed men to accompany us through the streets, three striding ahead of us, three behind. I did not entirely trust the Athenians' seeming acceptance of us. It would take only one dagger in the dark to slay the son of their conqueror.

As we walked through Athens' streets in the gathering shadows of evening, he said to me, "You realize that by sending me here, my father is robbing me of the victory celebration home in Pella."

"You got a hero's welcome here," I said.

"Smiling faces, Orion. But they smile out of fear. They are trying to deceive us."

"Perhaps so."

"Right now my father must be parading our troops through the streets of Pella. And then there will be the thanksgiving rites at the old capital in Aigai. And I won't be there for either one."

"They'll have celebrations when you return," I said.

He shook his head. "It won't be the same. *He* is getting all the glory for himself, making certain that all I get is left-overs."

"What you are doing here is very important."

Alexandros glanced around at the houses and shops crowding the street. It was late in the day, almost sundown. No one else was stirring, as far as we could see. The Athenians had emptied the street once they knew that Alexandros would be using it. Up ahead I could see the massive bulk of the Acropolis with its marble temples and the tip of Athena's spear catching the last glint of the setting sun.

"Important? This? I'm a messenger boy, that's all."

I said, "Ensuring the peace is king's work. Victory on the battlefield means nothing if the enemy isn't satisfied with the terms of the peace."

He did not reply.

"Your task is to make the Athenians realize that they have more to gain from peace than war. Your father sent you because Demosthenes has painted him as such a monster that it would be impossible for the Athenians to deal with him."

"Demosthenes," he whispered, as if he had just remembered where we were going, and why.

"You are not only Philip's representative," I reminded him, "you are his heir. The peace you arrange here should last into your own reign."

This time he looked at me squarely. "My father is still a vigorous man. I may not ascend to the throne for many years."

"You are young. You can wait."

"I am not good at waiting, Orion. When you have chosen glory instead of long life, waiting is hard."

"You sound like Achilles," I said.

"I want to be like Achilles: strong and glorious and famed forever."

"He was short and ugly and he slit his own throat," I blurted.

Alexandros jolted to a stop so suddenly that the guards behind us had to whistle to the guards up front to let them know they should stop too.

"How dare you defame the greatest hero of the Iliad?"

"I was there," I said. It was almost as if someone else were speaking. I heard my own words, and in a far corner of my mind I was astounded to be speaking them.

"At Troy?"

"At Troy. I was befriended by Odysseus and made a member of his house."

"That was a thousand years ago!"

"It was in an earlier life."

He grinned nervously. "You've been talking to that Hindi, haven't you? He believes in reincarnation."

"I have lived many lives. One of them was at Troy. I saw Achilles kill Hector. I saw Achilles take his own life when an arrow wound crippled him."

Alexandros shook his head like a man trying to rid himself of a bad dream. "Orion, I think you have taken too many blows on your head."

I knew he believed what I had told him but did not want to admit it, even to himself. So I said merely, "Perhaps so. Perhaps it was all a dream."

"Certainly it was."

We fell silent as we marched on to the house of Demosthenes. It was not as grand as Aeschines' house, where once again we were staying, but it was a large and handsome house with a whole detachment of uniformed city constables standing guard before it. Like Aeschines, Demosthenes was a lawyer. It must have been a profession that paid very well, I thought, judging from their homes.

Demosthenes knew we were coming, of course. His servants bowed us in through the front gate. He received us in the central courtyard, where gnarled fig trees provided shade by day. Now, with night's shadows creeping across the city, the courtyard was lit by lanterns hung from the trees' twisting limbs.

He stood as Alexandros and I approached, his eyes going wide at the sight of his shield. Our six-man guard stood out by the house's front gate, with the constables' detachment, within shouting range.

"I believe this is yours," said Alexandros, gesturing me to lay it on the ground at Demosthenes' feet. The man seemed to have aged ten years in the few days since Chaeroneia. His face was lined, a pallid gray, and his beard was ragged.

He stared down at the shield. It was unscratched. He had never come close enough to the fighting to have it marred.

"Wh-what do you w-w-want of me?" He could not look directly at Alexandros.

"Only to tell you that you have nothing to fear from Philip, King of the Macedonians. Despite all that you have said, despite your personal insults, he has instructed me to tell you that he bears you no ill will and he will not harm you in any way."

Demosthenes looked up then, his eyes more puzzled than surprised.

"But let me add this, Demosthenes," said Alexandros. "I, Alexandros, will one day be king of the Macedonians. And on that day you can begin to number the hours left to your miserable, lying, traitorous heart."

"T-traitorous? Whom have I b-betrayed?"

"The thousands of your fellow Athenians who died at Chaeroneia while you flung your shield and weapons away and ran to save your filthy neck. The brave Sacred Band of the Thebans, who fought to the last man because *you,* bought by Persian gold, talked them into making war against us. The people of your own city who trusted you to lead them to victory and now bless Philip's name for his magnanimity."

Demosthenes was trembling, but he managed to choke out, "So y-you intend to k-k-kill me once you g-gain the throne."

"You can run to the Great King, your secret master, but it will do you no good. Hide at the ends of the earth and I will find you," Alexandros snarled.

"My secret master?" Some of the old fire seemed to

rekindle in Demosthenes. "I have no m-master except the democracy of Athens!"

"You deny you took money from the Persians?"

"Of course not. I would have t-taken money from the dead souls in Hades if it would have helped to stop Philip."

"Little good it did you."

"Athens still stands," he challenged.

"Your people love Philip now. If you showed yourself on the streets they would no doubt tear you to pieces."

"Yes. Likely they would. Today. Tomorrow. But in time, perhaps a few weeks, perhaps a few months, they will come back to me."

Alexandros laughed.

And Demosthenes scowled at him. "You have no idea of how the p-people actually behave, do you? This is a democracy, princeling. Loyalty is not forced. Obedience is not coerced. Where the people are free to make up their own minds, they change their minds often." As before, the warmer his passion became the less he stuttered.

"Where the people are dazzled by demagogues," Alexandros countered, "they can be led by their noses by the man who tells the biggest lies."

"By the man who offers them the clearest vision of their own future," Demosthenes corrected.

"The same thing," said Alexandros.

"I will lead Athens again, sooner or later."

Nodding, Alexandros agreed. "Yes, I understand that a democracy will follow the smoothest talker. I hope they do make you their leader again. I hope it happens when I am king. Then I will smash you once and for all."

"You will try, I'm sure."

Alexandros took a step closer to Demosthenes. "I will crush you like a grape, demagogue." He scuffed a boot against the blue shield. "You'll need more than that to protect you, next time."

* * *

If Alexandros thought that Pella would ignore his return, he reckoned without his mother. We were only a small band: Alexandros and his Companions, and those of us of the royal guard who had been assigned to them. With the servants and horse handlers and mule drivers and all we came to fewer than a hundred and fifty men.

Yet the streets of Pella were decked with flowers when we returned. Crowds lined the streets as we made our way to the palace, cheering us and throwing even more flowers. Young women ran to us as we rode through the streets to beam smiles up at us and touch us with their outstretched fingertips. Boys pranced along beside our horses, proud to pretend they were part of us.

At the head of the palace steps, at the end of our procession, stood Olympias, resplendent in a red gown that swirled to the ground, her hair decked with garlands, her eyes bright with victory.

The king was nowhere in sight.

We were feted at a royal banquet. Even those of us in the guard were invited to recline on couches in the main dining hall and be served by comely young women and smooth-cheeked young men. Alexandros was up at the head of the hall, his mother beside him. Much wine was poured and most of the men became quite drunk. But neither Alexandros nor his mother did more than sip at their goblets. I drank freely, knowing that I never got drunk. Something in my body burned away the alcohol almost as quickly as I consumed it.

"Where is the king?" I asked Ptolemaios, on the couch next to mine. He was fondling one of the serving girls. Thais had elected to remain in Athens a while; he had complained loudly on the trip back to Pella that the woman was trying to drive him mad. And succeeding.

"Who cares?" he said. Then he returned to nibbling at the serving girl. She could not have been more than fifteen, but that was well past marriageable age among the Macedonians.

The dinner became rowdier. The young men began tossing morsels of food at one another. The more the wine flowed the more uproariously they laughed and bellowed obscene jokes back and forth. Olympias, up on the dais at the head of the hall, seemed to ignore it all as if she saw and heard nothing. She was deep in conversation with Alexandros, whose head was bent toward her.

At last they got up together and left the hall. Then the party became really raucous. Whole platters of food were hurled back and forth, goblets of wine sloshed through the air. Harpalos, the dour giant of the Companions, jumped atop a table and announced that he could make a roasted chicken fly as if it were alive. He pegged the seared bird halfway across the hall, narrowly missing dark-skinned Nearkos, who was intently slicing the skin off a peach in a single spiralling cut.

One by one, the Companions and guards staggered out of the hall, most of them with a girl or boy on their arms. Except for Ptolemaios, who brought two young women with him. "I'll forget all about her," he muttered. "At least, for tonight."

I got up from my couch and pushed past the few couples still carousing, heading for the door. I still wondered where Philip was and why he had not deigned to greet his returning son. And I hoped that Ketu was still somewhere in the palace; there was much I wanted to learn from him.

As I neared the door, however, I noticed a messenger boy scanning the spattered, littered hall. His eyes stopped on me.

"Are you the one called Orion?" he asked me.

"Yes."

"The queen summons you."

Glad that I had stayed out of the food fights, I followed him toward the stairs that led to the queen's rooms.

"She said I would recognize you by your size," said the lad. While some of the mountain people were big-boned, most of the Macedonians were much smaller in stature than I.

The lad smiled up at me as we started up the stairs. He held his lamp up to my face. "And your beautiful gray eyes," he added.

I knew that boys his age often sought a mentor who would guide them into adult male society. Homosexual relationships were an accepted norm between noblemen and pubescent boys. Usually the boy grew up to marry and raise a family, and then take on a boy companion at a later stage in life. From what I saw, Macedonian wives had closer bonds with their husbands than those in the cities further south, where wives were left at home and men sported with hetairai, professional courtesans like Thais. Still, men could remain lovers throughout their lives if they wished; Alexandros and Hephaistion seemed to be, although neither of them spoke about it and the other Companions only mentioned it jokingly when neither of them was within earshot.

"I am a stranger here," I said, "and only a member of the royal guard by the king's favor. I am not a nobleman."

"So I had heard," the boy said, looking a bit disappointed. He was ambitious, I realized. He would find someone other than a hired soldier.

The queen was in her small sitting room, where the window overlooked the palace courtyard. A stiletto-thin sliver of a moon had just cleared the dark bulk of the mountains. I could see stars glittering out in the night.

The room was lit by a single lamp on the table beside

the queen. Alexandros had apparently been sitting at his mother's knee. He scrambled to his feet as the messenger boy opened the door.

"Come in, Orion," said Olympias. To the boy she said, "You may go."

He closed the door behind me, although I did not hear his footsteps leaving. He had been barefoot, and he was slight of build. I gave the possibility of his eavesdropping no further thought.

Alexandros eyed me uneasily. He always seemed on edge, upset, when he met with his mother this way. Who knew what poisons she was pouring into his ears?

Olympias seemed content to have me stand at the doorway. She ignored me, reaching for her son's bare arm.

"Come, sit down again," she urged. "We still have much to talk over."

Alexandros looked uncertain, but after a moment's hesitation he sat on the floor again. For an instant I thought he would rest his head in his mother's lap.

"It is certain, then?" he asked, looking up into her coldly beautiful face.

Olympias nodded once. "As certain as the man's insatiable lust. He will marry her."

"But what will that mean to you, mother?"

"Better to ask what it will mean to you, Alexandros."

"He can't disown me. He can't ignore that I exist."

"He is a very clever man."

"But all the army saw me at Chaeroneia. I am a general now, equal in rank to Parmenio and the others."

"Orion," she called to me, "do you believe that if the army voted for a new king this night they would elect Alexandros?"

So that's why she wanted me. As a sounding board for her own opinions.

"He is greatly admired," I said.

"But not yet nineteen years old," the queen countered.

"The men trust him. At Chaeroneia—"

"Answer me truthfully. If the army voted this night, would they elect a nineteen-year-old over Parmenio? Or even Antipatros? Remember that their families are as old and noble as Philip's. They were all horse thieves together only a generation ago."

"I believe they would vote Alexandros king," I said truthfully. "Probably with Parmenio as regent for a year or so."

"You see?" she said to Alexandros. "You would get the title but not the authority. They will keep you from true power."

"But why this question?" I asked. "Has something happened to the king?"

"He's going to marry Attalos' niece, Kleopatra, the one he calls Eurydice."

"Marry?"

"The king may have more than one wife," Alexandros explained.

"He already has had several political marriages," said Olympias. "His marriage to me was to cement his alliance with the Molossians, originally."

"He fell in love with you," I said.

"He lusted after me, just as he's lusted after every wench with hair between her legs. And quite a few boys, too."

"I don't see it as a problem, Mother—as far as I'm concerned. I know it's a slap in your face, of course."

"Do you think I care about that?"

I thought she cared very much. But I kept my mouth shut.

"I think he hurts you," said Alexandros.

"And he humiliates you," she said, clutching at his shoulder. "He expects me to be so enraged at him that I will leave and return to my father in Epeiros. If I refuse to do that, he will divorce me. This little baggage he's marrying wants to be his only legitimate wife; that's Attalos' plan."

Understanding seemed to dawn on Alexandros' face. "Which means that if he has a son by her—"

"You will have a rival for the throne. Attalos will push for his niece's son because that will bring the throne to his house, his family."

"But not for many years," I pointed out.

She shot me a venomous glance. "He could have a new son a year from now. And *my* son will be pushed aside. He'll claim that he never fathered you, Alexandros. I know he will!"

"You told me that he didn't," Alexandros said, his voice hollow.

"I told you that you were fathered by Zeus," she said imperiously. "But Philip has always claimed you as his own."

"Until now."

"The clever dog will use your own godly heritage against you. He will call me an adulteress and you a bastard. Wait and see."

Again I broke in, "But all this is supposition. Philip hasn't even announced his intention to marry again."

"He will."

"Even if he does, even if he marries, it could be years before he produces a son. Alexandros will be a fully grown man, perfectly able to be voted king when Philip dies."

"Or he may not produce a son at all," Alexandros said.

"Yes," said Olympias. "He may not live long enough to sire a new heir."

Chapter 18

Olympias dismissed her son, but kept me with her. Like the slave that I was I followed her to her bed chamber where we made love until dawn amid her slithering, hissing snakes.

She did not need the special drugs that her vipers had injected into me other times. I was a cooperative slave that night, a willing lover. My body was unmarked by their fangs, although Olympias had sunk her own fingernails into my flesh more than once.

"You plan to assassinate Philip," I said to her as we lay together.

"Is that a question?" she asked lazily.

"No. An observation."

"And you will warn him of it, won't you?"

"I am loyal to Philip," I said.

"Not to me?"

"You can force me to do whatever you wish. That does not engender loyalty."

She laughed in the predawn darkness. "Come now, Orion, can you truthfully say that you don't enjoy what we do together?"

"My body certainly enjoys it."

"But your mind . . . ?"

I hesitated, not wanting to stir her anger. But I heard

my voice tell her, "I know what a trained bear must feel when he's made to dance."

She laughed again, genuinely amused. "A trained bear! Yes! That's what I want you to be: my trained bear."

I cursed myself for giving her a new source of amusement.

"Time for another performance, my great big bear," she said. "Must I find a whip to encourage you?"

I did not need a whip.

By the time the first pink flush of dawn was lighting the sky beyond her window, she returned to our earlier conversation.

"You will tell Philip that I plan to assassinate him, won't you?"

"If you don't prevent me, yes, I will."

"It's nothing that he doesn't know already."

I got out of the bed and went to the wash basin on the table across the room.

"Go ahead and tell him, Orion. Let him know what awaits him. There's nothing he can do to avoid it. Assassination is his fate. The gods have decreed it."

"The gods!" I spun around and faced her, still lying languidly in her bed. "There are no gods and you know it."

She laughed at me. "Careful, Orion. Men have been executed most painfully for blaspheming."

"For telling the truth," I muttered.

"Go," she said, her voice suddenly imperious. "Go to Philip and tell him the fate that awaits him. Tell him that it is ordained by the gods. There is nothing he can do to avoid it."

I left her chamber, Olympias' words and haughty laughter echoing in my mind. She said that Philip's assassination was ordained by the gods. As I strode along the empty corridors of Philip's palace in the dawn's gentle light,

I clenched my fists and vowed to do everything I could to stop her.

"Nothing is preordained," I muttered to myself. "Time itself can be bent and changed, not only by the so-called gods but by their creatures, as well. We create the future by our own actions."

And I swore that I would protect Philip with every ounce of strength in me.

I went back to my usual palace duties. By day we of the royal guard exercised the horses, trained our squires, oversaw the slaves who maintained our weapons and armor, shopped in Pella's growing market place for clothes and trinkets. And we gossiped, chattering among ourselves about Ptolemaios' madness over Thais, about the queen's scheming, about whether or not Philip truly intended to invade the Persian Empire.

Pausanias kept us busy and kept us sharp. He took his duties as captain of the royal guard very seriously, despite the sniggering jokes that the men made about him behind his back. I began to understand that the sly laughter had something to do with Attalos. Whenever anyone mentioned Attalos' name, or spoke about the prospects of the king marrying Attalos' niece, Pausanias' normally dour face darkened like a thundercloud.

I had to tiptoe around the subject, since it was so obvious that Pausanias was sensitive to the point of homicide about it, but at last I got Ptolemaios to explain it to me.

"A lovers' quarrel, from years ago. It got very nasty." Ptolemaios' usual smiling good nature turned grim at the memory of it. "You wouldn't think it to see him now, but when Pausanias was a youth he was quite beautiful. So much so that he became one of the king's lovers."

"Philip?" I blinked with surprise. "And Pausanias?"

Ptolemaios nodded grimly. "But the king never keeps

any lover for long. Soon he turned his eye to another lad who had been Attalos' lover."

I blinked again. This was starting to sound as complex as harem intrigues.

"Pausanias became very angry at losing the king's favor. He insulted the boy horribly, called him a womanly coward. A short time later the boy proved his manhood by saving Philip's life in battle. That was when Philip lost his eye."

"So the boy—"

"The boy died protecting Philip. Attalos was infuriated, but he kept his anger hidden. Attalos bided his time, that's his way. Months later he invited Pausanias to dinner, got him falling-down drunk, and then turned him over to his stable boys. They rammed him pretty well, from what I hear. Some say Attalos fucked him too."

"By the gods!"

"It could have started a blood feud between the two families; they're both high-born. So the king stepped in. Philip would not permit a blood feud; he absolutely forbade it. He smoothed things over by giving Pausanias the honor of becoming captain of the royal guard. But he didn't punish Attalos or even rebuke him."

Pausanias had grudgingly accepted the king's judgment in the matter. Philip had avoided a blood feud between two noble families that would have been costly and dangerous to his kingdom. But the affair still festered in Pausanias' mind; he still hated Attalos, that was painfully clear.

Each evening a handful of us were picked to stand guard during Philip's nightly banquet, which inevitably turned into a wine-soaked drunken circus. It was no surprise to me when Pausanias told me I would be on duty the night after my meeting with Olympias and Alexandros. What did surprise was that when Philip struggled up from his couch and lurched drunkenly toward his bed chamber, he crooked his finger at me to accompany him.

For the flash of an instant I felt a pang of fear, but then I told myself that I was not the kind of young boy that the king sometimes took to bed. And I certainly was not a shapely young wench. He wasn't *that* drunk.

As I followed him up the winding stone stairs to his bed chamber, I realized that he was not drunk at all. He limped on his bad leg and he leaned on the stone wall of the staircase for support, but he was able to climb the stairs unassisted otherwise.

Two young male servants were waiting in the bed chamber.

"Have you had any supper?" Philip asked me gruffly.

"Yes, sir," I replied. "Before coming on duty."

"Very well." He dismissed the servants with a wave of his hand, then sat wearily on the bed.

And he smiled at me, a wry, crooked smile. "That's the way I learn what my closest companions are thinking, Orion. I listen to what they say when they're drunk."

"I see."

"You've been with the queen." It was a statement, not a question. I realized that the entire palace was honeycombed with spies and counterspies and people who spied for both the king and the queen.

"It was not my choice," I said.

He grunted and leaned down to pull off his sandals. I went to help him but he waved me away. "I'm not as helpless as some people think," he muttered. Then he looked up at me. "She can entrance a man, I know. Her and those damned snakes of hers."

I said nothing.

"She's a witch, all right. I should have drowned her instead of marrying her."

"She bore you a fine son."

"That she did. And now she poisons his mind against me."

"She intends to assassinate you," I blurted.

Strangely, he laughed. "Does she now? Indeed!"

"Truly," I said.

"She's been intending that since Alexandros was born. Just waiting for the right moment."

"I think she will try soon."

He sat in silence for a few moments, the bedside lamp flickering shadows across his face. Then Philip shook his head. "Not yet. The boy's still too young. Never be elected king in his own right. Not yet."

"Are you certain?"

He wiped his beard with the back of his hand. Hunching closer to me, he said, "Orion, I have lived with the threat of assassination all my life. I surround myself with loyal men, and work hard to make certain they remain loyal. I change my royal guard often enough to make sure that no man stays so long as to be bewitched by her."

I leaned back slightly, away from him. "As I have been," I said.

He nodded. "Yes. I'm afraid you can no longer be a member of my guard. Or of Alexandros'. I'm going to have to send you out of the palace altogether."

"But I want to protect you."

Philip cocked a skeptical brow at me. "Yes, I believe you do. But *she* will get you to do her bidding, sooner or later, one way or the other."

I had no answer to that. He was probably right.

"I still value your service, Orion. I have an important task for you to do."

"What is it?"

"I'm sending this ambassador from the Persians, the one with the unpronounceable name—"

"Svertaketu," I said.

"Yes, the one you found with Demosthenes. I'm sending him back to the Great King with a message from me. I want you to head the escort I send with him."

"I would rather stay here to protect you," I said.

"That cannot be."

I bowed my head slightly to show I understood.

"In case you're curious, my message to the Great King is a peaceful one."

"I thought it would be."

"I want to assure him that I have no desire to make war on his empire. I will offer one of my family women in marriage to one of his male relatives. I want peace."

Before I could say anything he went on, "But—a king can't always get what he wants. I've created an army and I don't intend to see it rust away, or turn into an instrument for my generals to use against one another."

"Then what do you intend?"

"I want the Great King to understand that the islands in the Aegean are Greek, not Persian. Lesbos, Samos and the others were settled by Greeks centuries ago, they must be free of Persian overlords. And the cities on the Ionian coast, too: Miletos, Ephesos—those are Greek cities and should be as independent as Athens or Corinth or any other Greek city."

"Will the Great King agree to that?"

Philip smiled grimly. "Not without a fight, I'm certain. But I want *him* to be the one who starts the war. Then we'll have all the cities of the Greeks with us, instead of them taking Persian gold to work against us."

"But you said you wanted peace."

"And so I do!"

"Yet you make conditions that will lead to war."

He scratched at his beard briefly. "Does it seem strange to you that war can lead to peace?"

"No stranger than the fact that a rainstorm leads to sunshine."

His black eyebrows rose. "Aristotle's turned you into a philosopher, eh?"

"Hardly."

"Well, listen to a king's reasoning. We've beaten Athens and her allies. For the time being they're lying low, worrying about what I plan for them, surprised that I didn't occupy the city with my troops."

"Yes, that's true."

"Now then, if the Great King refuses to let the Greek cities and islands have their freedom, if he sends his army into Ionia or his fleet to Lesbos, don't you think the Athenians and all the others will rally to me, as the protector of those Greeks on the other side of the Aegean?"

I began to see what he was driving at.

He chuckled at me. "Ah, you do understand, don't you? By maneuvering the Great King to make war, I cement the loyalties of Athens and Thebes and all the rest."

"For a while."

"For long enough, perhaps."

"And what of Alexandros?" I asked. "He doesn't want merely to free a few cities. He wants to conquer the whole Persian Empire. And then go on from there."

Philip's grin dissolved. "My hotheaded son must learn that one doesn't always get what one wants."

I looked at that fiercely bearded face. "And what do you want?" I asked. "Truly, what is it that you desire? Not the king, but you, Philip, son of Amyntas. What is your heart's dearest wish?"

Philip did not respond for long moments. He seemed to be almost startled by the question. I guessed that he had been thinking as a king and a military commander for so many years that his own individual desires had long been hidden, even from himself.

At last he replied, "I want them to respect me. Those sophisticated men of good manners and high talk in Athens and Thebes and the other ancient cities. Those self-righteous demagogues who could never bring all the Greeks together in peace. I know what they call me: barbarian, savage, bloodthirsty dog. I want them to respect me; my power, my leadership, my restraint and mercy in dealing with them."

He took a deep breath, then went on, "I want *her* to respect me. I know that she only pretended to love me so she could get a son who would one day be king. All right, he will be king! But only because I have paved his way. Yet she calls me horse breeder, cattle thief, she says I stink of the stables and I think like a primitive tribesman from the hills."

Stretching out a battle-scarred arm, Philip said, "I built this city for her, Orion. I welded this nation together and made it powerful for her. And she sees it only as a chariot for her son to ride in. But that's why I did it. That's what I want: respect. I don't expect love from any of them, not even her, but I want their respect."

"You certainly deserve it."

Pushing himself up from the bed, Philip raised his hands over his head and cried out, "Look at me! I'm not even fifty years old and I'm half-crippled, half-blind, waiting for an assassin's knife or my own wife's poison. I've given my life to make something new and enduring, a nation of many tribes, many cities. No one has done that, Orion! No one in all of Greece. But I have, and I'll keep working at it because the instant I stop it will all fall apart. There's no end to my labors, no end except death."

I stood there, almost stunned by the passions my question had unleashed. Philip seemed to realize how much of his soul he had revealed. He let his hands drop to his side and shuffled off toward the window, pretending to look down into the darkened courtyard below.

"I did it all for her," he murmured, so low I could barely hear him. "I was a lad of eighteen, just about Alexandros' age, when I met her. I wasn't king; I had no prospect of being king. My two older brothers stood ahead of me."

He turned back toward me, his face a mask of memories and regrets. "She truly bewitched me, Orion. I wanted to conquer the world for her! I pushed both my brothers aside and seized the throne. I smashed the tribes who were carving up Macedonia. I made our army invincible. I worked for years to bring all of Greece together under my leadership. All for her. All for her."

I thought his voice was going to break into sobs.

"And she spurns me. Calls me foul names and refuses to lie with me. I put the world at her feet and all she can think about is how to put her son on the throne—*my* throne! She doesn't love me. She never did."

"She doesn't love anyone," I said. "She uses us the way a drover uses his oxen."

He cast his good eye on me. For long moments he was silent while a parade of emotions played across his scarred, bearded face.

At last he said gruffly, "You'd better go now. Prepare for your journey to Susa with that unpronounceable one."

I left him alone, staring into the past and his memories. Dawn was brightening the sky outside. Birds were stirring and singing cheerily out among the trees. But I felt far from cheerful. I wondered if I would ever see Philip again, alive.

BOOK II

OUTLAW

Death is not the worst; rather, in vain
To wish for death, and not to compass it.

Chapter 19

With two dozen picked men—none of them from the Macedonian nobility—I escorted Ketu from Pella to the capital of the Persian Empire. I realized why Philip had picked only commoners for this mission: he wanted no one from a noble family to be in danger of being held hostage by the Great King.

"The Persian Empire is so very, very large," Ketu told me as we rode toward Byzantion, "that the Great King has several capitals, one for each season of the year."

I was far more interested in his knowledge of the Buddhist way of life than his knowledge of the empire. I worried about Philip but was glad to be out of the reach of Olympias, free from her control, free from the intrigues of Pella. But Ketu's description of the Way, with its hope of achieving Nirvana and getting off the wheel of life, was what I wanted to know more about.

"The Buddha described it as the Eightfold Path," he told me. "It is the true road to enlightenment. The key to the Way is to reject all desire. Every craving, every wish, every yearning must be driven from your soul absolutely. Achieve true desirelessness and you achieve the final blessedness of Nirvana."

"Desirelessness," I repeated—somewhat dubiously, I admit.

"Oh yes, that is the key to it all," Ketu assured me. "The Buddha has instructed us thusly, 'The cause of human suffering is undoubtedly found in the thirsts of the physical body and in the illusions of worldly passion.' "

The illusion of worldly passion. That reminded me of what Aristotle had said about Plato's belief in pure ideas as opposed to physical sensations. The passions of this world seemed real enough to me, though.

" 'If these thirsts and illusions are traced to their source," Ketu intoned, " 'they are found to be rooted in the intense desires of physical instincts. Thus desire seeks that which it feels desirable, even if it sometimes causes death.' "

"But these instincts are built into us," I objected. "They are part of the human makeup."

"Yes, of course," Ketu agreed. "That is why it is so difficult to overcome them."

"Can a person overcome them?"

"The Buddha certainly did," he answered. "So have others. It is very, very difficult, of course, but not totally impossible." Then he fell back to his sing-song recitation, " 'If desire, which lies at the root of all human passion, can be removed, then passion will die out and all human suffering will be ended. This is called the Truth of the Termination of Suffering.' "

It sounded impossible to me. Remove all desire: food, drink, love, companionship, power, respect, the yearning for glory, the instinct for self-preservation, the yearning for justice—how could a man live without any desire at all?

As we rode to Kallipolis on the Chersonese, as we sailed across the narrow strait of the Hellespont into Asia, as we rode the dusty trails and rugged bare hills of Lydia toward Sardis where the Royal Road began, I begged Ketu for every scrap of information he knew about the Way.

In turn, Ketu was fascinated by my vague recollection

of earlier lives. Under his prodding each night, I began to remember more and more.

"The whole world was covered with ice and snow," I told him one night as we sat before our flickering camp fire. "Winter lasted all year long. There were giant beasts, like elephants except that they were bigger, and covered with shaggy fur."

Ketu's eyes glowed in the firelight as he listened. We always kept apart from the other men while we spoke of these things. I had no desire to have them laugh at me or, worse, spend the night arguing and tossing their own ignorant opinions around the fire.

"You remember Troy?" Ketu would ask.

"I was there when Hector almost broke into the Achaian camp and wiped out the Greeks."

"And Helen? Was she as beautiful as the legends say?"

"The most beautiful woman on earth," I answered honestly. I remembered that Helen and I had been lovers, but I did not speak of it. For all his lectures to me about the Eightfold Path and the need to remove all desires from one's soul, Ketu was far from desireless.

Often we camped among shepherds with the tinkling bells of their sheep lulling us to sleep. Once we reached the Royal Road, we spent most nights in caravansaries, old weather-worn inns along the main road leading into the interior of the land. Most of them looked as if they had been there for centuries.

In some places, though, the caravansaries were gutted, burned out, abandoned.

"This is not good," Ketu would mutter over and again. "This is not good. The power of the Great King must be weakening."

More than once we were forced to sleep alone in the dark wilderness with nothing but our guttering fire and the distant howling of wolves. But whether we slept in comfortable caravansaries or under the glittering stars, each night I gleaned more from Ketu.

" 'This is the noble truth of sorrow,' " he recited. " 'Birth is sorrow, age is sorrow, disease is sorrow, death is sorrow. All the components of individuality are sorrow. And this is the noble truth of the arising of sorrow. It arises from craving, which leads to rebirth, which brings delight and passion.' "

"But aren't delight and passion good things?" I asked.

"No, no, no!" Ketu exclaimed. "The noble truth of the stopping of sorrow is the complete stopping of craving, being emancipated from delight and passion. That is the noble truth of the Way which leads to the stopping of sorrow. That is the Eightfold Path."

Very, very difficult indeed, I thought.

By day our little band rode through the hilly wastes of Phrygia, sometimes alone, sometimes accompanying long mule trains loaded with timber and hides and grain from the rich farmlands along the fringe of the Black Sea. We passed other caravans coming from the east, stately camels and sturdy oxen carrying ivory from Africa, silks from far Cathay and spices from Hindustan. More than once such caravans were attacked by bandits and we helped to fight them off. Strangely, when we rode by ourselves, just the twenty-six of us with our horses and spare mounts and pack mules, no bandits bothered us.

"They can see that you are armed soldiers," Ketu told me. "They know that there is very little in your packs worth stealing. The caravans are much more tempting to them. Or a few travelers straggling along the road who can be slain easily and despoiled. But soldiers—no, I do not think they will try to molest us."

Yet, more than once I spied lean, ragged men on horseback eyeing our little group from a distant hilltop as we rode along the Royal Road. Each time I heard Ketu chanting to himself:

"I go for refuge to the Buddha. I go for refuge to the Doctrine. I go for refuge to the Order."

His prayers must have worked. We were not attacked.

As we inched toward the Zagros Mountains that bordered the Iranian plateau we saw the Great King's soldiers here and there along the road, usually near the wells or caravansaries. Their task was to protect travelers, but the roads were too long and the soldiers too few for such protection to be more than a token. Besides, they always demanded "tax" money in return for the little protection they gave.

"They're worse than the bandits," said one of my men as we rode past a checkpoint on the outskirts of a small town. I had just paid the captain of the local soldiers a few coins' "tax."

"Paying them is easier than fighting them," I said. "Besides, they are satisfied with very little."

Ketu bobbed his head as he rode on my other side. "Accept what cannot be avoided," he said. "That is part of the Eightfold Path."

Yes, I thought. *But still, it rankles.*

Ketu seemed more worried than angry. "Only a year ago I passed this way, heading for Athens. There were almost no bandits and all the inns were flourishing. The king's soldiers were plentiful. But now—the new Great King is not being obeyed. His power has diminished very quickly, very quickly indeed."

I wondered if his empire's internal problems would lead the Great King to agree to Philip's terms, so that he would not have to fight the Greeks with his diminished army. Or would he, like Philip, use a foreign foe to weld his people together in newfound unity?

My sleep was becoming more uneasy each night, more

restless. I did not really dream; at least, I remembered nothing in the morning except vague stirrings, blurred images, as if seen through a rain-streaked window. I did not visit the Creators' domain, nor was I visited by Hera or any of the others. Yet my sleep was disturbed, as if I sensed a threat lurking in the darkness nearby.

We posted guards, even when we camped with caravans that had their own troops with them. I took my share of guard duty. I needed little sleep, and I especially liked to be up to watch the dawn rising. Whether in the cold and windswept mountains or out on the bare baking desert, it pleased me deep in my soul to watch the stars slowly fade away and see the sky turn milky gray, then delicate gossamer pink, and finally to see the sun rise, huge and powerful and too bright to look at directly.

"They worship me," I remembered the Golden One saying, "in the form of the sun. I am Aten, the sun-god, the giver of life, the Creator of humankind."

I had given up all hope of reaching Anya, the goddess whom I loved. Those troubling half dreams tormented my sleep, dim indistinct visions blurring my unconscious mind, stirring forgotten memories within me. I wondered if I could ever achieve the state of desirelessness that Ketu promised would bring me the blessed oblivion of Nirvana. The thought of getting off this endless wheel of suffering, of putting a final end to life, appealed to me more and more.

And then one night she came to me.

It was no dream. I was translated to a different place, a different time. It was not even Earth, but a strange world of molten, bubbling lava and stars crowding the sky so thickly that there was no night. It was like being inside an infinitely-faceted jewel—with boiling lava at your feet.

Somehow I hung suspended above the molten rock. I felt no heat. And when I put out my arms, they were blocked by an invisible web of energy.

Then Anya appeared before me, in a glittering uniform of silver mesh, its high collar buttoned at her throat, polished silver boots halfway up her calves. Like me, she hovered unharmed above the roiling sea of seething lava.

"Orion," she said, urgency in her voice, "everything is changing very rapidly. I only have a few moments."

I gazed on her incredibly beautiful face the way a man dying of thirst in the desert must look at a spring of clear, fresh water.

"Where are we?" I asked. "Why can't I be with you?"

"The continuum is in danger of being totally disrupted. The forces arrayed against us are gaining strength with every microsecond."

"How can I help? What can I do?"

"You must help Hera! Do you understand? It's imperative that you help Hera!"

"But she wants to kill Philip," I protested.

"There's no time for argument, Orion. No time for discussion. Hera has a crucial role to play and she needs you to help her!"

I had never seen Anya look so pained, so wide-eyed with fright.

"You must!" she repeated.

"When can we be together?" I asked.

"Orion, I can't bargain with you! You must do as you are commanded!"

I looked deep into Anya's gray eyes. They had always been so calm before, so wise and soothing. Now they were close to panic.

And they were not gray, but yellow as a snake's.

"Stop this masquerade," I said.

Anya stared at me, open-mouthed. Then her face shifted, flowed like the boiling lava below me, and turned into Hera's laughing features.

"Very good, Orion! Very perceptive of you!"

"You *are* a witch," I said. "A demon sorceress."

Her laughter was cold, brittle. "If you could have seen the expression on your face when you thought your precious Anya had deigned to appear to you!"

"Then all of this is an illusion, isn't it?"

The seething ocean of magma disappeared. The jewel cluster of stars winked out. We were standing on a barren plain in Anatolia in the dark of a moonless night. I could see my camp, where Ketu and the soldiers slept. Two guards shuffled near the dying fire, their cloaks pulled tight around them. But they did not see us.

The metallic silver uniform Anya had been wearing had turned to copper red on Hera. Her flaming hair tumbled past her shoulders.

"Most of it was an illusion, Orion," Hera said to me. "But there was one point of truth in it. You must help me. If you don't, you will never see your beloved Anya again."

"What did you mean about the continuum being in danger of disruption?"

"That doesn't concern you, creature. You are here in this time and place to do my bidding. And don't think that just because Philip has sent you far from Pella that I can't reach out and pluck you whenever I choose to."

"Is Anya in danger?"

"We all are," she snapped. "But you are in the most danger of all, if you don't obey me."

I lowered my eyes. "What must I do?"

"When the time comes I will let you know," she said haughtily.

"But how—"

She was gone. I was standing alone in the cold night. Far in the distance a wolf bayed at the newly-risen moon.

The more I learned from Ketu about the Way the more I was attracted to it. And repelled, at the same time.

"The key to Nirvana is desirelessness," he told me over and again. "Give up all desire. Ask for nothing, accept everything."

The world is an endless round of suffering—that I knew. The Buddha taught that we endure life after life, constantly reborn to go through the whole pain-wracked cycle again, endlessly, unless we learn how to find oblivion.

"Meditate upon these truths," Ketu instructed me. "See everything around you as Nirvana. See all beings as Buddha. Hear all sounds as sacred mantras."

I was no good at all at meditation. And much of what seemed perfectly clear and obvious to Ketu was darkly obscure to my mind. The thought of final nothingness, the chance to escape the agony of life, was tempting, I admit. Yet, at the same time, oblivion frightened me. I did not want to cease to exist; I only wanted an end to my suffering.

Ketu would shake his head when I told him this. "The two are inextricably bound together, my friend, intertwined like the strands of a rope. To live is to suffer, to feel pain is to be alive. You cannot end one without ending the other."

"But I don't want an end to all sensation," I confessed to him. "In my heart of hearts I don't want complete oblivion."

"Nirvana is not oblivion," Ketu told me eagerly. "No, no! Nirvana is not a total extinguishing. All that is extinguished is the self-centered life to which the unenlightened cling. The truly real is not extinguished; indeed, only in Nirvana can the truly real be attained."

I could not understand his abstractions.

"Think of Nirvana as a boundless expansion of your spirit. Through Nirvana you will enter into communion with the entire universe! It is not as if a drop of water is added to the ocean; it is as if all the oceans of the world enter a single drop of water."

He was completely convinced of it and happy in his

conviction. I could not overcome the doubts that assailed me. If I achieved nothingness, I would never see Anya again. Never know her love, her touch. If I found the final oblivion I would never be able to help her, and from all that I had gleaned from Hera, she needed my help desperately. Yet Hera was keeping me from her. How could I break through Hera's control and—

I realized that I was far, very far, from being without desire.

On his part, Ketu remained fascinated by my claim to remember my earlier lives; at least, parts of some of them. For all I could remember were isolated fragments, a brief moment here, a snatch of a soldier's song, the great dust clouds of the Mongol Horde on the march, the burning fury of a nuclear reactor running wild.

One sunrise, after another troubled, tossing night of obscure fears and blurred memories, I sniffed the crisp breeze blowing from the northwest as the men prepared their morning meal. We had camped in the open, along the shoulder of the long, wagon-rutted Royal Road in the middle of flat brown scrublands.

"Lake Van is in that direction," I said to Ketu, pointing into the wind. "And beyond it is Ararat."

His big soulful eyes widened at me. "You know the sacred mountain?"

"I lived near it once, with a hunting tribe . . ." My words dwindled away because that was all I could remember: the snow-capped mountain, steam issuing from one of its twin peaks, shrouding the heights in clouds.

"A hunting tribe?" he urged.

"It was a long time ago." I tried all day to recall more, but the memories were locked away from me. I knew that Anya had been in that tribe with me, but there had been someone else. A man, the tribe's leader. And Ahriman! I remembered the dark, brooding danger that he threatened. I remembered the cave bear that killed me for him.

A week later a new memory assailed me. We were near the ruins of ancient Nineveh, the capital of the Assyrians, where the temples of Ishtar and Shamash once rose in glory. And mighty Sennacherib, who claimed that he himself had invented crucifixion as the most agonizing way to put his enemies to death. I remembered the rows of crosses lining the road as we marched back toward his palace—the grandest that had ever been built, he believed.

These were the memories that assailed my sleep. I had been in this ancient tortured land before, many times, many lives ago. The memories seemed to rise up from the blood-soaked ground like ancient ghosts, shifting, indistinct, tantalizing and almost frightening in a way. Anya was at the core of all these half-remembered lives. The goddess had taken on human form time and again, for my sake, to be with me, because she loved me. Was she trying to reach me now? Was she trying to break down the walls in my mind that separated us?

"I will never achieve Nirvana," I confessed to Ketu one night as we took our supper at a well-guarded caravansary. We were almost at Susa, at the end of the Royal Road. The Great King obviously had a firmer grip on the land here.

"It takes time," Ketu said gently, sitting across the table from me. We had been given a private booth since Ketu had told the innkeeper that he was an envoy of the Great King. "It takes many lifetimes to reach the state of blessedness."

I shook my head. "I don't think I'll ever get there. I don't even think I want to."

"Then you will continue to endure life after life. Continue to suffer."

"Maybe that's what we're supposed to do."

Ketu would not argue. "Perhaps," was all he said, keeping his convictions to himself.

But he was curious. "Two weeks' journey to the southwest is the mighty city of Babylon. What memories do you have of it?"

I concentrated, but nothing came forth.

"The hanging gardens?" Ketu prompted hopefully. "The great ziggurat?"

Something stirred at that. "Uruk," I heard myself say. "Gilgamesh the king and his friend Enkidu."

"You knew them?" His voice went hollow with awe.

I nodded, wishing that the memories would become clear to me. "I think I was Enkidu," I said. "I know that Gilgamesh was my friend."

"That was at the very beginning of time," Ketu whispered.

"No," I said. "It was long ago, but not at the beginning."

"Ah, if only you could remember more."

I had to smile at him. "You are not entirely desireless yourself, my friend."

Chapter 20

We arrived in Susa at last, and a mighty city it was, but I saw almost none of it. We "Greeks" were told to camp outside the capital's looming walls, while Ketu was escorted to the palace by a squad of the king's soldiers.

He came back a few hours later, looking unhappy.

"The Great King and his court have already moved to Parsa. We must go there."

Parsa was the springtime capital, a city unknown to Philip or even Aristotle. In time, Alexandros would call it Persepolis. We started out for Parsa, this time escorted by a troop of Persian cavalry, their horses glittering with gold-decorated helmets and silver-studded harnesses that jingled as we rode even farther east through gray-brown desert and hot, sand-laden winds.

When we finally arrived there, I saw that Parsa was magnificent, but it was not truly a city. The old Dareios, the one who had first invaded Greece nearly two centuries earlier, had built Parsa to be his personal monument. Laid out in the sun-baked brown hills on a flat terrace at the foot of a massive granite promontory, Parsa looked as if it had been carved out of the living rock itself. Indeed, the tombs of Artaxerxes and other Great Kings were cut deep into the cliff face.

Parsa was not a true city. It had no private homes, no

market place, no existence at all except as a residence for the king and court for a few months each spring. Oh, a scattering of people lived there all year long, but they were merely caretakers to keep the place from falling into ruin from one royal visit to the next.

Yet it was magnificent: far bigger than Pella, far grander than Athens. The king's palace was enormous; it had to be, to house his extensive harem. The meeting hall, where the court convened and the king sat to hear petitions, held a single room so large that fully a hundred pillars supported the vast expanse of the roof. Everywhere I looked I saw statues leafed in gold, gigantic reliefs on the walls of winged bulls, lions with men's heads on them, or human forms with animals' heads atop them. Among Philip's Macedonians the lion was a common symbol; in Athens all the statues I had seen had been of men or women—humans, even when they were representing gods and goddesses.

To me, this Persian architecture seemed heavy, ponderous, almost ugly in comparison to the fluted grace of the Parthenon. These massive, gigantic buildings were meant to dwarf mortal men, to awe them and impress them with the power of the Great King, much like the colossal palaces of the Pharaoh in his cities along the Nile. The cities and temples of the Greeks were much more human in dimension. Here the buildings were gigantic, decorated with gold and lapis lazuli, with ivory from Hindustan and carnelian from the mountains that were called the Roof of the World.

Yet despite all this display of wealth and splendor—or perhaps because of it—the palace seemed to me more pompous than majestic.

What was impressive was the fantastic variety of peoples at the court; a thousand different nationalities were bound up in this vast empire. To reach Parsa we had already travelled through Phrygia, Cappadocia, Syria and the ancient land of Sumer between the Twin Rivers, over the Zagros Mountains and the Iranian plain. Now I saw that there were even more lands and more peoples in the empire: swarthy Elamites and turbaned Parthians, olive-skinned Medes and dour lean Bactrians, dark men from distant Kush and eagle-eyed mountain dwellers from the Roof of the World. The Persians themselves were only a small minority among all these mixtures of peoples. The palace hummed with a hundred different languages, and buzzed with constant intrigues that made the machinations back at Pella seem like children's games.

Dareios had only recently come to the throne, after the assassination of the previous Great King. The empire was in turmoil as the new king struggled to bring its far-flung peoples under his central control. We had seen the signs of chaos as we had travelled on the Royal Road. Here in the magnificent palace at Parsa I saw that Dareios was working hard to solidify his hold on the throne.

We were given a small house in the section of the city where the army was quartered, not far from the palace. The men quickly learned about the king's harem and joked about how they would relieve the loneliness of so many women who had to wait upon the pleasure of one man.

"You mean he has a couple of hundred wives?" asked one of my men at dinner our first night there.

"They are concubines," explained Ketu. "Not true wives."

"But they're his?"

"Oh yes, they are certainly his."

"All those women for the king alone?"

"It is death for them even to see another man."

Another shouted across our dining table, "Can we get them to keep their eyes closed?"

"If a man is found among them," Ketu said, very

seriously, "he is dismembered, a little at a time, over many, many days. They start by cutting off his testicles."

That silenced their jokes, but only for a few moments.

"Might be worth it," one of the men muttered, "if you can work your way through forty or fifty of 'em before they catch you."

"Yah," said another. "By then your balls would be all worn out anyway."

To my surprise, Ketu asked me to come with him when he was granted his audience with the Great King.

"I want Dareios to see the kind of men that Philip has serving him," he told me. Then his face relaxed into a warm smile. "Besides, my friend, I think you are burning with desire to see the man who rules this mighty empire."

I had to admit that he was right. Another blow to my progress along the Eightfold Path.

Three days after we had arrived in Parsa, we were called to the great audience chamber of the hundred pillars. Ketu wore his best and most colorful robe, a striking pattern of bright red against lemon yellow. I had polished my bronze breastplate until it glowed like the sun. No weapons were allowed in the presence of the Great King, although I wore my dagger beneath the skirt of my chiton almost without thinking of it, it had become such a part of me.

There was enormous formality to an audience with the Great King. All morning one of the king's masters of protocol, an elderly man with shaking, palsied hands, instructed us on how we were to prostrate ourselves before the throne, how we were not to look directly at the Great King, what forms of address we were to use. Actually, I was to use no form of address at all; Ketu was to do all the talking.

We were marched to the great audience hall by a full squad of soldiers, gleaming with gold and silver. At the enormous double doors, four times higher than my head, heralds announced us, an honor guard in golden armor formed up ahead and behind us, and we paraded through that forest of obsidian pillars toward the distant throne. A throng of noblemen stood watching, their robes resplendent, pearls and jewels gleaming from necklaces and earrings and bracelets. Most of them wore rings on every finger of both hands, even their thumbs.

As we walked the endless distance toward the throne, I saw that it was of carved ivory in the form of a peacock, with jewels in its tail glinting in the sunshine from the great skylight above it. The man sitting on it seemed small and slight against that magnificent throne. His robe was heavy with gold thread, jewels bedecked him, and he wore a massive crown of gold and still more glittering gems. His black beard was curled and oiled. His slippered feet rested on a special stool, since the Persians believed their king's feet must never touch the ground.

Once we reached the foot of the throne the chief herald, standing to one side of the dais, spoke our names aloud once again. On that cue, we laid ourselves face down before the Great King. It rankled me to abase myself, but I reasoned that when in Parsa one does as the Persians do. I smelled great decadence here; all these jewels and formalities and shows of pomp spoke of the trappings of power rather than power itself. Philip's court, in contrast, was about as formal as a group of friends meeting to discuss the price of horses at the marketplace.

"The Great King Dareios Codomannus, lord of all the world from the rising to the setting of the sun, conqueror of . . ."

It took the chief herald several minutes to speak all the titles and honorifics of the Great King. His voice was powerful, and he gave each title a dramatic intonation. At length he said to us grandly, "You may rise and gaze on his magnificence."

Of course we had been instructed specifically *not* to look directly at the Great King. I clambered to my feet and gazed slightly off to his left, close enough to see him clearly.

Dareios III appeared much younger than Philip, although that might have been because he had led a much more comfortable life. His beard was so black that I thought it might have been dyed; it was curled and oiled like a woman's locks. His face seemed to be powdered; it was noticeably whiter than any of the other Persians I had seen. Sitting on his massive throne of ivory and inlaid teak he looked somewhat small, as if the throne had originally been designed for a much larger man. His robes were so stiff and heavy that it was impossible for me to tell much about the body beneath them. But I would not have been surprised if Dareios were soft and pot-bellied. The jeweled crown he wore must have been much heavier than a battle helmet.

No queen sat beside him. There was not a woman in the entire vast audience hall. Off to his left, however, sat a dozen older men, some of them in soldier's uniforms, others in robes: the king's advisors and generals, I surmised.

Dareios leaned slightly toward the chief herald and spoke in a near-whisper, "Ask my ambassador for his report."

The herald called out in his clarion voice, "Your report, ambassador of the Great King."

I understood their language as easily as I understood the tongue of Philip and Demosthenes. Why did the Great King tell his herald to ask for Ketu's report? Ketu spoke their language fluently. Then I realized that the Great King was considered too lofty to speak directly to his ambassador, or—horror of horrors—to have the ambassador speak directly to him. The chief herald was the go-between.

Bowing low, Ketu told the herald of Philip's desire for peace, and his demand that the Greek islands and the cities of Ionia be granted their freedom. He phrased it all very diplomatically, using words such as "dearest wish" and "friendly request" instead of "offer" and "demand." The chief herald relayed to Dareios exactly what Ketu had said, almost word for word, as if the king were deaf or his ears not attuned to hearing voices from the foot of his throne.

"Tell the ambassador that we thank him, and will in due time prepare a fitting answer for him to bring back to the Macedonian."

"The Great King, munificent and all-glorious, thanks his servant the ambassador and will, in due time, present him with his gracious and sagacious command to the Macedonian royal house."

I almost broke into a laugh at that word, "command," thinking how Philip would react to it.

The king mumbled something more to the herald, who turned to me and announced, "The Great King, ruler of the earth and leader triumphant of battle, demands to know the name and origin of the barbarian presented with the ambassador."

I was startled. He was referring to me. With only a moment's hesitation, I said to the herald, "I am called Orion, in the service of Philip, king of Macedonia."

Apparently my size had impressed the Great King, which may have been the real reason Ketu brought me with him to this audience. The Persians were not small men, but few of them had my height or the width of shoulder that I have. The king and chief herald buzzed briefly, then I was asked:

"Are you a Macedonian?"

"No," I said, unable to hide my grin, "I am from one of the tribes conquered by the Macedonians."

The Great King's eyes widened. I laughed inwardly at his brief loss of self-control, hoping that he truly realized that Philip's army was not afraid of size.

Inadvertently I looked directly at Dareios. Our eyes

met momentarily, then he looked quickly away, blushing. And I knew in that instant that the man was a coward. We were instructed not to look directly at him, not because it would rouse his imperial wrath, but because he did not have the courage to look at men eye to eye.

The chief herald dismissed us. Bowing, we backed away from the throne for the prescribed distance, then were allowed to turn our backs and walk like men from the hall.

But we did not get far. At the great doors a Persian soldier stepped before us.

"Ambassador Svertaketu, barbarian Orion, follow me."

He did not look like a Persian; his skin was more olive-toned and he was much bigger than the bejewelled dainty men I had seen at Dareios' court. In fact, he was the biggest I had seen in Parsa, nearly my own height and size. And a squad of six other equally big soldiers fell into step behind us as he led us out of the audience hall into the bright warm sunshine of the early afternoon.

"Where are you taking us?" Ketu asked.

"To where I have been commanded to bring you," said the soldier. His voice was deep, almost a growl.

"And where might that be?" Ketu probed.

"To see one of the Great King's slaves, in the palace. A Greek slave."

"Where are you from?" I asked.

He turned a level, cool-eyed gaze at me. "What difference does that make?"

"You don't look like a Persian. Your accent is different from the others we have spoken to."

He thought about that as we walked out into the sunshine and across the flagstone square between the audience hall and the palace proper.

"I am from Media, from the high hills where the old worshippers still tend their sacred fires. My people, the

Medes, conquered Babylon and created this great empire."

His voice was flat, his tone unemotional. Yet I felt there was a world of scorn and bitterness behind his words.

"You are descended, then, from Cyrus the Great?" Ketu asked. It was more a statement than a question. Cyrus had founded the Persian Empire ages ago.

"From Cyrus, yes. Though today the Medes are hardly more than one tribe among the many that compose the empire, still we serve the Great King whose power has come from Cyrus' mighty army. We serve, and we remember."

Another sign of unhappiness in the empire. Another man with an unsettled grievance. It began to look to me as if the vast empire of the Great King were rotting from the inside. Perhaps Alexandros could conquer it after all.

But all such thoughts flew out of my head when I saw the "Greek slave" to whom the Median soldier had been commanded to bring us.

Demosthenes.

"Don't look so surprised, Orion," he said to me, sitting at his ease in a cushioned chair in a luxurious palace apartment. A slave woman knelt in the far corner of the room. The table in the room's center was decked with a huge bowl of fruit and a silver decanter of wine chilled so well that its curved surface was beaded with water droplets. Demosthenes wore a long woolen robe of deep blue. He seemed to have recovered his aplomb since the last time I had seen him, or perhaps it was simply that he was not facing the fierce hatred of Alexandros. Still, he had grayed, and his eyes squinted beneath their bushy brows.

"You knew I was receiving the Great King's gold," Demosthenes said, leaning back in his chair.

"I did not know that you were his . . . servant."

"I serve Athens," he snapped. "And democracy."

"The Great King supports democracy?"

Demosthenes smiled uneasily. "The Great King supports anyone who can help him defeat Philip."

"Have you been exiled, then?" Ketu asked.

His smile turned grim. "Not yet. But Philip's friends are working hard to have the Assembly ostracize me. That's his way: show the open hand of peace and friendship while he gets his lackeys to stab you in the back."

"Why have you sent for us?" asked Ketu.

As if he suddenly realized that he was being less than polite, Demosthenes indicated the other chairs with his outswept hand. "Sit. Please, make yourselves comfortable. Slave! Bring cups for my guests."

Ketu sat. I walked over to the window and looked down. A lovely courtyard garden was being tended by ragged dark-skinned slaves. Through the open doorway I saw the Median soldier and his squad lounging out in the corridor.

"Why have you summoned us?" I repeated Ketu's question.

"I am now an advisor to the Great King. You might say that I have his ear. He has asked for my opinion of Philip's offer. I want to hear what it is for myself, from the lips of the Great King's ambassador."

"You don't need me for that," I said.

"No, there's something else that I want you for," said Demosthenes.

"What is it?"

"The ambassador first."

The slave brought us cups and poured the wine. It was cold and biting, yet warmed my innards as I drank of it. Ketu repeated Philip's offer and demands practically word-for-word.

"Much as I expected," Demosthenes muttered when the ambassador was finished, blinking nervously.

"What will be your advice to the Great King?" asked Ketu.

"That is for me to tell Dareios, not you," he answered, with some of his old haughtiness. "You will learn of his decision when he is ready to give it."

I thought I knew what Demosthenes would say to Dareios: refuse to surrender the cities and the islands, but make no warlike step against Philip. Demosthenes wanted to get Philip to start the war, so that he could tell the Athenians and anyone else who would listen that the barbarian king of Macedonia wanted to drown all the world in blood.

He looked at me as if he could read my thoughts. "You don't like me, do you, Orion?"

"I serve Philip," I replied.

"You think me a traitor to Athens? To all the Greeks?"

"I think that, no matter what you tell yourself, you serve the Great King."

"Yes! I do!" He pushed himself out of his chair to face me on his feet. "I would serve the Furies and Chaos itself if it would help Athens!"

"But you said that Athens no longer listens to your voice, no longer wants your service."

"That doesn't matter. The danger of a democracy is that the people will be misled, will be tricked into following the wrong road."

"I see. Democracy works fine as long as the people do what you want them to. If they vote otherwise, it is a mistake."

"Most people are fools," said Demosthenes. "They need leaders. They need to be told what to do."

"And that is democracy?" I asked.

"Bah! No matter what the people *think* they want, I serve Athens and the cause of democracy! I will use the Great King, the Spartans, the fish of the sea and the fowl of the air if it helps me to fight Philip and his bastard son."

It was my turn to smile. "You had your chance to fight them at Chaeroneia."

The barb did not bother him in the slightest. "I'm a politician, Orion, not a warrior. I discovered that at Chaeroneia, true enough. Now I fight in the way I know best. And I will beat Philip yet."

"I am a warrior, not a politician," I replied. "But let me ask you this question: would Athens and its democracy be safer under the Great King's authority, or under Philip?"

He laughed. "Yes, you're no politician at all, are you? You see things in black and white too much."

"So?"

"The Great King will leave Athens and the other cities of Greece alone, leave them free, if the threat of Philip can be eliminated. He wants the Ionian cities to remain in his empire. I am willing to let him have them in return for Athens' freedom."

Ketu spoke up. "That is the nature of politics: you give something to get something else. Give and take—favors, gifts, alliances . . . even cities."

"Aristotle told me," I said, "that the Persian Empire will inevitably engulf all of Greece. Athens will become a vassal of the Great King, just as Ephesos and the other Ionian cities are."

Demosthenes frowned. "Aristotle is a Macedonian."

"No—" objected Ketu.

"Stagyrite," said Demosthenes. "They've been part of Macedon long enough."

"But what of Aristotle's prediction?" I asked. "If he's correct, by helping the Great King you are slowly strangling the democracy you cherish so much."

Demosthenes paced the length of the room, all the way to the window and back to me, before answering. "Orion, I have a choice between Philip and the Persians. Philip is at

Athens' gates; the Great King is many months' journey away. Philip will swallow us up in a gulp, like a wolf—"

"But he has left Athens alone," Ketu pointed out. "He has not occupied the city with his soldiers nor demanded any political power in the city's government."

"Of course not. What he does is to place his friends in power, Athenians whom he has bought with gold and silver. He *uses* our democracy to serve his own ends."

"But he leaves your democracy untouched," I said. "Would the Great King allow that, if he were in Philip's place?"

"But he's not."

"He will be, sooner or later, if we can believe Aristotle."

Demosthenes threw up his hands. "Bah! This is getting us nowhere." He turned to Ketu. "Ambassador Svertaketu, I will ponder the terms you bring from Philip and make my recommendation to the Great King. You may go."

I took a step toward the door.

"Not you, Orion," said Demosthenes. "I have further words for you."

Ketu glanced at me, then made a small bow to Demosthenes and left the room. The soldiers outside snapped to attention and escorted him down the corridor, to his own quarters in the palace, I presumed.

Clapping his hands sharply enough to make the slave woman jump, Demosthenes said, "You too. Go. Leave us."

She hurried for the door.

"And close the door behind you!"

She did as he commanded.

"All right, then," I said. "What do you want of me?"

"Not him, Orion," said a voice from behind me. "I'm the one who has a message for you."

I turned and saw the Golden One, Aten, the self-styled god who created me. He glowed with energy. Golden hair, flawless face, body as strong and powerful as my own. He wore a magnificent robe of pure white, trimmed in gold. He had not been with us an instant earlier, and there was neither a door nor a window on that side of the room.

Glancing back at Demosthenes, I saw that he was frozen into immobility, like a statue.

"Don't worry about him," said the Golden One. "He can neither see nor hear us."

His smile was wolfish. A shock of recognition raced through me. He looked like an older Alexandros—so much so that he could have been Alexandros' father.

Chapter 21

"You recognize me," said Aten, smiling with self-satisfaction.

"Where is Anya?" I asked.

"Athena," he corrected. "In this timeplace she is known as Athena."

"Where is she? Is she here?"

His smile disappeared instantly. "Anya will be here briefly; near here, at any rate. At a mountain called Ararat. Do you know where that is?"

"Yes!"

"She wants to see you there, but she can be there only for a very short time. It's up to you to get there in time to meet with her."

"When?"

"As you reckon time, in five weeks. Five weeks from today's sundown. That is when she will appear at the summit of Ararat. Although why she continues to bother about you is beyond me."

"Can you take me there?"

He shook his golden head. "Orion, I am your creator, not a delivery service."

"But, five weeks—Ararat is so far away."

He shrugged. "It's up to you, Orion. If you want to see her, you will get there on time."

Sudden anger welled up in me. "What is this, another one of your childish games? Some kind of a test to see if your creature can be made to jump through another hoop?"

"It's not a game, Orion." His face went hard, grim. "This is deadly serious."

"Then tell me what's going on!" I demanded.

With an exasperated huff, Aten answered, "It's your own fault, creature. Anya took on human form because she felt sorry for you, and she found that she enjoyed being a human. She even thinks she loves you, whatever that means."

"She does love me." I said the words half as a hope, half to reassure myself.

"If it comforts you to think so," sneered the Golden One. "Anya seemed so taken by the attractions of human form that some of the other Creators have dabbled at it. Hera and I came to this era and began to play at making kings and emperors."

"You and Hera?"

"Does that shock you, Orion? I must confess that human passions can be very . . . intense. Almost satisfying."

"Hera wants to make the son she bore to Philip into emperor of the whole world."

"Bore to Philip?" Aten laughed aloud. "Don't be stupid, Orion."

"You fathered Alexandros!"

"As I said, Orion, human passions can be very amusing. Not merely the gross physical pleasures, but the excitement of setting one group against another, the chess game of armies and nations. It's exhilarating!"

"Then why do you need me?" I demanded.

"You are part of the game, Orion. One of my chess pieces. A pawn, of course."

"Hera said that the continuum is being threatened as never before. She said all of the Creators are in danger."

His condescending smirk faded. "It's all your fault, Orion," he repeated. "Yours and Anya's."

"How so?"

"Taking on human form and living human lifetimes. Phah!"

"But you're in human form," I said.

"Only when it pleases me, Orion. What you see now is merely an illusion." And Aten shimmered, shifted before my eyes, became a glowing sphere of brilliant gold, too bright to look at, like the sun. I had to throw my arms over my face. Still I felt the fierce intensity of his radiance.

"It is difficult to hold a conversation with a creature in our true form," he said, pulling my hands away from my eyes. He was a human again.

"I . . . understand."

He laughed at me again. "You think you understand, but you can't comprehend even a millionth of it, Orion. Your brain was not built to encompass our abilities."

I pushed my anger aside. "You said Anya will be at Ararat in five weeks."

"Five weeks' time. At sundown. On the summit of Ararat."

"I will be there."

He nodded. "It really doesn't matter if you are or not. Apparently Anya feels sorry for you. But truly, our work would be easier if she simply forgot about you."

"That's not what she wants to do, is it?"

"No. Apparently not." His face glowered with disapproval. "Well, I've delivered her message. Now I have my own tasks to accomplish."

He began to fade.

"Wait!" I called, reaching out to grab his arm. My hand went through emptiness.

"What is it?" he said impatiently, shimmering, almost invisible.

"Why am I here, in this timeplace? What am I supposed to be accomplishing?"

"Nothing, Orion. Nothing at all. But as usual, you've managed to make a mess even of that."

And he winked out like a candle flame snuffed by a gust of wind.

Demosthenes stirred, came back to life. He scowled at me, "You still here, Orion? I thought I had dismissed you with the ambassador."

"I am leaving now," I said, adding mentally, *for Ararat.*

The swiftest way to travel is alone. I knew I could not take the Macedonian soldiers with me, even had I wanted to. Their duty was to accompany Ketu back to Pella with the Great King's reply to Philip's offer, once Dareios got around to making his reply. That was my duty, too, but now I had a more urgent task to perform.

I had to get to Ararat, and that meant leaving my sworn duty to Philip and somehow getting out of Parsa despite all the soldiers guarding the palace city of the emperor.

So that night I stole a horse—two of the horses that we had ridden into Parsa upon, actually. I took them from the stables where our mounts had been put up. It was not particularly difficult. We exercised the horses every day, so the stable grooms were accustomed to seeing us. The two boys sleeping in the stables that night seemed more puzzled than upset that a man would want to exercise horses by the light of the moon. They soon settled back in their pallets of straw as I told them I would fit out my horse myself and did not need them to help me.

I walked the two horses to the palace gate. The guards were accustomed to keeping people from entering rather than leaving. Still they stopped me.

"Where do you think you're going, barbarian?" asked their leader. There were four of them that I could see, perhaps more in the guard house built into the palace wall.

"It's a nice night for a ride," I answered easily.

"There's an exercise course on the other side of the stables," he said. In the moonlight, his face looked cold and hard. The three guards with him all carried swords, as he did. I could see a half-dozen spears leaning against the side of the guard house.

"I want to get outside the city, have a good run."

"On whose authority? You can't leave the palace grounds without permission."

"I'm a guest of the Great King's," I said. "Isn't that authority enough?"

"A guest!" He tilted his back and laughed. So did the others. I leaped onto the back of the nearer horse and kicked it into a gallop before they realized what was happening. The reins of my second horse were in my hand and it followed right behind me.

"Hey! Stop!"

I leaned against my mount's neck, expecting a spear to come whizzing past. If they threw any I neither saw nor heard them as I clattered through the wide, paved avenues of Parsa, heading for the city wall.

They could not get a message to the guards at the wall faster than I could get there, I knew, but there was no time to waste palavering at the wall. I simply kept on going, since the gate was open. I could see the guards up ahead jerking their sleepy heads with surprise at the clopping of the horses' hooves against the paving stones. The gate was only partly open, but wide enough if I got to it before they could push it closed. Surprise has its advantages. They stood in stunned disbelief as I galloped toward them, reacting too slowly to stop me. I heard them shouting. One of them even stepped out in my path and waved his arms, trying to shy the horses off. But they had the bit in their teeth and they were not going to stop. He jumped aside and we dashed through the gate and out into the broad moonlit scrubland.

I took no chances on being pursued, but kept speeding along until we cleared the first small ridge beyond the city walls. Then I quickly changed mounts and started off again. By morning I was in the hills, and when I looked back I could see the city, standing against its cliff like a precisely-engineered square. The road was empty except for a wagon train coming toward the same gate I had left by.

I was free. On my own. And hungry.

Thus I became a bandit, a hunted outlaw. Perhaps "hunted" is too strong a word to use. The lands of the Persian Empire were vast, the soldiers of the Great King concentrated in the cities and larger towns, or used as guards to escort important caravans. Otherwise, a bandit had little to fear. Except other bandits.

For the first few days I nearly starved. I was moving north and west, staying off the Royal Road, heading for the high mountain country and Ararat. The land about me was semi-desert, sparsely settled. There were irrigated farms near Parsa, of course, to support the city. But the farther away from Parsa I rode, the fewer the people and scarcer the food.

The horses could crop the miserable scrub easily enough. And, after the rumbling in my stomach got loud enough to remind my brain, I realize that I would have to do what they were doing, at least for the time being: live off the land.

Ground squirrels and snakes are not the preferred delicacies of the highly refined palate, but for those first several days out in the open they were good enough for me. Then I found a band of farmers driving a herd of cattle toward Parsa. I thought about offering them to work in exchange for a meal, but they obviously did not need a stranger to help them with what they were already doing by themselves. And strangers would probably be immediately suspect. And they were heading in the wrong direction, anyway. So I waited for nightfall.

They posted a single sentry, more to keep the cattle from straying than in fear of bandits, I suspect. They had dogs with them, too, but I managed to work my way upwind and sneak past them all once the moon had set. My old skills as a hunter returned to me when I needed them. Did I do this on my own, or had Aten or Anya or one of the other gods unlocked part of my memory?

I made my way to their cook wagon. There was a dog beneath the wagon, and he began to growl menacingly as I approached. I froze, wondering what to do. Then another part of my memory seemed to open to me, and I recalled a time long ago, before the Ice Age, when Neanderthals controlled the beasts of the forest with a form of mental telepathy.

I closed my eyes and visualized the dog, felt his fear, his hunger. In a strange distorted way I saw myself through the dog's eyes, a dark figure against the starry sky, a stranger who smelled very different from the master and his kin. Mentally I soothed the dog, praised his faithfulness, added my scent to his category of accepted creatures, calmed him until he crawled out from under the wagon and let me pet him.

I rummaged quietly through the wagon's stores, took onions and dried greens and a pair of apples. Meat I could always find for myself. But I sliced a filet of raw beef from the carcass hanging inside the wagon and gave it to the dog. One good turn deserves another.

By dawn I was far from their camp, cooking a lizard spitted on a stick with onions. Then I resumed my northwesterly trek.

Twice I raided farmsteads. They were rare in this semi-desert hill country, but here and there flowed a stream, and then sooner or later there would be a village with lonely isolated farms scattered about it. The villages were walled, of course, but the farms were not.

Usually the men were out in the fields during the day. There was no war for them to worry about, and bandits generally picked on the towns or caravans where they could find gold or other valuables. Me, all I wanted was food.

I would leave the horses hidden some distance away in the trees and brush along the steam, then make my way to the farm house. They were made of dried mud brick, roofed with unfinished branches daubed with mud. I would burst in, sword in hand. The women and children would scream and flee. Then I would help myself to all the food I could carry. By the time the men came back from the fields I was long gone.

Mighty warrior, I told myself after each of those silly little raids. Terrifying women and children.

Then I came across real bandits.

The ground was rising, and off along the horizon I saw low-lying clouds that might have marked Lake Van. If it was the lake, I was more than halfway to my goal, with still two weeks to get there.

I camped for the night in a hollow and built a sizable fire. The nights were cold up here, but there were plenty of trees and windfalls for firewood. I ate the last of my latest farm fare and wrapped my cloak about me, ready for sleep. In two weeks or less I would see Anya. If Aten had told me the truth. The possibility that he was toying with me, as Hera had earlier, bothered me. Yet I had no choice but to push ahead. If there was any chance at all that Anya would be at Ararat, I was going to be there to see her.

I was just dozing off when I sensed them. A dozen men. More. Stealthily approaching my fire.

I always kept my sword beside me under my cloak. I

gripped its hilt now and rose to a sitting position, letting the cloak drop from my shoulders. Fourteen men, I saw, skulking around in the shadows beyond the firelight. All of them armed. Too many to take on, even for me.

"You might as well come in and warm yourselves," I said. "You're making too much noise for me to sleep."

One of them stepped close enough to the fire for me to see him clearly. Tall, well-built, scruffy beard turning gray, a scar across his left cheek. He wore a black leather corselet, stained and scuffed with hard use, and held an iron sword in his right hand. Bareheaded, but he looked like a soldier to me. Or rather, an ex-soldier.

"I don't have anything worth stealing," I said, still sitting. Then I realized that they would happily slit my throat for the two horses.

The others slowly came closer, forming a ring around me and the fire.

"Who are you? Why are you here?"

"My name is Orion. I'm heading for Ararat."

"The sacred mountain? Why?"

"He's a pilgrim," said one of the other men, with a wolfish grin. Like the first, he wore the black leather corselet of a military uniform.

"Some pilgrim," said the first.

"But that's what I am," I said, letting go of my sword and hauling myself to my feet.

"Orion the pilgrim, eh?" His voice was hard, suspicious.

"And what might your name be?" I asked.

"I'm Harkan the bandit, and these are my men."

I said, "Harkan the soldier, I would have thought."

He gave me a bitter smile that twisted the scar on his cheek. "Once we were soldiers. That was long ago. Now the Great King has no more use for us and we must make our own way."

"Well, soldiers or bandits, you can see that I don't have anything to steal."

"Except two fine horses."

"I need them to get to Ararat."

"Your pilgrimage is going to end here, Orion."

Fourteen against one are impossible odds. Unless I could make it a personal duel.

"I'll make you a wager," I said to him, trying to sound cheerful.

"Wager?"

"Pick your best two men. I'll fight them both at the same time. If they win, you get my horses. If I win, you let me go in peace. With my horses."

"A pilgrim who wants to fight. Who is your god, pilgrim, Marduk? Shamash? Who?"

"Athena," I said.

"A woman!" laughed one of the men.

"A *Greek* woman!" They all began to laugh.

Even Harkan was grinning at me. "And what weapon does your goddess want you to use? A spinning wheel?"

They roared with glee.

I raised my bare hands. "These will be enough," I said.

Their laughter cut off abruptly. I could see in their faces what they were thinking: *This is a madman. Either he is mad, or he truly serves the goddess Athena.*

"All right, pilgrim," said Harkan, brandishing his sword in my face. "Let's see what you can do."

"Who else will help you?" I asked.

The grin came back. "Who else? Just me and my sword. That's all I need."

I flashed out my left hand and gripped his sword arm before he could twitch. With my right I grasped his belt and lifted him off his feet. He yelled as I held him aloft and then tossed him to the ground so hard that he dropped his sword and I heard the breath *woof* out of him.

The others stood frozen, eyes wide, mouths agape.

Harkan climbed painfully to his feet. "Zoser, Mynash—take him."

They were experienced fighters. They moved warily, swords in hand, one to my left, the other to my right.

I feinted left, dived to my right, knocked Mynash off his feet with a rolling block and wrested the sword from his hand with a quick twist that made him yelp in pain. Zoser was swinging overhand at me. On one knee, I blocked his sword with Mynash's and then pounded his midsection with an uppercutting left that lifted him completely off his feet. As he landed flat on his back with a heavy thud I pricked the skin of his throat with the point of the sword, then spun and did the same to Mynash.

Harkan smiled grimly at me. "Can you take three at a time?" Before I could answer, he went on, "Four? Ten? Twelve of us?"

I had impressed him, but he was no fool.

"You agreed to a bargain," I said.

"That was only part of the bargain," he replied. "The rest of it is this: we are heading toward the country around Lake Van. Better pickings up there and fewer of the Great King's pretty soldiers to bother us. You're heading that way yourself, so until we reach the lake you are one of my men. Agreed?"

"I prefer to go alone. I need to travel fast."

"No faster than we!"

The bargain was clear. Accompany Harkan and his men or be slain here for my horses.

"As far as Lake Van, then," I said.

He stuck out his right hand. "Agreed!" We clasped forearms to seal the bargain.

They did not travel as fast as I did alone, but fast enough. Harkan's band was being hunted by the Great

King's men and they rode as if devils were hunting them down.

While I rode as if a goddess were calling me.

Chapter 22

From Harkan I learned that an empire always has troubles when a new king comes to the throne. Dareios III had been Great King for little more than a year. Apparently his first royal act was to poison his grand vizier—who had poisoned the man who had sat on the throne previously and then picked Dareios to be his pawn. This Dareios was no pawn. Yet many of the nations in the vast Persian Empire had immediately rebelled, wanting their own independence, before the new king could solidify his hold on the people, the government bureaucracy, the treasury, and the army. Especially the army.

"We're from Gordium," Harkan told me as we rode northward. It was a gray day, with a chill damp wind blowing down on us from the distant snow-capped mountains.

"Whoever holds Gordium holds the key to the heartland of all Asia Minor," he went on. "Our prince rebelled against Dareios, thinking that he could make himself Great King, with luck."

"He was wrong?" I prompted.

"Dead wrong," said Harkan grimly.

The Great King summoned troops from many distant lands of the empire, far-off Bactria, wild mountain warriors from Sogdiana, Parthian cavalrymen and even Greek mercenary hoplites.

"We were outnumbered ten to one," Harkan said. Then he ran a finger along the scar on his cheek. "That's where I got this. We were lucky to escape with our lives."

"What happened to Gordium?"

He did not answer for several moments, his eyes like dark chips of flint staring off into painful memories. The horses plodded on, noses into the damp wind.

"What usually happens to a city that's lost its battle? They burned a lot of it. Raped our women, killed half the population, sold off the children into slavery. They dragged our prince back to Susa in chains. I hear they spent almost a week killing him."

"Your own family . . . ?"

"Dead. All of them. Maybe my children escaped, but if they did they're slaves now."

I did not want to ask more. I could feel the pain that he had kept inside himself always before.

"I had a son and a daughter. He was eight, she was six. I haven't seen them since the day before the battle, almost a year ago."

I nodded, but he went on:

"Wounded and all, I sneaked back into the city that night, looking for them. My wife lay dead in our house. My mother too. The bastards had raped them both, then put them to the sword. Half the city was in flames. The Great King's men were looting everything they could carry. My children were gone."

I thought of the way Philip had treated Athens. And Perinthos and the other cities he had won in battle or through diplomacy. Yet Demosthenes and the Persians called him a barbarian.

"I escaped into the hills, found others who had done the same. This little band of ours, we were all soldiers, once."

"All from Gordium?"

"Most. Two from Cappadocia. One from Sardis, in Lydia."

Now they were bandits, fleeing from the Great King's vengeance. Living like parasites. Hunted men. And I was one of them.

By going north we were putting distance between the king's soldiers and ourselves. But the pickings were poorer the farther north we went. Until we came into the lake country, where there were good farms nestled in the valleys between the hill ridges, villages and market towns. And travelers on the roads.

We swooped down on the travelers. Most of them were merchants carrying precious goods such as silks, jewels, spices, wine. They were escorted by guards, of course, but we cut through them without mercy and took as much as we could carry.

At first I thought I could not kill men whose only fault was that they had goods Harkan and his bandits wanted to steal. But once the first spears were thrown, once the clang of blades rang out, all the old battle lust welled up in me and I fought as I had at Troy and Jericho and a thousand other placetimes. It was built into my genes, into the neural pathways of my brain. I took no joy in the killing, but I fought as if nothing else in the world mattered.

Afterward, when it was finished, when the blood lust ebbed away and I became sane once again, I did not like to look upon the bodies we had slain.

"What good are fine clothes and fancy jewelry to you?" I asked Harkan as we led a train of laden donkeys away from the dead bodies we had left in the road.

"We can sell them or trade them."

I felt surprised. "People will deal with bandits?"

He gave one of his rare, bitter laughs. "People will roll in cow dung, Orion, if they think they can profit by it."

I found that he was telling the truth. We sold off all the

goods we had stolen, even the mules, at the next village we came to. Harkan sent one of his men ahead to tell the villagers we were coming. By the time we arrived in their miserable, muddy central square the farmers and merchants and their wives flocked to our little group, picking over our stolen goods, bartering grain and wine and fruit for silks and gold-wrought cups and hides of thick-wooled mountain goats.

I noticed, though, that Harkan did not show the jewels we had taken from the merchant's chests, or from his dead body. Those he kept.

"They have no coin here, Orion. The jewels we'll sell in a market town, where they have coins of gold and silver."

"What good are gold and silver coins to you?"

"My children, Orion. If they're still alive they were sent to the slave market in Arbela or Trapezus or one of the port cities along the coast. I'm going to find them and buy their freedom."

I wondered if he would live long enough to find two stolen children in all the vastness of this huge empire.

We were close enough to Lake Van to see its waters glittering in the setting sun, far off on the horizon, like a sliver of gleaming silver. But Harkan's attention was on the caravan wending along the road below the ridge on which we had camped.

It was a big caravan. I counted thirty-seven donkeys laden with cargo, sixteen wagons lumbering along behind teams of oxen. And fully two dozen guards, armed with spears and swords, shields slung on their backs, bronze helmets glinting in the sun.

"Rich as Croesus," Harkan muttered as we watched from behind a screen of young trees and shrubbery.

"And heavily guarded," I said.

He nodded grimly. "Tonight. While they're asleep."

I agreed that would be the best tactic. But then I

looked into his hard dark eyes and said, "This is my last raid with you, Harkan. Tomorrow I set out for Ararat."

His gaze did not waver an inch. "If we're both alive tomorrow, pilgrim."

The men of the caravan were no fools. They arranged their wagons into a rough square for the night and posted guards atop them. The others slept inside the square, where they kept four big fires blazing. The horses and donkeys were herded into a makeshift corral by the stream that meandered along the side of the road.

Harkan had military experience, that I could see from the attack he planned and the crisp, sure orders he gave. There were fifteen of us, nearly fifty of them, all told. We had to use stealth and surprise to offset their numbers.

Only the two Cappadocians among Harkan's men were bowmen, so his plan was to kill the two guards nearest our position with arrows fired from the dark beyond the light of their fires.

"As the arrows are fired, the rest of us charge," he commanded.

I nodded in the darkness. As I made my way through the trees to the place where we had tied our horses, I thought once again that I would be killing men I had no grievance against, strangers who would die for no reason better than the fact that they had possessions that we wanted to steal.

I thought of Ketu and the lessons he had tried to teach me of the Eightfold Path. Desire nothing. I almost laughed aloud. But then I remembered his telling me about the older gods, the deities that the Hindis had worshipped long before Buddha. If all men are reborn after death, what does it matter if they are slain?

What was it he had told me that Krishna says in one of their poems? "Thy tears are for those beyond tears . . . The wise grieve not for those who live; and they grieve not for those who die—for life and death shall pass away."

All right, I told myself as I led my horse along the dark trail along the top of the ridge. *I'm going to help some of those men find new lives for themselves.*

Like a good general, Harkan had scouted the area thoroughly during the daylight hours. We moved as quietly as wraiths along the top of the ridge, and then led our horses carefully down the trail he had found to the road below. It was a cloudy night, damp and raw and threatening rain. We could see the bright blaze of the caravan's campfires up ahead. We stopped short of the dancing light the fires threw and mounted our horses. A cold drizzle began to sift down from the low clouds.

The two Cappadocians were still afoot. They crept a little closer, then a little closer still. I could see the guards atop the wagons, backlit by the campfires, perfect targets. One of them was standing; the other hunched down with his cloak wrapped around him. The Cappadocians knelt and fitted arrows to their bows. They pulled their bowstrings back to their chests and let loose.

At that instant we charged, leaving the two bowmen to mount their horses and follow us in.

I saw both the guards topple over as we yelled our wildest and drove our horses through the gaps between the wagons. Men were scrambling in the light of the fires, reaching for arms, rubbing sleep from their startled eyes. As my body accelerated into overdrive, the world slowed around me into a languid, torpid dream.

I speared a man who was clutching a blanket around him as he tried to shake his sword loose from its scabbard with one hand. His mouth went round and his eyes bulged as my spear penetrated his chest. I wrenched the spear free and he tumbled to the ground in slow motion, as if he no longer had any bones in his limbs.

A spear came hurtling out of the darkness. I ducked

under it and rode down the man who had thrown it at me. Wise in the ways of battle, he threw himself on the ground, flat on his face, to give me almost no target for my charging lunge. But in my overdrive state I had plenty of time to see what he was doing. As he slowly, slowly dropped to his hands and knees and then flattened himself onto his belly I adjusted the aim of my spear point and skewered him. His head jerked up and he screamed, his face distorted in agony. My spear dug into the ground and snapped as I rode past him.

Out of the corner of my eye I saw Harkan's horse go down, with him pinned beneath it. A half-dozen armed men were rushing to finish him off. I charged into their midst as I pulled my sword, slashing on both sides of me, taking arms from shoulders, splitting skulls into bloody pulps.

I dismounted and hauled Harkan's dying horse off his leg. He limped aside, tried to stand up and failed. I lifted him bodily with one hand and swung him up onto my horse. He still had his sword in his right hand. A lean swarthy warrior came at me with a spear, holding an oblong shield in front of him. I grabbed the spear with my left hand and wrenched it away from him, split his shield with one overhand blow of my sword and then disemboweled him.

Four of our men were down, but most of the caravan's guards were already dead or wounded. The merchants and their servants were fighting too, but not very effectively. I killed two more guards and was advancing on an overweight, paunchy merchant in a splotched robe when he threw down his sword and fell to his knees.

"We surrender!" he screeched. "We surrender! Spare us!"

Everyone froze for an instant. Harkan, up on my horse, pointed his sword at the guard who faced him on foot. The man took a step back, looked around and saw that no one was fighting any more, and threw his sword on the ground in disgust. He was a tall, rangy man with black skin, half naked, obviously roused from his sleep. But there was blood on his sword and fire in his eye.

"Spare us, spare us," the fat merchant was blubbering. "Take what you want, take *everything,* but spare our lives."

Harkan did that. He sent the merchant and the few servants he had left alive off on some of the donkeys, into the drizzling night, leaving all their goods behind. And their slain.

Six of the guards still lived, after Harkan's men had given their wounded mercy killings. They too were professional soldiers turned mercenaries in the turmoil of the Great King's accession to the throne.

"You can go with your former employer or you can join us," Harkan offered them.

The tall black man said, "What do we gain by joining you?" His voice was a deep rich baritone.

Harkan grinned viciously in the firelight. "An equal share of all we take. A price on your head. And the joy of following my orders at all times."

"I don't speak for the others," said the black man, "but I would rather take what fat merchants own than guard it for them."

"Good! What's your name? Where are you from?"

"Batu. From far away, the land beyond Egypt where the forest goes on forever."

The five other erstwhile guards also agreed to join Harkan's band, but grudgingly, I thought, without the unfettered enthusiasm of Batu.

By morning it was raining hard and Harkan's leg was blue and swollen from hip to mid-calf. He sat beneath the canvas shelter we had fashioned amid the trees back up on the ridge with his bruised leg stretched out straight and raised up off the damp ground by resting his heel on an overturned helmet.

"It isn't broken," he told me. "I've had bones broken before. It's only a bruise."

A sizeable bruise, I thought. But I had other thoughts in my mind.

"We lost four men last night, but gained six new ones."

"Batu is the only one I'd trust," Harkan muttered.

"Still, you'll have one man more than when I first met you."

He looked up at me. I was squatting on my haunches beneath his dripping canvas shelter.

"You're leaving?"

"Lake Van is in sight. I only have a few days left to make it to Ararat."

"You'll never cover the distance in a few days, pilgrim."

"I must try."

He made a snorting sigh. "If I could stand up I'd try to stop you from leaving. You're a valuable man."

"Only if I'm willing. I've got to leave, and the only way you could stop me would be to kill me. I would take a few of you with me if you tried that."

He grumbled but nodded. "Well, go then, pilgrim. Get on your way."

"I'll take four of the horses."

"Four?"

"You have more than you can use now."

"I could sell them in the next town we come to."

"I need four," I repeated.

"Four," he agreed sourly. But as I got up and started out into the driving rain he added, "Good luck, pilgrim. I hope your goddess is waiting for you up there."

"Me too," I said.

Chapter 23

Through the rain, and the sunshine that followed it, and the next rainstorm a few days later I galloped, driving my horses without stop. I changed them frequently but still they began to limp and fail beneath me. Two of them died before I came to a village. I stole two more, killing six men in a furious fight before I could break loose. I was bleeding and hungry, but I had four fresh horses with me as I continued my grim dash to Mount Ararat.

The rain turned to freezing sleet and then snow. The ground rose steadily. Again I drove the horses to their deaths, not caring about anything except reaching the summit of the mountain in time.

In the back of my mind I wondered how a Creator who could manipulate time the way I can travel across distance needed to have me at Ararat's summit within a certain span of hours. Why couldn't Anya wait there for me as long as she needed to, and then return to the placetime where she started from? It made no sense to me.

Yet I forged onward. The last of my horses gave out as I urged her on up the slope of the mountain. I slogged forward on foot, the snowcapped peak before me, shrouded in clouds and swirling gusts of snow that cast sparkling rainbows when the sun struck them.

I was half dead myself by the time I reached the summit, stumbling through waist-high drifts of snow. I had not eaten in days. My body had repaired the wounds I had suffered, but that sapped energy too, and I felt weak as a newborn baby as I staggered to the flat mesa at the crown of Ararat. The mountain was twin-peaked, so I had chosen the higher of the two. Summit meant highest point, I reasoned. There was an old volcanic vent there, silent and cold as the snow heaped upon it.

It was a whirling world of mist and snow, cold and wet and white. I could feel my body's heat leaching out of me, draining away into the deep cold wet snow, sucked away by the misty icy wind. I searched for hours or perhaps days through that white snowy wilderness. Alone. I was entirely alone. Was I too late? Or too early? It did not matter to me. I would meet Anya here or die.

At last I could not stand any more. I sank into the numbing snow, lost and alone, ready to die once again.

I was freezing. I could sense my body shutting itself down, trying to protect my cells from freezing—to no avail. The cold was seeping into me, the spark of life ebbing away.

I remembered another time, another place, when almost all the world was covered with snow and sheets of ice miles thick that stretched from the poles toward the equator. I had lived then, and died then, in the endless cold of a global winter. Died for her, for Anya, for the goddess I loved.

It was impossible to judge distances in that featureless misty snowscape. Somewhere out there I thought I saw a light, perhaps just the sparkle of crystals caught by a stray beam of sunshine breaking through the ice fog. Perhaps—

I struggled to my knees, to my frozen numbed feet. Shambling toward the sparkling light like a lurching snow monster, I saw that it was a glimmering silver sphere, no larger than my fist, hovering in the icy mist.

I nearly collapsed more than once, but at last I reached

it. The sphere hung in midair, shimmering like a soap bubble. I tried to look into it, as if it were a magician's crystal ball.

"Orion," I heard Anya's voice call faintly. "Orion, are you there? I can't maintain the discontinuity much longer."

"I'm . . . here." My throat was raw, flaming. My voice sounded as if it came from the pits of hell.

"Orion! I can barely see you! Oh, my poor suffering darling!"

"I'm here," I repeated. In that tiny glowing silver sphere I thought I could vaguely make out her form, standing alone, dressed in her metallic uniform, some kind of silvery helmet in one hand.

"I wish I could help you. I wish I could reach you."

"Just to know . . . you . . ." I had to force the words out. "It's enough."

"The crisis is upon us, Orion. We need your help."

I would have laughed if I had the strength. I was dying and they needed my help.

"You must return to Pella. You must obey Hera. It's important. Vital!"

"No. She's contemptible."

"I can do nothing if you don't obey her. No matter how it seems, I love you and I want to help you, but you must follow Hera's commands."

"She'll . . . murder . . . Philip."

"It must be. What she wants is what must be. Otherwise the entire strand of your present spacetime will unravel. We can't afford to have that, Orion! The crisis is too deep. We can't deal with anything more."

"She . . . hates . . . you."

"That doesn't matter. Nothing matters except resolving the crisis. You've got to stop fighting against us, Orion! You must do as Hera commands!"

I found the energy to shake my head. "Doesn't matter. I'm . . . dying."

"No! You mustn't die! We can't revive you. All our energies are committed. You've got to get back to Pella and help Hera."

I closed my eyes for a moment. Perhaps more than a moment. When I opened them the silver sphere had vanished and Anya's urgent, fearful voice was only a memory. I heard nothing except the keening wind, felt nothing except the numbness of freezing death creeping toward my heart.

Was it real? Had I really seen Anya, spoken my mumbled, half-frozen words to her? Or was it all a fevered delirium, the wild imaginings of a mind near death? Had I truly seen her or was I merely imagining what I wanted to see?

I floundered aimlessly through the waist-deep snow, for how long I have no way of knowing. I was like a ship without a rudder, a drunkard without a home. Anya wanted me to return to Pella and serve the witch Olympias, the self-styled goddess Hera. To murder Philip. To set Alexandros on the throne of Macedonia and start him on his bloody conquest of the rest of the world.

I could not do it. I could barely move my legs and force myself through the snow. The cold was getting worse, the wind sharper. It howled and laughed at me, stumbling and wallowing through the snowdrifts, lurching like an automaton set on a task it cannot understand.

Slowly, all sensation left me. Inexorably my strength ebbed away. I could see nothing, hear nothing, feel nothing. I fell a hundred times and struggled to my feet a hundred times. But the remorseless cold was too much for me. I pitched face down again and this time I could not get up. Little by little, the snow covered me entirely in a grave of icy white. My bodily functions shut down, one by one. My breathing almost stopped altogether; my heart rate slowed to one sluggish beat every few minutes, just enough to keep my brain alive. I dreamed, long jumbled strange distorted dreams of my previous lives, of all the times I had died, of the times I had loved Anya in all the various human guises she had assumed. For love of me. For love of a creature that her fellow Creator had fashioned to be his tool, his toy, his hunter and assassin and warrior.

I had been built to lead a team of warriors just like myself back to the Ice Age strongholds of the Neanderthals. My mission was to hunt them down and kill them all, every last Neanderthal man, woman, and child. So that my descendants, so-called *Homo sapiens sapiens* could inherit not only the earth, but the entire span of spacetime that made up the continuum. My Creators were my descendants, far-future offspring of the humans they had built and sent back into time.

But once you begin to tamper with the flow of the continuum you set up shock waves that cannot easily be controlled. The price of the Creators' meddling with spacetime was that they had to constantly strive to correct the waves they had set in motion. If they did not, their continuum would shatter like a crystal goblet hit by a laser blast and they would be erased from spacetime forever.

They had bound themselves to the wheel of existence, to the ordeal of endless lifetimes, endless struggle. And they had tied me to their wheel with them. I was their servant, to be sent into placetimes to do their bidding. But they had not reckoned on the possibility that their creature could fall in love with one of them. Or that one of them could fall in love with a creature.

I served the Creators because I was built to do so. Often I had no choice; my will was extinguished by their control. But I recalled that on more than one occasion I had found a way to circumvent their control, found ways to fight against them, to thwart them. The Neanderthals still existed in their own separate branch of the continuum because of me. Troy fell because of *my* thirst for vengeance, not Achilles'. I was slowly acquiring knowledge and strength. Even haughty Aten had admitted that I was gaining godlike powers.

That is why they wiped my memory clean and exiled me to this placetime. To get rid of me. To leach my mind of the abilities I had so painfully learned over so many lifetimes. To put me away until they needed me again.

I loved Anya. And now she was telling me that I had to obey murderous, scheming Hera, despite my own feelings and desires. But how could I obey anyone, lying frozen and as good as dead in the snow at the top of lofty Mount Ararat?

Chapter 24

For an immeasurable span of time I lay in abyssal cold and darkness. I could see nothing, hear nothing, feel nothing. My feeble thoughts, fading as my body froze, wandered to Ketu's concept of Nirvana. Was this the end of all sensation, the end of all wants and needs, the ultimate oblivion?

But somewhere in that dark nothingness I began to feel a hollow sinking sensation that gradually deepened into a wild, panicky impression that I was falling, plummeting through empty space like a meteor blazing across the sky. Abruptly I felt myself lying on a rough, uneven surface. Something hard was poking painfully into the small of my back. But the cold had gone; in fact, I felt comfortably warm as I sat up and opened my eyes.

I was sitting on a rocky hillside that descended to a heaving dark sea, where churning waves broke against the black boulders and sent up showers of spray. The salt tang of the sea reached me even up near the crest of the ridge where I sat, blinking away the memories of death, trying to adjust my mind to this new existence. There was a narrow crescent of sandy beach beyond the boulders, and then steep cliffs of bare rock. It was a gray day, yet not really chilly. The wind coming off the water was warm and wet, gusting fitfully. The trees up at the crest of the ridge sighed and rustled. I could see that the incessant sea breeze had bent and twisted them into hunched, lopsided forms like stunted arthritic old men.

I rose gingerly to my feet. I felt strong and alert. I knew I was a long way from Ararat, perhaps in a different era altogether. Then I realized that my clothing now consisted of a brief leather skirt and a leather vest so sweat-stained and cracked with age that it looked black. My dagger was still strapped to my thigh beneath the skirt. My feet were shod in rude sandals, bound to my ankles with leather thongs.

Where I was, and why I had been placed here, I did not know. I saw a trail threading through the rocks down the hillside to the narrow curving strip of white sand and an even narrower road that ran along the coastline. I headed for that road.

Then a new thought struck me. Who had sent me here? Hera, or Anya? Or one of the other Creators, perhaps—Aten, the Golden One?

By the time I reached the side of the road I felt like a blind man groping in unfamiliar territory, wondering which direction to take. To my right, the road followed the coast and then disappeared in a cut between two rocky cliffs. Far to my left, it swung inland from the beach and climbed up into the hills I had just come down from.

I decided to go to the right. The surf was rolling up peaceably enough on this narrow strip of sandy beach, but up ahead the waves smashed against the black rocks with thunderous roars. No one else was in sight, and as I walked along I wondered if Hera or the Golden One had sent me to a time before any human beings existed. But no, I reasoned: the road I followed was unpaved yet definitely the work of men, not an animal trail. I could see ruts in it worn by wheels.

As I walked along, the sun dipped below the dismal gray clouds, heading for the flat horizon of the even grayer sea. The road cut between the cliffs, then curved around another crescent-shaped beach. The coastline must be scalloped with these little beaches hugging the rugged hillsides, I thought. The sea was probably teeming with fish, but I had nothing with which to catch any. So when the sun touched the water's edge, red and bloated, I hiked up into the woods at the crest of the hills to hunt for my dinner.

By the time it was fully dark I was sitting before a small fire, hardening the point of a rough-hewn spear in its flames, digesting a supper of field mouse and green figs.

I started out along the coast road again at sunrise, my makeshift spear on my shoulder. Before long I came upon a fork; one branch continued along the coast, the other cut inland, up into the hills. I started up the hill road, thinking that it must lead somewhere. Yet for most of the day I saw no one else at all. Strange, I thought. Long ages of use had pounded the road hard and almost smooth, except for the ruts worn into it from the wheels of carts and wagons. Still I saw no one at all until well past noon.

Then I saw why no one else was using the road. In the distance, crowning a steep hill off to one side of the road, a walled city sat beneath the hot high sun. And what looked like a small army was camped outside its wall. It reminded me of Troy, except that this city was inland and the besiegers were not camped among their boats on the shore.

For long moments I hesitated, but finally I decided to follow the road to that camp. There must be some purpose for my being here, I reasoned. Perhaps this little war was it.

The discipline at the camp was extraordinarily lax, even compared to the unhappy camp of Philip's army before Perinthos. Men milled about, all of them armed but none of them in anything I could describe as a uniform. Most of them wore leather corselets. Their swords were bronze. They seemed to have no discipline at all.

Then a soldier in bronze breastplate spotted me. "You

there! Stand fast! Who are you and what are you doing here?"

He was young enough so that his beard was nothing more than a few wisps. His shoulders were wide, though, and his eyes as black as onyx.

"I am a stranger in these parts," I replied. "My name is Orion."

A few of the other men-at-arms gathered around us, eyeing me casually. I had to admit that I was not much to look at.

"Where'd you get that spear?" one of them asked, grinning. "Hephaistos make it for you?"

Their accent was much different from the Macedonians. It was an older variant of the tongue.

"I can just see the Lame One forging that mighty weapon up on Olympos!"

They all broke into laughter.

"Zeus must be jealous of him!"

"Naw, he probably stole it from Zeus!"

I stood there like a bumpkin and let them slap their thighs and roar with laughter. The young officer, though, barely cracked a smile.

"You are not from these parts?" he asked me.

"No. I come from far away," I said.

"Your name—you call yourself Orion?"

"Yes."

"Who was your father?"

I had to think fast. "I don't know. I have no memory of my childhood."

"Doesn't know who his father is." One of the men nudged his nearest companion in the ribs.

"I am a warrior," I said, realizing that there was no word for *soldier* in their dialect.

"A warrior, no less!" The men found that uproarious.

Even the young officer smiled. Others were gathering around us, making something of a crowd.

I dropped my spear to the ground and pointed to the one who was making all the remarks. "A better fighter than you, windbag," I challenged.

His laughter turned to a hard smile. He pulled the bronze sword from the scabbard at his hip and said, "Pray to whatever gods you worship, stranger. You're about to die."

I faced him empty-handed. Not a man offered me a weapon or made any objection. The windbag was an experienced fighter, I could see. His sword arm was scarred, his eyes focused hard on me. I simply stood before him, hands at my sides. But I could feel my body going into overdrive, slowing down the world around me.

The flex of the muscles in his thighs gave him away. He began to lunge at me, a simple straight thrust to my belly. I saw it coming, sidestepped, and grasped his wrist with both my hands. I flipped him over my hip and twisted the sword out of his hand in the same motion. He landed on his back with a thud like a sack of wet laundry dropped from a height.

Pointing the blade at his throat, I said, "My gods have heard my prayer. What about yours?"

He stared up at me with the terror of death draining the color from his face. I drove the sword into the dirt next to his head; he squeezed his eyes shut, thinking I meant to kill him. Then he realized he had not been harmed and popped his eyes open again. I reached out a hand to help him to his feet.

The others simply gaped.

Turning to the young officer, I said, "I seek to join your forces, if you will have me."

He swallowed once, then replied, "You must speak to my father about that."

I picked up my spear and followed him deeper into the camp, leaving the others muttering and milling about. The youth led me past a makeshift corral where horses and mules stamped and whinnied, raising dust and reek. There was a row of tents on its other side. We went to the largest one, where a pair of men in bronze armor and tall spears stood a relaxed guard.

"Father," he called as he stepped through the tent's flap, "I've found a recruit for you."

I ducked through and saw a solidly built man with thick gray hair and a grizzled beard sitting at a wooden table. He was obviously at his noon meal; the table was covered with bowls of steaming stew and fruit. A silver flagon stood next to a jeweled wine cup. Three young slave women knelt in the far corner of the tent.

The man looked oddly familiar to me: piercing jet-black eyes, wide shoulders, and beneath his half-opened robe I saw a broad, powerful chest. His bare arms bore heavy dark hair crisscrossed with white scars. He stared hard at me as I stood before his table, tugging at his grizzled beard as if trying to stir his memory.

"Orion," he said at last.

I staggered back a step with surprise. "My Lord Odysseus," I said.

It was truly Odysseus, whom I had served in the siege of Troy. He was older, gray, his face spiderwebbed with wrinkles. He introduced the young officer to me as his son Telemakos.

He smiled at me, although there was puzzlement in his eyes. "The years have been good to you. You don't seem to have changed a bit since I last saw you on the plain of Ilios."

"Are we in Ithaca?" I asked.

Odysseus' face became grave. "Ithaca is far from here," he murmured "My kingdom is there. My wife." The steel returned to his voice. "And the dead bodies of the dogs who would have taken my kingdom, my house, and my wife to themselves."

"The city before us is Epeiros," said Telemakos.

"Epeiros?" I knew that name. It was the city where Olympias was to be born.

Odysseus shook his grizzled head wearily. "After all the years that I have been away from my home and my wife, the gods have seen fit to take me away once again."

"The gods can be cruel," I said.

"Indeed."

Odysseus bade us both to sit down and share his meal. The slave women scurried out of the tent to bring more food while we pulled up wooden stools to the table. Although I had been a lowly *thes* when I had first met Odysseus, less than a slave, he had recognized my fighting prowess and made me a member of his house.

Now, as the slaves ladled the hot stew into wooden bowls for us, Odysseus told me his long and painful story.

When he left the smoking ruins of Troy to return to his kingdom of Ithaca, his ships were battered by a vicious storm and scattered across the wild sea.

"Poseidon has always been against me," he said, quite matter-of-fact. "Of course, it did not help that I killed one of his sons, later on."

He grew old trying to get back to Ithaca. Ships sank under him; most of his men drowned. One by one his surviving men deserted him, despairing of ever seeing Ithaca again, choosing to remain in the strange lands where they washed up rather than continue the struggle to reach home.

"And all that while, every unmarried swain in the lands around Ithaca was camping at my household door, courting my Penelope, laying siege to my wife and my goods."

"They acted as if they owned the kingdom," said Telemakos. "They even tried to murder me."

"Thank the gods for Penelope's good sense. She has the strength of a warrior, that woman does!" Odysseus grinned. "She refused to believe that I was dead. She would not accept any of those louts as husband."

The two of them went into great detail about how the aspiring noblemen behaved like a plague of locusts, eating and drinking, arguing and fighting, cuffing the servants, assaulting the women, and threatening to kill everyone in the household if Penelope did not choose one of them to marry.

"I finally made it back to Ithaca to find my kingdom in ruins and my house under siege by these swine."

Telemakos smiled grimly. "But we made short work of them, didn't we, father?"

Odysseus laughed out loud. "It was more play than work. After I felled the first three or four of them the others went dashing away like rats at the sight of a terrier. Did they think that a man who has scaled the walls of Troy and fought real heroes in single combat would be frightened of a courtyard full of fatted suitors?"

"We cut them down like a scythe goes through wheat," said Telemakos.

"Indeed we did."

"So the kingdom is safely yours once again," I said.

His smile evaporated.

"Their kinsmen have demanded retribution," Telemakos said.

I knew what that meant. Blood feuds, dozens of them, all descending on Odysseus and his family at once.

"Among the slain was the son of Neoptolemos, King of Epeiros. So the kinsmen of the others have gathered together here in Epeiros, preparing to march to Ithaca, take it for themselves, and slay me in retribution."

Neoptolemos was a name I had heard before: Olympias' father, if I recalled correctly. But Olympias would not be born for a thousand years. Neoptolemos must be a ceremonial name carried by all the kings of Epeiros. Unless—

"But we have marched here to Epeiros' walls," said Telemakos, "and laid siege to their city. With all of them bottled up inside the city walls."

The youth seemed rather proud that they had carried the war to their enemies, rather than waiting for them to strike Ithaca.

Odysseus seemed less enthusiastic. "It is a fruitless siege. They refuse to come out and do battle and we lack the strength to storm the city."

I remembered how long it had taken to capture Troy.

In a rare show of impatience, Odysseus banged the table with his fist hard enough to make the slaves cower. "I want to be home! I want to enjoy my last years with my wife, and leave a peaceful kingdom for my son. Instead the gods send me this."

How like Philip he sounded. Except that Odysseus seemed to love his wife and trust his son fully.

"I wish there were something I could do," I said to them. "Some way I could help."

The ghost of a crafty smile played across Odysseus' lips. "Perhaps there is, Orion. Perhaps there is."

Chapter 25

That night I slept outside Odysseus' tent. Telemakos, seeing that I had nothing except the clothes on my back and the crude spear I had fashioned, ordered his slaves to bring me a cloak and armor and proper weapons.

Strangely, Odysseus interfered. "A cloak only," he said. "That will be enough for Orion for this night. And tomorrow."

I did not object. Obviously he had some scheme in mind. Among the Achaians besieging Troy, Odysseus had been the wisest of the commanders. He could fight as well as any man, but he could also think and plan ahead—something that Agamemnon and Achilles and the others seldom did.

Morning broke and Odysseus summoned his rag-tag army before the main gate of Epeiros. Standing in his bronze armor, bareheaded, he raised his spear to the cloud-dotted sky and shouted in a voice powerful enough to crack the heavens:

"Men of Epeiros! Kinsmen of the dogs I slew in my home in Ithaca! Come out from behind your walls and fight! Don't be cowards. You mean to make war upon me because I defended my wife and my honor. Here I am! Come and make your war this morning. It is a good day to fight."

I saw dozens of heads rise up along the wall's parapet, many of them helmeted in shining bronze. But no one replied to Odysseus.

He raised his voice again to them. "Are you afraid to die? What difference does it make if I kill you here or before the walls of Ithaca? You have declared blood feud against me and my family, haven't you? Well here is your chance to settle the matter once and for all. Come out and fight!"

"Go away," a man's deep voice shouted back. "We'll fight you when we're ready. Our kinsmen are back at their cities raising thousands of men to come to our aid. When you see their dust on the road as they march here your blood will turn to water and you'll piss yourself with fear."

Odysseus laughed scornfully. "You forget, coward, that I fought on the plain of Ilios against the likes of mighty Hector and his brothers. I scaled the beetling walls of Troy with my wooden horse and razed the city to ashes. Do you think I fear a bunch of lily-livered milksops who are afraid to face me, spear to spear?"

The voice answered, "We'll see who's the coward, soon enough."

Odysseus' lips pressed into a hard angry line. Then he took a deep breath and called, "Where is Neoptolemos, king of this mighty city?"

No answer.

"Does Neoptolemos still rule in his own city, or have you taken over his household the way you tried to take over mine?"

"I am here, Odysseus the Ever-Daring," piped a weak, trembling voice.

A frail old man in a blue robe climbed shakily to a platform up above the main gate. Even from the ground before the gate I could see that King Neoptolemos was ancient, withered, wizened, more aged even than Nestor had been, his head bald except for a few wisps of hair, a white beard flowing down his frail narrow chest. His eyes were sunk so deep into their sockets that at this distance they looked like two tiny dark pits. He must have been nearly toothless, for the lower half of his face had sunk in on itself as well.

"Neoptolemos," said Odysseus, "it is a sad day when we must face each other as enemies. Well I remember my youth, when you were like a wise uncle to me."

"Well should you remember my son, the companion of your youth, whom you have slain in your bloody fury."

"I regret his death, King of Epeiros. He was among the suitors who tried to steal my wife and my kingdom from me."

"He was my son. Who will follow me when I die? His own son is only a child, hardly five years old."

Craning his neck at the blue-robed figure atop the city gate, Odysseus said, "A blood feud between us can do neither of us any good."

"Bring me back my son and there will be no need for a feud," the old man replied bitterly.

"Ah," said Odysseus, "that I cannot do. Even though I visited Hades himself during the long years of my journey home, he would not let me bring any of the departed back to the land of the living."

"You saw Hades?"

"Neoptolemos, revered mentor of my youthful days, if you knew the sufferings and toils I have had to endure you might forgive me even the death of your son."

I stood a few feet away from Odysseus, leaning on my knobbly makeshift spear, and watched him charm Neoptolemos into asking for a recitation of his arduous journey from Troy back to Ithaca.

The sun rose high while Odysseus spoke of the storms that wrecked his ships, of the enchantress Circe who turned his men into animals; of the cave of Polyphemos, one of the Cyclopes, and his cannibal orgies.

"I had to kill him or be killed myself," Odysseus related. "His father, Poseidon, stirred up even mightier storms against me after that."

"You know that a father feels hatred for a man who slays his son," said Neoptolemos. But I thought his thin, quavering voice was less harsh than it had been earlier.

Well past noon Odysseus kept on talking, holding everyone along the wall enchanted with his hair-raising tales. Slaves circulated among us with bowls of dried meat and fruit, flagons of wine. Odysseus took some of the wine, but kept on talking, telling his enemies of the dangers he had risked, the women he had left behind, in his agonizing urgency to return to his home and his wife.

"When at last I saw blessed Ithaca again," he said, his powerful voice sinking low, "my very own house was besieged by men who demanded the hand of my Penelope, and behaved as if they already owned my kingdom."

"I can understand the blood-fury that must have seized you," said Neoptolemos. "But that does not return my son to me."

"King of Epeiros," Odysseus replied, "a blood feud between us will bring down both our households. Your grandson and my son will never live long enough to father sons of their own."

"Sadly true," Neoptolemos agreed.

"And the same is true for all of you," Odysseus said to the others along the wall. "You kinsmen of the men I have slain would slay me and my son. But then my kinsmen will be obliged to slay you. Where will it end?"

"The gods will decide that, Odysseus," said the old king. "Our fates are not in our own hands."

I was thinking that if Neoptolemos and his grandson are killed in this pointless blood feud, his line will end here in the Achaian age. There will be no descendants to father Olympias, many generations down the time stream. *That* is why I have been sent here, I realized. But what am I to do about it?

"Perhaps there is a way for us to learn the wishes of the gods in this matter," Odysseus was saying.

"What do you mean?"

"A trial by combat. Single champions to face each other, spear against spear. Let the outcome of their battle decide the war between us."

A murmur arose among the men on the wall. Neoptolemos turned to his right and then to his left. Some of the men up there gathered around him, muttering, gesturing.

"A trial by champions would be a good idea, King of Ithaca," the old man finally replied. "But who could stand against such an experienced warrior as yourself? It would be an unequal fight."

None of the dandies up there dared to face Odysseus in single combat.

Odysseus threw up his hands. "But I am the one you seek revenge against."

Neoptolemos said, "No, no, Odysseus. As you yourself said, you faced mighty Hector and broke through the impenetrable walls of Troy. You have travelled the length and breadth of the world and even visited Hades in his underworld domain. Who among us would dare stand against you?"

Bowing his head in seeming acceptance, Odysseus asked, "Would you have me pick another to stand in my place?"

I saw Telemakos fairly twitching with eagerness, anxious to fight for his family's honor and his own fame.

"Yes, another!" rose a shout among the men on the wall. "Pick another!"

Odysseus turned around as if casting about for someone to select. Telemakos took half a step forward but froze when his father frowned at him.

Turning back toward the gate, Odysseus called up to Neoptolemos, "Very well. We will let the gods truly decide. I will pick this ungainly oaf here." He pointed toward me!

I heard snickers and outright laughter up on the wall. I must have looked like a country bumpkin in my leather vest and crude wooden spear. No wonder Odysseus had refused me better clothes and weapons. He had planned this ruse from the night before.

They swiftly agreed, and disappeared from the wall's top while they selected their own champion.

"Orion," said Odysseus to me, low and very serious. "You can save us all from a blood feud that will end my line and the old man's as well."

"I understand, my lord."

He gripped my shoulder hard. "Don't make it look too easy. I don't want them to know that they've been hoodwinked."

Telemakos, who had looked so disappointed a few moments earlier that I thought he would break into tears, was trying hard now to suppress a grin of elation.

At length the gates of the city opened and the men who had been lining the wall stepped out before us. Most of them wore bronze armor and kept a firm grip on their spears. Neoptolemos was carried out on a wooden chair fitted with handles for slaves to hold. They placed his chair on the ground and he got out of it, slowly, obviously in arthritic pain.

Before the fight could begin there were prayers and sacrifices and speeches to be made. It was late in the afternoon before the men cleared a space on the bare dusty ground and their champion stepped forward. He was almost as big as I, with a deep chest and powerful limbs. He wore a bronze cuirass, greaves, and a bronze helmet with nose piece and cheek flaps tied so tightly under his chin that I could see little more of his face than his light-colored eyes gazing out at me.

A young slave boy stood a few steps behind him, holding with both skinny arms a figure-eight shield of multiple layers of oxhide; it was so heavy it seemed it would topple the poor lad over at any moment. Another youth held a handful of long spears for him, their bronze tips glinting in the late afternoon sunlight.

His shield bore the figure of a single eye, and I remembered the eye of Amon that adorned the great pyramid of Khufu in distant Egypt. Was there some connection? I decided not. This was merely a variant of the evil eye that supposedly paralyzed opponents with terror.

I faced their champion with nothing but the crude spear I had hacked from the gnarled branch of a tree. Those pale eyes of his gleamed with the anticipation of easy victory. We circled each other warily, he behind his ponderous oxhide shield, which covered him from chin to sandals. Despite his solid build he was agile, light on his feet. I danced nimbly on the balls of my feet as my senses went into overdrive. I saw him pull his arm back so slowly that it seemed to take forever; then he hurled the spear at me with every ounce of strength in his powerful body.

I jumped to one side at last instant, and the crowd of men groaned as if disappointed that I hadn't been spitted on the sharp bronze point. My opponent half-turned and his squire handed him another spear. I merely stood my ground until he began to approach me again. Then I jabbed my spear at him, letting its point bang against his oxhide shield.

He grinned at me as he pushed his shield against my spear, using it like a battering ram, edging closer to me. "Don't run away, Orion," he half-whispered to me. "You can't escape your fate."

My knees went weak with surprise. Those tawny eyes glinting at me were the eyes of Aten, the Golden One.

"Don't look so shocked," he said as he jabbed his spear at me. "You've seen me take human form before."

"Why now?" I asked, backing away from him.

He laughed. "For sport! Why else?" And he rammed his spear at my midsection so hard and fast that I barely had the reflexes to flinch away. The sharp bronze point grazed my flank. The men crowding around us went "Oooh!" at the sight of my blood.

I knew that my pitiful tree branch would be no match for him. He had as much speed and strength as I; perhaps more. I danced backward several steps, and as he advanced toward me I lunged forward with all my might and aimed the fire-hardened tip of my spear at his eyes. He raised his shield to catch my thrust and my spear stuck in the layers of oxhide, forcing him backward a few steps.

Whirling, I dashed to the spear he had thrown at me. Now we were evenly armed, at least, although Aten still had that long shield and I had none. As I looked up I saw that both his young squires were tugging their hardest to pull my rude spear from his shield. It came out at last, sending them both tumbling onto their backs.

Now Aten advanced upon me again, and I held my spear in two hands. To the watching men it must have seemed like a moment from the battle for Troy, champion against champion, spear against spear.

For sport, he'd told me. He'd taken on human form and faced me in combat for sport.

"Are you prepared to die for sport?" I asked him.

"You tried to kill me once, do you remember?"

"No," I said.

"I thought I'd give you the opportunity again."

He feinted, then raked his spear point upward, catching my spear and nearly knocking it out of my hands.

Before I could recover he slashed downward again, slicing a long cut across my chest from shoulder to ribs. The watching men shouted their approval.

"I'm faster than you, Orion," Aten taunted. "And stronger. Do you think that I'd build a creature more powerful than myself?"

I jabbed at his exposed left foot, then swung my spear in my two hands like a quarter-staff and cracked him hard on his helmet. The men gasped. Aten staggered backward, his taunts silenced for the moment.

My mind was racing: *If he defeats me, Neoptolemos wins this dispute against Odysseus, and his grandson goes on to father the line that eventually gives birth to Olympias. If I defeat Aten, however, and Odysseus is the victor over Neoptolemos, what will happen to the royal line of Epeiros? Is* that *why Aten has taken human form and inserted himself into this fight? To make certain that I am killed and Olympias is born a thousand years down the time stream?*

Those were the thoughts running through my mind as we fought. They sapped my confidence, made me uncertain of what I should do. But each time I saw the golden eyes of Aten smirking at me from behind his bronze helmet, hot fury boiled up within me: *For sport. He is playing with me, playing with all the mortals here, toying with their lives and their hopes the way a cat torments a mouse.*

It seemed as if we fought for hours. Aten nicked me here and there, until I was bleeding from a dozen cuts and scratches. I could not get past his shield. He truly was as fast as I, perhaps even a little faster, so that whatever I tried to do against him he saw and protected himself against.

Once I almost got him. I jabbed straight at his eyes and as he raised his shield, covering his vision for an instant, I swept the butt of my spear across his ankles, tripping him and sending him sprawling to the dusty ground. But he immediately covered his body with the long shield, even as

I rammed my spear at him. The spear point caught in the shield and we became involved in an almost comical tug of war, me trying to wrestle the spear out of his shield, him struggling to his knees and then finally to his feet.

The men were roaring with excitement as they crowded close around us. I finally yanked my spear free of his shield, but the effort sent me staggering backwards into the crowd. I stumbled, slipped, and went down.

Aten was on me before I could blink. And I had no shield to hide behind. I saw his armored form looming over me, silhouetted against the brilliant sky, the sun at his back, his spear raised above his head as he started to plunge it into my heart.

There was nothing I could do except ram my own spear into his groin while he impaled me. We both screamed in death agonies and the world went utterly black and cold.

Chapter 26

Pain woke me. My eyes fluttered open. I was back atop Mount Ararat, lying in the snow, but now it no longer covered me completely. Much of it had melted away. I saw a clear blue sky above me, so bright it hurt my eyes to look upon it.

A snow-white fox was gnawing on my right forearm—a vixen, I could see from her gravid belly. *It must be spring or close to it,* I thought, *and she is so desperate for food up in this barren waste at the mountaintop that she will attack a corpse.*

But I was not dead. Not yet. Automatically I shut down the pain receptors in my brain, even as I clutched at the vixen's throat with my left hand so swiftly that she did not have time even to yelp. I ate her raw, unborn pups and all, and felt the nourishment streaming into my blood. My right hand was useless for the time being, although I had stopped the bleeding and wrapped the wound the vixen had made with her own pelt.

It took me days to get down from Ararat's summit. I had lain there in the snow for most of the winter, suspended in a frozen half-death while Aten or Hera or both of them used me to ensure the line of Neoptolemos so that Olympias could be born in this era.

Now I proved myself worthy of my name; I lived by

hunting, ferreting out the tiny rodents that were just beginning to come out of their winter burrows, tracking down the mountain goats and sheep on the lower slopes, even running down a wild horse over the course of several days until it dropped from exhaustion. So did I, almost.

By the time I was on the flat land again, with the smoke of distant farm houses smudging the horizon, my arm was healed and I felt reasonably strong.

I returned to the ways of the bandit. I had no other choice. My mission was to return to Pella, to do Hera's bidding, no matter how I might hate to obey her. I stole a horse here, raided a barn there, broke into farm houses, chased down stray cattle, did what I needed to do to stay alive. I tried to avoid people whenever possible and only fought when I had no choice. Even so, I killed no human—although I left several men groaning with broken bones.

I pushed westward, toward the setting sun, toward Europe and Greece and Pella and Philip and Alexandros. And Hera. There was no longer the slightest doubt in my mind: Olympias was Hera and had been all along. Her witchcraft was nothing more than the innate powers of the Creators themselves.

I rode night and day, sleeping only rarely as my strength returned to normal, pushing myself to get back to Pella as quickly as I could. In my dreams, on those rare nights when I did sleep, Hera kept beckoning me, but no longer with the enticements of her body. She commanded me the way a mistress commands the lowliest of her slaves. She urged me to come to her. She demanded that I hurry.

I did the best I could, crossing whole nations in days, avoiding the main roads and the bigger towns, hunting or stealing what I needed and pushing constantly on toward the setting sun.

Until at last I reached Chalkedon.

It was a large city, bigger than Pella, smaller than

Athens. A port city, across the Bosporus from Byzantion. Its streets were crooked, meandering down the slope from the city wall to the waterfront docks. Its buildings were old, in poor repair, dirty. Garbage stank in the alleys and even the main square looked dirty, uncared for. Inns and taverns were plentiful, however, and the closer I approached the docks the more the streets were lined with them. Knots of drunken sailors and keen-eyed merchants stood before open bars built into many of the house fronts, exchanging drinks and gossip, making bargains and deals for everything from Macedonian timber to slaves from the wild steppes beyond the Black Sea.

The busiest place in Chalkedon was the slave market, down by the docks. I was going to push past the crowd gathered there; I was looking for a cheap ride across the water into Byzantion. I had a few coins in a cloth purse I had taken from a horse trader who had made the mistake of travelling with only four guards.

But while I was trying to work my way through the crowd that filled the open-air slave market and spilled out across the street that led down to the docks, I stopped dead in my tracks. I saw Harkan.

He had changed his clothes and even trimmed his beard. Like most of the other men thronging the slave market, he wore a long plain coat over his more colorful robe, and covered his head with a felt cap. At a distance he looked like either a moderately prosperous merchant or the owner of a large farm who was shopping for hands to work it for him. But closer up, the scar on his cheek was clearly recognizable; so was the flinty look in his coal-dark eyes. I glanced around the crowd and spotted several of Harkan's men, also with their beards neatly trimmed, wearing decent clothes.

I pushed through the murmuring, jostling pack of men waiting for the market to open, heading for Harkan. He was turned slightly away from me, but his eyes kept searching through the expectant crowd, on the alert for danger. Then he saw me.

His eyes went wide as I came up beside him, but he quickly mastered his surprise.

"Your pilgrimage is over?" he asked.

I nodded. "I'm heading back to Pella. I have responsibilities there."

He nodded. "You look different."

"Different?"

"Calmer. More certain of yourself, as if you are sure of what you are doing now."

I felt a slight surprise at that, but inwardly I realized he was right. There was no turmoil within me now. I did not know exactly what I had to do, but I knew I must return to Pella and do Hera's bidding, no matter what it might be.

Then I looked squarely into Harkan's leathery face and realized for the first time that he reminded me of someone I had known. Another soldier, from long ago: Lukka the Hittite. He might have been Harkan's forebear, they looked so much like one another. In Harkan's eyes I saw something that I had noticed only once before, when he had spoken of his family. I realized why he was here.

"You are searching for your children," I said.

"If they haven't already been sold. I was told the people taken from Gordium were brought to the market here. They won't let anyone except the wealthiest buyers inspect the cages before the auctioning starts."

I thought a moment. "You are hoping to buy their freedom?"

"Yes."

"And then what?"

He shot a questioning glance at me. "What do you mean?"

"It will be difficult to continue your life as a bandit

with an eight-year-old son and a six-year-old daughter to take care of."

"What do you want me to do?"

"I don't know."

"Neither do I, pilgrim. For now, I'm seeking my children. What happens afterward, I'll worry about after I've found them. First things first."

I stayed at his side through the whole long miserable afternoon. The slave dealers paraded out their wares, one by one. Young women brought the highest prices; strong healthy-looking men young enough to work in the fields or the mines also made profits for the sellers. There were dozens of children, but they brought very little. Most of them were still not sold when the sun dipped behind the warehouses lining the docks and the auction ended.

Hardly a scattering of buyers was left in the square by then. The children, miserable, dirty, some of them crying, all of them collared by heavy iron rings, were led by their chains back to their pens.

While the slave dealers huddled off behind the auction block, counting their coins, the chief auctioneer climbed down wearily and headed toward the tavern across the square.

"It's a shame," said the chief auctioneer as we watched the children being led away. His leather-lunged voice was slightly hoarse from the long day's work. "We can't keep feeding those brats forever. They're eating up any profit we might make on them."

Falling in beside him, Harkan asked as casually as he could manage, "Where are they from?"

The auctioneer was a lean, balding man with a pot belly and cunning eyes. He shrugged his thin shoulders. "Here and there. Phrygia, Anatolia; we got a clutch of them from Rhodes, believe it or not."

"Have there been any from Gordium?"

He stopped walking and looked sharply at Harkan. We were more than halfway across the square, almost at the door to the tavern. "What is such information worth to you?"

Harkan's face became a mask of granite. "It is worth a life, auctioneer. Yours."

The man looked at me, then glanced back over his shoulder where the dealers were still gathered behind the block. A half-dozen armed men stood guard near them.

"You wouldn't get to utter a single word," Harkan said, his voice low with menace. "Now just tell me, and tell me truly. Have there been any children from Gordium here?"

"A month ago. Nearly a hundred of them. There were so many that the bidding went down almost to nothing. A bad show, a miserable show."

"Who bought them?"

"Only a few were bought in the open auction. The bidding was too low. We can't sell goods for nothing! Can't give them away! The dealers closed the auction when the bidding went down too low to satisfy them."

"So what happened to the children who weren't bought?"

"They were sold in a lot. To a Macedonian. Said he was from their king."

"Philip?" I asked.

"Yes, Philip of Macedon. He needs lots of slaves now that he's master of Athens and all the rest of the Greeks."

"This is the truth?" Harkan asked, gripping the auctioneer's skinny forearm almost hard enough to snap the bone.

"Yes! The truth! I swear it!"

"The few who were bought by men here," Harkan went on urgently, "were any of them an eight-year-old boy, with hair the color of straw and eyes as black as mine? Or a six-year-old girl with the same coloring?"

The auctioneer was sweating and trying to pry Harkan's fingers off his forearm. He might as well have tried to dig through the city wall with a dinner fork.

"How can I remember?" he yelped. "There were so many, how can I remember an individual boy or girl?"

"Let him be," I said to Harkan. "The chances are that your children are on their way to Pella."

He released the auctioneer, who dashed through the tavern's door without another word.

"To Pella. In Macedonia." Harkan drew in a great painful breath. "Then I'll never see them again."

"Why do you think that?"

"I know little of Philip and his kingdom, but I've heard that they don't tolerate bandits there. Philip's men keep the law. There's no place for me there."

I smiled at him and placed my hand on his shoulder. "My friend, Philip does not tolerate banditry, true enough. But he has the finest army in the world, and he is always ready to welcome new recruits."

I had heard that in ancient times heroes had swum across the Hellespont. Alexandros had sworn to his Companions that he would do it one day himself. Perhaps I could swim the Bosporus; it was narrower than the Hellespont, although its current was swift and treacherous. It would be far easier to buy a place on one of the ferries that plied between Chalkedon and Byzantion. And, of course, I could not expect Harkan or his men to swim.

His band had dwindled to nine men over the winter. The others had drifted off, tired of their bandit ways, trying to find their way back to their home villages or looking for a new life for themselves. I was glad to see that among the remaining nine was Batu. Harkan told me he was a strong fighter, with a cool, calculating mind.

"They say there are Macedonian troops in Abydos," Harkan told me, "down by the Hellespont."

"Truly?"

He shrugged his shoulders. "That's the word in the marketplace."

Philip's show of strength, I realized—holding a bridgehead on the Asian side of the water in case he ultimately decided to move the bulk of the army against the Great King. Diplomacy works best when it's backed by power.

"We'll get to Pella faster by taking passage across the Bosporus to Byzantion," I decided.

"That takes money, pilgrim. We don't have enough coin to buy passage for the eleven of us."

"Then how do you expect to buy—" I stopped myself in mid-sentence. I knew the answer before I finished asking the question. Harkan was saving whatever coin he had amassed to buy back his children.

So I said instead, "I know where there is coin aplenty."

Harkan grasped my hint. "The slave dealers?" He smiled grimly at the thought. "Yes, they must have more coins than old Midas himself."

"But they are always heavily protected," said Batu. "Their homes are guarded and they never venture into the streets alone."

"We are strong enough to overpower such guards," I said.

"Yes, I agree," said Batu. "But before we could take their coin to the docks and get aboard a boat, the city's guards would be upon us."

I nodded. He was right. Brute force would not work; the city was too small. An attack on one of the rich slave dealers would immediately bring out the whole force of guards and the first thing they would do would be to halt all the ferries attempting to leave the docks.

"Then we must use guile," I said.

Chapter 27

It rained that night, which was all to the good. I stood beneath the gnarled branches of a dripping olive tree, studying the house of the richest slave dealer in Chalkedon. Harkan and Batu were at my side, shoulders hunched, wet, miserable and apprehensive.

"The wall is high," murmured Batu, his deep resonant voice like a rumble of distant thunder.

"And the gods know how many guards he has in there," said Harkan nervously.

"Six," I told him. "And another dozen sleeping in the servants' quarters on the other side of the courtyard."

"How do you know that?" Harkan's harsh whisper sounded surprised, disbelieving.

"I spent all evening watching, from the branches of that big oak tree across the street."

"And no one saw you? No one noticed?"

"This is a very quiet street in a very rich neighborhood. My only trouble was getting past the constables' patrol down at the foot of the hill. Once I slipped past them there was no one on the street except a fruit vendor and his cart. I waited until he had gone around the corner and then climbed the tree. Up there the leaves were thick enough to keep me hidden. It was fully dark when I came down."

I heard Batu chuckle in the darkness.

"Is my report satisfactory?" I asked Harkan.

"For a pilgrim," he grumbled, "you have strange ways."

We agreed that they would wait out of sight in the deep shadows beneath the olive trees that lined the residential street. They would have to deal with any of the city constables or private guards who might pass by.

"The rain helps us," I said. "There will be no casual strollers this night."

"And it discourages the guards on the other side of the wall from roaming the grounds," Batu added.

I nodded. "If I'm not back by the time the sky begins to lighten, go back to the inn, gather up the rest of the men, and get out of town."

"You speak as if you were the commander, Orion," said Harkan.

I grasped his shoulder. "I speak as if I want you and your men to get away safely even if I am captured."

"I know," he said. "The gods be with you."

"They always are," I replied, knowing that he had no idea of the bitterness behind my words.

"Good luck," said Batu.

I shook my rain-soaked cloak to make sure it would not hamper my movements, then stepped from under the dubious shelter of the tree. The rain felt cold, almost stinging, although there was barely any wind at all. The wall surrounding the slave dealer's house was high, with spikes and sharp-edged potsherds embedded in its top. The groundskeepers had cut down any trees growing along the length of the wall. Its whitewashed surface was blank and smooth, offering no handholds.

So I ran from the olive tree, across the brick-paved street, and leaped as high as I could. My sandalled right foot slapped against the wall and I stretched my right arm to its limit. My fingers found the edge of the wall as my body slammed against it almost hard enough to dislodge me. Mindful of the sharp pottery bits and spikes up there, I hung for a moment by the fingertips of both hands, then pulled myself up until my eyes could see the top of the wall. It looked like a little forest of sharp objects.

Carefully I pulled myself up to my elbows and got one leg levered up onto the edge of the wall. There was not much room that wasn't covered with cutting edges or spikes. The one thing I worried about was the dogs. During my afternoon and evening observation of the house and grounds I saw several large black dogs trotting through the garden or lolling outside the doors, tongues hanging out and teeth big and white. The rain would help; dogs do not like being cold and wet any more than people do, and the steady downpour would deaden my scent. Or so I hoped.

I edged across the jagged potsherds and spikes and lowered myself slowly to the grass. Dropping to one knee, I waited long moments as the rain sluiced coldly down my neck and bare arms and legs. Nothing was moving in the dark courtyard. There were no lights in the servants' quarters and only one lamp gleaming feebly in the main house, through a window on the ground floor.

My senses hyperalert, I scuttled quickly to the closest window of the main house. Its shutters were closed tight. I heard a growl from their other side, low and menacing, a warning from the dog who had been sleeping inside. I backed away, then moved to the farther corner of the house and froze in my tracks. A guard sat there, trying to stay out of the rain beneath the overhang of the second story, his cloak wrapped tight around him, his chin on his chest—asleep or not, I could not tell.

I took no chances. Sliding along the wall almost like a snake, I was within arm's reach before he realized I was there. With one hand I muffled his mouth and with the other I chopped the back of his neck. I felt him go limp.

Then I sat him down again exactly as he had been, chin on chest, cloak secure around him.

I swung up onto the overhang and climbed to the second-floor window. It too was shuttered, but I gripped it by the slats in one hand as I hung there and forced it open with only a slight groaning, squeaking noise. Not enough to warn anyone, I hoped.

I pulled myself through the window and into the dark room. My eyes were fully adjusted to the dark and I swiftly saw that this was a bedchamber and that a woman lay asleep in the bed, tossing unhappily and muttering in her dreams. I tiptoed past her and went out into the corridor beyond her door.

It was a balcony, actually, that ran along all four sides of the house's inner courtyard. Sleeping chambers and other rooms lined its entire length. The area below was lit by that one feeble lamp I had seen from outside. It was a large central atrium, with rooms opening onto it. Peering through the polished wood railing of the balcony, I could see two guards squatting by the door, miserable in the chilly rain. The dog that had growled at me was pacing nervously across the flooring beneath the balcony on the far side of the atrium, his claws clicking against the stones. He looked up at me, ears pricked, but apparently he had been trained not to climb the stairs. He was a ground-floor dog, and for that I was extremely grateful.

Now the question was, where did the dealer keep his money? I smiled to myself in the shadows. In his own room, I was willing to bet. But which room was his?

I stood there for long moments, studying the area. The balcony was lined with doors, all of them closed. They were all single doors, except for those at the far end of the balcony, opposite the side where the stairs were. Double doors. Handsomely carved, at that.

Staying in the shadows along the wall, I made my way

swiftly and silently to those double doors. They were locked, of course. Very well. I retreated, testing each of the other doors as I went until I found one that opened for me. The room inside was unoccupied; it looked like a storage room, with shelves lining two of its walls. There was only a narrow slit of a window, but I pushed its shutter open and stuck my head out into the rain. The wall was smooth and straight; no handholds, no ledge or anything else to plant my feet upon. But there was the roof above.

I squeezed out through the narrow window, stood up precariously on its sill, and reached for the overhanging eave. The roofing tiles were slippery from the rain, but I managed to haul myself up onto the sloping roof. As quietly as I could, I edged across the tiles to the spot where the master bedroom must be. Leaning over the eaves I saw a double window. One of the shutters was even open a little. The master of the house liked fresh air. Good!

I swung down and went in through the window as silently as a shadow. And heard the growl of a guard dog.

I had no time to waste. The dog was standing before me, fangs bared. There was no time to try to soothe it; in another instant it would start to bark and rouse the entire house. Faster than it could react I seized it by the throat and yanked it up off its feet. It clawed at me and tried to snap at my face but I kept it at arm's length as I squeezed the breath from its throat. It jerked convulsively, then went limp. I eased the pressure of my hands. I could feel a pulse beat in its neck, heard it sucking in air. I let the animal down gently, hoping it would remain unconscious long enough for me to find the dealer's coins.

The embers of a dying fire glowed in the bedroom fireplace. The slave merchant lay asleep. I saw that his chamber had only a single door. There must be an anteroom out there, probably with guards on duty in it.

Looking around, I saw a massive cabinet standing in

one corner of the bedchamber. Tall as the ceiling, deep enough for a man to walk into, two ornate doors locked tight. There was a writing desk next to it.

There must be a key to those doors, I reasoned, and it must be near to the owner's hand. I tiptoed to the edge of his bed and saw that, sure enough, the key was on a chain around his neck. How to get it without waking him? *Guile,* a voice in my mind answered me. *Guile, not force. Remember, you don't want him to know that you've been here.*

Then I smiled to myself. Properly used, force can be a form of guile.

I went to the glowing embers of his fire, took the tongs from beside the fireplace, and lifted out a smoldering chunk of wood. I could hear the dog beginning to stir, whining. I blew hard on the half-burned ember and it glowed brighter. Then I swiftly crossed the room and touched it to the drapes of the windows, the clothing piled atop a chest, the bedclothes themselves. They began to smoke and smolder.

I pegged the ember back into the fireplace in a red arc of sparks, then gave the sleeping old man a mighty shove that knocked him flat onto the floor on the other side of the bed. Before he could raise his head I dashed to the open window and ducked through it, hanging outside in the rain by my hands.

"Fire!" I heard him screech. "Fire!"

Lifting myself to eye level I saw him run through the smoke to his door and fling it open. I felt the draft that immediately blew through the room, setting the smoldering bedclothes into real flames.

"Fire, you idiots!" he screamed to the startled guards in his anteroom. "Get water! Quickly!"

He dashed to that big double-doored cabinet and fumbled the key from the chain around his neck. With shaking hands he unlocked the doors and pulled them open. I could see in the growing light of the flames that he had several chests in there, and dozens of smaller boxes sitting on shelves. There were also row upon row of scrolls: his business records, I guessed.

The dog bolted past him and out the door as the window curtains burst into flame. The heat singed the hairs on the backs of my hands and made me duck my head below the window sill.

When I looked up again the dealer had tucked several boxes under his scrawny arms and was trying to lock the doors once again. The flames were licking higher; the canopy over the bed came crashing down and he finally gave up and dashed from the room.

I had only a few moments to act. I hauled myself through the window once again and went straight to the cabinet. Yanking its doors wide I pawed through several of the smaller boxes inside. They were all filled with coins. I took two of them to the window and tossed them on the ground, then raced back to the fireplace. Grabbing the largest half-burned log there, I blew it alight and then used it as a torch to set the scrolls afire inside the cabinet.

Heavy steps were pounding up the stairway, running along the balcony. Voices were yelling, dogs barking, women shrieking. Over them all I heard the piercing high screech of the slave dealer cursing at his men and screaming that the whole house would be destroyed.

Seeing the cabinet nicely ablaze I dashed back to the window and jumped to the ground below. I scooped up the two boxes of coins, ran through the night and the rain to the wall, stopping only to glance back over my shoulder at my handiwork. Smoke was pouring from the windows now, with flames flickering through. With a bit of luck the whole house would burn down.

I unlatched the front gate and stepped out onto the street as if I were walking to meet some friends. Which I did—Harkan and Batu were still beneath the olive tree.

"Time for us to leave," Harkan said. "The whole neighborhood is waking up."

I agreed, but held him up long enough to show him the two boxes of coins.

Batu's eyes went round. "I could return to Africa and live like a prince with that much money."

Harkan merely grunted. "You make a fine burglar," he said, "for a pilgrim."

Laughing, we left the slave merchant's house burning. *He will never know he's been robbed,* I thought. *Even if he suspects it, he will have no way to know who did it.* We could see the smoke even from the docks, once the sun came up.

Chapter 28

We found a ferry about to cast off from the dock and, after a quick haggle with its captain, all eleven of us trooped aboard. The captain was a good-sized man, his skin nut-brown from long years in the sun, his hair and beard just beginning to show flecks of gray. He eyed us suspiciously, but he hefted the bag of coins I gave him and gave the order to weigh anchor.

It was a fat little tub with a single mast and an open deck. The captain barked orders from a raised poop at the stern. Pens of goats took up most of the forward deck space, their smell overpowering until we got the wind behind us. Our men sat on the deck planks, resting their backs against bales of cloth and coils of rope or the boat's gunwales.

Slaves rowed us out into the channel, then the wind filled the boat's triangular sail and we cut through the harbor and out into the powerful current of the Bosporus. The boat began to bob up and down like a cork and most of Harkan's men began to turn various shades of green. The sailors laughed as their passengers moaned and staggered for the rail.

"Not into the wind, you fool!" roared the captain as one man after another emptied his guts into the churning water.

I went to the rail also, but well away from the seasick, vomiting men. I stared out at Europe across the way, the brown mud-brick buildings of Byzantion basking in the morning sunlight. Somehow I knew that this undistinguished collection of drab buildings would one day become a mighty city, a center of empire where palaces and churches and mosques would dot the skyline with magnificent domes and graceful minarets.

For now, though, Byzantion was little more than a strategically placed seaport, part of Philip's Macedonian hegemony.

"We're not getting any closer," Harkan murmured in my ear. I turned to him, surprised. He looked grim.

Batu came up beside me on the other side. "We seem to be turning around."

It was true. We were heading back toward the harbor of Chalkedon. The rest of Harkan's troop was too sick to notice or to care, sprawled on the deck or draped over the rail. The sail flapped uselessly and the stench of the goats washed across the deck, making matters even worse. Harkan gripped the rail with both hands, knuckles white, face pale green.

I looked up at the captain. There were signal flags flying from the stern. He was staring intently at the docks we had left barely half an hour earlier. Signal flags were fluttering from the pole back there. Then I saw that the sailors had all armed themselves with swords. Even the slaves had tucked clubs into their belts. Our weapons were stacked up forward, next to the goat pens, and none of our men was in condition to use them.

I headed for the captain's perch on the poop deck but two armed sailors stopped me at the ladder.

"Captain!" I called up to him. "What are you doing?"

"Returning a pack of thieves to justice," he said, with a laugh.

"What makes you think we're thieves?" I shouted.

He pointed to the signal flags. "Someone burned the house of an important person during the night. And you paid too much too easily for your passage this morning."

I thought over the situation for all of three seconds. Harkan's men were in no condition to fight; Harkan himself looked barely able to stand on his feet. The sailors were all armed and ready to start slitting throats. The captain was very pleased with himself; he would return a fraction of the coins I had given him to the dealer, and no doubt receive a reward for returning us to the city's authorities.

The two men before me were grinning smugly. Perhaps that is what decided me.

I grabbed each of them by the jaw before they could even flinch and banged their heads together so hard it sounded like an ax striking a sturdy old oak. As they slid to the deck, unconscious or dead, I whisked the swords from their belts and tossed them to the startled Harkan and Batu. Harkan fumbled and dropped his sword. Batu caught his cleanly and thrust it through the belly of the first sailor who came charging toward them. As he screamed Harkan recovered his sword and the two of them advanced against a half-dozen sailors, toward the rest of our troop who were still sprawled miserably on the deck.

I leaped up the ladder in two bounds, whipping out the dagger from its sheath on my thigh. A sailor in a ragged tunic was hanging onto the tiller with both hands. Next to him stood the captain, looking very surprised. The first mate stood between me and the captain, sword in hand. My senses went into overdrive. I saw the muscles in his arm flex, his legs tense as he prepared to move to my unguarded left. I feinted with my left forearm against his sword wrist and, stepping into him, drove my dagger under his chin and into the base of his skull. I stepped over his slumping body to face the captain.

He too had a sword in hand but he seemed to have no inclination to use it. I glanced over my shoulder and saw Harkan and Batu standing back to back over the seasick men, a circle of sailors and slaves ringing them with swords and clubs. The boat, unattended except by the one man at the tiller, was still drifting toward Chalkedon's harbor.

The captain said easily, "Put down your dagger or your friends will all be thrown to the fishes."

"You'll feed the fishes first, I promise you."

He smiled at me. "Kill me, and how will you sail this boat?"

I smiled back. "I watched your men this morning. I can sail this tub to Egypt if I need to."

His smile widened into a grin that revealed several missing teeth. "You don't lack confidence, thief."

"You have our money," I said. "Take us across to Byzantion as you agreed to do."

"Then when I return to Chalkedon they'll blame me for letting you escape."

"You have a few dead men to show that you didn't let us go without a fight."

He tugged at his beard, thinking, calculating. He knew that his crew could probably overpower Harkan and Batu, even though some of the other men were pushing themselves unsteadily to their feet, ready to fight despite their misery. But the battle would cost him more casualties and he had already lost his first mate and at least two other sailors. And he faced me alone—sword against dagger, true; but I could see that he did not like the odds.

I decided to sweeten the deal. "Suppose I give you the rest of the money I have."

His eyes lit up. "You would do that?"

"It would be better than fighting—for all of us."

He nodded quickly. "Done."

Thus we sailed to Byzantion and left the ferry and its

captain at the dock there. I felt happy to be back in Philip's domain. But Harkan had left the land in which he had been born and spent all his life. And he knew that he might never see Gordium again.

I found the barracks where Philip's soldiers were housed and announced myself as one of the king's guard, returning from Asia with ten new recruits for the army. The officer in charge, a crusty old graybeard with a bad limp, put us up overnight and provided us the next morning with horses. I was anxious to reach Pella. Harkan was just as anxious to track down his children.

We rode from one army station to the next, across Thrace and into Macedonia. Each night I could feel myself coming closer to Hera's power. I tried not to sleep. I went for almost a week without closing my eyes for more than a few moments at a time. But at last the night came when I could stay awake no longer, and as I sat on a cot in an army barracks, my back against the rough logs of its wall, I finally drifted into a deep slumber.

She came to me in dream, as she had before, beautiful, haughty, demanding.

"You are returning at an auspicious time, Orion," Olympias/Hera told me.

I was standing before her in that magnificent chamber that did not exist in Pella yet was connected to the palace by a gateway that spanned the dimensions of spacetime. Olympias reclined on a throne that was almost a couch, carved from green bloodstone veined with dark streaks like rivulets of dried blood. Snakes slithered at her feet, twined across the back of the throne, coiled around her bare legs.

I could not move, could not even speak. All I was able to do was to see her, decked in a gown of deepest black glittering with jeweled lights, like stars, her magnificent red hair tumbling past her shoulders, her yellow eyes fixed on mine. I could hear her words. I could breathe. My heart beat. But I know she could destroy me with a glance if she wished to.

"Philip has taken a new wife," she said, with a smile that was pure malice. "He has put me aside. I no longer reside in Pella, but have returned to my kinfolk in Epeiros. What say you to that?"

I found that I could open my mouth. My voice was scratchy, coughing, as if I had not spoken in weeks.

"You are allowing him to do so?" I asked.

"I am allowing him to write his own death warrant," Olympias answered. "And you, my obedient creature, will be the instrument of my vengeance."

"I will not willingly harm Philip."

She laughed. "Harm him unwillingly, then."

And then the pain struck me, wave upon wave of agony pouring over me like breakers rolling up on a beach. Through teeth clenched with anguish I managed to utter, "No. I will not."

The pain intensified as she watched, an amused smile flickering across her lips, her eyes smoldering with sadistic pleasure. I could not move, could not even cry out, but she seemed to sense every iota of the agony she was putting me through, and to relish each moment.

Normally I can control pain, shut off my brain's pain receptors. But I was not in control of my own body, my own mind. After an interminable time, though, the pain began to ease. I could not tell if I was regaining control of my own senses or if my tortured nervous system was simply beginning to fail under the continued stress.

Hera's face told me the answer. Her smile was fading, her pleasure waning. At length the pain ended altogether, although I still could neither speak nor move.

"This grows tiresome," she said peevishly. "You are strong, Orion. Perhaps we built you too well."

I wanted to answer her but could not.

"No matter. What must be done will be done. And you will play your role in it."

Suddenly I was awake in the barracks, still sitting against the rough log wall. Every part of my body ached. Even my insides felt raw, inflamed, as if I had been roasted alive.

At dawn we resumed our trek toward Pella.

"You are quiet this morning," said Batu as we rode along the inland road.

"You look as if you spent the night drinking," Harkan said, peering at me with those flinty eyes.

"Or wenching." Batu laughed.

I said nothing. But all that morning I was thinking that Olympias was biding her time, waiting for the proper moment to strike Philip down so that Alexandros could take the throne. That time was drawing near.

The stables were the best place to learn the latest gossip. Each village we came to was abuzz with the news from the capital. Philip had indeed married Kleopatra, niece of Attalos. Olympias, who had been his chief wife for twenty-five years, had truly been sent packing back to her brother in Epeiros.

"And Alexandros?" I asked.

The news was awful. At the wedding feast, oily Attalos had smugly proposed a toast that Philip and his niece produce "a legitimate heir to the throne."

Alexandros leaped to his feet. "You call me bastard?" He threw his wine cup at Attalos, opening a gash on the older man's forehead.

Philip, seemingly stupefied with wine, staggered up from his couch. Some said he pulled a sword from one of the guards in murderous rage and wanted to kill Alexandros. Others claimed he was merely trying to get between Alexandros and Attalos to prevent a bloody fight from breaking out. The entire hall was on its feet; mayhem was in the air. Whatever Philip's intention, his bad leg gave way and he sprawled clumsily to the wine-slicked floor.

Shaking with fury, Alexandros stared down at his father for a moment, then shouted, "This is the man who would take us across into Asia. He can't even get himself from one bench to the other."

Then he swept out of the hall, his Companions close behind him. Before dawn he and his mother had left Pella for Epeiros.

"He is still there?" I asked.

"So I hear. With his mother. In Epeiros."

"It's too bad about the Little King," said one of the stable men. "Bad business, his falling out with his father that way."

"But good riddance to the witch," said another as we exchanged our horses.

They were not going to get rid her that easily, I knew.

BOOK III

TRAITOR

Now o'er the one half-world
Nature seems dead, and wicked dreams abuse
The curtain'd sleep; witchcraft celebrates
Pale Hecate's offerings; and wither'd murder,
Alarum'd by his sentinel, the wolf . . .
Moves like a ghost

Chapter 29

At last we came to Pella, on a fine summer morning under an azure sky, with a cool breeze from the mountains moderating the heat of the sun. Harkan, riding beside me, murmured, "That's a sizeable city."

I nodded, and noted that Pella had grown noticeably, even in the two years I had been away. New houses reached up into the hills, new arcades and markets spread along the high road. A cloud of gritty gray-brown dust hung over the city, kicked up by the many corrals where horses and mules stirred and whinnied, by the building work going on everywhere, by the traffic streaming along the high road and into the city's streets.

As we rode into the city itself Batu laughingly complained, "Such noise! How can a man think in all this bustle?"

I had paid scant attention to the city's constant din before, but once Batu had said it I realized that the cities in Asia were much quieter and more orderly than Pella. Certainly the marketplaces were noisy with the cries of sellers and arguments of buyers, but the other sections of those ancient cities were sleepy in the hot sun, orderly and quiet. Pella was more like a madhouse, with the constant din of construction hammering everywhere, chariots and wagons and horsemen clattering through the cobblestoned streets, people laughing and talking at the top of their lungs on almost every corner.

No one stopped us or even paid us much attention as we rode up the main street toward Philip's palace. The people were accustomed to seeing soldiers; the army was the backbone of Macedonian society and these people did not fear their army, as the peoples of the Persian Empire's cities did.

But at the palace gate we were stopped. I did not recognize any of the guards on duty there, so I identified myself and told their sergeant that I had brought Harkan and his men to join the army. The sergeant looked us over with a professional eye, then sent one of the boys lounging nearby to run for the captain of the guard.

We dismounted and the sergeant offered us water for ourselves and our horses. Two of his men went with us to the fountain just inside the gate. They were treating us with civility, but with great care, as well.

"What's the news?" I asked the sergeant after slaking my thirst.

He leaned casually against the doorjamb of the guard house, in the shade of the doorway—within arm's reach of the clutch of spears standing there.

"There's to be a royal wedding within the month," he said, his eyes on Harkan and the men by the fountain.

"Philip's marrying again?"

That brought a laugh out of him. "No, no—he's still content with his Eurydice, for the while. She's presented him with a son, you know."

"A son?"

"A truly legitimate heir," the sergeant said. "No question about this babe being sired by a god." He glanced around, then added, "Or whomever the Molossian witch bedded down with."

"And what of Alexandros?"

The sergeant shrugged his heavy shoulders. "He had gone off to Epeiros with his mother when Philip married Eurydice, but the king called him back here to Pella."

"And he came back?"

"You bet he did. He obeyed the king's order, all right. He'd better, after all the trouble he stirred up."

I was about to ask what trouble Alexandros had stirred when the captain of the guard came tramping up to us, flanked by four fully-armed men. It was not Pausanias, but the officer of the day, a man named Demetrios. I recognized him; like me, he had been quartered in the barracks by the palace.

"Orion," he said, pronouncing my name like a heavy sigh.

"I've returned, Demetrios, with seven new recruits for the army."

He looked at me sadly. "Orion, you'll have to come with me. You're under arrest."

I was stunned. "Under arrest? What for?"

Harkan and Batu and the others came back toward us from the fountain. The sergeant stood up straighter and glanced at the spears resting by his side.

Demetrios said, "Those are my orders, Orion. From the king himself. You are charged with desertion."

Before a fight broke out I said, "Very well. I'm willing to accept the king's justice. But these men are volunteers for the army and they should be treated as such. They are professional soldiers, all of them."

Demetrios looked at them. "I'll see that they're well taken care of, Orion. But you must come with me."

"All right."

"I have to take your sword."

I unbuckled it and handed sword and belt to him.

Harkan asked, "What will they do to you?"

"It's all right," I told him. "Once I've had a chance to speak with the king this will all be cleared up."

Demetrios looked utterly dubious, but he did not contradict me. To the sergeant he said, "Take these men to the army barracks and have the officer in charge look them over. If they meet his approval, see that they're properly housed and equipped."

"Yessir," said the sergeant.

Then he turned back to me. "Come along, Orion."

Escorted by Demetrios and his four fully-armed guards, I marched across the palace courtyard and into a prison cell.

The cell was underground, beneath the palace, dark and so small that I could touch the walls on both sides without even extending my arms to their full reach. No window, except a barred slot on the heavy locked door. No bed; just a straw pallet on the bare dirt floor. And an earthenware jug for a chamberpot.

"I really hate to do this to you, Orion," Demetrios told me once we reached the cell. He came inside with me, while his men waited out in the dark corridor that was lit only by a weak shaft of dusty sunlight slanting in from an airshaft. "It's the king's standing order. The instant you showed up again in Pella you were to be arrested. For desertion."

"The king himself gave you this order?" I asked.

"No!" Demetrios seemed shocked to think that the king would speak to him personally. "Pausanias gave me the order, months ago. But it's from the king's mouth; he told me so."

"How many months ago?" I asked. "Was it when the Hindi ambassador from the Great King returned to Pella?"

"The Hindi . . ." Demetrios frowned with thought. "Oh, you mean the one with the name nobody can pronounce. No, I think it was before then. Yes, it had to be before then; I remember I was surprised that you'd be accused of desertion—of anything—because you were so far away in the Persian Empire. How'd the king know you'd deserted?"

Indeed, I said to myself. *How could he know what I was doing in Parsa before Ketu or anyone else returned to tell him?*

"I remember!" Demetrios said. "It was during all that hubbub when the king married Attalos' niece and Olympias stormed off to Epeiros with Alexandros."

"That's when the order was given?"

He bobbed his head up and down. "Yes, I remember it clearly now."

"And you received the order from Pausanias?"

"Yes."

"Well," I said, looking around at the stone walls of my cell, "please tell Pausanias I am back, and safely lodged in my new quarters."

In the dim light of the cell I could not make out the expression on his face, but Demetrios' voice sounded strained. "I will tell him, Orion. Believe me, I'm going to him right now."

"Thank you."

He left me alone in the cell. The thick wooden door, reinforced with iron strapping, swung shut. I heard the bolt shoot home. I was in almost total darkness, alone except for the dagger strapped to my thigh. Then I noticed a pair of red beady eyes glowering in the darkest corner of the cell. I would not be totally alone, I realized. There were the rats.

I had plenty of time to think. The hours dragged by slowly in that dark cell. I counted the days by the times that the jailor shuffled by and shoved a shallow metal bowl of thin gruel through the slot at the bottom of the door. It was decent enough. He took the chamberpot, too, when I left it by the slot. No one came in to change the straw, though.

I can go for many days without sleep, and I feared to lie down on that straw pallet and offer myself to the rats that chittered in the darkness. In the dim recesses of my memory I recalled Anya being killed by a pack of huge, fierce rats in the filth and slime of a city's subterranean tunnels. Her name was Aretha in that lifetime and I had been powerless to save her.

I tried to focus my thoughts on Pella and Philip and Olympias, on this time and place, on the commands that Hera had given me—and others.

There was no doubt in my mind that Hera was manipulating all of us now: Alexandros, me, even Pausanias. She had taken on human form and become Olympias, Queen of Macedon, the witch of Pella. She had created a son, Alexandros. She and Aten.

Seeing Anya take on human form and fall in love with one of their creatures, Hera did the same. And so did Aten, the Golden One, the cynical self-styled progenitor of the human race, the one who had called himself Apollo at Troy. They created Alexandros, the godling, the golden-haired offspring of the Golden One. Now Hera/Olympias was scheming to make him King of Macedon and eventually conqueror of the whole world.

"Why?" I asked in the dark solitude of my prison cell. "Why are they doing this?"

I knew there was only one way to find out. I had to face them myself, in their own domain. But to do that I had to put this body of mine into sleep, and leave it at the mercy of those hungry, baleful eyes.

Or did I? If one can truly master time, then I could leave this place in the continuum, seek out the Creators in their city by the sea, and return to this cell with no real time elapsed.

If I could truly master time.

For long hours I paced my cell, wondering if I could do it, trying to remember those other times when the Creators had moved me through the continuum to do their bidding. Their blocks against my memory were strong but I had a powerful motivation to break through: Anya had told me, on Ararat, that she was in danger. I wanted to be with her, facing whatever it might be at her side, ready to fight for her as she had fought for me so many times. Hera and the Golden One and perhaps the other Creators as well were all trying to keep us apart. Raw anger flamed through me. I would break through their control. I would do it even if it cost me my body, my life, my existence.

As I laid myself down on the damp, smelly straw, I smiled inwardly at the thought of Ketu and his Eightfold Path. Perhaps this time the Creators would end me forever. Almost, I felt glad of that possibility. Almost. But in my deepest soul I had no desire for final oblivion. I wanted to find Anya and know her love again.

I closed my eyes and willed myself to sleep. The last thing I sensed was the squeaking jabber of the rats.

I ignored them and concentrated on translating myself through the continuum to the city of the Creators. What were the physical sensations that I had felt those other times? A wave of infinite cold, as if my body had been displaced into the deepest reaches of empty space, out beyond the farthest galaxies, out where no star had ever shone. A falling sensation, weightlessness, and then—

I felt the warmth of golden sunlight seeping into my flesh. My eyes were still closed, but instead of blackness I saw a red glow brightening my lids.

Opening my eyes, I sat up and found myself on a grassy hillside dotted with wildflowers. White puffs of cumulus clouds dotted a deeply blue sky. A warm breeze made the flowers nod their colorful heads, the distant trees sway and murmur.

But there was no city. No ocean. No Creators. Nothing but an empty land stretching out to a rolling hilly horizon.

Slowly I climbed to my feet, looking for some sign of them. The Creators *had* to be here. Otherwise why would I have come to this placetime?

"Because you're something of a clod, Orion."

I whirled and there stood the Golden One with the sun at his back. He wore a short-skirted robe that seemed to gleam with a radiance of its own. His handsome face was frowning with annoyance.

"Orion, what are you trying to do? Don't you realize that every time you disturb the continuum like this we have to work to repair the damage you've done?"

"Where is Anya?" I asked.

"Far from here."

"What's going on? Why am I being held in Pella if there's a crisis so grave—"

"Stop this chatter!" Aten snapped. "You've been told more than once, Orion: your task is in the placetime where you've been sent. Do as Hera commands. Is that clear?"

"Not clear enough. I want to know what you are trying to accomplish."

His narrow nostrils flared angrily. "You want to know, do you? All right, I'll tell you. *You* ruined my plans for Troy. Do you remember that?"

He had wanted Troy to beat the Achaian Greeks and go on to establish an empire that would link Asia and Europe. I had thwarted him out of spite.

"That little game of yours unravelled the continuum so badly that we had to exert all our efforts to bring things back together again."

Good, I thought. Aten had gone insane then; he neglected to recall that little fact.

"We are still trying to repair the damage you've done. There *must* be an empire that unites Europe and Asia, even if it lasts only for a few generations. It is important. Vital!"

"So Alexandros—"

"Must succeed. If you ever expect to see Anya again, you must do as Hera commands. Do you understand that?"

I bowed my head and heard myself mutter, "I understand."

Aten shook his head and grumbled, "I must say, Orion, that you've been more trouble than you're worth. But you're strong, I'll grant you that much. I sent you to the Mesozoic again, back among the dinosaurs, just to get you out of our way until we needed you again. But somehow you showed up at Pella."

"Anya did that," I replied, with a certainty that surprised me.

He gave me a sharp look. "Perhaps she did," he mused. "Perhaps she did. When I wanted to put you in suspension, she insisted that I let you live out a life somewhere in the continuum."

"So I was to be stored away like a toy that you had grown tired of playing with."

"Like a tool that I wanted to keep available until I needed it again," the Golden One corrected.

"And now?" I asked.

"Now we face the gravest crisis of all, thanks in part to your infernal meddling."

"That is what Anya is doing, fighting against this crisis?"

"Orion, that is what we *all* are doing. We have no energy to spare on your antics."

"And Hera is manipulating the events in Macedonia?"

"That is her part of the crisis. Again, because of your stubborn resistance to our will."

"So what am I to do?"

He smiled thinly. "Nothing at all, Orion. You should have been put in cryonic storage, but I think your cell in Pella will do almost as well. Enjoy your new playmates."

He meant the rats, I knew.

Chapter 30

I opened my eyes in the darkness of my cell and saw the red hateful eyes of the rats surrounding me. Only a few heartbeats of time had elapsed since I had lain myself down on the moldy straw pallet, I reckoned. The rats were approaching me warily, sniffing at the odor of fresh meat but not yet excited into a feeding frenzy.

I sprang to my feet and they scattered to the corners of the cell, chittering with fear and disappointment.

Thus I spent my days, pacing the narrow confines of the cell, not daring to sleep. The only mark of elapsed time came when the jailor slid my gruel through the slot in the door and collected my chamberpot. Gradually I began to look on the rats as companions.

Using the skill I had learned long ago from the Neanderthals, I tried to put myself into the consciousness of the rats. Gradually I learned to see my cell through their eyes. I felt the gnawing hunger that drove them, so much so that I started to leave my miserable bowl of gruel unfinished and let them lap up the remains.

Day after day I perfected my rapport with them, to the degree that I could sit on the floor of my cell and go with them through the cracks between the cell walls, into their nests, along the tunnels that honeycombed the palace's cellars. Through the eyes of the pack's leader I visited the guard room and saw the giant humans lounging carelessly, dropping crumbs of bread and scraps of meat onto the floor—a feast for the pack, once the humans had left the chamber.

I even listened to the guards' conversations, although their voices sounded strangely deep and booming in the ears of my rats. It took some while for me to learn how to transduce the tones they were capable of hearing into words of understandable human language.

Another royal wedding was drawing near, I learned. But the more they spoke, the more bawdy jokes they made about the impending nuptials, the more confused I became. Alexandros was marrying Kleopatra, they said. Those were two of the most common names among the Macedonians. Did they mean Alexandros, the king's son? The Little King himself? And Kleopatra was the name of Philip's most recent wife, although he called her Eurydice.

It was Pausanias who cleared up the puzzle for me.

He came to visit me in my cell. One day I heard footsteps coming down the hall, and recognized that there was someone accompanying the shuffle-footed old man who brought me my food. Someone wearing boots. One of the rats happened to be near a crack in the corridor wall and I looked up through its eyes. Pausanias loomed like a moving mountain, shaking the rat's sensitive whiskers with each booted step.

The guard pulled the door open on its squeaking hinges and Pausanias ducked through the doorway into my cell. He carried a sputtering torch in his right hand. He had left his sword at the guard room, I saw.

"Leave us," he told the old man. "I'll call when I'm finished here."

The old man wordlessly closed the door and shot its bolt home.

"You've lost weight," Pausanias said, looking me over.

I saw his nose wrinkle. "And I must smell pretty bad, too," I said.

"That can't be helped."

"Why am I here?" I asked. "Why haven't I been allowed to see the king? Or to have a trial, at least."

"It will be over soon," he said. His face was grim, his eyes evasive.

"What do you mean?"

"After the wedding we can let you go."

"The wedding?"

Pausanias' lips turned down into a frown. "The king is giving his daughter to his brother-in-law."

"His daughter Kleopatra? Olympias' daughter?"

"She is to marry Alexandros, King of Epeiros."

"Olympias' brother?" I felt shocked.

He nodded sourly. "It smacks of incest, doesn't it? Marrying off his fourteen-year-old daughter to her own uncle."

"I thought that Olympias was living in Epeiros with her brother."

"She was. She has been returned to Pella."

Philip's statecraft, I realized. He was binding the king of Epeiros to Macedonia by marrying his daughter to him. Alexandros of Epeiros would no longer side with Olympias in their marital squabbles because he was marrying a Macedonian princess. Olympias no longer had a brother to take her side, to give her shelter, to possibly go to war against Philip for her sake.

"The One-Eyed Fox has outsmarted her," I muttered.

"Has he?" Pausanias made a bitter smile. "We'll see."

"And what of our Alexandros, the Little King? How is he reacting to all this?"

"He ran off to Epeiros with his mother when Philip

married Eurydice. But the king called him back to Pella and he came, obedient to Philip's command."

"He's chosen his father over his mother's wishes," I said.

"Don't jump to conclusions, Orion," said Pausanias. "Alexandros will be king one day. That's why he returned to Pella, to reinforce his claim to the throne. You know that Eurydice has born Philip a son."

"I heard."

"The babe will never become king of Macedonia. Alexandros is determined to succeed his father, no matter what."

I nodded my agreement. Then I asked again, "But what has this to do with me? Why am I being kept locked in this cell?"

"You deserted your duty," Pausanias answered crisply. "You ran away from the Persian capital and disappeared into the desert. Do you deny that?"

"No," I admitted.

"Deserters are usually hanged, Orion. I'm allowing you to live. You'll even have your freedom, once the wedding is over."

"What's the wedding got to do with it?"

He looked away from me again, as if there was something in his eyes that he did not want me to see.

"What's the wedding got to do with it?" I repeated.

"You're loyal to Philip," he muttered. "It's best that you're kept out of the way until it's finished."

I stared at him for a long, wordless moment. *Kept out of the way,* my mind echoed. *Until it's finished.*

I grabbed Pausanias by the shoulders and stared into his eyes. "You're going to assassinate the king!"

He did not deny it.

"Olympias has swayed you. The witch has you in her spell."

Pausanias laughed bitterly. "Jealous, Orion? She's thrown you aside for me. Does that bother you?"

"It frightens me. I'm frightened for your sake. And for Philip's."

"Philip." He spat the word. "That man deserves to die a dozen times over."

"You loved him once."

"Yes, and look what he did to me! He *knew* what Attalos had done to me and he did nothing about it. Nothing! I went to him for justice and he ignored me."

"He made you captain of his personal guard," I said. "That is high honor."

"Honor my ass! He didn't punish Attalos. After what that stinking hyena did to me he didn't lift a finger to punish him. Not even a harsh word."

"The king must avoid blood feuds."

But Pausanias did not want to hear reasonable words. "He threw a sop at me and let Attalos get away without a word. Then he marries the bastard's niece and makes a new princeling with her. And all the while he's laughing at me; him and Attalos, laughing at me every night, every time they see each other—"

His chest was heaving, his eyes wild with rage. His hands shook so badly that I feared he would drop the torch he was carrying and set my pallet afire. I knew he was speaking Olympias' words now. She was filling his ears with poison even deadlier than the venom her snakes carried.

Pausanias slowly pulled himself together. "None of this is your affair, Orion. You're not a Macedonian; perhaps you should be glad that you're not. You are an honest man and you feel loyal to the king, so I'm keeping you locked safely here until it's all over. Then you will be freed and you can go your own way."

"Don't do it," I urged. "Don't let her destroy you."

His twisted, bitter smile returned. "I was destroyed a long time ago, Orion. I have nothing to lose."

Weakened though I was by long days of imprisonment, I knew that I could overpower Pausanias. Perhaps I could force him to call for the guard to open my cell door. Perhaps I could overcome the other guards loitering in their chamber down the corridor. Perhaps I could reach the king and warn him.

Too many perhapses. There was no way I could protect Philip if I were cut down by the palace guard before I could reach his side.

Pausanias called for the jailer to open the door. I was tempted to try to force my way to freedom, but then I heard the tramp of a half-dozen men accompanying the old man. They were taking no chances.

I had learned to mark the passage of time through the rats. They were mostly nocturnal animals, although how they told the difference between night and day in the windowless cellar of the castle was beyond me. Still, when I peeked in at the guard chamber through their eyes, I could tell it was nighttime when the men there crawled into their bunks and slept. There were always at least six guards on duty, although they had little to do, even during the day.

I had no idea of when the royal wedding was to take place; only that it would happen soon. By listening to the guards' conversations I learned that it would not be at Pella, but at the ancient capita up in the mountains, Aigai. Apparently Philip was to depart for the old citadel within a day or so.

I needed more information. And help. Tentatively, I tried to control a few of my rat pack. Not merely use their senses as extensions of my own, but actively control them, make them do my bidding. I needed to find Harkan. Of all the soldiers and guards in Pella, only Harkan and Batu could I trust to help me.

I sent my rats ranging through the palace and barracks. It was dangerous for them; other packs attacked strangers in their territory. But I sent one "scout" after another scurrying along the warren of tunnels and hollows that honeycombed the palace. At last I found Harkan and Batu, still quartered together in the main barracks that adjoined the palace proper.

Now that I knew where they were, I had to reach them. That meant breaking out of my cell. But stealthily, without rousing the palace against me. Somehow I had to release the iron bolt that held my cell door locked. But how?

I knew that I could probably release myself from this placetime and travel across the continuum to the realm of the Creators, but then I would undoubtedly return to the same point in time and space that I had left; I would return to my cell. It was bitingly ironic: I could travel through uncounted ages and even span the distances between stars, but that ability was useless to me now. All I wanted to do was to get past my cell door. My barely understood powers of moving through the continuum could not help me. I had to rely on my own strength and wits.

I still had my dagger strapped to my thigh, so much a part of me that I took it for granted. One small dagger was not much of a weapon against all the guards of the palace. But it might make an effective tool.

Using the point of the iron blade I chiselled away at the wooden door at the point where the bolt slid into its iron groove on its other side. The wood was tough and old. I wondered how long my iron blade would hold an effective edge. All through the night I worked, forcing the blade's point into the iron-hard wood and working it back and forth until another splinter fell loose. From time to time I used the rats' eyes to check on the guards. They were snoring away in their bunks; even the jailor sat with his head down on the table, his evening's flagon of wine drained and empty.

After hours of unceasing effort, my blade scraped the hard iron of the door's bolt. I jerked back, shocked by the noise. It sounded loud enough to wake the sleeping guards, to me. But that was only my own fear and surprise; the guards snored on, undisturbed. Now the trick was to worm the blade into the bolt's slot and slide it open without snapping the dagger itself. My hands grew sweaty with the effort. Four or five times I felt the blade bending dangerously and withdrew it. The bolt remained stubbornly in place.

I stopped a while and tried to think of another way to get the stubborn door open. I tried using the edge of the blade to catch some surface roughness on the bolt and slide it out of its slot that way. But the blade merely scratched along the bolt without finding any real purchase, nothing but iron sliding across iron.

Finally I hacked at the wood to make a wider opening and then wormed my index finger into the rough opening. I felt the cool round iron of the bolt, pressed my finger against it and then slid my finger back a fraction of an inch.

The bolt moved. I pulled my finger out, moistened it slightly on my tongue, and tried again. Again the bolt slid back a bit. Slowly, slowly, I pulled it out until I felt the door give slightly under my pressing weight. Taking a deep breath, I pushed the door open. The hinges groaned and I froze. But none of the guards stirred, down the corridor. I placed my chamberpot in its usual spot, then opened the door only enough to squeeze through. I shut it and slid the bolt home again. From out here in the corridor it was impossible to tell that the door had been damaged. They would not know I had escaped until the jailor realized that I had not touched the next bowl of gruel he brought.

I was free! Almost.

Holding my dagger before me I tiptoed past the slumbering guards and up the stairway that led to the ground floor of the palace. Keeping to the shadows, I managed to avoid the few guards who stood sleepily on duty. I made my way to one of the courtyards and quickly decided that the safest and swiftest way to travel was across the rooftops.

It was difficult to recognize which part of the palace I was crossing, and where the troop barracks was, especially in the dark of night. But I saw that the sky to the east was turning milky gray; soon it would be too light for me to go scampering across the roof tiles without being seen. So I found a spot where a fig tree's branches shaded the roof. I gobbled a dozen of the ripe green figs, then settled in the tree's shade there on the hard tiles of the roof and had my first restful sleep in weeks.

Chapter 31

I slept without dreams, although when I awoke, late in the afternoon, I had the disturbing feeling that I had been discovered in my hiding place.

Peering over the roof's eave I saw slaves and servants bustling in the courtyard below: nothing unusual. A squad of soldiers marched past the gate, heading away from me. The sun was almost touching the mountains in the west. I smelled cooking odors, and wondered if there would be enough scraps from the evening's meals to keep the rats fed.

If my escape had been noticed I saw no evidence of it in the courtyard below. Probably my jailor had left my daily bowl of gruel at the locked cell door and taken my pot away with him. He would not suspect anything was amiss until he brought the next meal and saw that I had not touched the previous one.

Good. That gave me roughly twelve hours, more or less, to get to Philip. Then I smiled. If the rats in my cell ate the gruel I might have even more time. But I could not depend on that.

I needed help, and for that I had to reach Harkan. I spent the last few hours of daylight studying the layout of the palace from my rooftop hiding place. I located the troop barracks and plotted out a path across the roofs to get there. Then I waited until purple dusk had faded into the full darkness of night. The moon was rising as I scampered across the roof tiles toward the barracks, silent as a wraith. I hoped.

I waited several hours more, with growing impatience, to make certain that all the soldiers were asleep before I dared to enter the barracks. At last, with a nearly full moon lighting the parade ground almost brightly as day, I swung down from the eaves and through the blanket that hung across one of the barracks windows.

They were asleep, all right. Their snores and grunts and mumbles made the darkened barracks sound almost like a barnyard. I waited several moments while my eyes adjusted to the darkness, then began a tiptoe search for Harkan.

He found me.

As I tiptoed down the aisle between the rows of bunks, I sensed a presence behind me. I whirled and reached for the man's throat, determined to cut off his air and prevent him from awakening the others, only to see that he had a sword pointed at me. It was Harkan, naked except for his unsheathed sword.

"Orion!" he said, surprised.

"Shh!"

One of the men nearest us stirred in his sleep, but did not wake.

"I thought you were a thief," Harkan whispered.

"I was," I joked softly, "when I rode with you."

"Have they released you from prison?"

"I released myself."

In the shadows of the darkened barracks I could not see the expression on his bearded face, but his silence told me that he did not know what to say. I gripped his shoulder and together we walked quietly to the end of the long room.

"I must get to the king," I said as we stepped outside

onto the landing of the stairs that ran down to the parade ground.

"He left for Aigai this morning."

"Then I must go to Aigai."

Now, in the moonlight, I could see Harkan's face. He looked perplexed. "You're a fugitive."

"That was the queen's doing. The king will pardon me when he hears what I have to tell him."

"You think so?" another voice asked. A deep voice: Batu's. He stepped out of the inky shadow cast by the overhanging roof. Like Harkan he was naked, and armed with a sword.

I clasped his outstretched hand as I asked, "What are you doing out here?"

With a broad smile Batu replied, "I heard you scrabbling across the roof tiles. Harkan went to one end of the barracks, I went to this end."

"You two sleep very lightly."

"It comes from the life we've led," said Batu lightly. "Those others in there, they've been paid soldiers all their lives. Bandits don't sleep as well as they do."

I grinned back at him.

"But what makes you think the king will pardon you?" Batu asked again.

"Even if he doesn't, I have to warn him. Pausanias plans to kill him at the wedding."

Harkan scowled at me. "That's a serious charge, Orion."

"He told me himself."

"And the queen is behind it?"

"Yes."

"That means Alexandros is in it, too."

"Perhaps," I said. "He will certainly benefit from it—if we allow it to happen."

"We?" Batu asked.

"I need your help," I said. "I can't get into Aigai by myself."

They both fell silent for many moments. I could understand what was going through their minds. They had found employment, a roof over their heads, a place in the world here in Philip's kingdom. They were no longer outlaws, hunted, living in the wild little better than the beasts. And I was asking them to throw all that away, to desert their positions and fling themselves into the midst of the machinations being hatched by the witch-queen Olympias.

They would be fools to agree. Yet they owed their comfortable positions to me and they knew it. I had brought them to Pella and Philip's employ. If anyone had a right to ask them to give it up, it was I.

Before either of them could speak, my own mind hatched a plot of its own.

"Has Pausanias left for Aigai yet?"

"He departs tomorrow at first light," said Harkan.

"Then listen to me," I said, "Pausanias will send you scouring the countryside when he finds that I have broken out of confinement. He knows I will head for Aigai and he'll send you and most of the guard searching for me. All I ask is that when you find me you bring me to the king, not to Pausanias or the queen."

"How do you know Pausanias will send us?" Harkan asked.

"And even if he does, he will not send only the two of us," added Batu. "How can you be certain that we will be the ones who will find you?"

I gave them a grim smile. "Pausanias will send almost the entire royal guard, never fear. And *I* will find *you,* my friends. In the hills outside Aigai."

Harkan looked doubtful, Batu amused at my certainty.

"When does the wedding take place?" I asked.

"The night of the full moon."

I looked up at the fat waxing moon. "Three nights from now, I judge."

They agreed.

"Search the hills to the right side of the road before Aigai," I said. "I'll be waiting for you there."

Before they could argue I reached up to the edge of the eave and, after lifting myself onto the roof, ran toward the section of the barracks where Pausanias and the other officers slept in individual rooms.

I had no way of knowing which window was his. I simply swung myself through the first one I came to. It was not Pausanias, but the man stirred in his sleep as I leaned over him close enough to see his face in the darkness. Four sleeping rooms I went through before I found Pausanias. There were no guards in the corridor that linked the rooms, although I knew there was a perfunctory pair of men drowsing on guard duty down in the yard, before the door to the barracks.

At last I found Pausanias' room. He was tossing unhappily in his sleep, moaning slightly. The thin chiton he wore was soaked with perspiration.

I clamped my left hand over his mouth and pointed my dagger at his suddenly wide-open eyes.

"Dreaming of the queen?" I asked. "Waiting for her to invite you into her bed once again?"

His right hand moved slightly, but I touched the point of my dagger to the artery pulsing in his throat. He froze into immobility.

"Has she promised to make you regent here in Pella while her son goes off to conquer the Persians?"

I could see by his eyes that this idea was a surprise to him.

"Not even that?" I asked. "All she's offered you is her body? She certainly has you entranced, then."

He tried to say something but my hand muffled his words.

"Your cell wasn't strong enough to hold me, Pausanias. Now I'm going to the king and tell him what you told me. The next time you see me, you'll have a noose around your neck."

I sheathed my dagger. He shoved my hand away from his mouth and reached for the sword hanging beside the bed. I punched him solidly on his temple and he went limp, unconscious.

Then I ducked through his window and back up onto the roof, heading for the stables and a fast horse and the hills before Aigai.

Pausanias reacted almost exactly as I had expected. By the time I had swung off the road to Aigai and nosed my horse up into the brown hills, couriers on lathered horses raced to the old city's gates. Before the sun went down that day a troop of royal guards came up the road, riding almost as hard as the couriers, with Pausanias at their head. They made camp in front of the city wall, obviously to block my entry into Aigai.

Pausanias went inside. To the queen, I imagined, breathless to tell her of the danger to their plans that I represented. I smiled to myself as I made my own camp for the night. No fire for me. I was not ready to be caught just yet. I let my horse crop the scrawny grass pushing up through the rocky ground while I armed myself with a handful of small stones and went hunting. I killed a hare, skinned it and ate its meat raw. It was tough, but nourishing enough. Then both the horse and I drank at a shallow stream bubbling down the hillside.

She came to me in my dreams, of course.

Hera was furious. No sooner had I closed my eyes in sleep than I found myself standing before her in a chamber so vast that I could see neither its walls nor its ceiling. Enormous columns of gray-green marble rose like a forest, dwarfing even the many-columned hall of the Great King. Hera sat on a throne that glowed faintly, completely alone, magnificently beautiful in a flowing white robe that left her slim arms bare except for her jeweled bracelets and armlets, all in the shape of coiling snakes.

Staring down at me with fiery eyes, she snapped, "You are more trouble than you're worth, Orion."

I smiled at her. "I accept that as a compliment."

Her eyes blazed. She leaned forward slightly, hands clenching into white-knuckled fists, body rigid with tension.

I felt the beginnings of the pain she had inflicted on me before, but I fought against it, strove to banish it from my consciousness. It faded away before it became anything more than an annoying tingling.

Hera's face contorted into an even angrier frown.

"It's not working," I said. "You can't punish me the way you once did."

"You're being protected!" The thought seemed to surprise her.

"Or perhaps I've learned to protect myself," I said, not daring to hope that Anya was near. She was the only one who would protect me, I knew.

"Impossible. We wiped that capability from your mind before we sent you here."

"We?" I asked. "You and the Golden One?"

She did not need to answer; I knew.

"You failed, then. My memories are returning. My abilities are growing."

"We will destroy you, once and for all."

I thought of Ketu. "And grant me the release of oblivion?"

Hera glowered at me.

"The Golden One fathered Alexandros, didn't he? The

two of you are playing at kings and empires. Does it amuse you? Is there some point to it beyond your own pitiful entertainment?"

"You don't understand anything, Orion."

"Don't I? As far as I can see, you are serving the whims of Aten, the Golden One, whatever he's calling himself now. He wanted to create a Trojan empire that spanned Europe and Asia. I stopped him then. Now he gets you to help him create the empire he's wanted all along—by bearing his son, Alexandros, and allowing him to conquer the Persians."

"Alexandros will conquer the whole world," Hera said. "He must, or this nexus in the continuum will unravel disastrously."

"But Philip stands in his way. He has a new son now, one that he is certain comes from his own seed."

"Philip will die."

"At Pausanias' hand."

"Of course."

"Not if I can stop him."

"You mustn't!"

"Why not?"

Her anger had faded. Now she seemed alarmed, almost frightened. But she pulled herself together, regained her self-control. Hera leaned forward again and smiled coldly at me.

"Orion, consider: if this nexus unravels the fabric of spacetime, everything changes. You will be torn from Anya just as surely as the Earth will be destroyed in nuclear fire a few thousand years up the time-stream."

"And if I obey you and allow Philip to be assassinated?"

She shrugged her slim shoulders. "At least we will be dealing with a continuum we understand and can control."

"What is this great crisis that Anya spoke of? What is happening elsewhere in the continuum?"

Her face clouded over. "Problems so intricate that not even we Creators fully understand their implications. Anya is far from Earth, Orion, light-years off in interstellar space, attempting to deal with one aspect of the crisis."

"Is she truly in danger?"

"We are all in danger, Orion. The forces ranged against us are beyond comprehension."

Her usual haughty, taunting tone was gone. She was visibly fearful.

"How does this matter of Philip and Alexandros relate to Anya?"

I saw her draw back, a flicker of exasperation touching her face. "You *are* a stubborn mule, Orion!"

"Tell me," I demanded.

She heaved an annoyed sigh. "We cannot get out of this nexus until its flow is resolved, one way or the other!" Hera blurted. "We are locked into this placetime, Aten and I, and will be until the decision is made! Either Philip dies or Alexandros. Until one of them is killed, we cannot return to the continuum to help Anya and the other Creators."

"You're stuck here?"

Very reluctantly she admitted, "Yes."

I did not want to believe her, but suddenly much of what I had experienced made sense to me. When I had translated myself to the Creators' city it was empty and abandoned. Whenever I had left this placetime I had returned precisely to the same time and place again. If what Hera was telling me was true, she and Aten were trapped here also. That was why Anya could not come to me; she was enmeshed in this snare just as they were.

Without meaning to, without even thinking about it, I burst out laughing.

Hera's blazing anger returned. "You find this amusing?"

"Incredibly so," I answered. "Your meddling with the continuum has finally caught up with you. You sent me here to be rid of me, and now you're trapped here with me!"

I laughed until tears rolled down my cheeks.

Chapter 32

Hera disappeared so abruptly that I felt a jolt of physical alarm at finding myself back in the predawn cold of the hills near Aigai.

Pulling myself up to a sitting position, I waited and watched the dawn come up over the rugged eastern horizon. *So Hera and Golden Aten are trapped in this nexus of the continuum, unable to get away from this placetime unless and until either Philip or Alexandros dies,* I thought. *Unable to reach Anya and the other Creators. Unable to help them in their battle out among the stars.*

I got to my feet, wondering what I was to do. I could not let them kill Philip; he had been just and true to me. He was the one pillar on which the safety and prosperity of his people rested. Kill Philip and Alexandros would become king and immediately go chasing off for the glory of conquering the world. Years of wars and killing. To what end? Why should I help to make that come about?

Yet that is what Aten, the Golden One, had been scheming for all through the centuries since Troy. His vision of human destiny required an empire that brought together the wealth of Asia with the ideals of Europe. I remembered another time, another place, far to the east, when I was sent to assassinate the High Khan of the Mongols. Then my mission had been to *prevent* the Mongol empire from engulfing Europe.

Hera honestly seemed to believe that what we did here in this placetime had profound consequences for the space-time continuum as a whole. I had my doubts. I thought that Aten and the other Creators dabbled with the flow of the continuum, interfered with human history as a game among themselves, a pastime of the gods. They saw the human race as their creation, their playthings. Wars, empires, murder and human misery were simply amusements for them.

Yet Hera seemed frightened enough. And Anya was in danger, she said. Somewhere out among the stars Anya was fighting a battle for her life.

I shook my head. Maybe Hera was right: it was all beyond my comprehension. Yet I knew that what I was about to do would be pivotal. Aten and the other so-called gods had created me and a handful of other warriors to serve them, to be sent to specific critical points in the space-time continuum and alter the flow of events for the benefit of our Creators.

They created us, but we created them. I remembered it fully now. I remembered being sent back into the Ice Age to wipe out the Neanderthals. I remembered Anya taking human form to help me and the handful of creatures Aten had sent on that genocidal mission. I remembered how we survived the battles and the cold of centuries-long winter. How we peopled the earth. How we became the human race. How our descendants in the distant future became the Creators who made us and sent us back in time to start the chain of events that would ultimately lead to themselves.

All this I remembered as I stood in the chilly dawn of the worn, stony hills. But nothing in my newfound memories told me what I should do next. Nothing except the unshakable realization that Anya was the only one among the Creators to care enough about any of us to share our dangers, our pains, our fate.

I loved her. That much I knew without question. I thought she loved me. And she was in danger, far from this place and time.

The whinny of my horse snapped me out of my reverie. I had left the steed loosely tethered to a scraggly bush so that it could reach the sparse grass growing among the rocks without wandering off too far.

It had sensed someone approaching, I suspected. I crawled up atop one of the bigger boulders and, flat on my belly, scanned the slope of the rocky hill below.

Sure enough, there was Harkan in the armor of the royal guard, coming up the slope. He was alone. A pair of spears was tied to his mount's side and his sword rested against his hip. His helmet was tipped back on his head. He was peering at the hard stony ground, looking for some sign of me. If I just remained where I was he would pass me by a hundred yards or so and never know I was near. As long as my horse kept silent.

I decided, though, to keep the bargain I had made with him. Scrambling to my feet I called out his name. His head jerked up and he raised one hand over his eyes. The sun was at my back.

"Orion," he called back.

By the time I had climbed down from the boulder he had dismounted and was walking up to me, leading his horse with one hand.

We clasped forearms.

"I brought some biscuits and cheese," Harkan said. "I thought you might be hungry."

"Good. Let's have breakfast. It might look suspicious if you brought me in too early in the day."

He made a small smile and went to the pack his horse carried. There was a skin of wine in the pack, too. And a handful of figs. The sun was getting high in the morning sky by the time we finished. I stood up, wiping my hands on the hem of my chiton, and saw that rain clouds were building up in the east.

"Maybe we should get to the city before the storm arrives," I said.

Harkan nodded glumly. Then he held out his hand. "Your dagger, Orion. Pausanias knows you have a dagger. I'd better take it."

I felt a bit uneasy about that, but I slid my dagger from its sheath on my thigh and handed it to Harkan, hilt first.

"Thank you," he said. And that was all he said as we mounted up and began the ride downhill to the road and then up the road to hilltop Aigai. Harkan's silence bothered me; it was as if something was troubling him.

"What's the news?" I asked as we rode side by side.

"Nothing much," he said, not turning to look at me.

"Have you found your children?"

He gave me a sidelong glance. "They're in Aigai; they belong to the king now."

"Philip will give them back to you," I said. "Or sell them to you, at least."

"You think so?"

"Once you tell him that you're their father, he'll probably release them to you without payment."

"He likes silver and gold, they say."

"Even so, he knows what it is to be a father. He won't keep them from you."

Harkan nodded grimly, like a man heading toward battle.

"Pausanias was surprised that I broke out of my cell, was he?"

"Surprised is hardly the word, Orion. He's been in a frenzy. He wants your head on a spear and he's promised a great reward for whoever brings you to him."

"You're going to get the reward, then."

"Yes," he said, without enthusiasm.

We rode for a long, silent time. Something was obviously gnawing at Harkan. His children? The fact that he was turning me over to Pausanias?

I asked, "Where's Batu? Why isn't he with you?"

He did not reply at once. At length, though, Harkan said, "I thought it would look too obvious if the two of us brought you back. Too suspicious. Batu's riding through the hills on the other side of the road, with a full company of the guard. Searching for you."

I nodded and he fell back into silence once more.

Within a quarter-hour of our reaching the road, a whole contingent of guards galloped up to us.

"You've got him!" exclaimed their leader. "Good!"

He waved to a pair of riders at the end of his column and they trotted up to us. Chains jingled from the packs on their horses' rumps.

The guard leader gave me a rueful look. "Sorry, Orion. Pausanias' orders. You're to be manacled and fettered. He's taking no chances on your getting away again."

Harkan would not look at me, and the other guards seemed shame-faced to see one of their erstwhile comrades chained by the wrists and ankles. Even the two smiths who fastened the cuffs to me were almost apologetic as they drove home the rivets.

So I arrived at Aigai with my hands cuffed behind my back, my ankles chained together, tossed across the back of my horse with my head dragging down in the dust, trussed like a sacrificial offering. Which, I realized, Pausanias meant me to be. My only hope was to see the king before Pausanias killed me.

I got an upside-down worm's-eye view of Aigai's massive main gate and its thick wall, its dirt streets winding upward to the citadel at the very crown of the hill, and the even sturdier wall and gate of the castle proper.

But they did not take me to the king. Despite my protests they dragged me from my horse and down into the ancient dungeons of the castle that had been since time immemorial the seat of the kings of Macedonia.

"Take me to the king!" I shouted again as they locked me into a cell. My throat was getting hoarse from my unheeded demands. "I must see the king and warn him!"

To no avail. They dumped me into the dirt-floored cell, still chained. The last one to leave me was Harkan. He waited until all the others had filed out, then knelt beside me.

Ah-hah! I thought. *Now he's going to tell me that he'll return and get me out of this.*

But instead he whispered swiftly, "I'm sorry, Orion. It was you or my children. She's promised to give them back to me if I brought you in."

She. The queen. Olympias. Hera.

"She means to kill me," I said.

He nodded wordlessly and then left me lying there on the floor of the cell. The door clanged shut and I was alone in the darkness.

But not for long. My eyes were just adjusting to the gloom when I heard footsteps coming down the corridor outside. The door was unlocked and pushed open. Two jailers came in and, grunting, lifted me by my armpits to a sitting position and dragged me across the cell until my back was propped up against the rough stone wall.

They left and Olympias stepped into the cell. Pausanias came in behind her, holding a torch in his right hand.

"We should kill him now and get it over with," Pausanias muttered.

"Not just yet," said Olympias. "He may still be of value to us, once Philip is dead."

I saw the ageless eyes of Hera in her beautiful, cruel face.

"What value?" Pausanias snapped.

"You question me?"

He immediately yielded to the iron in her voice. "I just wanted to know—that is, he's dangerous. We should be rid of him."

"After Philip is killed," Olympias whispered. "Then you can have him."

"Do you think I won't go through with it?" Pausanias snapped. "Do you think I need a prize, a reward, to make me kill the king?"

"No, of course not," she soothed. "But wait until afterward. It will be better afterward, I promise you."

Pausanias stepped closer to me. "Very well. After." Then he kicked me with all his might squarely on the side of my head. As I slid toward unconsciousness I heard him growl, "I owed you that."

Chapter 33

I remained unconscious willingly, deliberately. My body lay in the musty cell, chained hand and foot, but my mind was aware and active. I sought out the city of the Creators once again, seeking the only refuge I could think of.

My eyes opened on that grassy hill above the empty and abandoned city. The sun glittered on the sea, the flowers nodded to the passing breeze, the trees sighed as they had sighed for a hundred million years. Yet I could not approach the city any closer than I had before. Once again that invisible barrier held me in its grip.

There was nowhere for me to go except back to Macedonia, back to that dark dungeon in Aigai, chained and helpless while Hera goaded Pausanias into murdering his king. There was no way I could get to Philip in time to warn him.

Or was there? If I could not get out of my cell to go to Philip, could I bring him here to this ageless bubble of spacetime to be with me? I paced along the soft grassy slope, thinking hard, noting absently that as long as I walked away from the city I was not hindered by the barrier.

How often had the Creators summoned me here? How many times had I made the transition from some place and time to this eternal city? I knew what it felt like so well that

I could translate myself here without their aid, without their even knowing it. Could I stretch that power to pluck Philip from Aigai and bring him here, even briefly, to warn him?

As I pondered the problem I thought I heard the faintest, subtlest echo of laughter. Mocking, cynical laughter that seemed to say to me that I had never moved myself through the continuum unaided, that I did not have the power to translate a molecule from one placetime to another, that everything I thought I had done on my own was really done for me by one of the Creators.

No, I raged silently. *I have achieved these things by myself. Anya told me so in a previous life.* The Creators were even becoming wary of my increasing powers, fearful that I would one day equal them despite all they tried to do to stop me. That is why they wiped my memory and sent back to ancient Macedonia. *But it didn't work. I am learning again, growing, gaining strength despite their betrayals.*

That mocking laughter was one of their tricks, I told myself—trying to weaken my resolve, my self-confidence.

I can *bring Philip to me,* I told them. *I know how to do it. I have the power.*

And Philip, king of Macedonia, appeared before me.

He seemed more annoyed than startled. He was wearing nothing but a thin cloth wrapped around his middle. His one good eye blinked in the sunlight, and I realized that I had taken him from his sleep.

"Orion," he said, without surprise.

"My lord."

He looked around. "What place is this? What's that city down there?"

"We are far from Macedonia. You might say that the city is the abode of the gods."

He snorted. "Doesn't look much like Mount Olympus, does it?" His body was covered with scars, old puckered white lines across his chest and shoulders, a raw ugly knotted gash along the length of his left thigh. He bore the history of all the battles he had fought.

"Pausanias told me that you're a deserter. Are you a witch, as well?"

I started to answer, then suddenly realized that Olympias had shown him other domains of spacetime just as she had shown me. Philip was not startled to be plucked from his bed and drawn to a different part of the continuum because *she* had done this to him previously.

"No, I'm not a witch," I replied. "Neither is your wife."

"Ex-wife, Orion. And I guarantee you, she is a witch."

"She's shown you other places?"

He nodded. "More than once, when we were first married. She showed me how powerful Macedonia could become if I followed her advice." Then he aimed his one good eye at me. "You're in league with her, then?"

"No. Quite the contrary."

"You have the same powers she has."

"Some of the same powers," I said. "I'm afraid she's much more powerful than I."

"More powerful than anyone," he muttered.

"She means to kill you."

"I know. I've known it for years."

"But this time—"

He held up a hand to silence me. "Speak no more about it, Orion. I know what she plans. I've outlived my usefulness to her. Now it's time for Alexandros to fulfill her ambitions."

"You want to die?"

"No, not particularly. But every man dies, Orion, sooner or later. My work is finished. I've done what she wanted me to do. She's like a female spider that must devour her mate."

"But it doesn't have to be that way," I objected.

"What would you have me do?" he asked, his fierce beard bristling. "If I want to stay alive, stay on the throne, I'll have to kill her and I can't do that, else she'll goad Alexandros into civil war. Do you think I want to see my people torn apart like that? Do you think I want to kill my own son?"

Before I could answer he went on, "If Macedonians make war on each other, what do you think the nations around us will do? What do you think Demosthenes and the rest of the Athenians will do? Or the Thebans? Or the Great King over in Persia?"

"I see."

"Do you? We'll be right back where we were before I made myself king." He pulled in a deep breath, then added, "And even if he's not my true son, that makes no difference. I won't murder him."

"Then they will murder you," I said. "Within a day or so."

"So be it," said Philip. "Just don't tell me who or when." He grinned sardonically. "I like surprises."

I shook my head in dismay and began to walk away from him.

"Wait," he called, misinterpreting me. "Will it be you, Orion? Is that what you're trying to tell me?"

Drawing myself up to my full height, I said, "Never! I'll die myself before I let them kill you."

That one good eye of his scanned me closely. "Yes, you would, wouldn't you? I never believed you had deserted."

He turned away from me and began to limp down the hillside toward the city. Before he had taken three steps he winked out, leaving me alone in that distant bubble of spacetime. I closed my eyes . . .

And opened them in the dungeon beneath the castle at Aigai. I was still chained hand and foot and the side of my head where Pausanias had kicked me throbbed with sullen pain.

There was no way for me to reckon time in that dark cell except for the beat of my own pulse. Impractical, yet for lack of anything better to do I counted beats the way an insomniac might count sheep. I could leave this cell and translate myself to the Creators' abandoned city, but I would always return to this same place, in the same chains. Like Hera, I was trapped here until the cusp of this nexus was resolved, one way or the other.

I gave up counting pulse beats when I realized that there were rats in this cell, just as there had been in the one at Pella. My cell mates, my companions, ready to gnaw off my toes or fingers if I did not wiggle them every now and then. The manacles on my wrists were so tight that a normal man's hands would have swollen painfully from lack of blood circulation. I consciously forced my deep-lying blood vessels to take over the work of the peripherals that were squeezed shut by the manacles. And I moved my fingers constantly to help keep the circulation going—and to discourage the beady-eyed hungry rats.

I heard footsteps shuffling along the corridor outside. They stopped at my door. The bolt squealed back and the door groaned open. My two jailers stood out there, one of them holding a torch.

Between them stood Ketu.

He pushed between the jailers and came into my cell. Kneeling beside me, he peered into my face.

"You are still alive?"

I made a smile for him. "I haven't achieved Nirvana yet, my friend."

"Thank the gods!" He straightened up and told the jailers to take me outside.

They had to drag me, grunting and struggling, to the big room at the end of the corridor. My heart thumped when I saw that the place was filled with instruments of torture.

"The king has ordered your release," Ketu reassured me. "This smith here—" he pointed to a sweaty, hairy, totally bald man with a bulging pot belly—"will strike off your chains."

He nearly struck off my arms, but after nearly half an hour of clanging and hammering I was free once again. My wrists and ankles were raw where the cuffs had chafed my skin, but I knew they would heal quickly enough. Ketu led me out of the dismal cellar and up into the fading sunlight of a dying day.

"The king's daughter has been safely married to Alexandros of Epeiros," Ketu told me. "Philip himself instructed me to set you free and give you all that you need to leave Macedonia. You may travel wherever you want to, Orion."

"The wedding is over?" I asked.

He was leading me to the stables, I saw. Ketu answered, "The marriage ceremony was last night. The feasting will last another two days, of course."

"Has anyone tried to assassinate the king?"

Ketu's liquid eyes went wide. "Assassinate? No! Who would dare even try?"

"A traitor," I said.

"Do you know this for certain?"

"I've heard it from the traitor's own lips."

"You must tell the captain of the king's guard, Pausanias."

"No, I must get to the king himself."

Ketu grabbed at my arm. "That cannot be. Philip gave me specific instructions. He does not want to see you. He forbids it! You are to take as many horses as you need and leave Aigai, leave Macedonia, and never return."

I stood there in the middle of the castle courtyard, near

the dusty stables. They smelled of hay and manure and the warm strength of the animals. Flies buzzed lazily in the purpling shadows of dusk. From far behind me I could hear the faint music of flutes and tambourines, and the raucous laughter of drinking men. Pausanias was there with the king. And Philip wanted me out of the way just as much as Olympias did.

"No," I said, as much to the gods as to little Ketu. "I won't let them kill him. I don't care what it does to their plans or to the fabric of the continuum. I won't let it happen!"

Pulling free of Ketu's restraining hand, I started toward the palace proper, where the wedding celebration was still going strong.

Ketu scampered beside me. "No, you must not! The guards have orders not to admit you. Philip does not want to see you. It will mean your death to try to force yourself upon his presence."

I ignored him and strode toward the big doorway where four men in armor stood guard.

"Come with me, Orion," Ketu begged. "We will travel the breadth of the Persian Empire and return to my land, to beautiful Hind. We will see the holy men and seek their wisdom . . ."

The only thing I sought was to save Philip, to shatter Hera's murderous plan, to protect the king who had shown me his trust.

"Please, Orion!" Ketu's eyes were filled with tears.

I left him standing there in the middle of the courtyard and approached the guards at the door. All four of them bore spears; two of them crossed their spears in front of the wooden double door.

"No one is allowed inside," said their leader. I recognized him as a barracks mate.

"I must see the king."

"I have my orders, Orion. No one means no one."

"Yes," I said softly. "I understand."

Swifter than his eye could follow I snatched his sword from its scabbard with my right hand while I drove the heel of my left beneath his chin. His head snapped back and I heard the spinal cord crack. Before the others could react I smashed the next guard on his helmet, splitting the bronze and the bone beneath it.

They both fell in slow motion as I turned to face the two men who still stood with their spears crossed in front of the door. I could see their eyes widening, their mouths gulping air in surprised shock. I drove my sword through the nearer one's chest so hard that it impaled him on the door. His companion was levelling his spear at me; a clumsy weapon when I was so close. I grabbed it with one hand while I kicked his kneecap out from under him. He went down with a yowl of pain and I pushed through the door, the dead guard still hanging from the sword through his chest.

I pulled it out and he dropped to the floor of packed earth. Bloody sword in hand, I went looking for Philip. And Pausanias.

Chapter 34

The castle of Aigai was old and grim, its ground floor nothing more than hard-packed dirt, the walls of the chamber I strode through made of rough-hewn stones, dark as the bloody sword I gripped.

I could hear the sounds of revelry coming from the main hall. The wedding had taken place the day before, from what Ketu told me, but the celebration roared on. Philip would be there, steeped in wine. Pausanias, as captain of the guard, would be in charge of protecting him. Olympias would be elsewhere in the castle, waiting to hear the wailing and cries of murder.

And Alexandros? Where would he be? Was he part of the murder plot? Did he know what his mother had set in motion?

There was another quartet of guards at the door to the main hall, each of them armed with spear and sword. Harkan and Batu were among them, I saw.

Harkan's bearded face went red once he recognized who was approaching. Batu smiled as if he'd won a wager. The lieutenant in charge stared at my bloody sword.

"Orion," he snapped, "what's going on?"

"They're going to kill the king unless we stop them."

"Kill the king? Who?"

"Pausanias."

"Are you crazy? Pausanias is captain of the—"

He never finished the sentence. Screams and roars of rage broke out from the other side of the door. Harkan threw the door open and we saw that the hall was in turmoil. Men were leaping across couches, servants and slaves were scattering in every direction, screaming in terror.

"The king! The king!"

I bolted past Harkan and the others, through the wildly scrambling crowd, toward the king. A dozen men clustered around him. I pulled them away, forced my way to Philip's side. He lay back against his couch, wine goblet locked in one frozen hand, his other clutched against his middle, his gut ripped open, hot red blood soaking his robe and dripping onto the dirt floor. It was a painful way to die.

"I trusted you," he muttered. "I trusted you."

And I heard Hera's bitter laughter in my mind. The vision from my old dream had come true. I stood before the dying Philip with a bloody sword in my hand and watched the light fade from his eye.

Harkan grabbed me by the shoulders. "This way," he said in a low voice. "Pausanias fled toward the stables."

As I ran back toward the door with him and Batu, I saw Alexandros standing on one of the tables, white-faced with shock, guarded by Antipatros and Antigonos and a dozen of his Companions. None of them had weapons on them, but if an assassin meant to reach Alexandros he would have to go through them first. Armed guards were pouring into the hall, though, through the doors at its far end.

"I swear by Almighty Zeus," Alexandros was shouting, his voice nearly cracking with emotion, "that I will find the assassins and deal with them as they've dealt with my father."

So now he's your father again, I thought as we left the hall. *And you are his son and heir to the throne. Hera and the*

Golden One will have their way; pity the Great King and his shaky empire.

The three of us raced across the courtyard to the stables. A half-dozen armed men barred the gate, but we cut them down without an instant's hesitation.

Pausanias was already on horseback when we broke in. Two other men were with him. Batu nailed one with his spear and Harkan knocked the other one off his horse, then drove his spear through the screaming traitor's chest.

Wild-eyed, Pausanias drove his mount straight at us. Dropping my sword, I stepped to one side as the horse thundered by and grabbed him around the middle. The two of us thudded to the dirt floor of the stable. I planted a knee on Pausanias' chest and pulled his own sword from its scabbard.

He stared up at me, gasping for breath. But his eyes became calm.

"It's done," he said. "Now you can do what you must. I don't care anymore."

I hesitated. Should I turn him over to Alexandros or give him a quick and painless death here and now? I thought of how he had slashed Philip and scalding anger boiled through me.

Harkan and Batu were standing over us. Quite calmly Harkan drove the point of his spear through Pausanias' throat. Blood fountained hot and red, splashing over me, as he jerked convulsively and gave a single gargling groan.

I looked up at Harkan.

He yanked the spear from Pausanias' dead body and said grimly, "She instructed us that there were to be no witnesses left alive, Orion."

I got to my feet. "That includes me, doesn't it?"

"I'm afraid so." He levelled his spear at my heart.

"Can you trust her?" I asked.

"My children are already safely at a farm up in the hills. That's where I'm going when this is finished."

"If she lets you live."

He shrugged. "Even if she doesn't, I'll know that my children are free."

I glanced at Batu. His dark face looked troubled, as if he could not decide which side he wanted to be on.

"Orion," he said, "I am not part of this. I did not know until this moment—"

"Then don't get involved now," I told him. "This is between Harkan and me. And the queen."

"She is a witch of great power," said Batu.

"Yes." I nodded.

"She can steal a man's wits from him."

"And his strength." I turned back to Harkan. His spear had not wavered a millimeter from my heart. "Go ahead, my friend. Do it and get it over with."

He hesitated.

"For your children," I told him.

Harkan took a deep breath, then plunged the spear into my chest with all his might. I felt no pain at all. Just darkness engulfing me, welcome, blessed nothingness.

I died.

Epilogue

This time death was like being in the center of a whirlpool, inside the heart of a roaring tornado. The universe spun madly, time and space whirling into a dizzying blur, planets and stars and atoms and electrons racing in wild orbits with me in the middle of it all, falling, falling endlessly into a cryogenically cold oblivion.

Gradually all sensation left me. It might have taken moments or millennia; I had no way to gauge time, but all feeling of motion and cold seeped away from me, as if I were being numbed, frozen, turned into an immobile, insensate block of ice.

Still my mind continued to function. I knew I was being translated across spacetime, from one cusp of the continuum to another. Yet for all I could see or touch or hear, I was in total oblivion. For a measureless time I almost felt glad to be free of the wheel of life at last, beyond pain, beyond desire, beyond the agonizing duty that the Creators forced upon me.

Beyond love.

That stirred me. Somewhere in the vast reaches of spacetime Anya was struggling against forces that I could not even comprehend, in danger despite her godlike powers, facing enemies that frightened even the Golden One and the other Creators.

I reached out with my mind, seeking to penetrate the blank darkness that engulfed me. Nothing. It was if there were no universe, no continuum, neither time nor space. But I knew that somewhere, sometime, she existed. She had loved me as I had loved her. Nothing in all the universes of existence would keep us apart.

A glimmer of light. So faint and distant that at first I thought it might be merely my imagination obeying my desire. But yes, it truly was there. A faintest, faintest glow. Light. Warmth.

Whether I moved to it or it moved to me mattered not at all to me. The glow grew and brightened until I seemed to be hurtling toward it like a chip thrown into a furnace, like a meteor drawn to a star. The light blazed like the sun now and I threw my arms across my eyes to ease the pain, delighted that I had eyes and arms and could *feel* again.

"Orion," came a voice from that blinding, overpowering radiance. "You have returned."

It was Aten, of course, the Golden One. He resolved his presence into human form, a powerful godlike figure with thick golden mane, robed in shimmering gold, almost too bright for me to look upon.

He stood before me in an utterly barren landscape that stretched toward infinity in every direction: a featureless plain of billowing mist that played about our ankles, an empty bowl of sky above us the color of hammered copper.

"Where is Anya?" I asked.

"Far from here."

"I must go to her. She is in great danger."

"So are we all, Orion."

"I don't care about you or the others. It is Anya I care for."

A faint hint of a smirk curled the corners of his lips. "What you care or don't care about is inconsequential, Orion. I created you to do my bidding."

"I want to be with Anya."

"Impossible. There are other tasks for you to perform, creature."

I stared into his golden eyes and knew that he had the power to send me where he chose. But I had powers, too, powers that were growing and strengthening.

"I will find her," I said.

He laughed scornfully. But I knew that whatever he did, wherever he sent me, I would seek the woman I loved, the goddess who loved me. And I would not cease until I found her.

Author's Note

While this continuation of the tale of Orion's struggles with his Creators is of course fiction, the details of fourth-century B.C. history are as accurate as I could make them. Throughout the novel I have used the Greek-style spellings for proper names, a practice that sometimes drives my copyeditors to despair.

Since I first read about Alexander the Great, when I was a child, I have been more interested in his father than in Alexander himself. And I think there are important lessons to be pondered in the story of Philip's life.

Without Philip there could have been no Alexander the Great. Philip II welded a dispirited and divided Macedonia into the first true nation-state of Europe. By force of arms, at first, but increasingly by diplomacy and clever use of military leverage, Philip made Macedonia supreme among the Greek city-states of the Fourth Century B.C. He was not merely a great general; he became a great statesman. He learned and grew during the course of his relatively short, arduous, painful life.

The struggle between ancient Athens and Philip's Macedonia has been painted by most historians as a contest between democracy and tyranny. So it was, although Athenian democracy was limited to free males born in the city, and Philip was not a tyrant in the modern, pejorative sense of the word. His authority had its limits.

For us, who have lived through a bitter Cold War and seen the collapse of the superpower that opposed us, it may seem uncomfortable to consider the parallels between fourth-century (B.C.) Athens and twentieth-century (A.D.) America. The city-state of Athens was overflowing with lawyers. Most of the great speeches that have come down to us over the intervening centuries were actually speeches made by lawyers who were trying to sway the Athenian council. In a sense, lawyers such as Demosthenes were the "media stars" of the day. They deliberately used every oratorical trick they knew to sway the crowds who came to listen to them.

Thus Athenian policy was often guided by bursts of emotion rather than carefully-reckoned reality, a danger that lurks in the shadows of every democracy—including our own. Athens was not conquered by Macedonia so much as made trivial by the growth of a new kind of nation-state. Eventually both Macedonia and Athens fell prey to the growing power of the Roman Empire. Could American democracy be cast aside, made trivial by new forms of corporate or governmental power? While our lawyers sue one another, are there Philips and Alexanders and Romans out there in other lands changing the very ground on which we stand?

For his part, Philip was a master of military might and diplomatic skill. Had a man of his caliber been running the Kremlin for the past twenty-some years, the Cold War might very well have been decided against us.

The problem with tyrants, though, even benevolent tyrants, is the problem of succession. Democracies, whatever other faults they may have, almost invariably produce peaceful changes of leadership. With kings and dictators, change usually means bloodshed. It was by no means certain that Alexander would automatically succeed his father to the Macedonian throne. He was young, and known to be impetuous. Philip had started a new family, formally divorcing Olympias and thereby placing Alexander's legitimacy in some doubt. Philip's assassination placed Alexander on the throne, and to this day most historians believe that if Alexander took no active part in the murder, he very probably knew of it and took no steps to prevent it.

Olympias stood at the center of these events, working with all her powers to assure that her son would succeed to the throne. That is what primate mothers do, whether they are chimpanzees or goddesses.

As soon as Alexander was accepted as king of the Macedonians, the tribes to the north and west rebelled, as they always did when a new king took the throne. Alexander spent a year quelling their desire for independence. Twenty-three centuries later, those Balkan tribes are still fighting among themselves.

Athens became restive and Thebes openly rebelled. Where his father was lenient, Alexander was genocidal. He stormed Thebes and burned that ancient city to the ground, selling its surviving inhabitants into slavery. The other cities, including Athens, bowed in terror to their new master.

Demosthenes fled Athens as Alexander at last launched his full-scale invasion of the rickety Persian Empire. He cracked it open like an overripe melon, besting Darius' armies every time they met.

The Great King was murdered by his own guards as he tried to flee Alexander's triumphant march through his empire. Demosthenes committed suicide, literally hounded to death by Alexander's implacable hatred. Alexander himself was accepted as the new god-king of the Persian Empire, but not even that satisfied him and he pushed across the Indus River into India, seeking to conquer the ends of the earth.

Inevitably he descended into the madness that plagues tyrants, growing suspicious of those closest to him. By his orders Attalus and his entire family were wiped out. Alexander's fevered paranoia began to fall upon his own Companions, friends since childhood. Torture and murder became his tools until even the army began to grow restive.

They rebelled in a sullen, grumbling refusal to march further into steaming Hindustan. He punished them by marching the army back toward Persia across barren desert wastes where more men died from thirst and heat than had been killed in his battles.

One of the casualties was Alexander himself. He came down with a fever and died in his thirty-third year.

His remaining Companions, including his half-brother Ptolemaios, gathered around his death bed and pressed him to tell them to whom he would leave his empire.

In his final moment Alexander gave his answer:

"To the strongest."

The surge and flow of ideas and armies between Europe and Asia has been one of the principal features of human history. In this novel, as in the earlier *Vengeance of Orion,* I made it a major aim of the Creators to fashion an empire that spans East and West. Alexander finally accomplished this, for a century or so. His empire broke apart into the separate kingdoms of his successors. By the time the Romans swallowed Greece, the Persians had reasserted themselves. The Roman Empire never penetrated eastward much beyond Palestine.

What of Orion and Anya and the other Creators? With all of spacetime as their arena, you can be sure that their story is not yet finished.

Acknowledgments

The epigraphs that begin each section of this novel are from William Shakespeare, *King Lear;* Karl von Clausewitz, *On War;* Sophocles, *Electra;* and Shakespeare again, *Macbeth.*